The Oracle

Clive Cussler is the author and co-author of a great number of international bestsellers, including the famous Dirk Pitt® adventures, such as *Havana Storm*; the NUMA® Files adventures, most recently *The Rising Sea*; the *Oregon* Files, such as *Typhoon Fury*; the Isaac Bell historical thrillers, which began with *The Chase*; and the recent Fargo Adventures which lastly included *The Grey Ghost*. He lives in Arizona.

Robin Burcell spent nearly three decades working in California law enforcement as a police officer, detective, hostage negotiator, and FBI-trained forensic artist. She is the author of ten novels, most recently *The Kill Order*. Burcell lives in Lodi, California.

TITLES BY CLIVE CUSSLER

The Oracle

CLIVE CUSSLER
and ROBIN BURCELL

MICHAEL JOSEPH
an imprint of
PENGUIN BOOKS

MICHAEL JOSEPH

UK | USA | Canada | Ireland | Australia
India | New Zealand | South Africa

Michael Joseph is part of the Penguin Random House group of companies
whose addresses can be found at global.penguinrandomhouse.com

First published in the United States by G. P. Putnam's Sons 2019
First published in Great Britain by Michael Joseph 2019
001

Copyright © Sandecker, RLLLP, 2019

Book Design by Kristin Del Roasrio

Printed and bound in Great Britain by Clays Ltd, Elcograf S.p.A.

A CIP catalogue record for this book is available from the British Library

HARDBACK ISBN: 978–0–241–38689–7
OM PAPERBACK ISBN: 978–0–241–38690–3

www.greenpenguin.co.uk

MIX
Paper from
responsible sources
FSC® C018179

Penguin Random House is committed to a
sustainable future for our business, our readers
and our planet. This book is made from Forest
Stewardship Council® certified paper.

CAST OF CHARACTERS

KINGDOM OF THE VANDALS, NORTH AFRICA, 533 A.D.

Gelimer—the last King of the Vandals, the Usurper
Tzazon—Gelimer's brother
Euric—Gelimer's next in command
Belisarius—general of the Byzantine Army

GELIMER'S ANCESTORS

Hilderic—penultimate King of the Vandals, murdered by Gelimer
Genseric—King of the Vandals who conquered North Africa and laid siege to Hippo Regia

THE PRESENT DAY

IN LA JOLLA

Sam Fargo
Remi (Longstreet) Fargo
Selma Wondrash—the Fargos' head researcher
Professor Lazlo Kemp—a Fargos researcher and cryptologist
Rubin Haywood—CIA case agent
Zoltán—the Fargos' German shepherd

IN BULLA REGIA, TUNISIA

Dr. Renee LaBelle—archeologist
Hank—site manager, Bulla Regia
Amal—Tunisian graduate student
José—Spanish graduate student
Osmond—Egyptian graduate student
Yesmine—Amal's mother
Warren—former site manager

TUNISIAN GANG

Tarek
Hamida
Ben Ayed
Monsieur Karim—Tunisian antiquities dealer
Leila—Karim's assistant

IN NIGERIA

GASHAKA GUMTI, FARGOS' SCHOOL FOR GIRLS

Pete Jeffcoat—Selma's research assistant, Corden's boyfriend
Wendy Corden—Selma's research assistant, Jeffcoat's girlfriend
Yaro—school caretaker, Monifa's husband
Monifa—school caretaker, Yaro's wife
Okoro Eze—tea farmer, Zara's father
Zara—student, Okoro's daughter
Jol—student
Tambara—student
Maryam—student
Jonathon Atiku—Nasha's uncle

IN JALINGO, NIGERIA

STREET THIEVES

Nasha Atiku
Chuk
Len

KALU BROTHERS

Bako Kalu
Kambili Kalu
Makao Oni (aka Scarface)—Area Boys gang leader

AREA BOYS

Jimi
Pili
Dayo
Den
Deric
Urhie
Joe

Whatsoever a man soweth,
that shall he also reap.

– GALATIANS 6:7 –

PROLOGUE

PART I

Ashes fly back into the face of him who throws them.
— AFRICAN PROVERB —

DECEMBER 12, 533 A.D.
Bulla Regia,
Kingdom of the Vandals, North Africa

The winter moon lit the paving stones as Gelimer, King of the Vandals, and his brother, Tzazon, galloped their horses through the old triumphal arch, past the theater, past the forum, past the still-elegant sleeping town houses. When they reached the center of the city, they veered left toward the old pagan tomb-lined highway leading out of Bulla Regia toward the hills. Once beyond the silent houses of the dead, they turned onto a long avenue filled with twisted shadows from the ancient olive trees. Their horses grew skittish as the silhouetted outlines of the neglected Temple of Saturn—the great god of the harvest—loomed up before them. A tangle of vines seemed to hold its crumbling, silver-tinged walls together, the entrance to the oracle's temple hidden in the hill behind the ruins.

The two men reined to a stop, tying their horses to one of the trees.

"This way," Gelimer said, leading Tzazon toward the temple, then up the stairs to the portico. They were met by a Moorish child, who seemed to appear out of nowhere.

She guided them over the porch of the temple, then beyond the ruins, deep into a cave in the hillside. Oil lamps hung from the ceiling at intervals, the shadows dancing across inscriptions carved into the walls. When they reached the heart of the cave, the girl stopped before an unlit chamber, Gelimer on one side of her, Tzazon on the other. Tzazon looked around. "Where is this oracle?"

The child raised her henna-traced hand in a gesture of silence. "Behold," she said, "the Sign of Saturn."

As their eyes adjusted to the dim light, they saw a tripod with glowing coals. Above this, a magic square seemed to materialize.

S	A	T	O	R
A	R	E	P	O
T	E	N	E	T
O	P	E	R	A
R	O	T	A	S

It glimmered for an instant, then vanished as the coals burst into flame. The flickering light revealed a girl not much older than the child who'd led them there. Sitting on a tall stool, she wore a turban, and was dressed in robes that shimmered like emeralds tinged with blood in the glow from the embers in the tripod. When she opened her dark eyes, she seemed to be looking straight at and through Gelimer at the same time.

The Priestess inhaled the fumes from the tripod. In a voice that seemed as thin as the wind whispering through the olive trees, she uttered her prophecy. "Saturn holds the wheels. The balance between Rhea, wealth and abundance, and Lua, destruction and dissolution . . . Hear, O King of the Vandals, the wheels have slipped. Lua reigns."

A chill penetrated Gelimer's heart. "Tell me, Sibyl, the meaning of your words."

"It is as it was foretold. As Gamma pursued Beta, now Beta pursues Gamma."

"Utter nonsense," Tzazon said. "A children's rhyme."

The Priestess inhaled. "Two lost already, at the tenth milestone."

The tenth milestone was where, in the attempt to rout the invading Byzantine Army outside of Carthage, their brother and nephew had met their deaths. Tzazon, unimpressed, spat. "She could have heard that from marketplace gossip. Or from one of Belisarius's spies. Tell me of *my* death, Sibyl, so that I can prevent it."

The Priestess turned his direction, her eyes as black as unlit coal. "Beware the third charge."

"The witch is mad," Tzazon muttered. "What does this even mean?"

The sibyl's unseeing gaze turned back to Gelimer. "Know, O King, the Saturnalia is upon us. To break the curse, the sacred scroll must be returned by one who is of royal blood. Death will come to one who is not."

"How?" Gelimer demanded. "How do I find this scroll?"

"The penultimate king sees it from the Underworld. The Usurper is blinded. He will lose that which he holds dear, until all that is left is shadow, and naught remains but vanity." Then, as if the power of her oracles had drained the energy from her slim form, the Priestess slumped in her chair and seemed to disappear.

Gelimer and Tzazon were alone with the child in the darkness.

"She's a Moor," Tzazon said to Gelimer after the child led them out. The two men walked from the temple ruins toward their horses. "She worships the old gods. How can you deceive yourself by listening to anything she tells you?"

"Deceive myself? You will be the next to die unless I find this scroll and return it."

"What is this curse you speak of?"

"It was cast as revenge from the very Priestess who helped Genseric win his conquest," Gelimer said. "Genseric stole the scroll, hid it, ordered the Priestess's death, then promised to destroy the scroll should anyone take up arms against the Vandals."

Tzazon stopped in his tracks. "You expect me to believe that something that occurred well over a hundred years ago has any effect on the here and now? You forget, brother, that these so-called oracles are masters of the vague turn of phrase. You hear what you want to hear."

"This oracle foretold Hilderic's death if he failed to find the scroll before the festival of Saturnalia, then return it to Hippo Regius."

"The only reason he is dead is because the Emperor Justinian would have tried to return him to the throne. It has nothing to do with prophecy and everything to do with protecting your kingdom."

"And what of the penultimate king's deathbed confession? How could she possibly have known that Hilderic's last words were about the map?"

"Servants talk."

"There was no one there except Ammatas, who thrust the knife into his belly at my orders. And he told no one but me. If I can find this scroll, and break the curse before we go to battle, I may yet save your life."

Tzazon freed the reins of his horse, then mounted. "Very well. Show me this map."

The two men rode back into Bulla Regia to the royal house that Gelimer had occupied after he'd deposed his cousin Hilderic from the throne. It was the same home that belonged to Genseric, after he had stolen the scroll.

And now, a century later, it was up to Gelimer to see to its return.

When they reached the royal house, a dozing groom who guarded the doorway rose to attention, taking their horses as they dismounted. The two men strode up the steps, through the great entrance, passing into the atrium, where Gelimer seized a burning torch from its sconce. The torchlight caused the mosaics on the floor to glitter like jewels beneath their feet as the brothers crossed the central hall to a marble staircase. That led down to a long mazelike corridor in the story underground, which protected the Vandal rulers from the summer heat.

At last, the brothers reached what had been Genseric's inner sanctum, then, years later, Hilderic's. The flickering light revealed a desk and chair of ivory and ebony. On the floor beneath it, a detailed mosaic from the old pagan mythology—Echo, behind one of two olive trees flanking the temple, pining for Narcissus, who lay at the foot of the stairs, the handsome youth gazing downward, his finger almost touching the blue and white pattern of the pool in front of the temple.

"I have searched this room, this house, a thousand times," Gelimer said. "There is no map."

"Perhaps it was Hilderic's final revenge. Sending you searching for something that doesn't exist. What exactly did he tell Ammatas?"

"That unless I faced my vanity, I would fail to see that which is right in front of me."

Tzazon grabbed the torch from him, pointing toward the floor. "Narcissus admiring his reflection. There's the answer to your riddle."

Gelimer stared at the shadows cast upon the mosaic by the dancing flame. Echo was looking at Narcissus, who seemed not to know she was there. Behind him was a building, which looked very much like the Temple of Saturn. "His reflection," Gelimer said as he repeated the sibyl's words in his head. *All that is left is shadow, and naught remains but vanity.* He looked up at his brother. "Vanity. That's the map. Narcissus is pointing directly at it."

"A map of what?" Tzazon said, scrutinizing the pattern in the blue and white mosaic beneath Narcissus.

PROLOGUE

PART II

War has no eyes.

— SWAHILI PROVERB —

DECEMBER 15, 533 A.D.
Tricamarum (50 kilometers west of Carthage),
Kingdom of the Vandals, North Africa

Gelimer held up his hand, signaling his army to a halt, as he and his brother, Tzazon, rode on alone to the top of the hill to survey the Roman encampment in the distance. A sense of fatality overwhelmed Gelimer as he studied the enemy, fifteen thousand strong. The sun glinted off the metal scale armor of the Roman cavalry and infantry as they sat around their fires, preparing their meals. "This is fruitless," he told Tzazon.

"Forget about the words of that witch-woman."

The sibyl's prophecy was all Gelimer thought about. Though he had sent men to search what was left of the now dry reflecting pool in front of the Temple of Saturn, they came up empty-handed. One man died after falling from his horse, the others refused to go back, fearing the curse. Gelimer had even tried to meet with the sibyl again, but they found her cave behind the temple abandoned. "I cannot lose you, too, Tzazon—"

His brother glanced at him in exasperation. "How can you trust in pagan prophecies?"

"I beg you, do not fight this battle. Go back to the stockade and guard our women and children. You'll give them courage."

"And look like a coward to my cavalry? Besides, it's my death that's foretold. Let me be the one to decide." He drew his sword, held it on high, and wheeled his horse to face his troops, crying, "Onward!"

With a mighty roar in response, the cavalry drew their swords and followed Tzazon into battle before Gelimer had a chance to countermand the order. Crossing the stream, they charged at Belisarius's center. On the right flank, Gelimer's troops held back.

Euric, his next in command, rode up beside him. "My Lord," he said. "Your men await your orders."

Gelimer rode over to the waiting troops, then held up his sword, repeating Tzazon's battle cry. "Onward!"

Euric raised his blade, shouting, "Hail, Gelimer!" They rode forth, bringing up the right flank as Tzazon took the center. Arrows flew toward them from the Romans, but the Vandals lifted their shields, rendering most of them useless. A few found their mark, the casualties dropping, but their ranks quickly filled, the Vandals repeating their battle cry as they drove into the ranks of Roman horsemen.

Swords clashed, the ring of steel deafening to Gelimer's ears. A Roman horseman charged, his spear poised toward Gelimer's chest. Gelimer parried with his shield, urged his horse around and brought his sword down, knocking the spear from his grasp. The Roman tried to draw his own blade, but Gelimer came in for the kill, driving the sharp tip beneath his armpit, knocking him from his mount. The king quickly turned, taking on a second horseman.

More Roman arrows pierced the Vandal ranks. Gelimer whirled his horse around, saw the archers riding behind the cavalry, and was about to call for his flank to work their way toward them, when suddenly Belisarius ordered the Roman Army to retreat.

The Vandals cheered, and Tzazon looked triumphant as he galloped toward Gelimer. "Cowards," he said. "You see? We have nothing to fear."

"Do not be so quick to judge," Gelimer replied, surveying the battlefield.

"They have twice the number of dead." Tzazon rode off toward his men, signaling them for their next attack.

Gelimer, unable to shake his sense of foreboding, watched Tzazon and his cavalry chase after the fleeing enemy as they tried to regroup not once but twice. The third time, the Roman horsemen ignored both the right and the left flanks, instead picking away at the center where Tzazon was fighting.

Beware the third charge . . .

"To my brother!" Gelimer cried to his men. "Protect him at all costs."

His cavalry galloped forward, scattering Romans in every direction. The Vandal warriors were superior horsemen and unparalleled with the sword, driving the enemy back as Tzazon battled a giant of a man.

The two fought bitterly, their swords clashing. The giant thrust his blade at Tzazon but missed. He tried to right himself, but Tzazon drove his sword into his enemy's shoulder, knocking him from his mount. As the man hit the ground, his sword fell from his grip. For the first time, Gelimer felt as though his Vandal Army had the upper hand.

Even Tzazon must have felt it. As he surveyed the battlefield, searching for the next Roman to kill, he caught sight of Gelimer. When their eyes met, Tzazon lifted his sword, crying out, "Hail to the King!"

Behind him, the giant stirred, grabbing his sword.

"Tzazon," Gelimer shouted.

Tzazon reined his horse around. Too late. The giant's sword arced toward him, striking his side between the plates of his armor. Tzazon faltered, his look one of surprise, as the giant thrust again, then pulled the blade from Tzazon's ribs. Tzazon's sword slipped from his grasp. He clutched his wound, staring at the blood. His horse, sensing the change in his master, suddenly reared, throwing him from the saddle.

"Tzazon," Gelimer cried as his brother struggled to his feet. A new strength surged through Gelimer's veins. He slashed at every Roman that came between them, the men falling in his wake. The giant leered when he saw Gelimer charging. He hefted the mighty blade and brought it crashing down on Tzazon's neck.

Gelimer's heart clenched. His pulse roared in his ears. He charged faster, driving his sword into the giant's chest, watching as he stumbled backward, dead before he hit the ground.

Gelimer slid from his horse, staring at his brother's fallen body. The battle raged on around him. The sounds dimmed, the world darkened.

"My Lord," Euric called. "We need orders."

Gelimer heard nothing.

"My King," Euric grabbed him by his shoulder. "Your men await your orders."

"All that is left is shadow . . ." He dropped to his knees. The battlefield was littered with the Vandal dead. His men. Tzazon's men. "Naught remains but vanity . . ." He struggled to breathe. "Tzazon . . ."

"He's dead," Euric said. "And you will suffer the same fate if we don't get out of here." Euric pulled him to his feet.

Gelimer remembered nothing afterward. Somehow, he found himself on horseback, following Euric, while the remnants of the Vandal Army fled in every direction.

CHAPTER ONE

———

A journey of a thousand miles starts with a single step.
— CHINESE PROVERB —

THE PRESENT DAY
La Jolla, California

Sam Fargo checked the figures for the second time. No doubt about it. There were several discrepancies in the accounting of the money that the Fargo Foundation had sent to fund an archeological dig in Tunisia. "It doesn't look good."

His wife, Remi, leaned toward the computer screen, her green eyes troubled as she scrutinized the numbers. She tucked a lock of auburn hair behind her ear, then suddenly rose, pacing the floor behind him. "How could this have happened? Renee LaBelle is one of my oldest friends. I can't just pick up the phone and start asking all these questions. It'll sound like I'm accusing her."

Sam swiveled his desk chair around to face her. Remi and Dr. Renee LaBelle had been roommates at Boston College and friends ever since. "As long as you two have known each other? I doubt she'll take offense. But if we don't reconcile our figures with hers, we're all going to have issues at tax time."

Remi stopped, looking at the monitor. "At least she backs up everything with ledgers. I remember her saying they had problems when they switched over to that new accounting program. That was right around the same time. Maybe there was a glitch. Something must have gotten entered wrong."

A very big glitch. And several somethings, Sam thought. A year ago, when Remi had suggested that the Fargo Foundation fund Renee LaBelle's archeological dig at Bulla Regia, he'd been against it from the very beginning. Though he and Remi had started the charitable organization to take on worthy projects of this type, he knew from experience that good friendships didn't always survive the discovery of bad money management. He'd mentioned this at the time, but Remi had her heart set on helping her friend, and had assured him that Renee LaBelle's past archeological projects had been very successful.

Unfortunately, that wasn't the case now. "We won't know anything until we sit down with her and go over the figures," he said. "Tell Renee our accountant is the one asking the questions. Like a tax thing. Which it is." Sam glanced at the clock. Just after ten in the morning. "What are they, eight hours ahead?" He picked up Remi's smartphone from the desk, handing it to her.

She pulled up a chair next to Sam. "Phone call or video? Video," she said before he could answer. "That's a little more personal. Don't sit too close. If she sees you, she'll think we're ganging up on her."

Sam leaned away from her as she made the call. Her friend's face filled the screen, her expression one of mild surprise. "Remi. Hold on. Let me step outside where it's a little quieter. I'm at dinner with the crew."

"Finish eating. It can wait. I just wanted to ask you a few questions about the books. For taxes."

"No. No. I've been meaning to call—"

"Who is it, LaBelle?" came a male voice in the background.

"Remi Fargo," she said. "Questions about the books."

A man's face appeared on the screen next to Renee's. "I've been telling LaBelle she needs to call you to set up a meeting."

Her friend nodded. "He has," she said, then seemed to realize that Remi had no idea who the man next to her was. "Sorry. This is Hank, our new site manager. Hank, Remi Fargo. She and her husband head up the Fargo Foundation. I'm sure Sam can't be too far away."

"Right next to me," Remi said, turning the screen to show Sam. He nodded at them.

Hank smiled. "So, what do you say? Set up a video call in a day or two? We know you must have questions."

Had it been a minor issue, Sam would have agreed. There was too much money unaccounted for, in his opinion, to handle it with a video call. "Turns out," Sam said, "we have to be in Nigeria next Monday. No reason we couldn't fly in a day or two earlier and stop off in Tunisia on our way. Might be easier if we all sit down together."

Renee LaBelle shook her head. "A slight logistics problem. We're in Kenya. Archeological conference. How long will you be in Nigeria? Maybe you could come by after?"

"Hard to say," Sam replied. "A week, maybe more." He and Remi were driving out to the southern edge of Gashaka Gumti National Park, where two of their assistants, Wendy Corden and Pete Jeffcoat, had been living these past few months, overseeing the construction of a self-sustaining school for girls. Though nearly finished, they'd fallen behind schedule, and their goal was to have everything done before the rainy season started. "We're checking in on one of the Foundation's projects."

Renee's face lit up. "Is that the school out in the bush? Do you actually have students yet?"

"We do," Remi said.

"Here's a thought," Renee said. "We could leave the conference a day early, meet you in Jalingo instead of flying all the way back to Tunis. Go over the books, pop out to the school . . ." She gave an apologetic smile. "Look at me, inviting myself. Last thing you need is us traipsing around while you're busy working."

Exactly what Sam was thinking. Hoping to avoid turning this into some sort of social visit, he nodded. "We'll definitely be busy."

Apparently, Hank was of the same mind, saying, "That's a bit much to be asking when they're trying to get work done. Don't forget, we'll have the crew with us." He nodded behind him.

Renee turned her phone so that the camera picked up a group of people seated around a table. "You've met Warren, of course." Her gray-haired site manager gave the slightest of nods, then went back to drinking his beer. "And one of my graduate students. Amal, say hi to the Fargos." A young woman in her early twenties, her long dark hair pulled back in a ponytail, lifted her hand, waved.

"Actually," Remi said, "that's even better. Isn't it, Sam?"

Clearly, he'd lost complete control of this conversation— assuming he'd ever had control of it to begin with. "How?"

"Having not one but two women come talk to the girls. A professor and one of her students. It's a brilliant plan."

Sam had no clue how his wife had landed on that idea. "Did you forget about the dorm we're supposed to be building?"

He wasn't surprised to find that Dr. LaBelle's mind worked in similar fashion to his wife's. She gave a nod in her colleagues' direction, saying, "We could always bring Hank. He's excellent at construction work."

"What about Warren?" Hank asked.

"Me?" Warren seemed surprised that he'd been singled out. "Too old for any heavy lifting. And someone's got to hold down the fort."

"Wait," Renee said. "It'll never work. The books are back in Tunisia."

"No problem," Remi replied. "We'll pick you up in Tunisia and we'll all fly out together."

"Wonderful idea. Don't you agree, Hank?"

"What? Yes. But we're on a tight schedule ourselves. I'm not sure how we'll—"

"Fortunately," Renee replied, "I'm the boss." She looked directly at the camera, smiling. "Get back to me with the details. We look forward to it."

Remi ended the call, looking very pleased as she set her phone on the desk. "That went well."

"Did I miss the part where we were supposed to be talking about the missing money?"

"We'll look at the books in Tunisia before flying out to the school. I'm sure there's a logical explanation."

He hoped she was right, because saying "I told you so" to your wife was never a good idea.

CHAPTER TWO

―――――

Return to old watering holes for more than water;
friends and dreams are there to meet you.

― AFRICAN PROVERB ―

Bulla Regia, Tunisia

A light breeze swept in as Sam and Remi leaned against their rented Audi RS at the edge of the archeological park. Sam looked at his watch, a few minutes past eleven. "You're sure Dr. LaBelle said ten-thirty?"

"Positive." Remi took out her phone and tried calling. "Voice mail. Do you think we should drive around and look for her? I'm sure this is where she said to meet."

Sam put his arm around her shoulders. "We can wait. How often does a guy get to stand close to a beautiful girl beneath a gorgeous blue sky?"

"Good point, Fargo," she said, leaning into him.

About ten minutes later, a midsize blue SUV pulled up.

Renee hopped out, waving to them. "Sorry. Warren normally takes over the supervision of our graduate students midmorning, but he never showed and I totally lost track of time." She quickly closed the distance, hugging Remi. "Rem-rem. So good to see you. I swear, you haven't aged a bit since the two of you got married."

"Nay-nay," Remi said and smiled. "How long has it been since we've heard those names?"

"Graduation," they said at the same time, then started laughing.

Both women had emerged with a master's in anthropology and history, though Remi's focus had been on ancient trade routes and Renee's in archeology. And, other than the two being slim, they looked nothing alike. Remi, with green eyes and red hair, stood a half head taller than the petite blond-haired, blue-eyed Renee. Their first names, however, had caused quite a bit of confusion for their unfortunate professors—and most of their friends—quite simply because they were always together and the two names were so similar. When someone dubbed them Rem-rem and Nay-nay to avoid any confusion, the nicknames stuck up until Renee left Boston College to pursue her Ph.D. in archeology.

Remi linked her arm through Renee's. "It's been far too long," she said, still feeling a bit sensitive over the real reason they were meeting. "No problems taking the time off? To come out to the school?"

"The timing's perfect. No one's going to miss us for a few days." Renee smiled at Sam. "You're sure you don't mind us tagging along, Sam?"

"Looking forward to it."

Renee laughed at the look he gave Remi. "Just not to the same degree, perhaps?"

Sam winked at her. "Happy wife, happy life."

"You married a smart man, Remi." She laughed again, then nodded toward the rolling hills and blue sky in the distance. "That's where we're headed. Before we drive out there, I thought you might want to see some of the older digs first. You have time, I hope?"

"Nothing planned," Sam said.

"Perfect. They've made a lot of progress restoring the mosaics since our college days." She grabbed her shoulder bag from her car, locked the car, and led them toward the entrance.

Because an earthquake destroyed much of the city, little remained of the villas except for the occasional column, the crumbling walls, and the theater, where the bishop Augustine had once harangued the citizens of Bulla Regia for living in a sinkhole of iniquity. The ruins of what had been two-story Roman luxury villas were unprepossessing. The ground level had been occupied in the winter so residents were able to take advantage of the warmth from the sun. In the summer, they took refuge from the intense heat in the underground chambers, many of which survived the massive quake.

Renee led them along the ancient paving stones, talking about the history of the site, then paused along the way to point out the striking detail of some of the mosaic work of the paths they were walking on. Renee led them along the ancient stones, talking about the history of the site, when Remi stopped, pointing to a group of people in the distance. "Could that be Warren and Amal?"

Sam glanced up as the woman and three men disappeared behind some ruins.

Renee shaded her eyes, looking that direction as well. "That certainly looked like Amal. She gives tours to earn extra money for school. I can't think why Warren would be there, though. Especially when he knew you were coming, and I needed him at the excavation site this morning." She gave one last look that direction, then led them toward a low rectangular parapet. "Careful," she said as they peered down some twenty feet below into a peristyle courtyard supported by six granite columns. Above the columns were large hexagonal windows, which let light into the subterranean corridors. "This is one of my favorites," she said as they descended the stairs into the heart of the villa. She stood off to one side, allowing them to see the splendor of the richly colored floor mosaics.

Remi crouched down for a better look at the intricately detailed sea creatures and twin cherubs astride dolphins, one carrying a casket of jewels, the other a mirror, gifts for a haloed Venus borne in triumph by two centaurs. "Amazing."

"That's what I think every time I come into work." Renee sighed as she looked around, then started up the steps. "Who'd have thought all those years ago that we'd be living our dream?"

"We did," Remi said.

Sam laughed, no doubt thinking about all the scrapes they'd gotten into and escaped from over the years. "Not quite how you'd planned, though. Eh, Mrs. Fargo?"

She looked over at him, laughing as she took his hand. "Not even close."

Renee was waiting for them at the top of the stairs. "What you two consider fun the rest of us consider extreme." She suddenly turned, her eyes going wide, as someone grabbed her shoulder bag, then pushed her down the stairs.

CHAPTER THREE

A tree does not move unless there is wind.
— NIGERIAN PROVERB —

Sam caught Renee as she tumbled down. Once he had her safely on her feet, he raced up the stairs. The man who had grabbed Renee's bag was now rummaging through it by the time Sam emerged. He looked up, then took off. Sam chased him along the paths and out to where their cars were parked as a dark SUV pulled up, tires kicking up dust as it skidded to a stop. Sam breached the gap between them as the driver reached over and threw open the passenger's door. The thief looked back, saw Sam, and threw the bag at him.

Sam flung it aside, lunged, grasping the man's shirt but losing his grip as the man jumped in the SUV. The vehicle sped away. In the few seconds it took to see that there was no license plate on the back, the thief rolled down the window, tossing Renee's wallet out.

Sam ran over, picked it up, and returned for the bag as Remi and Renee hurried toward him.

He handed both to Renee. "You're not hurt, I hope?"

"No. More humiliated than anything," she said, looking inside her wallet to see what was missing. "There's been an uptick in thefts around here, especially around our site. Had I been smart, I would've left my bag in the car."

"Did they take anything?" Remi asked.

"A couple dinar, but that's it. If I had to guess, they thought I was some rich tourist, not a poor archeologist." She dropped the wallet into her purse, then patted her pant pocket. "Keys right where they belong . . . I say we get out of here."

"You don't want to call the police?" Sam asked.

"Had they taken something important like my keys or ID, I would. This? Not worth the time."

When they reached their cars, they followed Renee past the main archeological park toward the foothills, parking behind her when she finally stopped.

"That's our site," she said as they walked across the uneven ground down the hill to where Hank stood watching two younger men who were kneeling by a marked-off area, carefully brushing away dirt from the dig site. "Not much to look at from here, but extraordinary up close."

Hank saw them and walked over. "Ah, the Fargos. A pleasure to meet you in person."

"Likewise," Sam said, shaking his hand.

"Has Warren come back?" Renee asked.

"Not that I've seen." Hank's brow furrowed. "You look a little green around the gills, LaBelle. Everything okay?"

"Purse snatch. Failed, I should add. Sam ran after the guy and got it back for me."

He glanced at the bag on her shoulder. "After the rash of robberies in the area, you need to be careful."

Sam nodded toward the two men working in the field. "What's going on out there?"

"That," Renee said, "is the new site that may or may not be another villa. Last year we made a topographical survey, did some coring, and dug several test pits. No serious excavation until that's all done, but there's plenty to be found on the surface."

Hank twisted off the top of his stainless steel water bottle.

"Though not nearly as exciting as the underground villa we're already excavating. You should take them to see the rest of it in person. It's spectacular. And now that we have electricity in there, we can actually work at night."

"That can wait. I want to introduce the Fargos to my grad students," she said, nodding out toward the field to the two young men. "José's from Spain, Osmond's from Egypt. I've told them all about your escapades. José's a hobbyist treasure hunter. He'll get a kick out of meeting the two of you."

"You'll miss the good daylight," Hank said. "Those two can wait."

"Good point." She smiled at Sam and Remi. "Shall we?"

Sam eyed the men, who seemed to be waiting eagerly. "I'll introduce myself and catch up to you."

"I'll go with Sam," Hank said. "Better fill a bucket if you really want to show it off."

"We will." Renee smiled as she looked over at Remi. "You have to see this . . . Did I mention there's a curse?"

CHAPTER FOUR

Hurry, hurry, has no blessings.
— SWAHILI PROVERB —

W hat curse?" Remi asked as Renee led her toward the villa. "Not that I believe in that stuff, but it was something about the last Vandal King's brother being brutally killed because of it." Renee stopped in her tracks, grinning. "With all the thefts going on around here, it just occurred to me that I should post warning signs. *Property Cursed. Violators Will Suffer a Violent Death.*"

They laughed, then continued down the uneven path for several more minutes to an area cordoned off with a chain-link fence. A padlock and chain hung on the open gate, and yellow caution signs warning *Excavation in Progress* were posted around the perimeter.

Renee pointed to their left. "Somewhere over there is where we think the stairs are located. Buried beneath tons of rubble and centuries of dirt."

"I thought they'd discovered most everything there was to find and that the work now was all about preservation."

"Exactly what I thought, until I got to know Amal." She gave a conspiratorial smile. "That's when I learned about the curse. That was the hook of her thesis. But the idea that the city extended farther than anyone had previously believed came from a strong oral history about Bulla Regia passed down through the women in her family. See that house up there?" she said, pointing past the dig site. "That's where she lives with her mother. The olive grove covering the entire hillside and all the land just beyond it has been in their family for generations. The university rents the house there at the bottom of the hill for our crew."

A gust of wind swept through the ancient trees, swirling the twisted branches. "A warning, no doubt," Remi deadpanned as spent leaves fluttered to the ground.

"Let's hope not. Last thing I need is to deal with the remnants of a centuries-old curse. Heaven knows it's caused enough problems around here these last few months."

"What sort of problems?"

"Trying to get local help. Somehow, word about the curse got out and, next thing we knew, no one would even step foot on our site." She removed the chain, pushing the gate open. "Thankfully, our graduate students are nonbelievers. They've been great at picking up the slack."

"Curse aside, what was in Amal's history that brought you all the way out here?"

"Her photograph of a charcoal burner—or, rather, the lid to one—sitting on her mother's mantel. According to Amal, her grandmother found it when she was a girl not too far from where we're digging." She handed Remi a hard hat. "The site is shored up with support scaffolding, but there's always danger of a loose chunk falling from the molded-stucco ceiling."

Remi tucked her sunglasses into her shirt pocket, then put on the hard hat. She followed Renee onto a wooden deck structure surrounding an opening from which an aluminum ladder protruded. Next to it, on the deck, sat a metal bucket and a thick coil of rope. "How deep is it?" asked Remi, peering down into the space.

"About eighteen feet." Renee preceded her down, leading her through a jungle of scaffolding, platforms, and pulleys. "Just wait until you see the floor mosaic."

The temperature dropped noticeably as they descended, and it took some time for Remi's eyes to adjust to the softly lit chamber. She could make out the dusty masonry of thin, flat horizontal bricks typical to Roman Empire buildings of the second century. At one end of the room was a large arched entranceway, behind which were huge masses of masonry where the ceiling had apparently collapsed. A work light was clamped to the railing on the first platform, its thick orange extension cord looped halfway down the side just above the rubble. "Remnants of the earthquake." Renee turned on the light, aiming it toward an area marked off with yellow and black caution tape, one end tied to the scaffolding, the other secured to a wooden sawhorse. "We're lucky so much of this survived."

She turned the light off and the two climbed down the ladder. At the bottom, she opened her canteen and poured water onto a portion of the mosaic. When the liquid washed away the film left by mineral accretions, the mosaic patterns shimmered with a remarkable depth, some with semi-precious stones, revealing a temple with a man lying on the bottom step. "Isn't it stunning?"

"Gorgeous."

"The man lying along the bottom step of the temple and looking down into the water is supposed to be Narcissus. You can see Echo there behind the tree on the other side of the temple. She's exquisite." Renee tried to brush what remained of her water over the floor. It quickly evaporated. "Or she would be. You really need enough water to get the full effect. I'll go fill the bucket."

"I'll go with you," Remi said.

"It's not that far to the water tank. Take your time, have a look around. Just stay on this side of the yellow and black tape."

Renee climbed up the ladder through the maze of squeaking scaffolding and decks, then pulled herself out.

Remi walked beneath the scaffolding that filled most of the anteroom, looking at the patterned mosaic, trying to imagine what it must have been like to live in that area centuries ago. Some of the mosaic pieces had come loose along a crack that ran beneath the rubble all the way across the floor to the other side of the room. She bent down for a closer look as the wind gusted into the chamber, causing the scaffolding and deck boards to creak like the hold of a ship. Closing her eyes against the sting of dust wafting down, she waited for everything to calm. Soon, all was quiet and she turned her attention back to the mosaic, admiring the workmanship and wondering how long it had taken to place each tiny piece.

"Still there?"

Remi looked up, saw her friend silhouetted above her on the top deck. "Still here."

"Might want to move away from the opening in case I spill water on you. It's a crude system, but try to guide the bucket so it doesn't hit the mosaic when it lands." She lifted the pail onto a hook, the rope creaking in the pulley as she turned the crank. The bucket was no more than a few feet down when a loud crack startled them.

"What was that?" Remi asked. Drops of water hit her as the bucket swung high over her head.

It took a moment before Renee answered. "The pulley, I think."

"Whatever it was can't be good. Maybe we should skip the water."

Renee, still holding the rope for the bucket, nodded. But when she tried to straighten up, there was another crack and the water-filled pail rushed downward. Attempting to stop it, she slammed her foot on the coil of rope. It ripped out from beneath her foot, wrapped around her leg, and knocked her over the side of the scaffolding. Suddenly she was the one falling as the bucket flew upward. Remi braced herself in an attempt to break her friend's fall. But the rope went taut and the woman jerked to a stop, dangling above Remi's head, too high for her to reach.

"Are you okay?"

"Holy . . ."

It wasn't until Renee started spinning that Remi realized the rope wrapped around her leg was the only thing holding her up. "Grab the scaffolding," Remi shouted.

Renee reached out, caught one of the pipes, and pulled herself to a stop. Several seconds passed before she gave what sounded like a small laugh. "Remember that frat party we went to our first year? This feels like that hangover."

"It's going to feel a lot worse if you fall." Remi pulled out her phone to call Sam. No signal.

"You think that extension cord's strong enough?"

Remi eyed the length of orange cord hanging down the side of the scaffolding. "Not sure that's a good idea. Hang on. I'm going to climb up. Maybe I can pull you onto the deck and cut the rope." But the moment she stepped onto the ladder, she heard another loud crack as dirt and debris fell from above.

She froze. One more step and she'd bring the entire thing down.

CHAPTER FIVE

———

If opportunity doesn't knock, build a door.
— AFRICAN PROVERB —

The moment Sam heard the crash echoing across the field, he whipped around. "What was that?"

"No idea," Hank said.

Sam raced down the hill, past the water tank, seeing the remnants of an observation deck constructed over a large opening in the ground. "Remi?"

"Down here," she shouted. "Renee's caught in the rope. The deck gave way."

Relief flooded through him on hearing his wife's voice. When he reached the deck, he tested its surface with one foot. It felt solid and he stepped on, leaning forward to peer in. Several boards were broken near the entrance. A crushed bucket was wedged against a pulley system, its thick rope disappearing below. What he didn't expect to see was Remi's friend hanging from that rope, stretched out between it and the ladder like a trapeze artist caught mid-performance.

"LaBelle," Hank shouted, running toward the deck.

Sam held his hand up. "Stop. I'm not sure how much weight it'll support."

Hank halted at the edge. "Is she okay?"

"So far. Do you have any rope?"

He nodded.

"Bring it here."

Hank ran to his car, unzipped a thick canvas duffel bag in the back, and returned with a rope, which he tossed to Sam. "What can I do?"

"Park your car as close to the deck as you can," Sam said, unwinding the long coil, fashioning a harness.

Hank did as he asked, then joined Sam. "Can't we just pull her up with the rope from the pulley?"

"This is safer," Sam said, not wasting time to explain the hazards of such an idea. The rope wrapped around her leg, the damage to the scaffolding, the precarious anchoring of the ladder to it—never mind if any of it fell during their rescue attempt—it all put Remi in danger.

He anchored the rope to the tow hook beneath the car's front bumper, slid into the harness, and edged his way toward the opening. The A-frame over the deck that held the pulley had collapsed. Fortunately, a deck beam and the aluminum ladder remained intact, both strong enough to have stopped the bucket wedged between them while still holding the weight of Renee LaBelle. "Remi, move back. I'm coming down."

He lowered himself into the chamber, bringing himself level to Renee, noting a trickle of red blood in the hairline above her forehead. "Anything broken?"

"Not unless you count my pride."

"You think you can grab on to my shoulders and hold on piggyback all the way up?"

"No question."

Sam gripped her wrist as she reached across his back with one arm, wrapping tight, before letting loose of the scaffold. He glanced down, saw Remi off to the side, watching.

She gave him a look of relief once he and Renee reached the top, then shouted up to Sam, "You are planning to come back for me?"

"Have I ever left you behind?"

"There was that time in . . ."

Sam waited until Hank had helped Renee from the deck before turning back around and looking down at his wife. "Never left you behind without a good excuse."

"I'm sure you had a good reason."

Sam stepped out of the harness and lowered the apparatus to his wife. She slipped into it and he pulled her up and out, helping her from the deck. "Remind me what that reason was again?" he asked, once she was on solid ground.

"The details are a bit fuzzy."

"Conveniently fuzzy."

She kissed him. "Why rehash old history?"

They walked arm in arm over to the car, where Renee was seated, examining her left ankle and calf, which looked swollen and bruised. She smiled at Remi. "Twice in one day. Guess there really is something to that curse."

Hank hovered over her, asking, "Are you sure we shouldn't get you to the hospital?"

"I'm fine. I hit my head on the ladder. It's already stopped bleeding. Remi, tell him I'm fine."

Remi took a closer look at her friend's head. "I think you might need a couple of stitches. When's the last time you had a tetanus shot?"

"I have no idea. And what about lunch? We were all supposed to sit down together and go over the books."

"The books can wait," Remi said.

"I agree, Mrs. Fargo." Hank turned a stern eye toward Renee. "You're going to the hospital, LaBelle. We can all have a good laugh over how you ended up where you did once they patch you up."

Hank drove Renee, while Sam and Remi followed in their rental car. About fifteen minutes after they arrived at the hospital, a young woman with long dark hair raced into the lobby, looked around, and made a beeline to Renee. "Dr. LaBelle."

Renee smiled. "Amal, you didn't need to come all the way out here."

"I had to see if you were okay," she said, slightly out of breath.

"I'm fine. Probably just a sprain."

"Or a break," Hank said, "we can't verify until X-rays."

Amal clasped Renee's hand, then let go as she seemed to notice Sam and Remi for the first time. "Mr. and Mrs. Fargo. Sorry. I didn't mean to ignore you. I'm Amal."

"A pleasure to finally meet in person," Remi said. "We thought we saw you out giving a tour earlier."

Amal seemed taken aback. "No. That wasn't me."

"My mistake," Remi said. "Anyway, we're so glad you've agreed to come out to the school."

"It's all very exciting, if not overwhelming." She turned toward Sam, smiling at him as she reached out to shake his hand. The moment their fingers touched, she jerked back, then suddenly clasped her throat, looking as though she couldn't breathe.

CHAPTER SIX

A friend is one who knows everything about you
and still wants to be your friend.
— AFRICAN PROVERB —

S houldn't we call for a doctor?" Remi asked as Hank led Amal
to the chair next to Renee.

"She'll be fine," Hank said, patting her hand.

Renee nodded. "Poor thing has panic attacks. Just needs to catch
her breath."

If Amal heard them, she gave no indication. Her dark eyes held a
vacant stare as she muttered something under her breath that
sounded like "Sat-er . . . Sat-er . . ."

Remi looked at Hank, then Renee, noting both seemed very calm
over the whole thing. "You're sure she's okay?"

"I promise," Renee said. "Give her a minute. She tends to drift
off and utter odd words. The French and English I get, since those
are the languages she grew up with. It's the Latin and Greek that are
somewhat surprising."

"Studying archeology?" Hank said. "Maybe not so surprising."

"Good point. Anyway, she'll be fine."

In fact, almost as soon as Renee finished talking, Amal blinked a
couple of times. "I had one of my attacks, didn't I?"

Renee nodded.

"I don't know why this happens to me. Maybe I should go home.
If I hurry, I might be able to catch my taxi before it leaves."

"Don't be silly," Renee said. "Hank can give you a ride."

"No." She gave an embarrassed smile and stood. "I don't want to leave you stranded."

"You won't," Hank said. "The Fargos have their car here. I'm sure they'll get her home just fine."

"Not until after lunch," Renee said. "I'm starved."

Hank laughed, then guided Amal out.

Remi waited for the doors to close after them, before asking Renee about Amal's health.

"Her doctor thinks they're mild seizures brought on by stress. Needless to say, she doesn't drive because of it."

Sam asked, "You think she's okay going out to the school?"

"If we can get her there, yes. Frankly, I was surprised we were able to get her out to the convention. Unfamiliar surroundings seem to affect her more and she tries to avoid them. But she loves children, so I think the school will be a great trip for her."

"Renee LaBelle?"

They looked up to see a nurse enter the lobby, pushing a wheelchair. Renee raised her hand and the nurse rolled the chair toward her and helped her into it. "Let's get that X-rayed, shall we?"

A good hour later, Renee was discharged, a bandage on her forehead, a pair of crutches for her wrapped ankle, and complaining about the tetanus shot in her left arm. "That thing hurt worse than the three stitches in my head."

Remi laughed. "You think it hurts now? Wait until tomorrow."

"Cheery thought," she said, leaning on her crutches, waiting for Sam to pull up in the car.

"You're sure you still want to go to lunch?"

"Positive. Where are we going? I'll text Hank to let him know where to pick me up."

They decided on the Fargos' hotel, since it was fairly close to the hospital. Sam walked both women in but didn't take a seat. "I've got some phone calls to make. I think I'll order room service and let you two catch up." He leaned down, kissed Remi, then left.

Renee, having taken a pain pill at the hospital, ordered a virgin Bloody Mary, while Remi ordered the real thing. When the drinks arrived, Renee lifted her glass. "To old friends, the best kind."

"To best friends, the best kind." Remi raised her glass, touching the rim to Renee's before taking a sip. "Whoa! That is one spicy drink."

"Just the way I like it."

The waiter returned with their lunch and they picked at their food, talking about everything but the reason the Fargos were in Tunisia to begin with. Remi waited until they were nearly finished eating before broaching the subject. "About why we're here . . ."

Renee sighed. "I know you have to look at the discrepancy in the books."

"I hate this."

"Not as much as I do. Hank told me I needed to call you. I . . ." She set her drink on the small square napkin, looking Remi in the eye. "I don't know why I didn't say something sooner, but Hank thinks that Warren's been skimming money from the dig. I thought for sure Hank was wrong, but when he showed me the pages in the ledger, there was no doubt. Warren denied it when Hank and I confronted him. He was even going to sit down with you and Sam this morning. He promised to straighten everything out when you got here, but then he never showed, the accident happened, and, well, now you know."

Her words came out in such a rush, it took Remi a moment to process them. "Warren?" She tried to reconcile the man she'd met with what her friend was telling her. "I don't believe it. He seemed so—"

"Quiet? Unassuming?"

"Well, yes, but I thought that was just a thing. Not that he was a crook."

"That's the only thing that makes sense." She paused as two men walked into the restaurant, standing off to the side, their gaze landing on Remi and Renee a second longer than Remi felt comfortable with. The men looked away and Renee continued on, saying, "When Hank took over the books and found those discrepancies, I was shocked."

"How long ago was this?"

Renee hesitated, looking distinctly uncomfortable at Remi's question. Finally, she gave an embarrassed smile. "Two . . . Three weeks before you called."

Sam was not going to take this well. "You should have said something."

"I know. I guess Hank and I were both hoping we were wrong. But with Warren taking off on the very day you and Sam show up . . . ? I still can't believe he'd do this to me." She gave a ragged sigh. "The biggest reason is, I was embarrassed. All that money you gave us. Gone."

Before Remi had a chance to comment, the strangers hovering near the entrance started toward them. While highly possible that they were simply two men interested in polite conversation with two women sitting alone at a table in a bar, her gut instinct told her otherwise. She edged her hand toward the silverware, wrapping her fingers around the handle of the knife, and quickly assessed which of the two she'd take down first.

CHAPTER SEVEN

*Cross the river in a crowd
and the crocodile won't eat you.*

— AFRICAN PROVERB —

I 'd hate to see you cut your visit short, Mr. Fargo."

"I'm just glad you're both okay, Pete," Sam said, cell phone to his ear, as he took the stairs down to the lobby. "So we make a little side trip before we drive out. I know Remi will agree. This school is near and dear to her heart."

"The biggest issue is that it's going to delay us. The project . . ."

That was something Sam definitely wanted an update on. But he saw his wife in the restaurant just then. "You can tell me about it when we get there. Let me go break the news to Remi."

He dropped the phone in his pocket, barreling past the two men who were also walking that direction. They took one look at Sam and did an about-face. Sam noticed Remi's gaze on them as they made a hasty departure. "Did I miss something?"

"Not sure," Remi said. "Your untimely arrival sort of put a damper on things."

Renee glanced out toward the men as they pushed through the lobby doors and made for the parking lot. "Honestly, I thought they were merely trying to pick us up."

Remi casually slipped the knife she'd palmed onto the table, her smile telling Sam she thought otherwise. "Something on your mind?"

He glanced out the window as a dark sedan took off, the car's tinted windows preventing him from seeing in. While the location of the hotel was fine, they had driven through some sketchy areas on the way back from the hospital. It wasn't unheard of that guests at hotels were often victimized, especially if they looked like helpless women who'd make easy targets. "Change of plans," he said. "We're leaving tomorrow."

"Why?" Remi looked at her friend, then back at him. "I thought we had at least another day."

"Something came up," he replied. "Supply truck for the school never made it."

"What do you mean 'never made it'?" Remi asked.

"Highway robbery. I'll tell you in the car while we drive Renee back."

HANK STARED IN SURPRISE WHEN SAM OPENED THE FRONT DOOR, holding it for Renee as she hobbled into the house she shared with the other archeologists. "LaBelle," he said, jumping up from his desk chair to assist her. "I would've picked you up. You should've called."

Sam waited for Remi to enter and closed the door after her. "No sense having you make a special trip out when we were right there."

"Well, thank you," Hank said, helping her into one of two armchairs. He eyed the soft bandage around her ankle. "No break, I see."

"More bruised than anything else," she said. "They want me to stay off it for at least five days."

"Five days? That's not bad." He took her crutches and leaned them against the wall. "So, why the serious face?"

"Their friends from the school were robbed," Renee said. "They even stole their truck."

"That's terrible." He looked at Sam. "What happened?"

"A band of robbers pulled alongside the truck somewhere between Jalingo and Serta. They pointed a gun, forcing Pete to the side of the road. Yaro, one of the caretakers, was with him. They took the truck and their cell phones, then left them stranded in the middle of nowhere."

"No one was hurt, I hope?"

"Fortunately, no. Unfortunately, Remi and I have to leave tomorrow. The school van's in the shop being repaired, so they have no transportation should any emergencies arise. Selma's arranged for a new truck, and we need to pick up a duplicate order of the stolen supplies." Selma Wondrash, their Hungarian-born head researcher, wore a lot of other hats in the Fargo household, which allowed the Fargos to continue pursuing their charitable operations uninterrupted. "We'd like to get back on schedule before Lazlo flies in."

"Who's Lazlo?" Hank asked.

"One of our researchers," Remi said. Though Professor Lazlo Kemp's specialty was cryptography, they'd hired him on full-time when he proved invaluable at helping Selma with her work. Remi smiled at Renee. "Can't wait for you to meet him."

"Two academics in one room?" She grinned. "I'm looking forward to it."

"What?" Hank said. "Surely, you're not still thinking of going, LaBelle? You're injured."

"It's only a sprain. Besides, we're hanging out at a school, not trekking through the jungle. Wouldn't miss it for the world." She directed her gaze to Sam. "As long as you think it's safe."

Sam, halfway hoping they'd back out, knew his wife was excited about bringing the two women to the school as positive role models for the students. And in this case, he happened to agree with her. Too many young girls were discouraged from getting an education, especially those living far afield in the smaller villages. As much as he'd prefer to head out without them, being able to personally talk to someone like Dr. Renee LaBelle or one of her graduate students could have a huge impact on the girls. "I'm not worried. Safety in numbers. We'll have the truck and a rental car. Two vehicles and the extra people should discourage anyone from thinking we're an easy mark."

Renee nodded. "Works for me. What about you, Hank?"

"Well, it's not that I don't want to go. I thought we weren't leaving until day after tomorrow."

"It's only a day early."

"Even so, I'll have to make some calls," he said. "Rearrange some appointments. You'd better tell Amal about what happened. She's in the kitchen with Osmond and José."

Amal seemed hesitant about going after hearing about the robbery. When José volunteered to take her place, Renee shook her head. "They're looking for women to inspire the girls. Amal, I know this will be a wonderful experience for you."

"But," Remi said, "only if you're comfortable. We'll understand if you choose not to go."

The young woman looked at everyone in turn, her face filled with uncertainty. Her gaze settled on Renee. "What do you think I should do, Dr. LaBelle? I mean, a robbery . . . ?"

"I'm not worried a bit." She put her hand over Amal's and smiled. "If anyone can get us there safely, it's the Fargos."

CHAPTER EIGHT

If you have health, you have hope,
you have everything.
— AFRICAN PROVERB —

Taraba State, Nigeria

The capital of Taraba State, Jalingo, was situated in the savanna-covered foothills not too far from the highest peak in West Africa, Chappal Waddi—the so-called Mountain of Death. The school was situated farther southwest, between the Gashaka Gumti National Park and the village of Gembu. Since that was a good six-hour drive from Jalingo, the Fargos secured hotel rooms for everyone, intending to set out the next morning after a good night's rest.

Once they arrived at the hotel, they decided to have dinner in the on-site restaurant. Sam and Remi stepped off the elevator to find Renee and Amal waiting for them in the small lobby. "Where's Hank?" Sam asked.

"He'll be down in a minute," Renee said. "Something about a phone call and a small fire to put out."

In fact, he met them in the restaurant just a few minutes later.

"Everything work out?" Sam asked as a waiter set out glasses of water for each of them.

"It did," he said, taking a seat. "I was trying to arrange a crew to come in to fix that decking. That blasted curse."

"Tell me about it," Renee said, exasperated. "Over fifteen hundred years ago. You'd think they'd get over it by now. Hard to get locals to come in and work because of it."

"Yes. No need to worry now, at least as far as the decking's concerned. They've agreed to do the work." He raised his water glass in a toast. "Here's to a successful trip."

"Hear! Hear!" Renee said.

Hank took a sip, then looked over at Sam, his expression sobering. "Had we been smart, we'd have brought the books with us to go over. I'm assuming LaBelle has already told your wife that we believe Warren may have been skimming funds."

"That would explain the financial hit," Sam said. As much as he wanted to discuss the embezzlement of the Foundation's funding. "The books aren't going anywhere and we can talk to Warren when we get back. Obviously, the more pressing matter is getting the truck and supplies to the school."

"I agree," Hank said. "That far south, they can't possibly depend on a delivery from Jalingo every time they need something. Surely there's somewhere closer?"

"They get the basics from Gembu, a village about two hours' drive south. But the roads around Gashaka Gumti aren't the best. What we're hoping to do is make the school self-sustaining for exactly that reason. So they won't have to depend on anything or anyone. Unfortunately, this truck robbery set us back."

"I can imagine," Hank said. "That was pretty brazen. But I've heard highway robbery out in the bush isn't uncommon."

"Not just the bush," Renee said. "I was reading the newspaper in the lobby. It seemed like every other article was about the increasing gang activity in Jalingo."

"Big-city life," Sam said. "It's almost a given, no matter where you go in the world."

"I suppose so," Hank said. "But rural life down here can be bad. Aren't you worried about Boko Haram and the like?"

"That's always a worry," Sam replied. The terrorist militant group, based in northeastern Nigeria, was known worldwide for suicide bombings as well as kidnapping women and children, and had been trying for years to establish a stronghold farther south. While the school's isolation made it an attractive target, Jalingo, less than a day's drive, was a large enough city to have a strong police and military presence. "They're more active up near the northern Nigeria border."

Hank was about to comment when instead he glanced at Renee. "Are you okay, LaBelle? You seem a little pale. It's not your ankle, is it?"

"No." She gave a tired smile. "I'm sure I'll feel better in the morning, but after the conference and my accident, I've hit a wall."

"I'll go up with you," Hank said, helping her with her crutches.

She nodded. "I think what I need is a good night's sleep." She put her hand on Remi's shoulder as she looked at Sam. "What time do you want to leave in the morning?"

"Nine should work."

"See you then."

The next morning, everyone but Renee had gathered in the lobby. Amal paced the floor, talking softly to herself. "You can do this. You can do this . . ."

Remi and Sam gave her space, pretending not to notice. Hank watched her a moment, then joined them. "I hope she'll be okay. The convention was a big step for her. The stress exacerbates her anxiety, which apparently causes these mild seizures."

"Does she take medication for it?" Remi asked him.

"I'm not sure," he said as the elevator door opened.

Renee stepped off, her face pale, her eyes watery. "I hate to cancel at the last second, but I've been sick to my stomach all night. I've definitely caught some bug, and my ankle's a bit more swollen."

Amal took a tentative step toward her. "I'll stay with you, Dr. LaBelle."

"I don't think it's anything serious, but you probably shouldn't get too close. I'll be fine. What I need to do is prop my foot up and rest, just like the doctor said. You should go."

"Without you? What if something happens?"

"If we had a crystal ball and knew everything bad that was coming down the chute, we'd all be paralyzed. Venture out, spread your wings."

"But—"

"Have faith in yourself, Amal. You might be surprised. Besides, the Fargos will take good care of you."

"But the girls," Hank said. "They're expecting you, LaBelle. Never mind that you can't stay here alone."

"I'll be fine. I checked with the hotel. They're actually happy to have me stay." Renee gave a tired sigh. "I'm sorry, Remi. Maybe I'll recover in a day or two . . ."

Remi looked at Sam as though he had some power over the situation.

"Her health is more important," Sam said. "If she gets better, we'll swing by and get her after we pick up Lazlo from the airport. Until then, the girls are going to have to make do with a site manager and graduate student."

CHAPTER NINE

*A difficult journey will make you daring
and harden your will.*

— AFRICAN PROVERB —

Makao clutched the steering wheel of his white extended-cab Toyota Tundra pickup as it bounced from one pothole to another on the long stretch of washed-out road a couple of hours outside of Jalingo. A thin film of red dust covered everything inside the cab, including the black dash bearing the smudged fingerprints from his passenger Jimi, who braced his left hand against it while gripping his right around the barrel of his assault rifle.

Makao glanced in the rearview mirror to the backseat where two more men rode, both cradling their rifles in their laps. All three passengers were *agberos*, criminals he'd trained from a young age after picking them up over a decade ago on the streets of Lagos.

Men who would do his absolute bidding, no questions asked.

Every one of them had started off as Area Boys, the name given to the mostly harmless pickpockets and thieves that infiltrated every busy street in the populous city. Most worked in loosely based gangs run by low-level crooks. That was how Makao got his start, rising through the ranks, making enough money to buy some form of respectability, even a position in the local government. And, it was where he learned that law enforcement tended to look the other way unless their hands were forced, usually due to the actions of those boys with a predilection for violence.

That was why he and his crew had to flee Lagos. To avoid being arrested for murder after a series of robberies gone wrong. A helpful tip from one of his police friends on the take had allowed them to escape, until such a time when all the witnesses could be eliminated.

His reputation, thankfully, preceded him, and it didn't take long before he dominated the larger criminal enterprises in Taraba State. And though he was trying to maintain a low profile, when Tarek called him about the job, it was one he simply couldn't pass up. The potential payoff was too great, with his share making the predawn departure into the middle of nowhere very much worth it.

"There." Jimi pointed out the dusty windshield toward a stand of trees to their left at the base of the rolling hills that led up to the forest in Gashaka Gumti.

Makao slowed the pickup and rolled to a stop. "This should work. There's nothing but grass for miles. We'll see them the moment they try to run—if they try."

He set the parking brake, left the engine running, then waited for the dust to settle before opening his door. To the north, the direction they'd come from, a few trees dotted the savanna that stretched out on either side of the road beneath a cloudless blue sky. They were headed southeast, and he turned that direction, eyeing the road where the pavement—or what remained of it—started again just before the bend. A half mile past, a thick stand of trees created some natural cover.

He slapped the side of the truck. "You two gather leaves and grass. Jimi, get the bag. We'll set up here."

The men left their guns behind, hopped out of the truck.

Jimi walked around to the back, lowering the tailgate, grabbing a large black vinyl satchel by its strap. The contents jangled as he dragged it from the bed of the pickup. "Where do you want me to drop them?"

Makao pointed to the narrowest stretch of road. "There."

Jimi trudged over, shaking the contents of the bag into the road, the dark gray tire spikes scattering across the ground. Once the bag was empty, he kicked dirt across the spikes until they were nearly as red as the road.

Makao leaned against the side of the truck, lighting up a cigarette, waiting for the men to finish tossing grass and leaves over everything to hide the hazard. "Not too high," he said. "We don't want them driving around it."

If they did, his men would shoot out the tires, the plan of last resort. In his opinion, these things always worked best when no shots were fired.

A few minutes later, he took a final drag of his cigarette, then blew out a plume of smoke, eyeing their work. They'd done a fairly good job camouflaging the spikes. He dropped his cigarette into the dirt and stomped it out with his boot heel. "Let's go."

The men jumped back into the Toyota and he drove around the hidden spikes, following the bend past the trees, searching for an area wide enough in the forest's edge to park the truck where it wasn't visible from the road.

His vehicle hidden, they found a spot beneath the trees and settled in for the long wait. Makao checked the message from Tarek on his phone, looking at the pictures of the Fargos and their Land Rover, smiling to himself.

This was going to be easy money, no doubt about it.

CHAPTER TEN

If you want to go quickly, go alone.
If you want to go far, go together.
— AFRICAN PROVERB —

After breakfast, Sam, Remi, Amal, and Hank stopped to pick up the new supply truck, with its canvas cargo cover, that Selma had purchased for the school. The sight of the Mercedes Zetros 4×4, meant to handle the rough mountain roads, seemed to make Amal nervous. Perhaps, Remi thought, it was a reminder that they'd be miles away from anywhere should she have one of her attacks. The moment Sam took possession of the keys, Amal turned a worried glance Remi's way. "I hope you won't be upset, but I'm just not sure about going. I can stay with Dr. LaBelle until she's better."

"Of course I'm not upset," Remi said. "Disappointed, yes, because I know the girls will love you. But you have to do what's right for you."

Sam walked up a moment later. "We're ready to go."

"Amal's changed her mind. We need to take her back to the hotel."

"Honestly," Amal said. "I'd be glad to take a taxi."

Hank, overhearing Amal, looked up from his phone. "Remember how you worried about the conference? That turned out okay. And in a couple of days, Dr. LaBelle will be joining us."

Remi gave her an encouraging smile. "He's right. We'll have fun.

And if, for some reason, you feel as if you need to come back, we'll bring you home."

The moment she nodded in agreement, Sam held out the Land Rover key fob to Hank. "Any chance I can have you drive the car to the surplus store? It'll give me a chance to go over the truck controls with Remi. Just in case."

"Absolutely," Hank replied.

Remi climbed into the truck, then turned a shrewd glance toward her husband. "You didn't seem terribly broken up when you thought Amal wasn't coming."

"Let's just say I was being pragmatic. If she didn't come, Hank wouldn't come. We'd probably get a lot more work done without entertaining a couple of outsiders."

"Spoilsport. A slight inconvenience to us, but worth the trouble. Think how much those girls would benefit talking to a young university student like Amal." She gave an exasperated sigh as she buckled her seat belt. "Not that I intend on driving this thing unless I absolutely have to, show me what I need to know."

After a quick lesson, Sam headed into the central part of town, eventually reaching a crowded street filled with vendors selling goods beneath large umbrellas, their bright colors faded from the sun.

Pedestrians and motorbikes weaved in and out of the slow-moving traffic. Horns beeped, music blared, and the cacophony of bartering between shoppers and sellers filtered in through Sam's open window as he navigated his way down the street at a snail's pace.

"There it is," Remi said, pointing to a storefront farther down the block.

Sam stopped in front of the building to let Remi out, motioning for Hank to pull up alongside him. "Find somewhere to park and come back here."

Hank nodded, started to idle forward, stopped to let Amal out of the car before taking off again.

"Watch out for pickpockets," Sam called out. Remi waved to him as he drove to the back of the store, parking the truck in front of the loading dock. By the time he returned, Hank jogged up.

"Apparently," Hank said, slightly out of breath, "parking around here is at a premium. Had to leave the car around the corner." He eyed the dilapidated-looking warehouse. "Wouldn't a bigger store get you better prices? It'd definitely get you a nicer place to shop."

"That it would," Sam said. "But Pete and Wendy prefer to work with the smaller businessman, trying to keep the money local."

Hank wiped his brow, then looked out across the street at a restaurant. "Are you going to be a while? I'm starving and dying of thirst. Probably should have eaten a bigger breakfast." He glanced at Sam. "Or am I being presumptuous? I should have asked if we had time."

"No," Sam said. "You're fine. Remi and I just wanted to add a few extra things to our replacement order. They'll still have to load the truck. Maybe an hour?"

"Plenty of time," Hank said. "Amal? You're welcome to join me."

"Thank you, no. I'm going to wait here in the shade. Stretch my legs a bit."

He crossed the street and stopped in surprise as a group of children ran up and surrounded him, some actually tugging on his shirt. At first he shook his head, but then reached into his pocket, pulling out some coins, tossing them into the air. Thinking to make his getaway, he turned, only to run into more kids coming in from the other direction. For a moment, it looked as though he'd be mobbed, but a police car drove by and the children scattered.

"Let's hope he was smart enough to hold on to his wallet," Sam said. He looked at Remi. "Shall we?"

"I'll meet you inside." She glanced over at Amal, worried about leaving her out there alone. "Are you sure you wouldn't like to come in with us?"

Amal, looking at her phone, dropped it, staring almost in disbelief as it hit the ground.

Remi, concerned, picked up the phone, tried to hand it to her, but from the expression on the young woman's face, it was almost as if Remi wasn't even there. "Amal . . . ? Are you okay?"

CHAPTER ELEVEN

No matter how good you are to a goat,
it will still eat your yam.
— NIGERIAN PROVERB —

It was several seconds before Amal moved. She waved as though trying to clear cobwebs in front of her. "Throw back . . . your veils . . ." she said in French. And then, as quickly as it came over her, she seemed fine. "I . . . I think I had one of my spells."

"It certainly looked like it." Remi, afraid to leave her behind, guided her into the store. "Maybe you should wait in here until we're done shopping."

"Good idea."

The white-haired clerk, seeing there was some sort of issue, brought out a plastic chair and placed it next to his counter. "I'll watch her."

"Thank you," Remi said. She hovered over the young woman a few moments.

"I'm fine," Amal said. "Really."

"We'll only be a few minutes."

"Go. Please. I promise I'll sit right here until you get back."

Sam nodded toward Remi. "Sooner we get this done, sooner we can get on the road."

"IT WAS SO ODD," REMI SAID, ONCE THEY WERE OUT OF HEARING. "Almost as if she was looking right through me." She followed him down the aisle, accessing the text Wendy had sent that morning of the additional items they needed for the school. "Ten buckets."

Sam's attention was on a boy, about twelve or so, standing near the endcap, peering at them through the shelves of liquid detergent. He'd been one of the children who'd crowded around Hank just before he'd walked into the restaurant across the street. "Buckets of what?"

"Of what?" Remi looked up, her green eyes filled with exasperation. "Seriously, Fargo. You're beginning to worry me. Buckets for the school."

"Sorry." He glanced at the list on her phone, glad that the bulk of supplies were preordered, and waiting to be loaded on the truck out back. "Ten buckets," he said.

Remi eyed him, then the boy at the end of the aisle. "You can't think he's any sort of problem. The first gust of wind would blow him away."

Sam looked over at his wife, almost surprised. They were usually on the same page when it came to potential threats. "It's not him I'm worried about. It's his gang of pickpockets and thieves waiting outside for us. You saw them surround Hank."

"You're worried about Hank? Living in Tunisia, I imagine he's got plenty of experience avoiding—"

"Not him. Us. We've been marked as a target."

"Noted," she said, going back to the list. "Except I'd amend that to you being marked as a target. I seriously doubt that I have anything they want."

In that respect, Remi was correct. Prepared for their trip into the bush, she was dressed in khaki slacks and an olive green button-down shirt. They both knew this area of Jalingo was rife with gangs, which was why Remi wasn't carrying a purse or wearing any jewelry. Amal, Sam noticed, had taken the same precautions. Remi, like

Sam, was carrying a concealed gun, hers in a slim holster beneath her shirt, his holstered behind a secret panel in his safari vest. Other than that, the only thing Sam carried that might fall prey to a pick-pocket was his wallet—not that he was worried. He'd moved his billfold up to his top vest pocket, zipping it tight, before he ever left the supply truck.

With the last item checked off, they reached the front of the store, where Amal still waited. Sam paid for the supplies, arranging to have everything boxed and stacked on pallets for delivery. The clerk read the name on the purchase order. "Fargo . . ." he said. "That sounds familiar. We just filled this earlier in the week. The girls' school near Gashaka Gumti, yes?"

"It never made it," Sam said. "This time, we're delivering it personally."

The man turned a dubious glance toward Remi and Amal, then back to Sam. "These days, the roads can be dangerous. It might be better to pay someone to deliver it for you."

"We appreciate your concern, but we'll be fine. What time will it be ready?"

The man looked over the paperwork, picked up the phone, talked to someone in a melodic language Sam didn't recognize. "They just started to load the truck. Maybe an hour?"

"We'll see you then."

The clerk nodded, caught sight of the boy, who was pretending interest, reading the label on a jug of bleach near the front door. "Out of here, you." The boy left, and the clerk turned to Sam, handing over his copies of the purchase order and receipt. "Terrible thing, what is happening here. It used to be only in the big cities like Lagos. Now, it's everywhere. I've heard that the boys are forced to steal."

"Who's forcing them?" Remi asked. She had a particular soft spot for children and championed any cause that might help.

"Street gangs. And now we have Boko Haram."

Sam perked up. "You think they're responsible for the robbery of our supply truck?"

"Boko Haram? No. Around these parts, that'd be the Kalu brothers. Those kids work for them. Be careful, whatever you do."

"We will," Sam said, tucking the invoices into his pocket. "Thank you."

He, Remi, and Amal left. Amal nodded toward the restaurant. "Hank's still in there."

Sam glanced over, seeing several of the children, including the boy who'd been watching them inside the store, mingling around the door of the restaurant. "Time to collect him," Sam replied. Hank walked out the door almost as soon as Sam stepped off the curb. One of the children shouted, and Sam heard a corresponding shout farther down the block. "That can't be good," he said to Remi.

A group of kids raced up to them, clearly a distraction, as they tried to cross the street toward Hank. Remi elbowed Sam. "Don't let them steal the truck keys. If anything happens to that—"

"We'll never hear the end of it from Selma," he finished. He dug the keys from his pocket, gripping them tight, as several boys ran straight for him, holding their hands out, begging for money and candy in heavily accented English.

No sooner were the three of them surrounded than Sam spied their Land Rover driving by, a boy, barely tall enough to see out the windshield, at the wheel.

Remi stopped short. "That's ours!"

"Call the police," he said, breaking into a run as the vehicle continued down the street, its progress hampered by pedestrians and traffic.

The distraction had never been about taking anything from them. It was about delaying them long enough to find the car after they'd stolen the keys from Hank's pocket.

The pretend beggars scattered like rats as Sam gained on the slow-moving vehicle. The boy at the wheel panicked when he saw Sam chasing him. He hit the brakes, threw open the driver's door, about to jump out. When Sam came closer, he scrambled toward the passenger's door instead. With no one at the wheel, the car rolled down the street, angling to the right—directly toward a flimsy-looking chain-link fence surrounding a massive liquid petrol tank with a bright red *Danger. Explosives* sign posted on it.

CHAPTER TWELVE

Do a good deed and throw it into the sea.
— EGYPTIAN PROVERB —

S am sprinted faster, reached into the open door, grabbed the
steering wheel, yanking it to the left, away from the liquid petrol tank. He jumped inside, guiding the truck to a stop just
inches from the fence. The kid, eyes wide, threw himself at the
passenger's door, working the handle.

"I'm not going to hurt you," Sam said, turning the car ignition off.

The boy, unconvinced, rammed his shoulder into the door, the
chain links rattling as he tried to force it open.

Remi ran up. "Nice save, Fargo." She peered into the still-open
driver's door at the boy, his futile efforts to escape hampered by the
fence. "No one hurt, I hope?"

"Not that I can tell," Sam replied as a police car pulled up behind them.

A uniformed officer approached, standing next to Remi, peering
in at the boy, then saying something, his tone harsh.

The boy's dark eyes widened and he shook his head, pressing
himself farther into the door.

Sam, who barely understood the thickly accented English, was
surprised when Remi smiled sweetly at the officer, saying, "You're
mistaken, sir." Her gaze landed on Sam as she added, "This boy
wasn't the thief at all. He was waiting for us in the car when it rolled

away. It's our fault for leaving the keys in the ignition. Isn't that right, Sam?"

It didn't matter that Sam had no idea what his wife was talking about, or that they'd caught the boy dead to rights. He recognized that look in his wife's eyes. "Exactly. I must have left it in neutral."

The officer, not convinced, focused on the boy. "You didn't try to steal it?"

Again, the boy shook his head.

"No harm, no foul," Sam said.

Finally, the officer gave a curt nod. "Let me get my report form."

Sam, at the driver's door, blocking the kid's only route of escape, waited until the officer was out of earshot. "What gives?" he asked Remi. "He almost got away with the car and all our luggage in the back. We're just going to let him go?"

"Not him. Her."

Surprised, Sam took a closer look. A fine layer of dust covered the child's dark skin and close-cropped hair. She was a good half head smaller than the other boys, thinner, more delicate-looking, and her dark eyes widened in shock as though surprised they had discovered her secret. "Regardless. The girl's a car thief." He turned the full force of his glare on the kid. "Why'd you take our car?"

She hesitated for the barest of seconds, looking from Remi to Sam, perhaps sensing that whatever answer she gave could make the difference between being arrested or turned loose. "I found it."

"You found it?"

Before he could question her further, she turned a pleading gaze toward Remi. "If they find out I'm a . . . You won't let him take me, will you?"

"Of course we won't," Remi said. "What's your real name?"

"Nash . . . Nasha." The girl, seeing the officer returning with his clipboard, covered her face with her hands, making a loud sobbing noise.

"Do something," Remi whispered. "We are not letting them arrest her."

It didn't matter that Sam was certain the girl was faking tears for their benefit. What did matter was that Remi had made up her mind. Hoping he wasn't going to regret this decision later, he headed off the officer a few feet from their car. "Look," Sam said. "There's no damage to our car. Or the fence. Any chance we can make a quick report and be on our way? We're delivering supplies to a girls' school that's being built out near Gashaka Gumti. It'd be nice to get there before dark."

Remi, doing a superb job of blocking an immediate view of the girl, smiled at the officer as he mulled it over. He pulled a pen from his shirt pocket, angled it over the clipboard, then looked at Sam. "Name?"

"Sam Fargo. My wife, Remi Fargo."

"What's the boy's name?"

"Nash," Remi said.

"Nash . . . ?"

Sam looked at Remi, who in turn looked at Nasha. The child wiped her tears. "Atiku."

"Age?"

"Eleven."

The officer turned his attention to Sam. "You understand there's a fine for leaving your keys in the car?"

Paying on the spot was standard fare in this country. "Of course," Sam said as Remi gave a subtle nod to her left. He looked that direction and saw Hank patting his pockets, his expression turning to one of disbelief as he realized the keys had been stolen from him. Sam handed Remi his wallet, then left to divert Hank before the officer saw him. "Why don't you wait with Amal in the shade. No sense all of us getting involved. Remi can take it from here."

Realization dawned on Hank, the moment the officer took off in his patrol car, without their thief in custody. "That pickpocket stole the keys from me. He should be in jail."

"Easy," Sam said as Hank tried to move past him. Though he wasn't drunk, Sam could smell the alcohol on his breath. "It keeps us all from having to come back for court."

"Court?"

"Exactly. Remi and I don't have that time. Do you?"

He shook his head. "No," he said, leaning around Sam, trying to see what Remi was doing. "Is your wife really giving that kid money?"

"Of course not," Sam said, though knowing Remi, she probably was. He led Hank back across the street. "Don't you think it's a little early to be drinking?"

"Apparently not," he said, patting his pockets once more. "What if they got my wallet?"

CHAPTER THIRTEEN

———

You cannot beat a child to take away its tears.
— AFRICAN PROVERB —

Nasha stuffed the money into the pocket of her pants, not even bothering to count it, half tempted to say nothing about where it came from. Something told her that if any of the Kalu brothers learned of the generosity of the Fargos, they'd try to exploit it, then punish her because she had the misfortune of getting caught stealing the car. It'd be worse if one of them somehow discovered how it was she'd managed to avoid being turned over to the police. She'd survived this long on the streets because no one had realized the secret she'd taken such great pains to hide, especially from the Kalu brothers.

Being a girl was bad enough. Being an orphaned girl was worse. They were the ones who disappeared, never to be seen again.

Racing across the street, she dodged a car that suddenly pulled away from the curb. She didn't stop until she reached the alley, out of sight of the police, the Fargos, and anyone else who might see her. When she was alone, she dug her hand into her pocket, counting the thick wad of bills, and almost crying real tears when she realized how much the Fargo woman had given her.

Chuk, one of the boys from her uncle's village, ran up behind her. "Did you get anything?"

She nodded.

Small, like Nasha, his eyes widened when he saw the wad of bills she pulled from her pocket. "How much?" he asked.

"I don't know." She handed a few bills to him, then gasped when she saw his swollen cheek. "Who did that?"

"No one," he said, crumpling the money in his fist. "I fell."

She didn't believe him for a moment, but she was too excited by the Fargos' gift. "Put that away before someone sees it or they'll take it from you."

He stuffed it into his pocket, then walked alongside her. "You won't leave me here, will you?"

Nasha was surprised by the hurt in his voice. "Why would you say that?"

"Because now you have enough money to go home."

What she didn't have was enough to take him with her. "I promised we'd stay together. I meant it." They reached the door of the ramshackle furniture repair shop where she and all the other boys lived. The moment they entered, Chuk ran down the hall. Nasha hung back in the front room, filled with broken chairs. Counting off half the money to go toward their bus tickets, she stuffed that into her pocket, kept out the rest to turn over, and knocked on the door to Bako Kalu's room.

Bako lowered his beer can, his eyes narrowing as she walked in. "What are you doing back? Why aren't you with the others?"

She held out the paper bills.

He snatched them from her hand, tossing them onto the table next to a heap of coins and wrinkled bills. The sight of that other money surprised her. Frightened her. When she looked at him, he leaned forward, pointing at her with his can. "You're not holding out on me?"

Heart thumping, she told him no.

He cocked his head toward the door. "Get out."

She backed to the door, then hurried down the hallway to the small room she shared with Chuk and some of the other boys.

Checking to make sure no one else was in there, she moved the rags that doubled as her bed, pulled the money from her pocket, and lifted the floorboard.

Her breath caught.

Empty. All of it gone.

"So, it's true."

Nasha spun around, seeing Bako glaring at her from the doorway. And behind him, Chuk and one of the older boys, Len. Chuk wouldn't even look at her.

Bako crossed the room, grabbing her by the arm, ripping the cash from her hand. "You steal from me? After all I've done for you?" His grip tightened, his face filled with disgust, as he held out his hand for the rest of the money.

"That's all there is, I swear."

He eyed it, then her. "If you weren't so small and nimble, I'd toss you back where I found you." He shoved her against the wall, pain shooting across her shoulder as she hit the wood siding. Gritting her teeth, she tried not to cry out.

"Quit your whining," he said, before turning his attention toward Len. "Go get my brothers. We're going to get that truck and their car."

"How?" Len asked. He'd been the lookout in the store. His job was to delay their marks, giving them time to steal the Land Rover.

"Same way we took the last one."

The boy shifted on his feet.

"What is it?" Bako asked him.

"I don't think you should. This man. He's not like the others. He watched us. He knew. I think he's—"

"He's what?"

"Dangerous."

Bako's black eyes narrowed as he lifted his shirt, revealing the butt of a gun. "So am I. If he puts up any fight, we'll kill them all. Very simple. Now go."

The boy ran out the door and Bako's attention returned to Nasha.

Pulse pounding in her ears, she cowered in the corner. He grabbed the hammer from the table, his gaze boring into her for several seconds. "You remember what happened to the last boy who stole from me?"

She nodded, tucking both hands beneath her arms. Chuk stood in the doorway, looking sick to his stomach. Not as sick as she felt. He was the only one who knew where she hid the money.

Heavy footsteps in the hallway drew Bako's attention. He turned to see both of his brothers and Len shuffling into the room past Chuk.

The oldest, Kambili, leaned against the doorframe. "What's so important we had to come running?"

"Remember that truck we robbed a few days ago?" Bako said. "From the girls' school? They're back."

"No. We don't hit the same people. Too dangerous. They'll know to expect us."

"Yes. But this time may be easier and more profitable. Len here tells me they have many friends."

"How many?"

"Four. Three of them are Americans. And they're carrying cash."

"You're sure?"

He nodded, weighing the hammer in his hand as though testing his grip.

Kambili focused on the hammer. "What are you doing with that?"

"Nash stole their car, but got caught. So, one strike for getting caught. The other for stealing from us."

"That boy is one of our best pickpockets. You'll end that if you smash his fingers."

Bako slapped the flat side of the hammer's head against his palm, his gaze locked on Nash the entire time. "He's also one of our best beggars. Think how much more he'll bring in if he's injured. Sympathy."

Bako took a step toward Nash, raising the hammer.

"But not now," Kambili said, stopping him. "If you're serious about taking that truck, you need to leave now."

Bako glared at Nash, then suddenly smiled, his stained yellowed teeth looking like fangs. "Later is better. I can take my time. One finger at a time." He tossed the hammer onto the washstand, pushed Chuk from the room, and followed his two brothers out the door, slamming it closed.

Nasha heard the key turn in the lock, their footsteps receding down the hallway. She ran to the door, tried to open it, and slid to the floor, her knees giving out beneath her.

Bako had caught another boy stealing and had smashed every finger of his right hand. Two had become infected and had to be amputated. Though the boy had tried pickpocketing with his left hand, he couldn't, and now had to beg to earn his keep.

Nasha, like her mother, was ambidextrous, able to use both hands equally. Even so, she wasn't about to wait around and risk losing any of her fingers. She'd long ago given up any hope that her uncle was returning for her or Chuk.

The bus tickets had been their only hope.

And now that the Kalus knew they couldn't trust her, they'd be watching her every move. The longer she stayed, the greater the danger.

Girls like her didn't stand a chance. They disappeared like her aunt.

The door handle jiggled. "Nash? Are you mad at me?"

"You shouldn't have told."

"I just wanted to see how much we had. Bako caught me."

She looked at the hammer, unable to tell if that was rust or dried blood on its head. And though her stomach turned at the sight, she picked it up, strode to the window, smashing the glass from the frame.

The door handle jiggled harder. "Nash. I'm sorry. You can have my money."

She climbed up onto the sill.

"Don't leave me! . . . Nash . . . You promised."

She could still hear his cries as she raced down the alley.

CHAPTER FOURTEEN

A child is a child of everyone.
— SUDANESE PROVERB —

After a quick lunch at the same establishment that Hank had gone into earlier, the Fargos were ready to hit the road. Sam left to get the truck, while Remi, Hank, and Amal waited near the recovered Land Rover. Remi gripped the keys tight, not taking any chances that the pickpockets might return. Curiously, the street was empty of all but a couple of the boys, who watched them from a distance.

As Sam drove up in the truck, Remi unlocked the driver's door of the Land Rover. "Let's hit the road."

"You sure you don't want me to drive?" Hank asked. "I know I had a drink, but I'm fine. I was thinking about the books, and Warren, and the embezzlement . . . I had one shot. That's it."

He seemed perfectly sober to Remi, but they were in a foreign country with a rental car. "Why don't you ride with Sam in the truck," she said. "It'll give Amal and me a chance to get all our girl talk out of the way. You boys won't be bored during dinner. Win-win, right?"

Hank nodded, walking to the truck.

Remi looked at Amal, asking, "Does he typically start drinking this early in the day?"

"Not that I've ever noticed," Amal said. "Then again, the convention was the first time I've really spent much time with him outside of the dig site."

She followed Remi to the car and the two rode in companionable silence. It wasn't until they reached the open road that the conversation started to flow again. Remi glanced over at her. "I hope you don't mind my asking, just in case it happens again while we're out, but about your . . ."—*anxiety attack* didn't seem like the right description—". . . exactly what happens to you?"

"I guess the best way to describe it is, I disappear into myself."

"Is there a medical reason?"

"Depends on which doctor you ask, but the general consensus is that it's like a mild seizure. It almost feels like my brain is buzzing. Like I'm instantly asleep and I get a flash of a dream, then wake up."

"Do you remember them?"

"The dreams? Sometimes. Especially if someone reminds me of what I did or said. Apparently, I tend to say a lot."

"Well, in this case, you were swatting at something while talking about throwing back veils."

Amal laughed. "I felt like I was in a cloud, a fog, and everyone was gone. I think I was trying to clear it away. Anyway, to answer your question, I don't think it's dangerous. Usually my family just makes sure I don't fall."

"Sam and I can do that. I promise."

"Enough about me, how did you and Dr. LaBelle meet?"

"College," Remi said, and they spent the next part of the trip discussing dorm life. Long after the town of Jalingo had disappeared, the rough paved road turned into a pockmarked ribbon of red dirt, evidence of past flooding having washed the asphalt away. Within minutes, a thin film of dust covered the windshield, making it difficult for Remi to see. She turned on the wipers, then called Sam's cell phone. "You mind if we switch positions? I'm Braille-driving back here."

"Something we didn't think about with a second vehicle. You take the lead. I'll hang back until you get far enough ahead to keep the dust to a minimum."

"Thank you, Fargo. Very gentlemanly of you."

He slowed, allowing her to pass. She drove alongside the truck, doing a double take when she thought she saw someone peeking out from beneath the canvas cargo cover. "Sam, there's someone hiding in the back of the truck."

Sam pulled to the side of the road.

Remi parked beside him. "Wait here," she told Amal, setting the emergency brake, before meeting Sam alongside the truck. She pointed to the canvas covering near the tailgate. When he started to reach for his gun, she waved him off. "I think it's our pickpocket."

Sam lifted the corner of the canvas.

Nasha stared out at them, her eyes going wide, her expression one of panic. "You can't stop," she said. "What are you doing?"

"What're we doing?" Sam glanced at Remi, then back at the girl. "I'm asking you the same."

Hank jumped out of the cab, walking back toward them. "What the . . . ?"

Sam waved for him to be quiet and turned his attention to Nasha. "Why are you hiding in the back of our truck?"

"I want to go with you. Please . . ."

"You can't," Sam said. "You need to be at home, with your parents. Where are they?"

"Gone. Everyone. My uncle was supposed to come back for me." She turned toward Remi, her hands clasped together. "I know I'm only a girl. But I want to go to school."

Her simple statement caught Remi by surprise. "Sam . . . ?"

He eyed the girl, then Remi. "How about we work on getting this load secured first?"

The load was secure, but she nodded, saying, "Good idea."

Smiling at the child, she pointed toward the one spot of shade near the front of the truck. "Why don't you wait there, where it's cooler, while I help my husband."

Nasha nodded, did as she was told.

"Well?" Remi said as Sam pulled the canvas back in place.

Hank looked at the two of them, his expression incredulous. "How do you know this isn't another scam? So you don't turn her over to the police?"

"We don't know," Sam said as Amal got out and joined them.

"What's going on?" she asked.

"You can't be seriously thinking of taking her?" Hank said. "There's got to be laws against that sort of thing."

"Sam . . ." Remi leaned over, speaking softly. "She's just a girl."

All four glanced toward the front of the truck, where the child paced nervously, her attention on the road behind them. Remi looked that direction, wondering what she was looking at. The flat road stretched for mile upon mile through the flat grassland. If there was anything out there, Remi couldn't see.

"Hank's right," Sam said. "We can't just start yanking stray kids off the street without permission from parents or guardians or authorities. They'll shut down our school in a heartbeat if that gets out. We've got to take her back. Now."

"To where?" Remi said. "You heard her. She has no family."

"The police. You know we have no choice."

Amal gripped Remi's hand. "I want to go back, too. I have a bad feeling about this."

The last thing Remi expected was for Hank to champion her cause. "Mrs. Fargo is right. If we drive back now," he said, "that creates another delay delivering the supplies."

"It can't be helped," Sam said. "We're going back."

"Thank goodness," Amal said, looking infinitely relieved.

Sam pulled the knot on the canvas cover tight, then glanced at

Remi, clearly unable to resist her look of pleading. "We'll track down her next of—"

"Hurry!" Nasha raced toward them, pointing. "You need to leave!"

Remi shaded her eyes, seeing the glint of sun reflecting off the windshield of a vehicle in the distance.

"Now!" Nasha screamed. "Before it's too late. They're coming."

"Who?" Hank asked, looking startled.

"The Kalu brothers," she said. "We have to go. Please."

"Remi," Sam said.

"Already on it," she replied, opening the tailgate of the Land Rover and digging out a pair of binoculars from one of the packs. She tossed them to Sam.

"A yellow car?" Nasha said.

Sam lifted the binoculars, watching until the vehicle neared enough to see the color. "Definitely yellow. Are you a part of this? Supposed to distract us?"

She shook her head, her eyes pleading. "They have guns. They're going to rob you. I . . . I thought you might get to the school before they found you."

Sam glanced at Remi. "Going back's out of the question. For now."

"What about the truck?" Remi said. "As heavy as it's loaded, we're not going to outrun them."

"No. But maybe we can find a better place to make a stand."

"A stand?" Hank said. "You can't be serious."

Sam ignored him, looking through the binoculars in the opposite direction. "What the . . ."

"Sam?"

He handed Remi the binoculars, then pointed farther up, near the bend in the road. "About halfway between here and the trees."

Remi swept her gaze across the stretch of rutted dirt, at first seeing nothing alarming. "Empty road."

"Take a closer look."

She adjusted the focus, noticing that what at first glance appeared to be dried brush and leaves strewn across the roadway actually formed a fairly straight line. Too straight for it to be natural. Which meant it was covering something. "Tack strip? We're being chased into an ambush?"

"If I had to guess, the other half of that ambush is just around the bend, by those trees."

"What if we drove around the tack strip?"

"We run into whoever's waiting for us on the other side."

Remi glanced back at the yellow vehicle speeding toward them from the opposite direction. She looked around for cover. With nothing but long grass on either side of the road, they had nowhere to go.

And very little time to come up with a plan.

CHAPTER FIFTEEN

*A good plan today is better than
a perfect plan tomorrow.*
— AFRICAN PROVERB —

Sam took one last look through the binoculars, then handed them back to Remi. "Remember that time in Mozambique?" he asked.

"Yes. But we have two cars to move and an ambush coming from both directions. How—"

"Put the Land Rover in neutral."

"You, Fargo, are brilliant." Remi grabbed Nasha's hand, pulling her away from the truck.

Sam jumped into the driver's seat, starting the engine, while Hank climbed into the passenger's seat. "What's going on?" he asked Sam.

"We're creating a diversion for the women."

The color drained from Hank's face. "Us?"

"You should probably get out and wait with them."

"No. I'll wait here."

Sam glanced at Remi through the open window, waiting for her to move the car.

"Amal," she shouted. "Take Nasha and wait by the side of the road." Remi bent down, looking into Nasha's dark eyes. "You stand next to my friend. Wait for me."

She nodded her head.

"I'll be right back. I promise."

The girl let go, then ran toward Amal. Remi hopped into the Land Rover, started it and drove about twenty feet in front of the truck, leaving the vehicle in neutral before returning to where Amal and Nasha waited. The moment she was clear, Sam hit the gas, made a three-point turn, and spun the tires, kicking up enough dust to cover for the women as they ran to the side of the road toward the brush.

Hank glanced in their direction, but the dust hid them from his view. "Where're they going?"

"Trying not to be targets," Sam said, moving his foot from the brake to the gas pedal. The truck lurched forward.

"But . . ." Hank gripped the dash as the front of the truck tapped the rear bumper of the Land Rover, pushing it forward. "Are you insane?"

"There's a tack strip up ahead. And if that growing cloud of dust just beyond the bend in the road belongs to whoever placed it there, we're about to encounter some very nasty people."

"But that kid—"

"Thinks there are two men in that yellow car who plan to hit us from behind. In other words, we're about to be ambushed."

Sam stopped the truck, allowing the rental car to drift forward on its own, hopefully far enough that their attackers wouldn't realize that the women were hiding much farther back. With one foot on the brake, he hit the gas again, spinning the tires, raising a dust cloud so thick he hoped no one from either direction would know if anyone was hiding in the truck or had abandoned it. Which was the point.

Sam drew his gun, checked his phone to make sure the ringer was off, then looked over at Hank. "Follow me."

Hank's gaze widened at the sight of Sam's pistol. "I . . . I can't."

"If they come in shooting—"

"I'll take my chances," Hank said.

"Suit yourself." Foot on the brake, he stepped on the gas again, raising even more dust, before shutting off the truck and opening the door. "If I were you, I'd get down on the floorboard. If you're lucky, the engine block will stop any stray bullets."

CHAPTER SIXTEEN

Patience can cook a stone.
— AFRICAN PROVERB —

Stay low," Remi said. Amal started to part the long grass, but Remi grabbed her arm. "Not there. They'll see the broken stalks." She pointed to a natural break in the vegetation. "That way. Hurry."

Amal scrambled into the space. Remi turned to guide Nasha in after her, surprised when the girl pulled a thick but loose clump of grass from the dry ground, using the root ball to erase their tracks from the side of the road. A moment later, she scurried into the field after Amal, grabbing a handful of dirt, rubbing it into her short dark hair, attempting to blend into her surroundings.

Remi, both fascinated and horrified that a child that young was proficient in camouflage techniques, belly-crawled next to them, drew her gun, then double-checked her phone to make sure the ringer was off. Just in time, too. She peered through the tall grass to her left, watching the yellow vehicle's tires bouncing across the ruts in the road, jarring its occupants.

The car drove past. It skidded to a stop about fifteen feet behind the Fargos' supply truck. Dust rose and drifted on the wind as two men got out, their backs to the women. They stood behind their open doors, each holding a handgun, aiming at the truck.

"That's them," Nasha whispered. "Two of the Kalu brothers. Bako is the one closest to us."

"Whatever happens," Remi said, "keep your head down and don't make a sound."

She nodded.

Remi had a clear shot of the man standing behind the front passenger's door just fifty feet away. Unfortunately, the driver was on the far side of the car. If she took the shot, she risked giving up their position—something she wasn't about to do unless left with no other choice. Though she and Sam had successfully used this tactic just outside Mozambique, the two of them splitting up to take out their enemy, neither had to worry about trying to protect three other lives at the same time.

She set her cell phone on the ground in front of her, calling Sam's number. "We're in place. I take it you and Hank made it to the sidelines?"

"He wouldn't leave."

Her gaze flew to the supply truck. A complication they hadn't expected or needed. She had little time to worry about it. Another dust cloud in the distance—this one from the opposite direction—grew rapidly. Within seconds, the square front end of a white pickup came into view, the vehicle slowing as it veered around the suspicious layer of leaves and grass stretched across the road. It skidded to a stop in front of the now empty Land Rover and, beyond it, their supply truck. Both doors of the pickup opened, but no one got out. Their tinted windows blocked Remi's view.

Crack! Crack!

Two shots hit the dirt in front of the white pickup. The shooter, the driver of the yellow car, draped his arm over his open door, his handgun haphazardly pointed toward the new visitors. "This cargo belongs to us. Leave."

"Didn't see that coming," Remi whispered. "Different groups?"

"Looks like it," Sam said. Ears ringing from the gunshots, she barely heard his low voice coming from her phone. "This is not going to end well."

Though she couldn't see Sam, she knew he was positioned on the same side of the road to her right—which meant he had a far better view of the pickup's occupants. The driver stuck both hands out his open door to prove he wasn't armed. "Don't shoot," he shouted. Tall and slim, he had a scar running down the left side of his face. He stood next to his truck, staring at the Kalu brothers. "I'm sure we can work this out in a friendly manner."

"Scarface," Nasha whispered.

"Makao?" Bako seemed shocked to see him. "I . . . I didn't know it was you."

"So I see. Turn around and we'll just forget this happened." Makao gave a semi-smile to his would-be attackers.

Bako's brother motioned with his gun. "This cargo is ours."

"Keep it." Makao rubbed at the scar on his cheek, then slid behind the wheel. He backed the pickup, made a three-point turn, but instead of driving off, he stopped the vehicle. Two men pointing assault rifles jumped up from the pickup bed. A deafening rat-a-tat-tat followed as they peppered the Kalu brothers, their bodies jerking from the force of the bullets. Nasha stifled a sob as they slumped to the ground. Though Remi wanted to comfort the child, she didn't dare let down her guard. Thankfully, Amal reached over, placing her shaking hand on the child's shoulder, whispering something in her ear.

"Remi?" Sam's low voice from her phone brought a sense of relief. They were in this together. They'd get out of it the same way.

"We're fine," she said as the two shooters hopped out of the pickup bed. They circled around the far side of the Fargos' Land Rover, aiming their rifles at it. One glanced in, then pointed toward the supply truck. They walked past it, the lower part of their legs visible beneath the truck's chassis. When they reached the cargo area, one stopped behind the rear wheel. The other continued on, eyeing the Kalu brothers sprawled on either side of the yellow car. Deciding they no longer posed a threat, he turned back toward the truck, pulling up the canvas to look underneath. "No one back here," he shouted.

Makao, who remained at the driver's door of the white pickup, said something to his passenger. The man got out, walked toward the supply truck, his weapon aimed at the door behind which Hank hid.

Remi followed him with her gun sight. "Sam . . ."

"Do not take that shot, Remi. They'll know where you are."

She kept her finger on the trigger. "We can't just—"

"Yes. We can. There are two more gunmen on the other side of the truck. Without a way to draw them out, we're trapped."

He was right. Both men had taken cover, one behind the rear wheel, the other behind the front, no doubt aiming at the truck's door in case someone came charging out on that side. "This worked so much better in Mozambique," she said.

"Yeah, well, there were about five less gunmen."

A sharp intake of breath from Nasha caught her attention. "Look, Mrs. Fargo. Bako's moving."

She followed the direction of the girl's gaze, seeing Bako on the ground, slowly reaching for his gun. "Sam. By the yellow car. He could be our distraction."

"They'll kill him before he ever gets a second shot. We need something else."

Once again, her husband was right. Unless they found a way to draw those other two onto this side of the supply truck, they'd still be outgunned and outmanned. Her gaze hit on the Land Rover. "Amal, where's your phone?"

"In the car."

"Get ready, Fargo." Remi slid her phone toward Amal and raised her gun sight, taking aim. "Time to even those odds."

Sam's soft laugh sounded in the phone just before Amal called the number. A moment later the faint but shrill ring of her phone sounded from the open car window.

Scarface held up one hand. "Wait," he said, then walked toward the Rover.

Remi smiled to herself when she saw one of the two men on the far side of the supply truck move toward the engine block, his head and shoulders visible over the hood. "Come on . . ." she whispered, hoping the remaining gunman would step into view.

To her right, Scarface reached into the window and pulled out Amal's purse, fishing out her phone. When it stopped ringing, Amal ended the call. He narrowed his gaze, tossed the phone and purse into the car, and looked over at the man standing next to the supply truck. He nodded.

The gunman yanked open the truck door, pointing his weapon inside.

Hank cowered on the floorboards, covering his face with his arms. "Don't shoot," he cried.

CHAPTER SEVENTEEN

A fight between grasshoppers is a joy to the crow.
— BASOTHO PROVERB —

S am, his finger on the trigger of his Smith & Wesson .38, watched with clinical detachment as the gunman pulled Hank from the truck's cab. Like Remi, Sam was belly-down in the grass, his phone set out in front of him. The screen lit up as Remi called him back. He answered, then gave a quick glance toward the lone survivor sprawled in the dirt near the yellow car. The man slowly lifted his gun in a vain attempt to take down his four attackers. He was bleeding out fast and Sam didn't know if he'd even have the strength to get off a shot.

"Hold . . ." Sam said softly into his phone. Remi, an expert sharpshooter, could easily drop the man holding the gun to Hank, and was no doubt worried about his safety. At the moment, Sam didn't care if Hank lived or died. He wasn't about to risk his wife's life, or that of Amal and Nasha, because the man was too stupid to follow instructions.

The gunman pointed his weapon at the archeologist's chest. "Where are the others?"

Hank scooted back, hitting the side of the truck, looking around in desperation, whether for them or to escape, Sam couldn't tell.

"Tell . . . me . . . where . . . they . . . are . . ." With each word, he shoved the barrel of his gun against Hank's chest.

"They just ran."

"Which direction?"

"I . . . I didn't see." Hank's gaze flicked to the side of the road. "Too much dust."

Crack!

Bako's shot went wild.

The two gunmen on the other side of the truck spun around, spraying bullets at the yellow car in a deafening barrage. The third gunman grabbed Hank, using him for a shield, blocking any chance of Sam taking him out. "Remi," Sam shouted into the phone.

She fired before he finished saying her name.

The gunman fell to the ground, taking Hank with him. The man near the front of the truck stepped out into the road, belatedly realizing the shot came from the grass. He swung his rifle in Remi's direction. Sam fired twice. He fell back against the truck.

Makao, seeing his men fall, ducked behind the Land Rover, then raced to the pickup, jumping in. The lone surviving gunman raced after him, grabbing on to the tailgate as the vehicle sped off.

Sam kept his sights on the truck, waiting until the dust settled to make sure it wasn't circling back. Finally, he glanced in Remi's direction, not yet seeing her in the tall grass.

He grabbed his phone. "Remi . . ."

"Here."

"Keep the others down. Let's make sure it's clear."

They rose at the same time, guns at the ready, and walked toward the three vehicles.

The only thing moving was Hank, his breathing shallow, his face pale, as he struggled to his feet, trying to push the dead man off him.

"Stay there," Sam ordered and moved to the right as Remi moved to the left, checking the downed men, kicking any weapons out of reach in case anyone had miraculously survived.

They were all dead.

"Clear," he called out.

"Same," Remi said as they met on the other side of the supply truck. They circled back. "It's safe," she shouted. "You can come out."

Amal and Nasha slowly rose, the young girl reaching for Amal's shaking hand as they made their way through the tall grass.

Sam eyed the dusty pair. "Nice job blending in."

"The child's a natural," Remi said, then, in a lower voice, added, "I hate to think how she knows what she knows."

That sort of knowledge didn't come from living in the city—or a peaceful village. "Definitely makes you wonder," Sam replied, leaning down to pick up one of the fallen assault rifles. He turned on the safety and slung the gun across his back.

Hank rose to his feet, leaning against the truck, his frightened gaze landing on Nasha. "You stole my keys. Those men were after you."

Nasha ducked behind Amal.

"Pointing fingers gets us nowhere," Sam said, not wanting to spend any more time there than necessary. The longer they remained, the greater the risk those robbers would return with reinforcements. "Remi, make sure we haven't missed any stray guns. Hank, why don't you have a seat in the car, turn on the AC. Amal . . ." He was about to order her to join Hank. Seeing her ashen tone, he tempered his voice. "Are you going to be okay?"

She gave a faltering smile. "I . . . I think what I need is fresh air."

"Nasha," Sam said. "Come with me." He started walking toward the Kalus' bullet-riven car, then stopped when he realized the kid hadn't moved from Amal's side. Instead, she watched him with a healthy dose of suspicion and wariness.

Remi cleared her throat and he looked at her blankly, raising his brows in hopes she'd clue him in to whatever she was thinking.

"Nasha," Remi said. "I think my husband wants to ask you a few questions in private. You can trust him."

She shook her head. "I don't trust any man."

Of that, Sam had no doubt, especially coming from a child who knew the skills she knew. "Remi?"

She held her hand toward the girl. Nasha took it and Remi guided her toward Sam, who was standing near the dead men by the supply truck. The girl refused to look at the bodies.

As much as Sam hated what he was about to do, he didn't have much choice. "I need you to look at them. Do you know them?"

She hesitated, slowly turned, her gaze skimming across their faces before turning back, pressing herself into Remi's side. "No," she whispered.

He led her past the supply truck toward the yellow car. "You know them?"

She glanced at them, then quickly looked away. "Yes."

"Who are they and why are they here?"

"I told you. The Kalu brothers. They came to rob you."

"Why?"

"Because you stole their car."

"You mean you stole the car."

"I found it. I only stole the keys. But the Kalus said it was theirs. And they wanted your truck. They stole the last one."

"Did they send you?"

She shook her head but refused to look at him.

"Nasha . . ." He saw her shoulders tensing and kneeled down in front of her. "Why did you come?"

She stole a glance at the dead man on the passenger's side and looked at Sam, her dark eyes welling with tears. "Bako wanted to smash my fingers because I . . . I tried to hide the money that Mrs. Fargo gave me."

Had the man not already been dead, Sam would have killed him right then and there. He stood, trying to reconcile what had happened with what little he'd learned from her. "You think they called some friends to help them?"

"No," she whispered.

"The men in the white truck. You're sure you've never seen them before?"

She shook her head. "I've only ever heard of Scarface. The Kalus work alone. They have no friends."

Sam gave her shoulder a gentle pat. "No more questions. Why don't you wait in the car. You'll be much cooler in there."

Nasha shook her head again. "I don't like that man."

"Hank?" Remi asked. "Why?"

"Because he doesn't like me."

"To be fair, you did steal his keys."

"He was easy." Nasha glanced toward Amal. "What's wrong with your friend?"

Remi saw Amal's distant gaze. She was either in the middle of one of her seizures or about to have one. "She'll be okay. Do you think you can hold her hand and get her to the car?"

Nasha, no doubt anxious to get away, nodded, then hurried toward her.

Remi joined Sam by the Kalus' vehicle. "Amal had another seizure."

"All things considered, it's not surprising. If she's not better by tomorrow, we'll bring her back."

"What about Nasha?"

"There is no way in hell that I'm taking her back to Jalingo. You heard what she said he was planning to do to her."

Remi looked at the dead man. "I suppose it would be a total waste of ammunition to put another bullet in him."

"Definitely. More importantly, Nasha said the Kalu brothers

worked alone. So who is this Makao that the Kalu brothers seemed to know?"

"You have to admit that the two groups meeting here in the middle of nowhere is an interesting twist of fate."

Sam was a firm believer that twists of fate were a very rare occurrence. "Whoever this other group was, it had nothing to do with the street thieves from Jalingo."

"Agreed." Remi nodded toward the guns she'd collected in the back of the supply truck. "We've got enough firepower. I say we go find these guys."

CHAPTER EIGHTEEN

We desire to bequeath two things to our children;
the first one is roots, the other one is wings.

— SUDANESE PROVERB —

E asy does it, Annie Oakley," Sam said, noting the fire in his wife's green eyes. "We're not turning vigilante with a kid in the car."

"We can send her ahead with Hank and Amal. You and I can—"

"Remi."

"Fine," she said. "We call the police. But what about Nasha? All that's going to do is involve her and us in a lengthy investigation. What if they try to take her back? You heard what she said. There's a third Kalu brother waiting for her."

"We skip the part that says any of us were involved."

"Until they realize that the bullets in half of the bad guys don't match the bullets in the other half."

Sam took a good look around, trying to make sure there was nothing that could tie them to the scene. "Considering that we're taking all the guns with us, I don't think that's going to be a problem. This is what the cops back home call *no human involved*."

"And what if they start investigating?"

"Somehow, I doubt the two that got away are going to give us up."

"Good point." They walked back toward the cars and Remi nodded to the tack strip farther up the road. "What about that?"

"Take it with us. I'd hate to see someone else run over it."

THEY GATHERED THE ROAD SPIKES, THEN LEFT AS SOON AS SAM called the police to report what looked like a shoot-out between two groups on the road. Once again, he had Hank join him in the supply truck. If they were attacked again, Remi was armed and could protect the women.

Hank didn't argue with Sam's decision. In fact, he didn't say much at all. Sam glanced over at him about twenty minutes into their trip, noting the still-pale pallor of his face. "You okay?"

"A bit shaken, is all," Hank said. "I . . . I had no idea . . ."

"No idea what?" Sam asked, turning his attention back to the road.

"You and your wife both carry guns?" He nodded to the Land Rover driving in front of them.

"Depends on where we are."

"What about at the school?"

"What about it?"

"Guns. Children. It seems to me that'd be a bad mix."

"So are terrorists. Which is why some on our staff there are also armed. There's never a time the girls are left without protection."

"It doesn't scare the children?"

"They're not even aware."

"I suppose that's best." He was quiet for several moments, then looked over at Sam. "You don't think they'll come after us? The men who got away?"

"Why would they?"

"Revenge? You killed their friends."

"If they do, we'll be ready."

AFTER SEVERAL HOURS, THEY PASSED THROUGH BALI, THEN SERTI, where the military barracks were located. Eventually, the winding road meandered through the lush forests and thick undergrowth of Gashaka Gumti National Park. The sun hung low on the horizon by the time Sam neared the property belonging to Okoro Eze, a tea farmer who lived just outside the park's border. His property extended to both sides of the road and included the easement that led up to the mountainside parcel that the Fargos had purchased for the school.

Sam followed the single lane on the southeast border of the plantation. Down a long drive to the right, next to a stand of eucalyptus trees, he saw Okoro's small house and an outbuilding, the solar panels on the former's roof looking oddly out of place as electricity of any kind was a rarity this far out. The panels were there because the Fargos had paid for their installation since the Mambilla farmer, a widower, had refused money for the use of his land. A hardworking man, he was grateful that his daughter, Zara, had a nearby school to attend and could get the education he felt she deserved.

Okoro and Zara's situation was, unfortunately, hardly unique. The lack of transportation combined with the long trek through rough terrain of steep slopes and deep gorges made it difficult for most girls living in the scattered villages this far out on the Mambilla Plateau and surrounding areas to even think of attending school. The idea had been Wendy and Pete's after they'd spent one of their vacations hiking through the vast national park. With the Fargos' blessing, and the Foundation's money, the two had returned to Nigeria to bring their dream to fruition.

Just past Okoro's home, Remi turned off onto a dirt road to the left. Sam, in the heavily laden truck, followed at a much slower pace. One day, they hoped to get the road paved, but for now it was a good thirty-minute series of sharp turns through the montane forest just to get to the school. About midway up, they passed a wooden sign announcing

LOWER GASHAKA TRAIL
WATCH OUT FOR PEDESTRIANS

About a quarter of a mile higher, just before the next hairpin turn, a second warning sign announced *Upper Trail*. It was another fifteen minutes before the steep, winding road started leveling off. The last half mile was a straight shot to the school, which was set on its own plateau in the forest, the landscape protecting it from flooding during the rainy season.

Pete met them at the open gate and Wendy stood on the porch just outside the office. In their twenties, they were both tall, tanned, and blond, Pete's hair cut short and Wendy's pulled back into a ponytail. Pete waved them in, then locked the gate behind them.

Chickens scurried as Sam idled forward across the wide graveled drive. He parked in front of the main building, a long one-story bungalow, its whitewashed siding tinged orange from the late-afternoon sunlight. It was one of four almost identical buildings—the office/staff quarters, the cafeteria/classrooms, and two dorms, one not yet finished—all constructed in a circle around a large courtyard just visible between the structures. To Sam's right, at the far end of the grounds, about a half-dozen girls were kicking a ball back and forth in what looked like a half-field version of soccer.

The weather up here was significantly cooler than in Jalingo, something Sam noticed the moment he jumped out of the truck. He walked back to Pete, who was making his way from the gate. "A little later than planned," Sam said, shaking hands with him. "But we're here."

Pete glanced at Hank as he helped the women unload their luggage from the back of the Land Rover. "I thought you were bringing three guests? Who's missing?"

Sam followed the direction of his gaze as Wendy joined them. "Dr. LaBelle fell ill. She's hoping she can make it later in the week."

"Probably best," Wendy said. "Last thing we need is a bunch of sick kids."

"We did, however, pick up a hitchhiker." Sam nodded toward Nasha as she slid out of the backseat of the Land Rover.

Once the introductions were made, Remi gave Wendy a hug, then hugged Pete. "Good to see you both. We've missed having you at the house, but, boy, this is amazing. To think that six months ago it was nothing but an empty meadow."

"It's coming along," Pete said. "Hoping to finish the roof and—"

Wendy, apparently noticing Amal's shaky stance, said, "We can talk about that later. Let's get them settled. Looks like you all had too much excitement for one day."

"I think everyone needs a little down time after our experience on the trip here," Remi agreed.

As she herded everyone through the door, Sam and Pete remained behind, Sam calling out, "We'll catch up with you in a moment."

"You got it," Wendy said, then followed the others in.

Pete saw the bullet holes in the side of the truck, glancing over at Sam.

"A little trouble on the road here. Long story. I'll tell you later," Sam said, looking back to make sure they were alone. He waited until everyone disappeared inside, the door closing behind them. "They're gone. Now, about this other project you and Yaro are working on . . . No one knows?"

"No one," Pete said. "Wendy's managed to cover for us. Just like you asked."

"Good. Let's have a look."

CHAPTER NINETEEN

The child of a rat is a rat.
— MALAGASY PROVERB —

P ete led Sam toward the courtyard, stopping when he saw several girls racing toward them from the picnic benches. "Then
again," Pete said, "maybe tomorrow morning will be a better
time to discuss that project. They'll all be in class." He glanced back
at the holes in the supply truck. "I'm definitely curious to know what
happened there."

"That should probably wait, too," Sam said as several more girls
emerged from one of the buildings to join them.

It wasn't until they all sat down to dinner at a separate table from
the students that Sam explained about the attempted robbery.

Pete sat back in his chair, looking from Sam to Remi. "You think
it was the same group who stole our last truckload of supplies?"

"In fact, the same yellow car followed us after we left the city.
The girl we brought in was part of it. She's the one who tried to steal
our Land Rover."

"That little thing?" Wendy said, looking over at Nasha, who
stood at the end of the line. One of the older girls was directing what
utensils she should put on her tray. "Is she even big enough to see
over the steering wheel?"

"Barely. She was part of a much larger crew of young boys."

"Doing what?"

"Distractions," Sam said. "General thievery. And scouting for new victims. If I had to guess, the kids targeted Pete and Yaro the moment they arrived at the warehouse in Jalingo to pick up the supplies. They never had a chance."

Wendy, her attention still on Nasha, finally turned toward Sam. "You think it's safe to have brought her here?"

"I think so," Remi said. She looked over at Amal. "What do you think?"

"Me?" She seemed surprised that anyone was bothering to ask her opinion. "I . . . I think she had to have been desperate to hide in the back of a truck. Especially knowing the Kalus would come after her."

Hank also watched the child, his look troubled. "No doubt I'm prejudiced because I was the unwilling pickpocket victim. But I've seen her type before in Tunisia. She won't be able to help herself. Things will turn up missing."

"Maybe so," Remi said. "But if not for her, we'd have driven right into an ambush. She's the reason we fared as well as we did."

"That, Mrs. Fargo," Hank said, "was sheer luck. How do we know if her gang was or wasn't part of the ambush?"

"I guess we don't," Remi said. "But she did say the Kalu brothers worked alone."

"The word of a thief," he replied, "is worth nothing."

Amal, her face pale, her food untouched, pushed her chair back. "If you'll excuse me, I think I'll go lie down."

Hank started to rise. "Are you okay?"

"Fine. Just tired after everything that's happened."

Sam, not wanting the conversation to devolve further, took a good look around the building. "You've made a lot of progress since we were out here last. Keep this up and you two will be back in California, hitting the beach, in no time."

"It's been moving along," Pete said. "The mess hall was finished a couple of weeks ago."

"We'll be glad when the second dorm is done," Wendy added.

"What happened to the idea of one large dorm?" Remi asked her.

"After thinking about it, we figured one for the younger girls, one for the older. I think it'll be easier in the long run."

Sam lifted his water glass. "Well done."

"Agreed," Remi said, lifting her own glass. "To Pete and Wendy."

A loud crash interrupted their toast and the four looked over at Nasha and saw her looking horror-stricken, her tray on the ground in front of her, the soup splattered across the floor.

Remi started to rise, but Wendy stopped her. "She'll be fine. Watch." Within seconds, three older girls converged on Nasha, one whisking her back to the food line while the other two quickly cleaned up the mess. "Zara, Tambara, and Jol," she said.

"Part of the Four Musketeers," Pete added. "Joined at the hip."

"Who's the fourth?" Remi asked.

"Maryam," Wendy replied, nodding to the girl who was standing behind the counter, helping serve up the food. "We have a rotation schedule for chores. Today's her turn on kitchen duty."

"Glad to see so many girls getting along," Remi said.

Wendy laughed. "Don't get me wrong. They definitely have their squabbles. But they want to be here. They quickly learn that everything goes much smoother when they work together."

Sam was impressed, and it wasn't long before Nasha had a new tray and was seated at the table with the other girls. She ate her food, her watchful gaze taking in everyone and everything. Even so, Sam decided that Hank was right. She had the distinct appearance of someone who was casing the place and he mentioned it to Remi as they readied themselves for bed that night. "I'll be surprised if we don't find a few things missing along the way."

"I'm less worried about her than I am Amal. I don't think she's well. Maybe we should drive her back to the hotel to stay with Renee."

They had pushed their cots together and were lying on top of them side by side. "After what she's been through today, it's expected. If she wants to go back tomorrow, we'll take her." Sam put his arm out, drawing Remi toward him. "Nice shooting, by the way."

"Likewise, Fargo." She snuggled against him and was asleep within seconds.

The next morning at breakfast, Amal looked considerably better, declining the offer of a return to Jalingo. When they finished eating, Pete and Wendy took the Fargos, Hank, and Amal on a tour of the compound. Pete, having been instrumental in the design and layout, pointed out the solar panels on the south-facing roof of the building that housed the staff quarters and cafeteria. "By the time we're done," he said, "the entire school should be completely self-sufficient, including being energy autonomous. We've also installed a water purification system at the well."

The compound was surrounded by a tall, slatted chain-link fence with a gate, which they kept closed and locked. The quadrant of buildings surrounded the large courtyard garden of raised planter beds with a well set in its midst.

"Goats?" Hank asked Pete when he heard bleating coming from the other side of the dorm.

"We have to keep them fenced in behind the dorms or they eat everything in the garden. The chickens," he said, nodding to the few nearby, who were pecking at the ground, "have free rein."

Amal watched as a few girls holding handled baskets wandered the grounds searching for eggs. "No wonder breakfast tasted so good."

"Fresh every day," Wendy said. "Now, if we could teach the hens to lay their eggs in one spot, we'd have it made."

"What's that building?" Hank asked, pointing to a circular structure between the finished dorm and the dorm still under construction.

"Our supply shed," Pete said. "We wanted to keep it central."

The four bungalows had wood siding. This, however, had an almost smooth whitewashed plaster exterior. The morning sun glinted off what looked like round tiles, each with a star in the center, inset throughout the plaster. Remi ran her hands over one. "Plastic water bottles?"

"Filled with dry soil," Pete said. "Lay them like bricks with the bottom facing out, mortar them with mud, and you get the double benefit of insulation and strength." He looked around, then leaned in close, speaking softly. "Even better, it makes the buildings bulletproof. Safer for the girls. We decided to test the structural strength here. Eventually, we'll do the same to the other buildings."

Wendy nodded. "A shame we have to think that way, but with so many of these terrorist groups against educating women, it was a necessity."

"I like the setup," Sam said, giving a nod of approval as he looked around. He especially liked the way the buildings surrounded the courtyard, making it very defensible. He turned toward Pete. "You have that inventory list?"

Pete held up the clipboard. "I had a feeling you'd want to go over that."

"Let's get started." He put his hand on Remi's shoulder. "I'll catch up with the rest of you in a bit. No sense boring all of you with paperwork."

"Just make sure you're back in time for the hard labor." She smiled at Wendy. "Let's go see those classrooms."

"This way," Wendy said, leading Remi, Amal, and Hank out of the courtyard.

Sam and Pete walked off the opposite direction, Sam looking

over the clipboard, which was nothing more than a copy of the invoice he'd picked up from the warehouse in Jalingo. They pretended interest in what was on the paper until the others disappeared inside. As soon as the door closed, Sam glanced at Pete. "Let's take a look at this thing."

CHAPTER TWENTY

In the moment of crisis, the wise build bridges,
the foolish build dams.
— NIGERIAN PROVERB —

Pete led Sam around to the back of the circular shed. To their left was the pen with a couple of dozen goats. The two full-time live-in staff members, Yaro and his wife, Monifa, were feeding the animals. When Yaro saw them looking at the dirt piled behind the shed, he said something to his wife, then walked over and joined them.

"Yaro," Sam said, shaking hands with him.

"Glad you made it out here, Mr. Fargo."

Sam nodded at the dirt. "I see you've made good progress."

"Slow, but steady," Yaro said.

"Let's go see how it's coming along."

Yaro led them back to the courtyard garden area, gesturing to one of the raised beds, this one with seedlings planted in neat rows, some sort of squash by the looks of the leaves. "That's how we get rid of it."

"So far, so good," Pete said. "No one's seemed to notice that no matter how much dirt we shovel from the pile, it doesn't seem to get smaller."

"How far did this get you?" Sam asked him.

"About the size of a decent basement, which should hold everyone."

"Stocked?"

"With the basics. Air vents hidden beneath the buildings." He pointed to the raised foundation of the dorm and schoolroom, grilles visible under each but looking like they belonged to the main structure. "I'd say with what's down there, they could last a good week to ten days."

"Longer," Yaro said, "if we can double the size and get more water stored."

Sam studied the rows of planters, noting they were mostly complete. "There's enough lumber in the back of that truck for at least five more planters, in addition to shoring up your cellar," Sam said, taking a look around the courtyard. "Just not sure where you plan to put more of them."

"Behind the dorms," Pete replied. "Wendy calls it functional greenery. It'll hide the goat pen."

Yaro glanced over at his wife. "Monifa has told me that the girls are growing suspicious of the dirt. She's told them it's a secret project for the garden. So far, that's kept them from asking more questions."

Sam nodded in approval. "Looks like the two of you thought of everything. Let's go see this cellar."

He followed Pete and Yaro to the shed. Pete opened the door, then stepped back, giving Sam a view inside. Gardening and building tools lined the wall and shelves. The three men entered, Pete closing the door behind them. When he turned a hook on the wall counterclockwise, Sam heard a soft click underneath the wooden floor next to a wooden pallet piled high with empty burlap sacks. Pete pressed on one of the planks with his foot. Another click sounded and the trapdoor raised up slightly.

"The knothole is the handle," Pete said, lifting it open the rest of the way, revealing a dark tunnel accessed by a ladder leading straight down.

Sam leaned over, looking in. "How long until it's done?" he asked, his voice echoing into the space.

"At the pace we're going . . ." Pete thought about it a moment. "Assuming we can get the extra planters built, a couple of more weeks. It's all about having a place to hide the dirt. Like I said, no one's commented that the mountain of soil behind the shed doesn't shrink." Pete closed up the tunnel and the three men stepped out of the shed. "What we really need is to finish that second dorm and open up more beds. There's a lot of interest from the neighboring villages."

Considering the nearest village was over ten kilometers away, Sam was impressed. "Word's getting around?"

"Definitely," Yaro said.

"But," Pete added, "until we hire more staff, get the planters built, and get the roof on the new dorm, we can't take any more girls on. We want to make sure we have enough beds. More importantly, that the cellar can hold everyone we bring in."

Sam gave him a hearty slap on the back. "Good thing I brought help. Speaking of, we should probably catch up to them."

"I'm assuming you haven't told Remi's friends about the tunnel?"

"No. And I'm not planning to. For the same reason I don't want anyone telling the students. All it takes is one word overheard by the wrong person when they think no one's listening. Remi's friends will be gone in a couple of days. None of this affects them in the least."

Pete closed the shed. Yaro returned to help his wife, and the two men crossed the courtyard toward the classroom building. Inside, they found Remi and the others standing in the doorway of one of the main rooms, where the girls were seated at desks listening to a young woman speaking French and diagramming a sentence on the chalkboard.

Hank stood just outside the doorway, looking back at Wendy. "Why is she teaching French? Isn't English the official language of Nigeria?"

"This close to the Cameroon border, we figured it was important for the girls to be fluent in both."

"She seems young to be teaching."

"Zara," Wendy replied, keeping her voice low, "is sixteen. But she's bright in most subjects and extremely gifted in languages, with a knack for retaining almost everything she's ever read. Much like Mrs. Fargo," she added, looking over at Remi. "Under normal circumstances, Zara might have been fast-tracked through the lower levels and already be at the university. Her father's the one who brought her here. You passed his farm on the way up. He said she'd never be allowed that sort of education if she remained where she was."

"She'll get there," Remi said. She motioned Sam to her side. "Look," she whispered, pointing toward the back of the classroom where Nasha was seated, a small chalkboard in front of her on the desk, a navy backpack still strapped to her shoulders, her complete attention on the instructor.

Wendy smiled. "She's had some schooling, but it's clearly been a while. She reads and spells at the level of someone in kindergarten or first grade. Still, she wants to be here. That's half the battle."

Remi linked her arm around Sam's as they left, the group walking down the hall toward the office. "Did you see how happy she was? She hasn't taken that backpack off since they gave it to her."

He saw—which was going to make it that much harder when it came time to tell the poor girl she wouldn't be able to stay.

Remi, no doubt reading his mind, leaned in close, her voice low, heartbroken, as they walked. "You said we weren't taking her back."

"If we can't find out who's responsible for her, you know we won't have any choice."

She crossed her arms, her frustration evident. "Then we need to find them. Someone in this gang she was running with must know something."

"Possibly."

"Good. I vote you go talk to the last Kalu on your way to pick up Lazlo. I'll see if I can't get directions to his lair for you."

"You realize Jalingo's an hour and a half away from the airport?"

"Close enough, Fargo," she said as Hank caught up to them.

"Hope I'm not interrupting." He smiled at the group. "Just wondering about this building we're supposed to be working on."

It turned out that Hank was as proficient with a hammer and nails as Dr. LaBelle had claimed and they made good progress that first day and the next, finishing up some of the framing. While they worked, Amal, who was doing much better, spent time with the girls in the classroom, discussing archeology.

At their lunch break, they sat around the mess hall table, Remi nursing a blister on her hand from the hammer she'd been wielding. Sam helped apply a new Band-Aid. "A good pair of gloves should help."

"Oh, no," Amal said, indicating the food line where Nasha stood. "I hate to say it, but Hank was right. She can't really help herself."

Sure enough, Sam saw Nasha look around, then stuff something into her backpack.

Wendy happened to walk into the cafeteria at that very moment, catching the child in the act. "Here, now. What're you doing there?"

Nasha spun around, nearly dropping her tray. "Nothing."

"Are you hungry?"

She shook her head.

Wendy squatted down in front of her. "There's plenty of food to go around. You don't need to take it."

Nasha hid the small pack behind her back. "I might be hungry later."

"You can ask later. The food's not going anywhere. I promise." Wendy held out her hand.

The girl hesitated, then reluctantly reached into her pack, pulling out several rolls.

Sam, watching this, felt Remi's gaze on him.

"Do something," she said. "Nasha needs to know she's safe."

"Me? What about—"

Clang! Clang! Clang!

"Emergency bell," one of the girls shouted, and they all went running.

CHAPTER TWENTY-ONE

The road to success is always under construction.
— AFRICAN PROVERB —

S am took a quick look around, not seeing anything out of the ordinary, as the sharp bell rang. "Planned drill, I hope?"

"It is," Wendy said, earning a look of relief from Amal. Wendy apologized for not warning them, stood, and called out, "Emergency bell. Time to go." She guided Nasha to the door after the other students, then looked back at Sam. "You're welcome to finish your coffee."

Sam rose. "A drill's a drill. Lead the way, Wendy. We won't know what to do if we don't practice."

Remi, Hank, and Amal followed him from the mess hall out to the courtyard, where they found most of the students rushing to line up behind the four oldest girls, who stood by a stone marker on the ground. There was a lot of talking and laughing among the children while they waited.

Amal smiled when the two smallest girls realized they were in the wrong line and scurried to their proper places. "Haven't done one of these since grade school," she said to Remi. "Not sure I'd know what to do."

"Same, here," Remi said, laughing. She glanced at Sam, her relief evident. Though they'd both been worried about Amal's health after their attack on the road, she'd had no seizures since, and seemed to be enjoying her time with the girls.

About two minutes later, Pete walked out into the courtyard, nodding at Sam, Yaro, and the women as he passed. He took a position in front of the girls, holding up two fingers. They stopped talking, their attention on him. "Nicely done," he said loudly.

The students clapped briefly, wide smiles on their faces.

He waited for quiet again before proceeding. "What if you don't hear the bell but you know there's an emergency?"

In unison, they shouted, "We come to the shed."

"A fire?" Pete said.

"We come to the shed."

"An earthquake?"

"We come to the shed."

"A shooting?"

"We come to the shed."

Pete raised his brows.

One of the older girls shouted, "We find cover."

"Correct," Pete said. "What's cover?"

As one, they said, "A safe place to hide."

Remi reached over, taking Sam's hand in hers, saying nothing. She didn't need to. He nodded as Wendy looked over at them, whispering, "Like I said, a sad but necessary reality."

AFTER THE DRILL, THE GIRLS WENT BACK TO LUNCH AND THEN THE classroom with Amal. The other adults returned to their framing of the new dorm, Sam and Pete on the roof, Hank and Remi down below.

"Pete," Hank called out. "Any more nails? I'm running low."

Pete, working next to Sam at the peak of the roof, looked down at Hank. "There's some in the shed. Hold on a sec. I'll go get them."

"No trouble," Hank said. "I can go."

Pete glanced at Sam, who gave him a slight nod. Unless someone knew where to look, that tunnel was going to remain a secret. "Yeah, sure," Pete said. "Should be a case of them on the shelf, right side as you enter."

Hank headed toward the shed and returned a few minutes later. "You realize you only have a couple of boxes left. We'll be out by the end of the day."

"That doesn't make sense," Pete said. "I thought we had an entire case."

Sam surveyed the roof, where he and Pete had almost finished the installation of the plywood sheathing. Down below, Remi and Hank had made considerable progress on the siding. "Well, among the four of us, we've gone through quite a few."

"I could've sworn we had more," Pete said. "I'll drive into the village tomorrow and pick up whatever they have, then put in a new order."

"We could send Remi."

"Send me where?" she called out. She moved away from the building, looking up at Sam.

"To Gembu, in the morning. Figured you could take Amal. Show her around the village."

"I'm sure she'd love the trip."

AROUND FIVE THE NEXT MORNING, BEFORE ANY OF THE KIDS WERE up, Sam and Pete took their coffee and walked the grounds, trying to determine everything that needed to be accomplished before the start of the rainy season. They stopped in front of the shed but didn't go in. The ground there, and in the courtyard around it, seemed fairly level. "What about flooding?" Sam asked. "Even though I know we're on a plateau, I'd hate to see all that work ruined after the first big rainstorm drains into the shelter."

"You can't tell from here, but the buildings and courtyard are actually built on a slight mound. It's why we picked the sight. Most of it should drain outward."

"Just in case," Sam said, "let's make sure to order a couple of pumps."

Out front, the chickens started clucking louder than usual for that early an hour. Sam glanced that direction yet couldn't see anything between the two buildings.

"Odd," Pete said, looking at his watch. "The girls don't usually feed the hens until around six."

The sound of a car engine turning over stopped them short. "Who is taking off this early?" Pete asked.

Couldn't be Remi, Sam thought. She wasn't planning to leave for the village until after breakfast. There was only one person he knew who was brazen enough to take a car without permission. "Nasha."

CHAPTER TWENTY-TWO

Those who are absent are always wrong.
— CONGOLESE PROVERB —

Remi and Monifa were cracking eggs open into an industrial-sized stainless steel bowl when Remi heard the heavy footfalls echoing across the courtyard into the open door of the kitchen. "What on earth?"

Wendy, who was closer to the door, set down her butcher knife next to the half-chopped potato to look outside. "Sam and Pete just ran out to the front."

The three women hurried into the courtyard and followed the men between the buildings. Through the open gate, Remi saw their Land Rover driving off, but the dust trailing up behind it prevented her from seeing who was behind the wheel.

"What's going on?" she asked Sam.

"Good question," he said. "You happen to know where Nasha is?"

"Nasha? Why would she take it?"

He looked over at Pete. "Get the truck keys."

Amal apparently heard the commotion, almost running into Pete on his way into the office. "Is something wrong?"

As much as Remi didn't want to believe it, she couldn't think who else might be responsible. "Sam thinks Nasha stole our car again."

"What?" Amal glanced toward the dusty speck on the horizon. "That's not possible. I just saw her."

Sam looked over at her. "You're sure?"

"I'll show you." She walked them through the courtyard and pointed toward the shade trees. Nasha, a basket over her arm, collecting eggs.

"If it wasn't her," Remi said, "then who was it?"

Wendy and Pete exchanged glances, Wendy saying, "There's no way any of the girls would take the car. They're all honest to a fault—never mind I don't think any of them know how to drive."

"Hank," Sam said.

He certainly had access to the keys, Remi realized. "Why not say something? 'Hey, I'm taking the car for a spin.'"

"A spin?" Sam looked over at Amal as though hoping she had some explanation.

"An early drink?" she said. "Maybe he wasn't thrilled to find out the school was dry."

Pete drew his gaze from the dirt road as the Land Rover headed downhill, disappearing around the bend. "Should we go after him?"

"Let's wait," Sam said. "If he's not back by lunch, Remi and I can go looking. We can pick up the nails then."

Pete nodded. "I'll lock the gate."

Sam watched him walk off, then turned toward Remi, his expression dark.

Unfortunately, Sam's and Pete's anger failed to lessen by the time they all sat down to breakfast. "Leaving the gate unlocked?" Pete said. "What if we'd all been in bed? What if—"

Wendy reached for the coffee carafe, pouring herself another cup. "We're all in one piece," she said. "Maybe we should wait until he returns and find out what he has to say."

Four hours later, Sam, who was tacking tarpaper on the roof, saw the Land Rover approaching. "He's back."

Remi was down below, sweeping construction debris from the subflooring. Pete was filling a wheelbarrow with dirt from the endless pile behind the shed. As Sam climbed down from the roof, Pete pushed the barrow toward one of the half-empty planters in the courtyard, asking, "What do you want to do?"

"I brought him here," Sam said. "I'll talk to him."

Pete agreed, then went back to work.

Remi followed Sam out of the courtyard to the front of the school, somewhat worried on Hank's behalf. She knew that Sam felt responsible for every one of those girls. When they'd begun looking into building the school, security had been first and foremost in his mind. He'd spent countless hours with Pete and Wendy on the design, making sure that the local contractors they'd hired were the best. When these same contractors weren't able to finish the second dorm, he and Remi had dropped everything so that they could come out to help. In less than two days, Professor Lazlo Kemp was flying in for the same purpose.

With the rainy season bearing down on them, time was of the essence. Having to stop work after the delay caused by the theft from the first supply truck and now the lack of nails put them even further behind schedule. And Sam's face reflected that. He stood there, his arms crossed, jaw ticking, waiting for the car to pull up to the gate.

"Sam . . ."

He glanced over at Remi, but said nothing.

"Don't do anything you'll regret."

"Like put my fist in his face?"

The classroom door opened and the girls hurried out, most running toward the mess hall. A few, however, wandered toward the front, Nasha included, curious about what the adults were doing in the drive. "Don't forget that there are a lot of little pitchers with big ears." She nodded toward the girls.

"What if I promise to hit him quietly?"

"Maybe I should talk to him instead. After all, Renee's my friend, and he's here because of his connection to her."

Sam nodded. "I'll get the gate." He walked over, opened it, then closed and locked it after Hank drove the Land Rover through.

Hank got out of the car, holding up a carton of nails as if that explained his five-hour trip. "Figured we wouldn't get much done without them. I bought all they had on hand in the village. Ten boxes."

"Very kind of you," Remi said. "Except that Amal and I were supposed to go."

"Thought I'd save you the trip. Amal's a lot more useful around here with the girls than I could ever be." He reached into the car, pulling out a large cardboard box, no doubt containing the other cartons of nails. When he turned, he looked at Sam, who had walked up, his expression stony. "Before you say anything, I realize that I left the gate open in my haste to get out before anyone woke up."

"You did," Sam said.

"Yes, well it may turn out to be a good thing. Not the gate, my trip into town." He hefted the heavy box and closed the car door with his hip. "While I was there, I saw a man getting out of a white pickup truck. There was a definite scar running down his cheek."

CHAPTER TWENTY-THREE

Rain wets the leopard's spots,
but it does not wash them off.
— ASHANTI PROVERB —

Remi glanced back behind them, seeing Nasha standing next to Amal. Worried that the child would overhear what Hank was saying, she turned to the courtyard, trying to keep her smile light. "Nasha, wouldn't you like to join the other girls at lunch? I promise you, they don't bite."

Nasha shook her head.

Amal dug her phone out of her pocket, holding it up. "Let's go take some pictures. It'll be fun."

She hesitated, then took Amal's hand.

Hank watched as they disappeared into the courtyard, Amal showing Nasha how to work the camera on her phone. "You might want to watch that one. I saw her out early this morning when I took off."

"Amal?" Remi asked.

"No. The pickpocket. She was sneaking around out there," he said, indicating the part of the courtyard where Pete was shoveling dirt into one of the planters. "When she saw me, she ducked. Definitely suspicious. Probably hiding something."

The girl reminded Remi of a cat. Agile, light on her feet. Just yesterday, Remi had seen her in one of the shade trees in the lunch area, watching the girls below, who had no idea she was hiding up above them. "She was collecting eggs."

"That's not what it looked like to me," Hank said.

"She's just a kid," Sam said. "I'm more interested in hearing about this man you saw."

"There's not much to tell. He got out of his truck and was walking into the marketplace as I was loading the nails into my car. I don't think he saw me, as busy as it was. I can't say for sure he was one of the men who attacked us out on the road. I suppose it could have been a coincidence. The only reason I noticed him was because of the white truck and the scar on his face."

"So you weren't followed?" Sam asked.

"I don't see how." Hank glanced toward the girls lingering in the courtyard, then back at Sam and Remi. "I realize now that it was foolish for me to take off without telling anyone. I am sorry. Truly." He shifted the heavy box in his hands, saying, "I'll just put these in the shed."

"By the dorm would be better," Sam said. "We'll be working there after lunch."

Remi watched him walk off, then looked over at her husband. "Should we be worried?"

"That's a long stretch of road with nothing between where we were robbed and that village. Like he said, it could be coincidence. Just in case," he said, pulling out his phone, "I'll call Selma and have her move up Lazlo's flight. Couldn't hurt to have an extra body around. Especially if we have to go into the village for anything." He called the number and put the phone to his ear, telling Remi, "Let Pete know."

"I will," she said. Sam walked toward the office and Remi headed to the courtyard, where Pete was dumping yet another wheelbarrow of dirt into one of the planters. She related what Hank told them about seeing the man in the village. "Sam's calling Selma now to get Lazlo on an earlier flight out," she said as Hank walked up, looking suitably apologetic.

He watched Pete work. "That's some fertile-looking soil."

"Lucky for us it's fertile land. We're just moving it around, trying to put it to better use." He wiped the sweat from his brow, then leaned on his shovel. "Not as exciting as a dig in Tunisia, I expect."

"No," Hank said, bending down and picking up something from the grass near the side of the planter. He closed his hand around the item, staring out toward the two shade trees, where Nasha and Amal stood, watching the girls jumping rope.

Pete followed the direction of his gaze. "So, what is it you're looking for out there?"

"What?" Hank, focused on the girls, looked back at Pete and Remi almost startled.

"In Tunisia?" Pete said.

He suddenly laughed. "Right. Forgot what we were talking about for a second. The usual. Excavating ancient Roman villas," he said as a bell rang twice.

"Lunch." Pete rested the shovel against the wheelbarrow. "Guess we better head in and wash up."

"Remi," Hank said as she was about to follow Pete. He opened his palm, showing her a gray carpentry nail a little over two inches long. "I have a feeling this is why we ran out."

Pete looked over at them as he pulled off his leatherwork gloves. "What are you talking about?"

Hank showed the nail to Pete. "The pickpocket we brought back, Nasha. I've seen her taking things. If I had to guess, she's the reason the nails ended up missing."

Pete eyed the nail and gave a casual shrug. "Maybe it fell there when they built the planter."

"I doubt it. If you don't believe me, take a look for yourself." He stepped back and pointed.

Remi and Pete walked over. One or two they could dismiss as being missed when they were building the planter. But there were at least a hundred or more stashed between the grass and the base of the planter, which made her wonder where the rest of the nails were stashed. Remi looked out toward the picnic tables, where Nasha and Amal sat in the shade. Nasha looked up from Amal's phone, surveying them as though she knew she was the topic of conversation. "I'll talk to her about it."

Hank gave Remi a knowing look. "Don't be surprised if she lies about where she found them."

"Ease up," Pete said. "The kid's had a hard life."

"I'm not being critical," Hank replied. "Stealing may very well be so ingrained to her survival, she's not even thinking about it. Can't change a leopard's spots."

Remi was glad Nasha wasn't within hearing distance. "I'm sorry," she told Pete after Hank left.

"For what?"

"Everything. Hank leaving the gate unlocked, Nasha taking things."

"At least he wields a good hammer. And we've made up for a few days of lost work since he's gotten here. The kid . . . ?" They both looked out to the picnic area.

Remi's cell phone buzzed in her pocket and she pulled it out, seeing a photo Amal had texted to her of a chicken that had hopped up on one of the picnic tables. The caption read *Frum Nasha*.

Remi looked up in time to see Nasha returning the phone to Amal. "Our newest girl seems to be assimilating quickly," she said, showing the text and photo to Pete.

"What does Sam say about her staying? Assuming we can tame those sticky fingers of hers."

"Not unless we get permission from her guardians or the government. I'm just worried that if she is orphaned, there'll be too much red tape and she'll somehow end up back on the streets."

"You're probably right."

"I was hoping Selma might be able to find something. So far, nothing. There's just not enough information out there about the girl. She tends to shut down when we try to question her."

"What about Amal?" he said. She and Nasha were bent over the phone, for the moment the best of friends. But when Nasha glanced up and saw they were still watching her, she ran off. "They seem to have a good rapport with each other. Maybe she can break through and get a few more details on the girl's background."

Remi nodded. "Good idea."

After picking up her lunch tray, Remi joined Amal at the picnic table. "You seem to be doing better."

"Much better. Yesterday I thought about going back, but I looked at Nasha and I thought that if such a tiny girl can go through all that, surely I can."

"Speaking of, where'd she go?"

"Out there." Amal nodded to where several girls were jumping rope, chanting a poem about a robber coming in through the door. Nasha, her coveted navy pack strapped to her shoulders, stood on the sidelines, watching with a look of longing until she noticed Remi's and Amal's attention focused on her. She ran from the courtyard, just out of sight. "She's a natural with an iPhone. But, then, most kids are."

"I'm worried about her," Remi said. "Hank saw her hiding something this morning just before he took off. A stash of missing nails. I'm hoping I didn't make a mistake bringing her here, but I can't see turning her over to protective services. I hate to think where she might end up."

Amal looked over at Remi. "I would have done the same thing. Brought her here, I mean."

"Do you think you can talk to her?" Remi asked. "We need to find out where she's from if we hope to get permission to bring her in."

"Me?" Amal's glance strayed toward the girl. "I . . . I could try."

Remi smiled to herself. When she'd last spoken to Renee on the phone, her friend had mentioned that Amal tended toward the shy side, keeping to herself and rarely interacting with strangers. In fact, that was one of the reasons Renee had been insistent about sending Amal on to the school without her. Even after the traumatic events on the road from Jalingo, the young woman certainly seemed to be coming into her own out there. For a few moments, they sat in peaceful silence, watching the younger girls jump rope. Eventually, Nasha peered around the corner at them.

Remi nodded toward her. "What do you suppose we'll find in that backpack she never takes off? Or up in that tree she hides in?"

"I know exactly what you'd find. Food. And about anything else that isn't nailed down, including some of those missing nails." She smiled at the pun. "I've talked to her quite a bit. She's a sweet girl, but that sort of behavior won't stop until she starts to feel secure."

"How do you know so much about this?"

Amal watched as the older girls now jumped and she smiled. "Originally, my major was in child psychology. And I might have continued in that direction except I had one of my seizures one afternoon and the person helping me brought me into the wrong lecture hall. It happened to be Dr. LaBelle, talking about the part of Tunisia where I grew up. The more I listened to her, the more I realized I was supposed to be there. It felt right. Like all those stories my grandmother had told me about the people who lived centuries ago were meant to—"

She stopped when one of the girls raced across the courtyard toward them, calling out, "Mrs. Fargo. Miss Amal." She stopped in front of them, out of breath, pointing toward the mess hall. "Come quick. I think Mr. Hank is dying."

CHAPTER TWENTY-FOUR

If you give bad food to your stomach,
it drums for you to dance.
— AFRICAN PROVERB —

S am lifted the final roll of tarpaper over his shoulder and was about to climb up the ladder when Remi and Amal ran past him toward the mess hall. "What's going on?"

"It's Hank," Remi called out.

Which didn't tell him much. He lowered the heavy roll to the ground, then followed them into the cafeteria. Hank was leaning over a garbage can, heaving. A half-dozen girls stood on the other side of the room, their hands over their mouths, looking as though they were seconds from getting sick themselves. The acrid scent hit Sam the moment he walked in.

"Is he dying?" one of the girls asked.

"I doubt it," Sam said, opening up one of the windows.

Remi scooted the kids out the door, grabbed a roll of paper towels, and returned to his side. "Maybe you should check on him."

"Me?" Sam said, eyeing the mess on the floor near Hank's feet. Apparently, he hadn't quite made it to the trash can when he became ill. "What about that whole he's the friend of your friend thing?"

"That was when he was in trouble. This is different."

"How?"

"He's sick. What if he's contagious?"

"So it's okay if I get sick?" he said as Pete walked in, saw what was going on, then did an immediate about-face.

She smiled sweetly. "If that happens, I'll promise to take good care of you."

Sam took the towels and walked over to Hank, noticing his pale, clammy skin. "You okay?"

"I feel like—" He pivoted toward the garbage can, racked with the dry heaves. "I'm fine."

"You don't look fine." Sam tore off several sheets, giving them to the man.

Fingers shaking, Hank wiped his mouth and dropped the spent sheets into the garbage. "Hoping it's just something I ate from the market this morning and not something contagious. Maybe I caught whatever bug LaBelle had when she got sick at the hotel."

He handed the entire roll of paper towels to Hank. "Do me a favor and clean that up the best you can. If you are contagious, we wouldn't want anyone else to get sick."

Hank tore off several sheets, again wiping his mouth. "Is it my imagination? I get the feeling that you don't like me."

"I'm reserving judgment."

Hank glanced past him to where Amal and Remi waited near the doorway, and, just beyond, a group of curious girls peering in to see what was happening. "I don't think I should be here," he said. "I wouldn't want to get the kids sick. Maybe I should drive back to Jalingo and get a hotel room. Maybe even a doctor's appointment. I'll probably need medical clearance to even get on a plane."

He was right about that. Ever since the Ebola crisis, the airlines were under orders to disallow passengers with a fever. "If you are sick, you shouldn't really be driving yourself. Let's hope it's food poisoning."

Sam moved to the doorway, anxious to be in the fresh air.

Remi crossed her arms, giving him the look. "You're making him clean it up himself?"

"It's not like he's dying or anything."

Amal laughed. "I do like your husband."

Remi gave him a quick jab with her elbow. "Good thing I do, too." She glanced at Hank, her smile fading. "Let's hope he's better after a good night's sleep."

BUT THE NEXT MORNING, WHEN SAM AND REMI WENT TO CHECK ON him, Hank was still sick. He looked at them from his cot, his face pale, his hand resting on the edge of a bucket that Pete or Wendy had brought to him.

Hank gave a wan smile when he saw them. "Sorry to be such a burden. Something tells me this isn't food poisoning."

Remi moved closer, putting her hand on his forehead. "You do feel a bit warm."

"I think I might need to see a doctor. I'd be glad to drive myself into Jalingo. I don't want to take anyone away from work."

"Get some rest," Sam said. "We'll be back in a few minutes."

"Well?" Wendy asked. She, Pete, and Amal stood just outside the office, waiting for the prognosis.

"He looks pretty sick," Sam said.

Remi nodded. "I know he didn't ask, but maybe we should offer to fly him back to Tunisia. It's not like we're going anywhere in the next week. And you have to go pick up Lazlo anyway."

"He'd never make it through Immigration without a medical clearance." Sam glanced behind Remi at the closed door. "More importantly, I'm not overly thrilled with the idea of putting a sick man with our crew. I'll drive him in."

"I'll go with you," Pete said.

"No. If he really did see this Makao character in the village, I'd rather you stayed to help Remi. If we have any hope of keeping on schedule, you're better off here. Besides, I have an appointment with the last of the Kalu brothers," he said as the dorm room door opened and several girls emerged, walking toward the mess hall.

"What sort of appointment?" Pete asked.

"The kind that works better when I'm by myself."

Pete nodded. "I'll go in and tell him to pack his things." He emerged a minute later, carrying the man's duffel bag, dropping it on the porch. "He's washing up now. Maybe you should eat a quick breakfast while you can."

Wendy had a plate ready for Sam the moment he and Remi walked into the mess. Remi took her cup of coffee and sat next to him as he ate. "I could always go with you."

He shook his head. "Until we assess if that threat at the market-place is real, Pete and Wendy need you here."

She agreed. "Let's hope your trip back to Jalingo is less eventful than the trip here."

Thirty minutes later, they were ready to leave. Hank, carrying a bucket, emerged from the building, his hair still damp from his shower. As Sam opened the tailgate of the Land Rover, Hank set the bucket down next to his duffel on the porch, then suddenly kneeled, riffling through the duffel. "Someone's gone through my shave kit." He pulled out a black toiletries bag, a look of desperation on his face as he searched through it.

Still kneeling, Hank looked around the grounds, his gaze landing on Nasha, who seemed inordinately interested in whatever he was doing. When he stood, she darted around the corner, out of sight.

"Anything missing?" Sam asked.

It was a moment before he answered, finally zipping the bag and dropping it into his duffel. "Nothing important."

"Good. Grab your bucket. It's a long trip."

CHAPTER TWENTY-FIVE

There are many colorful flowers on the path of life,
but the prettiest have the sharpest thorns.
— AFRICAN PROVERB —

The car just came down the hill. They're passing the farm now."
Makao held up his hand, signaling for his crew to stop
talking so that he could hear what was being said on his cell
phone. Eight men in all, they were gathered round their two vehicles
parked near the road just outside of Gembu. "You're sure it's the
same car we saw in the village? The Land Rover?"

"No doubt."

"How many passengers?"

"Two men. The driver had yellow hair. That's all I could tell."

"Good. Which way did they go?"

"It looks like they're headed back toward Jalingo."

"Perfect." Jalingo was a good six-hour drive, double that for the
return trip. It would give him and his men plenty of time to work.
"The four of you stay there. If they come back, call." Makao smiled
as he returned his phone to his pocket. "They've left."

Jimi was watching him. "You think one of them is this Fargo?"

"So it seems." It wasn't hard to confirm the names, Sam Fargo
and his wife, Remi. All the villagers in Gembu knew of the school
they'd built up in the forest. It made finding them extremely easy.
What hadn't been easy was coming up with a way to get to the
school without running into Sam Fargo himself. Verifying that he

was actually at the wheel on the way down the hill heading toward Jalingo made Makao's job a lot simpler. That meant that the dangerous half of the Fargos was gone. He had a feeling that Remi Fargo was like most beautiful rich women, able to wield a credit card, but beyond that not much of a threat. She'd want to protect the children, which would be her weakness.

He'd make sure to use that to his advantage.

Though he'd gone over the plans once with his men, he wanted to make sure there was no confusion. After their failed robbery out in the bush, he knew better than to leave anything to chance. Never before had he encountered anyone like Fargo, the man who'd been driving the truck. The way he'd created the dust screen to hide from view . . .

If there was one thing Makao admired, it was brilliance. Had Fargo not killed two of his best boys, he'd be far more appreciative of how he'd lost the upper hand in that failed ambush. Typically, he didn't dwell on collateral damage, but in this case he was taking it personally. His swift loss had made him look like a fool in front of his own men and it took every ounce of his willpower to ignore such a blow and carry on. As much as he relished the idea of personally putting a bullet in the head of the man responsible, that particular joy would have to wait.

Makao had a far more profitable goal. And even though he felt certain they could move in now, patience was the key.

The school was set high on the hillside, open ground surrounded by thick forest. A single winding dirt road leading up to the compound made getting to it without being seen nearly impossible. Yet the relative isolation meant that they wouldn't have to worry about anyone else suddenly showing up. More importantly, he was bringing enough men to ensure that if they were seen, any attempt to stop them would be quickly ended. Sam Fargo may have thwarted their ambush out in the bush, even making off with a couple of his automatic rifles, but with Fargo gone Makao doubted that anyone at the school was about to pull one out and start shooting.

In fact, he was counting on it.

From everything he learned from his inquiries in the village, the school was not officially open yet. The staff was too small to present an obstacle to eight men armed with AK-47s.

"When do we go in?" Jimi asked.

Though he wanted to wait for dark, he needed enough light for their initial entry. "We'll wait a couple of hours, then hit hard and fast. I don't want to give anyone time to call for help."

"What if some of them escape?"

"I doubt it. This is the only road in," he said, tracing his finger along the map. "If anyone gets past the farm, either direction, they'll call."

"What if they go up?"

The possibility always existed, but he doubted anyone would make the attempt. The trek was far too dangerous, especially with young girls. "Only a fool would go that way. These people aren't fools." He studied the map one last time and looked up at his men. "Load up. It's time to go."

CHAPTER TWENTY-SIX

*No matter how beautiful and
well crafted a coffin might look,
it will not make anyone wish for death.*

— AFRICAN PROVERB —

The distinct feeling of being watched came over Remi as she sat alone at the staff table in the cafeteria, reading the expense report that Wendy had given her earlier that morning. When she glanced up, she saw Tambara, Jol, and Maryam quickly look away from her, then shyly back.

Tambara elbowed Jol, whispering something, and all three walked over. "Mrs. Fargo?" Jol said, looking to her two friends, who nodded in encouragement. "Miss Wendy said that you're a great treasure hunter."

Maryam added, "And that you've found gold all over the world."

"We've found a lot of things all over the world," Remi said as Amal and Nasha walked up to the table, lunch trays in hand.

Jol gave Nasha a pointed look. "You don't have to wear your backpack everywhere. No one's going to steal it."

"I know," Nasha said, putting her tray on the table next to Remi's. "I like it."

Maryam and Tambara giggled, their attention now on Amal as she took the seat on the other side of Nasha. "Are you married?" Maryam asked.

"No."

"Why not?"

Amal looked down, her expression bittersweet. "There was somebody. Once."

Maryam's eyes widened. "What happened?"

Remi cleared her throat. "Girls . . ."

"It's okay," Amal said. "I think I liked him more than he liked me is all." She gave a wide smile, looking around. "Aren't you missing a Musketeer?"

"Zara's napping," Maryam said. "Goat-milking duty this morning." Tambara and Jol concurred.

Nasha looked up from her lunch with sudden interest. "What's a Musketeer?"

"A character," Amal said. "From a book called *The Three Musketeers*."

"I want to be a Musketeer. I can milk goats."

"You can't," Tambara said. "There's no such thing as five Musketeers."

"There's no such thing as four," Nasha said.

"D'Artagnan," Maryam replied.

Nasha looked at Amal. "Who's that?"

"An honorary Musketeer."

"See?" Maryam said. "So there are four."

Nasha scrambled from her seat, glaring at her. "I hate you. I hate all of you," she shouted, then ran from the mess hall.

Remi glanced at Amal, who raised her brows slightly. Both had been warned by Wendy to let the girls work out their own problems. Even so, Remi was torn about whether she should follow Nasha, especially when Maryam gave a dramatic sigh, saying, "She's so immature."

"She's eleven," Remi pointed out. "Maybe we could be a tiny bit nicer?"

Maryam nodded, her gaze moving to the floor. "Sorry," she whispered.

Jol, not to be dissuaded from their earlier conversation, looked eagerly at Remi. "We want to know how you can do all those things when you're just a girl."

"Just a girl?" Remi said. "What makes you think girls can't do that sort of stuff?"

The three young ladies shrugged their shoulders. Tambara elbowed Jol again. "Ask her," she whispered.

"Ask me what?" Remi said.

"About that time you and Mr. Fargo were trapped in a shipping container in France."

They had to have been talking about her and Sam's search for the stolen prototype of the first-ever Rolls-Royce Silver Shadow. "How'd you hear about that?"

"Miss Wendy told us," she said. "Weren't you scared?"

Nasha suddenly raced back into the cafeteria, pointing out the door. "Mr. Fargo is back."

Remi smiled at the girls. "Tell you what. I'll share a fun story of one of our adventures after lunch."

"Promise?" Maryam said.

"Promise."

Remi followed Nasha out into the courtyard to the front of the compound, curious. "You're sure?"

"Positive." Nasha led her across the drive to the locked gate.

Something must have happened, because Sam wasn't due to return until the following night. Remi peered between the two posts of the fence, seeing what looked like a mini dust storm in the distance. A gust of wind blew from the south, clearing the cloud enough for her to see the white truck and an SUV behind it. A chill swept through her. "That's not Sam," she said.

Nasha's breath caught. "Scarface . . ."

"Go tell Wendy to ring the bell. If you see anyone, tell them to meet at the shed. Hurry."

Nasha raced across the graveled drive, clucking chickens scattering in every direction.

Remi pulled on the chain at the gate, making sure it was secure, as the bell started clanging from the office.

Within seconds, girls flew out the doors into the courtyard, lining up as they'd been taught. Pete stood at the forefront, his tanned face etched with concern, as Remi ran in. "What's wrong?" he asked.

"Get the girls in the tunnel. The man in the white truck. With reinforcements."

Pete ran to the shed, opening the door wide as the girls gathered outside it, frantic, unsure about this sudden drill, undoubtedly picking up on the quiet urgency of the adults. The bell rang several more times, then Wendy rushed into the courtyard carrying three packs—hers, Remi's, and Pete's. Monifa and Yaro ran out of the mess hall, taking a position behind the girls, as Pete stepped out of the shed, holding two fingers high. The girls stopped talking, their eyes on him.

"Listen up," Pete said. He pointed toward the shed. "I want you all to follow Miss Wendy down the ladder as quickly and as quietly as you can."

"A ladder?" someone asked. "For what?"

"Is this a drill?" one of the girls asked.

"No. It's not."

Panic filled their faces as they looked around, trying to find the threat.

Wendy handed Remi her pack, then took the hand of the first girl, leading her to the tunnel. "Quickly," she said, her voice and demeanor the epitome of calm. "And no talking." Remi pulled the Velcro from the hidden slot in her pack, wrapping her fingers around the butt of her Sig Sauer but not drawing it. After seeing the fright on the girls' faces, she knew the sight of a gun might send them over the edge. Not surprisingly, their attention wasn't on her and instead was on Pete, who hurried them into the shed. Nasha brought up the rear, looking back toward Remi as Pete led her in. "Down you go," he said.

"I don't want to go," Nasha said.

"It's safer."

"But I know where—"

Remi, hearing the vehicles outside the gate, realized they had seconds. "They're here." Apparently, that was enough to send Nasha scurrying to the ladder. Remi looked at Pete. "You first."

"Sam will kill me if anything happens to you."

"Nice try. I'll be right behind you," she said, suddenly realizing Amal wasn't there. Drawing her gun, she moved to the shed door, opening it just enough to look out. The courtyard was empty and eerily quiet. So far, though, whoever had arrived hadn't yet breached the gates. She closed the door and moved to the tunnel, hearing Wendy's soft voice, taking a head count of the students.

Remi looked over at Pete. "Is Amal down there?"

He squinted into the tunnel just as Wendy's panicked voice said, "We're missing four girls."

Remi peered down the ladder, just able to make out Wendy's face below her. "Who's missing?"

"Maryam, Tambara, Jol, and Zara," Wendy said.

Remi recalled three of the girls running off when Nasha came to tell her about the car. "You're sure they're not here?"

Nasha squeezed in front of Wendy, looking up at Remi. "I know where they are," she said, scrambling to the top before Wendy could stop her. "I saw them after I left the office."

"Saw them where?" Remi asked.

"In the dorm. Miss Amal went to find Zara, and the girls followed her. But something happened to Miss Amal again. They couldn't wake her."

"A seizure," Remi said.

Pete started to open the shed door. "I'll go look for them, Mrs. Fargo."

Crack!

The single gunshot echoed through the compound. Nasha ducked behind the raised trapdoor. The girls in the tunnel started screaming.

"Hush," Wendy said from the top of the ladder. "Don't make a sound."

Remi moved next to Pete and looked out the door, thankful the courtyard was still empty. No doubt someone shot the lock off the gate. Putting her hand on Pete's shoulder, she looked him in the eye. "Whatever you do, don't come out until Sam comes back. He'll know to look for you."

"We can go together."

"No." Remi didn't doubt Pete's sincerity or bravery, but she also knew that with so many girls to care for, Wendy, Yaro, and Monifa were going to need his assistance to survive until help came. "I'll be fine. I promise. Get that tunnel closed and keep them calm. Their lives may depend on it."

"I will."

Pete followed Wendy down the ladder.

Remi slung her pack over her shoulder, knocking her phone from her back pocket to the floor. Before she had a chance to retrieve it, she heard the sound of car doors slamming, then the crunch of gravel beneath booted feet as someone shouted, "Search every building."

CHAPTER TWENTY-SEVEN

Do not let what you cannot do tear
from your hands what you can.
— ASHANTI PROVERB —

Remi glanced back, unable to see her phone in the shadows cast across the rough planking from the north-facing window. With seconds to spare before the men reached the courtyard and saw her, she slipped out.

"Where is everyone?" a man asked from somewhere out front.

"Keep looking. They're in here somewhere."

The deep, gravelly tone was undoubtedly that of the scar-faced leader of the ambush, Makao. She had no idea how many men were out there with him, all probably armed with the same sort of assault rifles they'd used during the ambush. As much as she wished she'd had the foresight to open the safe and retrieve the two she and Sam had recovered, she knew it would've wasted valuable time. Their goal had been to get the girls into the tunnel without being seen.

That goal hadn't changed.

Her Sig Sauer was woefully inadequate, and, until she was able to get the four girls and Amal into the tunnel, she wasn't about to risk getting into a firefight with who knew how many men.

She was relieved to find the dorm unlocked. Just before she slipped inside, she took one last look at the empty courtyard, praying it would remain deserted long enough for her to get everyone out and to the shed. She locked the door behind her and looked around for the missing girls, seeing nothing but bunk beds, neatly made, and a wardrobe against the wall between every other bed. A few wardrobes, she noticed, had doors partially open, and she checked the closest to see if anyone was hiding within.

Deciding the girls would have to be contortionists to fit inside, she crossed to the other end of the dorm, stepping through the bathroom doorway past the large, industrial-sized laundry hampers piled high with used towels. She quickly ruled out the open toilet stalls on one side, as well as the curtained shower stalls on the other. Her gaze landed on the two hampers. Before she had a chance to look, she heard someone rattling the handle of the exterior door, followed by a loud crash as someone kicked it open.

Trapped, she ducked between the hampers, holding her gun on her knees, listening to the heavy footsteps clomping across the floor. The top of the hamper blocked her from seeing out the door, which was to her left, but she had a partial view of the large mirror over the row of sinks to her right and watched the reflection of the two men looking around the dorm. Both carried pistols, one with an AK-47 slung across his back.

"Nobody here," the first said.

The second man looked toward the bathroom, a pale jagged scar on his face cutting from his cheekbone to his jaw. "In there."

The two walked over, their booted feet scuffing across the wooden floor. Remi slid down as far as she could, moving her finger from the trigger guard onto the trigger. She had nine rounds, one in the chamber, eight in the magazine. She could easily take both men, but the others were bound to start firing at anything and everything. Not willing to risk the girls' lives, she lowered her weapon, kept watching the men's reflections, knowing that if they glanced in the right direction, they'd see her.

But neither man looked her way. Instead, they focused on the showers and toilets, pulling back the curtains and pushing open the door of each stall.

"Empty," Scarface said. They turned, the other man brushing against the hamper as he stepped through the doorway.

Relieved, Remi leaned back against the wall, watching their reflection as they strode across the dorm and out the door. Another man joined them, saying, "Nothing. They're all gone."

Scarface turned around, looked into the seemingly empty dorm. For a moment, Remi thought he'd seen her, but then he turned away. She caught sight of him in the mirror, his smile sending a chill down her spine. "Burn the place to the ground."

CHAPTER TWENTY-EIGHT

Be a mountain or lean on one.
— AFRICAN PROVERB —

You two," Remi heard Makao call out. "Get the gasoline."

Hoping the man was bluffing, Remi remained where she was between the two hampers, until she heard a sobbed whisper from the right. "I'm scared."

"Shhh," came a second voice to her left.

Relief swept through her. "Amal?"

"Yes."

"Thank goodness. How many?" Remi asked.

"Five of us. I . . . I had one of my spells. The girls heard the gunshot and were afraid to leave the dorm."

"They're safe."

"What if they burn—"

"Let's hope it doesn't come to that." Remi stood, peering out far enough to see two men walk past the open doorway. When she saw their gasoline cans, she realized she had no choice but to give herself up. "Don't come out unless I tell you."

Holstering her gun in the hidden panel of her pack, she shoved it against the wall and dropped a couple of towels over it. She stepped from the bathroom and quietly crossed the dorm, her hands raised above her shoulders as she walked out the door. She counted eight men, each armed with a pistol at the hip and an AK-47, the majority of which were aimed at the various doors of the buildings.

"I'm unarmed," she said as they turned, aiming at her.

That the men didn't fire the moment they saw her gave her some hope that they were under orders to take everyone alive.

Which meant they weren't terrorists bent on killing girls who were being educated.

That did not, however, rule out terrorists bent on kidnapping girls who were being educated.

One of them patted her waist, looking for a holster. "Nothing."

Scarface held her gaze, then looked past her through the doorway. "What's your name?"

"Remi," she said. "Remi Fargo."

"Where is everyone, Remi Fargo?"

"I'm alone."

"Then you won't care if we burn down each building? Starting with this one?"

Remi said nothing, still hoping he was bluffing. He flicked his head. The two men holding the gasoline cans started splashing fuel on the wainscot at opposite corners of the dorm.

"Stop," she said.

Makao's smile turned triumphant. "Call them."

"They're just children. No need for guns."

He studied her for a moment, then said something in another language, one she didn't understand. They lowered their weapons. He pointed his gun at her. "If anything happens, you'll be the first to die."

She nodded and moved away from the door, drawing his aim toward her and away from the girls. "Amal," she called. "Bring the girls out. Keep your hands up and they won't shoot."

The massive hampers creaked as the girls climbed out. A moment later, Amal led them to the threshold, hesitating at the sight of the armed men.

"Over here," Remi said, holding out her hand. They refused to move. The looks on their faces broke her heart.

This was supposed to be their safe haven.

She had failed them.

Makao eyed the girls, then turned toward Remi, his gaze boring into her. "Where are the rest? All the others?"

"We're the only ones here. Everyone else left this morning. To Jalingo."

"You expect me to believe the entire school is gone?"

"Believe what you will. They're not here."

He called one of his men over. "Ask Dayo if any cars came down from the school."

The man nodded as he pulled out his cell phone and moved off to make a call.

If Makao had someone watching the road, it had to be at the tea farm at the bottom of the hill. Hoping she was wrong, she glanced over at Zara, glad to see the child hadn't realized the danger to her father.

With only one road in and out, they'd never get past the farm without being seen—assuming they could even escape.

A moment later, the man returned. "No cars since the Land Rover left this morning."

Makao glared at her. "You lie."

"Think whatever you want," Remi said. "They're gone. We're all that's left."

He stared at her a moment, then stalked up to the girls. "Where are they?" he demanded.

"I don't know," Zara said, bursting into tears. "When I woke up, everyone was gone."

The raw and painful truthfulness convinced him in a way nothing else could. He turned back to Remi.

"What do you want?" she asked.

"I think that'd be obvious. I hope you know someone with enough money to buy your freedom."

"If you think my husband will turn over one cent without proof of life for each one of us, you're making a grave mistake."

He laughed. "We just need to keep you alive long enough to collect the ransom. After that, I don't care much about what my men do to you."

"You harm one child and—"

He stalked over, grabbing her by her collar, pulling her until she was inches from his face. "If you knew what was good for you, you'd shut your mouth and cooperate. Am I clear?"

He twisted her collar so hard, she felt a prickling sensation across her face from the loss of circulation. "Very."

Finally, he loosened his grip on her shirt, his face filled with disgust as he shoved her back against the building. "Tie them up. I don't want anyone getting away. Then search the buildings again."

CHAPTER TWENTY-NINE

———

Sticks in a bundle are unbreakable.
— KENYAN PROVERB —

Nasha lifted the burlap sacks she'd hidden beneath and crept from the corner, listening to the men walking around in the courtyard outside the supply shed. She glanced at the trapdoor, saw it was securely closed, wondering if Mr. Pete and Miss Wendy would even notice she was gone. Probably not, she decided. She wasn't like the other girls.

People tended not to notice her.

It was, after all, what made her a successful thief.

Then again, Mr. Hank had noticed her. But only because she'd stolen his keys. She didn't feel the least bit of guilt over seeing him leave, though she was sad to see Mr. Fargo go. He also tended to watch her closely, yet she sensed that he was different. He watched his wife closely, too.

She liked that.

It reminded her a bit of her uncle, how he had watched her aunt when Nasha first came to live with him. That was before Boko Haram had killed everyone who tried to stop them as they invaded the school, taking the girls hostage. So many of her friends were gone. By the grace of God, she'd escaped to her uncle's home, even though he lived in the shadow of a Boko Haram stronghold. He'd had the foresight to shave her head and dress her in boy's clothes. "No more

Nasha. Nash is now your name," he'd said, putting her to work in the field with the other male children, who were, for a while, too young to catch the eye of the terrorists in their hunt for new fighters. A self-educated man, her uncle had a saying for every situation. When she'd complained after the first day about a blister on her hand, he'd told her, "A blister will heal, yet—"

"When can I go to school?" she asked, not wanting to hear yet another of his old proverbs.

Her statement had angered him and he slammed his fist on the table, scaring her. "Everything you learned in school, you forget. You are no longer a girl. Even to the boys you work with— especially Chuk," he said, naming her one friend in the village. "He's too young to keep that a secret. Tell them nothing. Do you understand?"

"No," she replied, tears springing to her eyes.

"A whisper released is like feathers soaring in the wind. You cannot catch them to take back. And you never know where they might land."

"But—"

He grabbed her blistered hand, pain coursing through her fingers as he squeezed them between his. "If they find out you're a girl, they'll take you away. They'll . . ." His gaze flicked to an empty chair at the table, where her aunt used to sit. He paused and gave a deep sigh. He'd never spoken about what had happened to her, why she was no longer there, and Nasha had never dared ask.

"I'm sorry," she said, having no idea what she'd done to rouse his anger.

He said nothing at first, just watched the tears slipping down her cheeks. Realizing he still held her hand, he let loose, suddenly pulling her into his arms. "No more crying. You're a boy now. You're Nash."

"But I'm not."

"You are. And you can never tell anyone different. If they find out . . ." He held her away from him, looking deep into her eyes. "I'll get you out of here. However long it takes. But until then, you must do as I say. Understand?"

She nodded. "But when can I go to school?"

"They hunt the schools. Destroy them. Take the girls. It's not safe."

And that she did understand. She'd seen the empty building, listened to the wind whistling through the broken windows.

Her uncle was determined that would not be her fate. For the next six weeks he disguised her right beneath the terrorists' noses, sending her to work the fields by day and hiding her at night. Her best friend in the village, Chuk, thought she was a boy. Her uncle refused to let her tell him the truth. Their life was lonely, hard, but filled with love. At night he read to her from an old tattered book of proverbs that had been borrowed decades ago from the library in Jalingo, a day's bus ride from his village. "Someday," her uncle told her, "we'll take the bus and get a new book."

That day never came. One night, her uncle shook her awake. "Time to go."

"It's too early. The sun isn't even up."

"Nasha," he said, not dropping the *a* at the end of her name for the first time since she'd come to him. "Move. Quickly."

She roused herself from her cot, reaching for the lantern.

"No light," he said, handing over her clothes.

She dressed in the dark. And he put her in the back of a borrowed truck along with a half-dozen other boys who were destined to become the next unwilling soldiers of Boko Haram. They picked up Chuk last. A year younger than her, he started crying as the truck bounced along the dirt road on their way out of the village.

Nasha took his hand in hers. "We'll stay together, like my uncle says. And watch out for each other. Okay?"

"Promise?" Chuk said.

"Promise."

Her uncle drove them to Jalingo. He'd made a deal with someone who promised to take care of the boys until he could come back for them.

That had been well over a year ago.

The man he'd entrusted had pocketed the money, leaving the boys to fend for themselves.

Some of them ran off. Nasha, Chuk, and one other boy, Len, were picked up by the Kalu brothers as they wandered the streets of Jalingo. They may have escaped Boko Haram but they'd landed in a completely different hell, of that she had no doubt. The oldest Kalu brother, Kambili, had always told them this was their fate. This was what society's rejects deserved.

As much as she tried not to believe him, a part of her figured there was some truth to his words. Wasn't that why bad things kept happening to her?

Shaking off the old memories, especially the hurt of Chuk's betrayal, Nasha crept toward the partially open shed door and peered out. She startled when she saw Mrs. Fargo, Miss Amal, and the four older girls surrounded by men with rifles.

Frightened, she glanced toward the closed trapdoor, longing for the feeling of security, wondering if anyone would let her in if she were to knock.

Still, she hesitated. Those girls down there might not be like her. But once she had been like them, thinking there was nothing else in the world but loving parents and a new day. And as much as she wanted to return to that life, free from Boko Haram and the likes of the Kalu brothers, she refused to knock on the door. If someone heard her, every one of those girls would be in danger.

Heavy footsteps scuffed across the courtyard toward the shed, and she hurried back to her corner, kicking something as she scrambled beneath the burlap sacks. She looked out, saw a small square thing near the door, too far to reach without exposing herself. Mrs. Fargo's phone, she realized, her heart beating so hard, she was sure that the man who walked into the shed could hear each and every thud.

CHAPTER THIRTY

He who is sick will not refuse medicine.
— AFRICAN PROVERB —

Sam pulled up to the lobby doors of the Jalingo hotel, parked, then pushed the hatch release button, looking forward to having Hank and his bucket gone from the car. Thankfully, whatever had plagued the man seemed to have let up once they were on the road, though he still looked pale and weak. "I'll get your bag," Sam said.

"Appreciate it."

Sam walked around to the back of the Land Rover, grabbed Hank's duffel from the cargo, as Renee LaBelle hobbled out the lobby doors on her crutches, her own bag slung over her shoulder.

"Don't close that," she said as he slammed the tailgate shut.

Hank hauled himself and his bucket from the car. "LaBelle?" he said, looking at her travel bag. "Where are you going?"

"I left a voice mail on Remi's phone. I thought that's why you were here. Well, why Sam was here. Why are you here?" she asked Hank.

"Sick." He held up the bucket. "I didn't want to pass anything on to the kids. I figured I must have picked up what you had."

"I'm fine," she said. "I think it was a bout of food poisoning or a very quick bug. Anyway"—she smiled at Sam—"seeing as how you're here, can I catch a ride with you to the airport?" She gave a pleading smile. "I've made a late-night flight back to Tunis."

"Everything okay?" Sam asked.

"Unfortunately, no. There was a break-in at the dig site. Luckily, I think it was interrupted before too much was disturbed, but I need to get back right away."

Hank put his hand on her arm. "I'll go with you."

"Au contraire," she said, acknowledging his bucket.

"Really," he said, quickly setting the pail at the curb. "I'm feeling better already."

"Even if you were, the flight's booked full. Besides, you look like death warmed over. You'd never get through airport security."

"She's right," Sam said. "They'd quarantine you before you ever made it through the terminal."

Renee looked at her watch. "Hate to rush you out of here. My plane leaves in a few hours."

Sam took Renee's bag from her, slung it over his shoulder, then set Hank's bag at his feet. "And I have to pick up Lazlo."

Hank looked at Sam in disbelief. "But—"

"Get some rest," Sam said, opening the tailgate with a key on his fob and depositing Renee's bag. He helped her into the front passenger's seat, put her crutches in the back, and walked around to the driver's side. "Couple of days, you'll be right as rain. Oh, and thanks for your help with the dorm. Appreciate it."

Sam slid behind the wheel as Renee buckled her seat belt. She rolled down her window, waving at Hank as they drove off. "Room service," she called out. "They serve a mean chicken broth."

When it was clear Sam was driving into town instead of out, Renee looked over at him. "Shouldn't we be heading the other way? Airport? Lazlo?"

"Gotta make a quick stop first. Sorry. Should have warned you."

He drove to the street where Nasha had stolen the keys from Hank, parking the Land Rover in front of the warehouse store. He looked over at Renee. "You think you can drive the car?"

"My right foot is fine. Why?"

"Good." He took her crutches from the back, bringing them around to her. Once she was behind the wheel, he said, "Sit here, doors locked, engine running. I don't want you falling prey to the pickpockets."

"What exactly are you doing here?"

"A little chat with the remaining Kalu brother. I need some background on that kid we found."

"The pickpocket? Why?"

"Long story," he said. "If I'm not back in half an hour, drive yourself to the airport and send Lazlo back for me."

"Sam, what kind of chat are we talking about?"

"I guess that depends on how forthcoming the man is with his information."

"Isn't he part of the same group who stole your truck? Are you sure you should be doing this by yourself?"

"I'll be fine." He started to walk off, stopped, and rapped on the hood of the Land Rover. "Might want to roll up that window. Like I said, pickpockets."

Within moments, the kids swarmed around Sam, at first begging, then quickly backing off as though suddenly recognizing him and recalling their last encounter. A few followed at a safe distance as he turned the corner and ducked into a doorway, waiting for them to catch up. He didn't wait long. Two boys rounded the corner and he stepped out, blocking their path.

"Don't run off," he said as they started backing away. "I've got a deal for you."

They stopped, eyeing him warily. One tilted his head back, trying to look defiant. "What sort of deal?"

"I need to talk to Kambili Kalu. Where can I find him?"

"You can't. He finds you."

The other boy added, "If he wants."

"The thing is," Sam said, "I'm a bit short on time." He fanned out some bills in front of them. "Tell me where he is and I'll make it worth your while."

CHAPTER THIRTY-ONE

*If you don't stand for something,
you will fall for something.*
— AFRICAN PROVERB —

The kidnappers lined up the women against the siding of the unfinished dorm, tied their hands behind their back and ordered them to sit. Remi, Amal, Zara, Jol, Maryam, and Tambara huddled together. Though tears slid down the girls' cheeks, they remained stoic.

Makao ordered his men to search the buildings a third time. "There's a ladder," he said, nodding to the one Pete had used to get on the roof. "Maybe there's an attic in one of these buildings. Search every corner, anywhere someone might hide."

"This is my fault," Amal said after the men moved off. "Had the girls not stopped to help me, they'd have been safely away."

"No," Zara said, near tears. "The only reason anyone was in there was because I was too tired to wake up. And then we heard the gunshot and—"

"It's no one's fault," Remi said, looking over at them. "And we're going to get out of this."

"How?" Amal said.

"I'm not sure. Yet."

One of the men looked at them. Amal waited until he turned away, then whispered, "Do you think they're Boko Haram?"

Remi thought about the attack on the road and the men who'd been hiding in the back of the white pickup. The road spikes would have disabled their vehicles, which meant they weren't in it for the truck, the rental car, or the cargo. At least not the cargo meant for the school. Undoubtedly, they'd been after hostages. These men had enough firepower to ensure that anyone they came up against would quickly surrender without a fight. "I have no idea. But whoever they are, there's no doubt they're holding us for ransom."

Zara looked at her in alarm. "My father doesn't have any money. Who'll pay?"

"My husband will." But only as a last resort—that, Remi kept to herself. Right now, she needed the girls to remain calm. "Everything's going to be fine. I promise."

Her words sounded hollow even to her. A loud crash, then another and another, all coming from the dorm, startled the girls as the men ransacked the school.

"What are they doing?" Maryam asked, her voice shaking.

"Looking for the others."

"But where are they?"

"Not here," Remi said.

The answer seemed to confuse the girls, but Remi didn't have time to come up with a plausible explanation. Noises came from every direction as the men searched. "Makao," one of the bandits called out from the cafeteria. He walked over, looking in the door, the two talking intently. Remi wondered what they'd found that was so interesting.

"Look," Tambara whispered. "At the shed."

She turned to see Nasha peering out the door, watching the men standing by the mess hall. As much as Remi wanted to call out to her, tell her to stay there, she didn't dare make a sound, even when the girl slipped out, ducking behind one of the planters. A moment later, she belly-crawled to the edge of the wooden box, looking out through the long tussock of grass that grew up at the corner of the bed.

Zara took a breath. "What's she doing?"

Remi shook her head at Nasha, warning her away, but the girl darted toward them, scrambling into the space between Remi and Zara just as Scarface looked back to check on them. He watched them for several seconds, and Remi leaned forward, trying her best to block his view of the girl.

Apparently not realizing they'd gained an extra hostage, he returned his attention to whatever the man was telling him about what he'd seen in the mess hall.

Remi glanced over at Nasha, relief mixed with worry. If Makao connected her to the missing girls . . . Knowing they might have only seconds, she said, "Do you remember how to send a picture on a phone?"

She did. "Amal showed me. The button with the little white cloud. And then I press the camera button."

"Good. I dropped my phone somewhere in the shed. If you find it, I need you to send a message to Sam. But you have to unlock the phone first."

"How?"

"You'll see the numbers when you press the round button at the bottom. Seven-one-two-two."

"Seven-one-two-two."

"When the screen comes up, take a photo and send it to Sam."

"How do I find his number?"

"Unless someone else texted me, it should be the top number on the messages."

"What do I say?"

"*Help.* Do you think you can do that?"

She nodded.

"Good girl. If he calls, tell him they have men watching down near the farm." From the corner of her eye, she saw Zara look over at her in alarm, tears clouding her eyes. "He needs to know."

"Okay."

"And no matter what happens, don't let them see you. I want you to hide."

Nasha looked at the other girls, then Remi, her chest rising in defiance. "No. I won't. I might be just a girl, but I want to fight." She lifted her chin, daring Remi to refuse her.

Remi searched the girl's determined face, knowing without a doubt that if she didn't give the girl some direction, Nasha would engage the enemy on her own. She seemed to fear nothing, which was what worried Remi. If she turned into a mini rogue agent, doing whatever she wanted, chances were good she might be caught. Far better to keep her safe so that if all else failed she could warn Sam. "You can help, if you promise to do exactly what I say. If it's too dangerous, you have to hide."

"I promise."

The other girls looked from Remi to Nasha, their eyes filled with uncertainty. Remi outlined her plan, starting with her pack hidden beneath the towels between the hampers. Nasha listened intently, nodding, as Remi told her what she wanted done. "If you can't get to my pack, don't worry. What's more important is the road spikes we found. They're in a box in the shed."

"I know where they are."

"Good. You'll have to get the box out without them seeing or hearing. Maybe the girls and I can create a distraction."

"Like the boys do when we pickpocket?"

"Just like that. If we can't make one, you need to wait. I'm going to try to get us moved to the office. That will be closest to the truck and the keys. There's a window in the office bathroom." Remi, about to tell her that the window should be open, glanced over at Makao, shocked to see him looking their direction.

His eyes locked on hers and he drew his gun, then stalked across the courtyard toward them.

CHAPTER THIRTY-TWO

An army of sheep led by a lion
can defeat an army of lions led by a sheep.
— GHANAIAN PROVERB —

Within seconds he stood in front of them, pointing his weapon at Remi's chest. "There are twenty trays and food in the cafeteria, waiting to be served. Where is everyone?"

"I told you. Gone. Some of the kids were sick. We were worried it might be contagious, so we did an emergency evacuation. They won't be back."

"The food—"

"You're welcome to wait, but it'll be a long one."

Makao started to turn away when he seemed to notice Nasha for the first time. He scrutinized her for several interminable seconds, his gaze narrowing, when two of his men appeared from the back of the compound.

"The place is deserted," one of them said. "But there's a huge pile of dirt behind that building." He pointed toward the supply shed. "We can't figure out where it came from."

Scarface looked at Remi for an explanation. "Well?"

"Honestly, I have no idea," she replied, grateful his attention was no longer on Nasha. "I've only been here a few days. But I'd assume it's topsoil from the firebreak around the school." She nodded toward the garden area. "They've been using it in the planters."

She hoped he'd believe the partial lie. The area outside the fence was plowed regularly as a firebreak to separate the forest from the school, but it was clearly contaminated with grass and weeds—which easily could be seen if they walked outside the courtyard for a closer look.

He seemed to buy it. Her relief was short-lived when his interest focused on the shed. "And why is that building round? Different from the others?"

"It was an experiment in recycling." From the corner of her eye, she saw the older girls looking at the shed. Keeping her voice nonchalant, she added, "They filled the plastic bottles with dirt and used them for the walls."

He studied the structure. "What's in it?"

"Tools. Feed for the goats and chickens. Nothing much."

"I want to see this bottle building." He and two men walked toward the shed, stood in front of it a few moments, discussing something she couldn't hear.

Nasha had an innate sense of timing. The moment the men looked away, she dashed toward the planter, ducking out of sight.

Amal stared after her, then leaned toward Remi. "You're sure that's a good idea?"

"Worst case? They catch her and she ends up here with us."

"You're positive about that?"

If anything happened to Nasha, Remi would never forgive herself. But she'd seen the child in action, feeling certain that she had the skills to survive. "Yes."

For the first time since they were captured, a sense of hope filled her. "Say nothing," she told the other girls as Nasha scurried toward the picnic benches and behind the tree. A moment later, they saw the branches above moving. "Whatever you do, don't look up there. If they find her . . ."

The girls reluctantly tore their gazes from the shade tree and watched as Makao pushed open the door. A clatter inside sent him and the other men back a step, all of them pointing guns into the building. As Makao nodded to the man on his right to go in, she prayed the girls down in the tunnel stayed silent.

The guard entered, his weapon at the ready.

Remi forced herself to breathe evenly. If Amal or the girls suspected that building was anything more than an empty supply shed, they'd all be in trouble.

The guard finally appeared in the doorway—then stopped to pick up something from the floor before stepping out.

Her heart skipped a beat.

Please don't let it be my phone . . .

"What is it?" Scarface asked.

He held up something too small for her to see. "Nails. I think they fell from the shelf when the door hit it."

Scarface nodded.

Thanking the stars that Hank had stacked the nails in so precarious a place, Remi let out a breath she didn't even know she'd been holding. Nasha was safe. Wendy, Pete, and the students hadn't been discovered.

For the moment.

Amal leaned toward her again. "What if Nasha can't figure out how to work the phone?"

"Sam will know something's wrong when he can't get in touch with me." No doubt Sam had dropped off Hank at the hotel and was on his way to town to find out what he could about Nasha from the remaining Kalu brother. She only hoped the delay wasn't going to cost them, since he still had to pick up Lazlo from the airport. If—and it was a big if—Pete and Wendy somehow had cell reception in the tunnel, Sam already knew of their plight and was on his way back. If not, it was up to Nasha to tell him—assuming she could get back into the shed, then find and work the phone.

Right now, though, they needed to get into the office. Without those truck keys, they'd have no way of getting out of there. That part of the plan was going to take a little more finesse, she thought, watching as the man tossed the nails back into the shed. When he returned to stand guard over them, Remi said, "How long are we going to be here?"

"Long enough."

"And when we have to use the bathroom?"

"Do you think I care?"

"You better do it soon. Or whoever ends up riding with us is going to wish they'd listened."

Maryam glanced at Remi, then at their guard. "I need to use the bathroom."

"So do I," Zara said.

"I do, too," Tambara added.

Makao looked over at Remi, suspicious. "You put them up to this."

"I assure you, I said nothing. Lock us in the dorms, if you must. We can use the bathrooms, and the girls' beds are there. They can rest while you're . . . doing whatever it is you're doing."

"Where else are there bathrooms?"

"In the small building, out front. But there's only one door and it's crowded. We'd have to sit on the floor."

"I don't care where you have to sit." He looked over at Pili. "Move them there. They'll be easier to watch."

Pili ordered the hostages to stand, taking hold of Remi's arm. "Get going."

The girls filed out of the courtyard and across the graveled drive toward the office, Remi, still held by the guard, bringing up the rear. Makao walked in first, taking a look around on his own, then exiting. "Leave them inside."

"What about our hands?" Remi asked. "At least tie them in front."

"I'm sure you'll make do." He looked at the guard. "No one in or out. You do not leave this doorway."

"Understood."

The moment he walked out, leaving Remi and the girls alone, she smiled.

CHAPTER THIRTY-THREE

The strong do not need clubs.
— SENEGALESE PROVERB —

The two boys led Sam through a maze of streets and pointed down a narrow alley. "It's a secret where Kalu lives," one of the boys said. "You can't tell anyone."

"Promise," Sam said, paying them. They ran off and he continued past the dilapidated buildings, most with rusty corrugated tin roofs. Not much of a secret, he thought, reading the sign over the door, its faded red paint peeling and flaking from the warped wood.

KALU & SONS
FURNITURE REPAIR

To the right was a broken window, the shattered glass glittering on the ground just below it. Checking the alley in both directions and seeing no one, Sam stepped up to the door, pounding on the frame.

No answer.

He pounded again, then waited. Reaching down, he turned the knob. It was unlocked and he stepped to the side and pushed it open, looking into a workroom piled high with broken chairs. Judging by the thick dust and cobwebs, he doubted anyone had attempted to repair anything there in years. "Kalu," he shouted.

A boy, maybe a year or two younger than Nasha, poked his head out of a room near the end of a dim hall and ducked back when he saw Sam. A moment later, a man stepped out of a different room. He bore a striking resemblance to the Kalu brothers. He closed the distance between them, crossing his muscular arms as he towered over Sam. "Who are you?" he asked, his voice deep.

"Sam Fargo. I'm here for information."

"If you were smart, Sam Fargo, you'd leave. I don't invite strangers into my home." Kambili seemed to be sizing him up. Apparently, Sam didn't appear to be much of a threat because the guy didn't draw the gun that was clearly in his waistband. His gaze flicked out the door, then back. "Who's with you?"

"I came alone."

"A shame." He picked up the leg of a broken chair.

"Here, now," Sam said, putting his hands out. "Just trying to have a civil conversation."

Kambili leered. "I'm not the civil type." He swung.

Sam jumped to one side as the club whistled past.

"Look," Sam said, grabbing a broken chairback. "All I want is a little information—"

Kambili swung again. Sam lifted the back. The club bounced off the top and flew from Kambili's grasp, clattering against the wall.

Eyes narrowing in anger, he reached for his gun.

Sam charged, ramming the broken chair into Kambili's gut.

He doubled over, grabbing at the chair. Sam drove it up, smashing his jaw. As Kambili staggered back, Sam grabbed the man's gun, then shoved him into an old desk chair on casters. "Maybe you didn't hear me. I want information."

Kambili glared at him. "I'll kill you."

"In the meantime," Sam said, tossing the chair back onto the pile of broken furniture and pointing Kambili's gun at him, "I need you to answer a few questions about a boy who used to work for you."

"I have"—his voice came out as a rasp—"a lot of boys. In and out. Who can keep track?"

"A boy named Nash."

"Thief."

"Where did he come from?"

"I don't know. A man who brought him and the others, just dumped them on the street."

Sam reached over and picked up the fallen chair leg. "Let me jog your memory a little."

"No, I swear."

Sam took a step forward.

"Wait. There is someone. I just remembered. Chuk. One of the boys who arrived with Nash is from the same village."

"Call him."

"Chuk," he shouted, never taking his eyes off Sam. "Get in here."

A moment later, the same boy Sam had seen earlier walked into the room, his eyes widening at the sight of the oldest Kalu brother sitting in the chair, his face injured.

"Tell him," Kambili ordered.

"Tell him what?" the boy asked, looking at Sam.

"Nash," Sam said. "Do you know him?"

He nodded.

"Where's he from?"

Chuk's gaze flicked from Sam to Kambili, then back. "He lived with his uncle on a farm."

"Where?"

He shrugged. "Near Maiha."

Kambili gave a sharp tilt of his head and the boy ran off. "There. You got what you came for."

"That wasn't so hard, was it?" Sam said, backing toward the door.

"You ever show up in Jalingo again, I'll kill you. My brothers will kill you."

"Not likely." Sam emptied the rounds from the man's pistol, shoving them into his pocket along with the empty gun. "Is this a good time to offer condolences? Wait. You don't know, do you?"

"Know what?"

"Your brothers are dead. If you're wondering, it wasn't me."

Kambili stared, shocked. "Who?" he asked.

"Good question. You know a guy with a big scar running down his face? Drives a white pickup?"

Several seconds ticked by as Kambili just stared. "You lie. Why would Makao kill my brothers?"

"Apparently, they were squabbling over my supply truck. The second one, since your brothers stole the first."

"That doesn't make sense."

"That your brothers stole my truck?"

"No. That Makao would. He wouldn't waste his time. My brothers would know not to mess with him."

"Not sure they got the memo. About this Makao—I killed two of his men. You think he'll take that personally?"

Kambili gave a wary smile but the gleam in his eye was real. "I think he'll kill you. Slowly."

Sam drew his own gun and aimed at Kambili's chest. He closed the distance between them. Sweat beaded on the man's forehead. Sam lifted his foot onto the chair and shoved it back so hard, Kambili's head slammed into the wall. Dust rained down from the ceiling. He sat there, too stunned to move.

Sam pushed open the door, then looked back at him. "By the way. If I ever hear that you hurt one of these boys, or any others, I'll come back and smash every one of your fingers right before I kill you."

"DID YOU FIND WHAT YOU WERE LOOKING FOR?" RENEE ASKED AFTER Sam returned to the car.

"I did," he said, texting the information he'd learned to Selma. He checked the time. Lazlo was probably wondering where he was. "Let's get you to the airport." He pulled out into the street, noticing the kids were decidedly absent. Word traveled fast.

Renee leaned back in her seat, suddenly looking over at him. "Does this have to do with the people who tried to steal your truck?"

"Sort of."

"Remi told me what happened. I'm surprised Hank wasn't insistent on you taking him back right then. I swear, he's afraid of his own shadow."

"Considering one of the men put a gun to his head, he did surprisingly well."

"They did what?"

He looked over at her and back at the road. "Remi didn't mention that part?"

"Apparently not." Quiet descended for several minutes and then she sighed. "Look, Sam—"

"We don't have to talk about that now. It can wait. Really."

"No, it can't," she said. "And maybe it's better Remi's not here. I know we should've said something earlier, but Hank was hopeful we'd figure out where the money went. He did. It turned out Warren had a gambling problem—and, well, it wasn't like we could've returned the money."

"No word to anyone?"

"A note. Apologizing and saying it was his fault."

"To think I actually liked that guy."

"Really?" Renee said. "He was so unassuming and quiet."

"That's what I liked about him." He glanced in the rearview mirror, then at her, curious. "Excavations of that nature aren't cheap. How're you getting by?"

"Let half the crew go, utilize graduate students, like Amal, and tapped into my retirement. We're not exactly in a position to complain. Nor were we about to ask for more money until we knew what happened to it."

He slowed for a truck that turned in front of him. "I had Selma hire an investigator to find him," he said as his phone rang. He picked it up from the console, not recognizing the number except that the area code was Tunisia. He angled the screen toward Renee. "Someone you know?"

"That's Amal's number."

No doubt she was calling to see what he'd found on Nasha, he thought. "Hello."

"I have your wife."

CHAPTER THIRTY-FOUR

*The tiger that prowls quietly
doesn't mean it's intimidated.*
— AFRICAN PROVERB —

S am felt as if someone had gut-punched him. Unable to breathe
as he processed the words, he let his foot off the gas.

"Sam," Renee whispered. "What's wrong?"

He shook his head at her, checked the mirror and pulled over,
hoping, praying, he'd misunderstood. He put a finger to his lips, signaling for Renee to remain quiet. "Who is this?" he demanded.

"Makao."

"Put my wife on the phone."

The man gave a cynical laugh. "In case there's any confusion,
I'm the one who gives the orders. I'll decide when and if you get to
talk to her."

"What is it you want?"

"Aren't you the least bit interested in who else I have?"

Sam forced himself to take deliberate, even breaths, quelling the
fear and anger coursing through him. "Who else?"

"Some very scared girls. How much would that be worth to a
man of your means?"

"That depends on the proof that my wife and the others aren't
hurt."

"She mentioned that might be an issue." Sam heard Makao's
voice, muffled, then saying, "Your husband wants to talk to you."

"Sam?"

"Remi. Are you okay?"

"I'm . . . we're fine. There's si—"

The sound of the phone being moved quickly, air hitting the mic, then Makao saying, "Satisfied?"

"Let's cut right to it," Sam said. "What is it you want?"

"One million."

"Naira?" he asked.

"Dollars. U.S."

"If I find out you've harmed my wife or anyone else at that school, not only won't you see the money, I'll kill you and everyone involved."

"You have twenty-four hours. If you involve the police, we'll kill them all."

The line went dead. Sam immediately called Selma, listening to the line ring.

"Sam?" Renee said, watching him. "What's going on?"

"Someone's kidnapped Remi and the girls."

"Amal?"

"I'm assuming so since it was her phone."

Renee's hand went to her mouth, shocked. "Now I know why Remi never answered my texts."

He wanted to tell her it would be fine, but Selma answered and he briefed her on what he knew. "No one's called you?" he asked, thinking that surely if Pete or Wendy were safe they would have phoned him or Selma immediately.

"No one," Selma said. "What would you like me to do, Mr. Fargo?"

"Two things. First, go through the school contacts. Is there anyone there we can trust who might be able to get us intel?"

"Zara's father's the closest. I'll see what I can find. What else?"

"I need a million dollars ready to go." He'd do everything he could to save his wife and the girls with her. As much as he wanted to head straight to the school, taking the extra time to get Lazlo first was a wiser course of action. "I'm on my way to the airport now."

"I'll text Lazlo to let him know. The police—?"

"Can pick up the pieces when I'm done."

"Understood. I'll get on it right away, Mr. Fargo."

Sam dropped the phone into the cupholder on the console, forgetting for a moment that Renee had been there listening the whole time. He looked at her. "We better get going."

"Are you sure you don't want me to cancel my flight?"

"Positive," he said. "Lazlo's already here. And you have your own emergency to handle."

"Is that a polite way of saying I'll only get in the way?"

He attempted a smile. "Sorry, but yes."

"Don't apologize for the truth."

The rest of the trip was made in silence, Sam replaying the phone conversation in his mind, trying to determine if there was anything he'd missed, some bit of information that he could use.

Nothing came to mind.

When they reached the airport, Sam texted Lazlo to meet him out front. When he walked out the doors, his duffel slung over his back, Sam idled forward, parked at the curb, and pressed the hatchback release.

He got out, retrieved Renee's crutches as Lazlo walked over, offering to carry her bag into the airport for her.

"It's not heavy," she said. "You need to get going."

Sam gave her a quick hug. "Take care, okay?"

She clasped his arm. "I don't want to call and tie up your line or Remi's while you're in the middle of all this. Let me know as soon as you find them. Please."

"I will. Hope you get everything straightened out yourself."

Lazlo dropped his duffel into the cargo area, slammed the tailgate shut, then got in the passenger's seat. "Selma told me. Have you heard anything?"

"Not yet. We're heading to the hangar to pick up my gear bag from the jet. If we're going after these guys, you need a gun." Sam started to pull out, looking in his rearview mirror, surprised to see a stranger running after them, shouting. He hit the brake, looked again in the rearview, and saw Renee waving one of her crutches at him.

He backed toward her and lowered Lazlo's window. "What's wrong?"

She leaned inside the car. "I just received the strangest text from Remi. *Hep.*"

"Hep?"

"There's a photo." She held the phone out showing him an underexposed image on the right-hand side of what he assumed was the inside of the supply shed, with a view out the door to an overexposed image of the courtyard and several people seated on the ground in front of the dorm.

At first glance, it appeared that someone had taken the photo by mistake—and he would have thought exactly that were it not for the ransom demand he'd just received. He enlarged the picture. Though blurry, there was no doubt he was looking at Remi, Amal, and four girls seated next to them.

He double-checked the phone number showing as the sender of the text.

Definitely his wife's.

But if Remi was being held captive, who had sent the photo?

CHAPTER THIRTY-FIVE

The brave man is not he who doesn't feel afraid,
but he who conquers that fear.
— AFRICAN PROVERB —

Nasha gripped the phone in her hand. Getting into it was easy. But working it was an entirely different matter. She had no idea who she'd sent the photo to. Or if they'd even know what it meant. The only other photo she'd ever sent was to Mrs. Fargo and Miss Amal had helped her do it. But when Nasha pressed the button that showed the little white cloud, all she saw was a list of names—and the one at the top was not Sam. It started with an *R*. Confused, she wondered for a moment if it was *Remi* spelled wrong. But it couldn't be because this was Mrs. Fargo's phone.

She tried to blink away the tears that threatened, worried she'd made a terrible mistake. Suddenly the phone buzzed, the screen lit up, and she saw Mr. Fargo's face in a small circle near the top. Her fingers shook as she touched the green phone button at the bottom and his picture filled the square like a small movie.

"Nasha?"

She nodded.

"Where are you?"

"In the shed. Miss Wendy rang the bell and everyone got into the tunnel, but Mrs. Fargo went back because some of the girls didn't come. I didn't want to leave her, so I hid."

"You did good. Who's there?"

"Scarface. He brought a lot of other men. They were looking for all the other girls, but Mrs. Fargo told them they left. Miss Amal is with her, and some of the older girls, but I don't remember their names."

"Can you show me?"

"They'll see me."

"Not if you stay hidden. Turn the phone so my picture faces out. I'll see what the phone sees."

She turned the phone, showing him the inside of the shed.

"Is there a way I can see outside?" he asked.

She pulled aside more of the burlap she'd been hiding under and crept toward the partially open door, careful to avoid the spilled box of nails. She held the phone low, waving it around, before backing toward her hiding spot, afraid to remain too long in the doorway.

"Where's Remi and the girls? I don't see them."

She turned the phone around so that she could see Mr. Fargo's face again. "I think they moved them to the office."

"Nasha, do you know how many men there are?"

"A lot. There were two cars. The big white truck and another one. They have the big guns like when they killed the Kalus." The memory frightened her, but she tried not to cry. "Are you coming back?"

"It's going to be a while. I'm in Yola. At the airport."

A tear trailed down her cheek. "I'm scared."

"Nasha," he said. "Whatever happens, you stay in the shed. Understand?"

She nodded.

"If they take Remi and the others, she'll know what to do. Do not let them see you. Okay?"

"Okay."

"I'm coming for you. Stay—"

The picture turned black. "Mr. Fargo? Are you there?"

Her heart clenched. She was supposed to tell him about the farm and the men waiting there.

Worried, she pulled the burlap over her head, leaving a space big enough for her to see out the door. For the next hour she waited and watched, eventually realizing that these men were just like the Kalu brothers. Because they carried guns, they didn't seem to care about their surroundings.

One of the bandits passed yet again just a few feet away from her. He had done it over and over. In a moment, he'd walk between the buildings to smoke and talk to another man coming from the opposite direction. They wouldn't move until they finished smoking. And they'd leave in the same direction every time.

That was something she knew how to work with.

Mr. Fargo had told her to stay put, but she didn't think she should wait. She looked at the phone screen to make sure that his face was no longer there, worried that he'd try to stop her.

The screen was still black—even when she tried to push the buttons—and she shoved the phone into her pack, then looked out the door, waiting until the man with the gun met up with his friend. As soon as their cigarette smoke drifted into the courtyard, she crept out.

CHAPTER THIRTY-SIX

*The length of the rope determines
the movement of the goat.*
— AFRICAN PROVERB —

M akao sat on the edge of the desk, scrutinizing the two women and four girls who were seated on the floor against the wall beneath the window. He lit a cigarette, then tucked the lighter into his pocket, as he focused on the red-headed woman. "You must know the combination to the safe."

Her gaze flicked to the storage closet behind him on the other side of the desk. Next to it, against the wall, was a tall safe, too heavy to move. A small bathroom was located next to that, the window open to let in fresh air.

"I don't know it," she said. "I've been here only a few days."

"New? You seem to be the one in charge. The school is named after you," he said, walking toward the open doorway, looking out. The sun had dipped behind the trees, the long shadows across the grounds disappearing as darkness descended. Two of his men were standing beside one of the trucks in the drive, one lighting a cigarette. Makao started to turn away, when his eye caught on something moving low across the ground behind them. He could've sworn he saw a very small girl out there. About to call out to his men to take a better look, he paused when a chicken strutted from beneath the pickup. Shadows playing tricks, he decided. Watching a moment longer, he turned back toward the Fargo woman. "I asked around in the village. There was a man who bought every last box of nails, apparently for the Fargos' school for girls. I'd think that if a school is named after you, you'd have the combination to the safe."

"You'd think wrong."

"Is there money in there?"

"If there is, there can't be much. Everything is paid for by credit card."

"Even in the village? I find that hard to believe." He took a long drag on his cigarette, watching her as he blew out the smoke. Her green eyes held his, but she didn't rise to the bait. She held no fear, he noticed. In fact, everything with her seemed calculated. He glanced at the other woman and the girls, all who refused to look at him.

"Where are you taking us?" she demanded.

"Somewhere safer. As I said, you'll be held for ransom." He walked to the door, again looking out. The two men had returned to their patrol and he scanned the grounds, once again seeing something or someone moving around their cars. Whatever it was, it was far too big to be a chicken. "Jimi."

The young man who'd been stationed at the open gate looked back at him.

"Stand here at the door. No one in, no one out."

Makao strode across the graveled drive toward their parked trucks, circling each one, ducking to look underneath. Chickens. He kicked some gravel at them, sending the birds running, and looked over at the large truck he'd tried to ambush several days back, noting the canvas covering the cargo bed seemed to be moving. He walked up, pulled the canvas up, and looked inside, unable to see anything in the dark interior.

Deciding it was empty, he dropped the flap and turned as two of his men emerged from the courtyard to investigate the noise. "Did you see anyone out here?" he asked.

The men glanced toward the office, where Jimi stood outside the door, then at the now unguarded gate. "No," one said as they heard loud bleating in the courtyard.

A moment later, three goats came trotting out between the buildings and toward them. "What the . . ." He glared at his men. "Where'd they come from?"

"There's a pen behind the buildings, on the other side."

"Go close it up."

The pair took off, running through the courtyard. When they started yelling and swearing, he gave a quick look toward the office and ran after them into the darkened court. The bleating grew so loud, he couldn't hear what his men were saying. He didn't need to. Dozens of goats poured into the yard, some jumping up onto the planters, others darting past him. The ruckus brought his other men running. They stared at first, then suddenly tried to herd the goats, holding their arms wide, attempting to block the animals from going around them.

"You fools," he said. "What're you doing?"

"They're getting away. You said you didn't want any noise."

"I meant no shooting." While there wasn't much down the hill beside the long, winding dirt road between the school and the main highway, he knew full well that there were plenty of scattered and remote enclaves. Gunshots were bound to be noticed. More importantly, his boss, Tarek, wanted the hostages alive and unharmed.

The goats calmed for a moment until one of them knocked a couple of tin buckets stacked on the edge of a planter to the ground, sending them into a frenzy again. Suspicion grew as he surveyed the chaos and then the buckets, which he didn't recall seeing before. He grabbed the arm of the nearest man. "If one of you didn't open that pen, there's someone else here. How many hostages do we have?"

"Six. Two adults and four girls."

A flash of memory hit him from when the hostages were lined up against the building, right before they'd moved them all into the office "I saw five girls earlier. One of them's missing."

"Why would they let the goats out?"

"A distraction, you idiot." He pushed him away. "Go find whoever did this."

"Where are you going?"

"To make sure the rest of our hostages are still there."

One of the goats brushed up against his leg and he tried to knee it. The creature merely jumped out of the way and trotted out of the courtyard. Cursing, Makao followed it to the front of the compound and feigned lunging at it, watching in satisfaction as it trotted across the drive toward the open gate.

He glanced at the office door, where the light spilled out across the wooden porch onto the gravel. The man he'd posted stood guard, oblivious to his growing unease as he hurried that direction.

CHAPTER THIRTY-SEVEN

*A flea can trouble a lion more than
a lion can trouble a flea.*
— KENYAN PROVERB —

Two things taunted Remi. The orange-handled scissors jutting up from the penholder on the desk a mere six feet away and the keys to their supply truck, hanging on a hook by the door just over her head. The odds were against her from the beginning, but she wasn't willing to give up. Nasha, she hoped, would make her way here, get the keys, and . . . Well, Remi hadn't yet worked out how they were going to get to the truck. They'd need one heck of a distraction. And until that moment, getting to either the scissors or the keys without being seen by the guard posted outside would be impossible.

Redoubling her effort to loosen the plastic ties binding her hands behind her back did little more than chafe the skin at her wrists. Amal, who was trying to do the same, was so far holding up well. Remi couldn't help but worry about her since she was the weak link in her plan. If it was stress that triggered Amal's episodes, then she could have one at any moment. "How's it going?" she whispered to her.

"No luck."

Remi looked at the other girls. Tambara and Maryam shook their heads. Jol was clearly attempting to get free. Zara had her head on her knees, undoubtedly worried about the mention of her father's farm. "Zara," Remi whispered. "You have to try."

"What if something happened?"

"Sam will check on your father. I promise. Keep trying," Remi said, hearing the bleating of the goats coming from the yard. A lot of bleating, she realized.

Maybe the distraction she was hoping for.

Scooting closer to the door, she leaned far enough to see past the threshold between the guard's legs. Goats everywhere. One hopped up onto the porch, its hooves clopping on the wood. The guard chased it off, momentarily leaving his post.

Didn't matter how they'd gotten loose, she was going to take advantage of it.

Tucking her legs beneath her, she maneuvered onto her feet and backed toward the desk, keeping her focus out the door, grateful the guard was engrossed in the livestock and not them. A quick glance over her shoulder, she saw the scissors and reached back, linking one pinky through the handle. With one eye out the door, she lifted them from the cup.

A scraping noise from the bathroom alerted her to Nasha's arrival. Remi looked back to see her little face peering out.

Remi gripped the scissors, then eyed the guard, worried by the sight of Makao cursing the goats as he strode from the courtyard to the drive. Realizing they had very little time, she glanced toward Nasha. "Did you call Sam?"

She nodded.

"What'd he say?"

Her eyes downcast, she clasped her hands together. "To stay in the shed, that he was coming." When she looked up at Remi, it was as though she was hoping for forgiveness. "But the screen turned black before I could tell him about the farm and I couldn't hear him anymore."

Zara leaned forward, her expression imploring. "How will Mr. Fargo know to warn my father?"

"He'll know," Remi said. She didn't have the heart to tell Zara that the warning was for Sam. If Makao's men were holed up down there, chances were good that Zara's father was already a prisoner—assuming they hadn't killed him first. "Sam's very resourceful." She indicated the hook. "Nasha, the keys to the truck."

Nasha glanced up at them, then back, clearly troubled. "Do you think Mr. Fargo will be very mad that I didn't tell him?"

"No. Of course not." Hoping to get Nasha back on task, Remi was about to remind her of their mission. But when she looked outside, she saw Makao bearing down on them fast. "You need to hide."

"But the keys."

"Now," she whispered and hurried back to the corner, sliding against the wall and to the floor. Remi slid the scissors toward Amal and looked over at the girls, their eyes wide as they watched Nasha scurrying beneath the desk.

"Look away, girls," Remi whispered.

None too soon. Makao stormed in, pulling Remi to her feet. "Where is she?"

"Where's who?"

"The girl. The little one."

"There's just us. Everyone else is gone."

His eyes bored into hers. "What were you doing by the desk?"

"Nothing," she said. "I heard the goats and wondered what was going on. That's it. I was worried they were getting loose."

"I don't believe you. There were five girls outside. One was sitting between you and her," he said, nodding toward Amal. "Where'd she go?"

"Makao."

He turned to see one of the men walking in, carrying a cardboard box. "Look what I found sitting by the round building."

Makao shoved Remi against the wall, grabbed the box, then tossed it onto the desk with such force it tipped over, scattering road spikes across the floor. "Why would I care about that?"

"I don't think it was there earlier. I saw something moving by the cars."

"Something moving?" He pointed out the door. "There's a lot moving out there. Goats. Everywhere."

The man looked, nodding. "But—"

"But what?"

"I saw a bunch of buckets there, too. They weren't there before. And someone was throwing eggs at our cars."

Eggs? Definitely not part of Remi's plan. Apparently, Nasha had been busy, using the distraction with the goats to move around the compound without being seen.

Makao strode toward the door, looking out, glaring at Remi as he pulled her along with him. "Where . . . is . . . the . . . girl . . . ?"

"I have no idea what you're talking about."

He pointed out the door. "Then who did that?"

"Did what?" She stepped forward, drawing the attention toward her instead of the desk where Nasha hid. "You realize we have a lot of chickens? They lay eggs all over the place."

"On our windshields?"

Remi looked at the truck keys just inches from her face, then slid her gaze past them out the door.

Right now, her priority was to keep Nasha from being discovered since she was the only one who had a chance of getting the keys without being seen. "Chickens . . . Pesky little things."

Makao ignored her, his attention on the man who found the box. "See if there's anyone else out there." After he left, Makao returned his attention to Remi. "Where are the keys to that truck?"

"Our truck?"

He took a step forward, putting his hand on the butt of his holstered gun. "Play dumb and see what happens."

"Hanging on the wall by the door," she said.

He plucked the keys from the hook. "Jimi."

The guard at the door stepped inside.

"Load them in the back," Makao said, tossing him the keys. "We're getting ready to move out."

The man tucked the keys into his pocket and took Remi by the arm. "Let's go."

He shoved Remi toward the door, then ordered Amal to her feet. "Get up," he demanded again when she failed to move.

Remi looked back, saw Amal's vacant stare, worried, not only about her but the scissors. "She can't hear you."

"What's wrong with her?"

"It's like a seizure," Remi said. "You need to give her a few moments." When the other four girls glanced toward Nasha's hiding place, Remi cocked her head toward the door. "Everyone up," she said. "Amal will be fine."

As the girls stood, Nasha, gripping a road spike, burst from beneath the desk, screaming like a banshee. Makao tried to catch her. She jammed the spike into his hand. He jumped back, swearing. She charged full force into the other man, driving the spike into his arm. By the time he realized what was going on, she was through the door.

The guard spun around, trying to catch her, but Remi blocked his path. He shouldered her into the doorframe, knocking the breath out of her.

"After her," Makao yelled.

Nasha leaped to the drive, darting around the goats as the guard lunged toward her. Within seconds, several other guards appeared and the chase was on. She escaped them all, sending the goats into a panic, running in every direction.

Makao, looking at the blood dripping down his hand, swore again, finally calling the guard back. "Jimi."

When the guard returned, empty-handed, Makao nodded at the girls. "Load them up."

"Her, too?" he said, jerking his head toward Amal, her expression still empty.

"Send one of the other men back for her." As Jimi took Remi by the arm, forcing her out the door, Makao added, "If you find that other girl, kill her."

CHAPTER THIRTY-EIGHT

When you see a turtle on top of a fence post,
you know he had some help.
— AFRICAN PROVERB —

Amal started to come to the moment the other guard arrived to help. Makao, blood dripping down his fingers, didn't move from the door until Jimi led the hostages to the truck. The moment the Fargo woman was safely in the cargo bed, he returned to the office, looking for a first aid kit. He found one in the bathroom, and was applying a bandage to the gash, when he heard someone traipsing around on the gravel outside the office. Pressing the bandage tight, he walked to the door, saw Jimi searching for something on the ground.

"What're you doing?"

"I'm looking for the truck keys."

"I gave them to you."

"And I put them in my pocket. They must have fallen."

"The hostages?"

"They're tied up in the back of the truck."

Makao glanced across the graveled drive, inspecting the canvas secured over the cargo area. "You left them? Alone?"

A loud crash somewhere in the courtyard startled the goats and sent them running.

"The girl." Makao took a step in that direction and stopped. "Get back to that truck."

"What about the keys?"

"Forget the keys. We have two cars. Three prisoners in each. The rest of you can ride in the back of my pickup." He started toward the courtyard.

"Why us? Put them in the back of your pickup."

Makao stopped in his tracks, resisting the urge to smash his fist into the man's head. "Imagine some farmer sees the girls as we're trying to smuggle them out—without being seen. Get over there. Now."

Jimi hurried toward the truck, searching the ground as he walked. Makao took one last look around, then left for the courtyard to investigate. He had a sneaking suspicion about those buckets, almost certain he'd seen them earlier in the day, stacked inside that round building. The girl who attacked them in the office had to have moved them. Maybe she was in there now, he thought, pulling open the door to the shed. Moonlight angled in, casting its pale glow across the trail of dirt tracked across the floor planks.

He felt along the wall for a light switch, found one, flicked it on. A bulb overhead lit up the space and the dirt trail seemed to disappear in the light. He turned it off and the trail reappeared, and led to a pallet on the far side of the room. On top of it were stacked empty burlap sacks, the pile looking disturbed . . .

A child that size could easily be hiding beneath, he thought, stalking over and lifting them. Finding nothing, he tossed the sacks to the ground, distracted by the sound of a heavy engine starting. Jimi must have found the keys, he thought, seeing the footprints leading toward the pallet. Too many footprints for just one girl . . . He squatted for a closer look, his suspicion rising when he realized that all the prints seemed to disappear right there. A knothole in one of the floorboards caught his eye and he started to reach for it.

"Stop! Stop!"

Makao jumped to his feet, racing out of the shed, and through the courtyard, in time to see the Fargos' truck rolling toward the open gate, Jimi running beside it, trying to open the driver's door.

The rest of his men ran into the yard. "Pili," he called to the closest. "Climb in the back."

Pili ran toward the truck and vaulted onto the back bumper. The canvas whipped open. Amal, her hands no longer tied, kicked out as Pili reached for her. He missed, tried again, but she kicked him in the chest and he fell to the ground, writhing in pain.

Jimi raised his gun, ready to shoot. "No," Makao called out. "No guns."

"They're getting away."

"After them," Makao shouted as he ran to his pickup.

He shoved his key into the ignition, starting it, waiting for his men to jump in the back, while Pili and his group got into the SUV. They sped out the gate, but Makao had to lean to his left in order to see around the egg dripping down his windshield. He accelerated, gaining on the truck, swearing at the dust kicking up, all of it sticking to the egg. When he turned on the wipers, the blades smeared the sticky substance across the glass, turning it into mud. Just able to see through a small patch on the left of the windshield, he stabbed at the gas, glad the truck was four-wheel drive. When he approached the first hairpin turn, the back end started swaying, then fishtailed as he hit the brakes.

Figuring it was the rough road, he attempted to steer into it—until he heard the steady thump-thump of the rim and rubber hitting as they rolled down the hill.

"What's wrong?" Jimi asked.

"Flat." He slowed to a stop, got out, and saw both rear tires almost peeled back from the rims. He waited for Pili to catch up, watching the headlights bouncing wildly as it came to a stop behind his. He ran up the hill, saw the mess of egg and dirt smeared across the windshield, and knew without a doubt the rear tires would also be flat.

Pili got out, swearing.

Makao looked over the damage, realized they'd have to cannibalize the wheels from Pili's SUV to get his truck working. He ordered his men to change the tires.

"We're going after them?"

"Why wouldn't we?" He walked to the side of the road, looking down the steep slope, catching a glimpse of the headlights through the trees before they disappeared farther down the hill. The sight angered him.

They'd been set up.

"You two, go back," he said. "Burn the school down."

The two men grabbed the gas cans from the back of his truck and trudged up the hill toward the open gate, while the others got to work changing the tires.

He took out his phone, calling Dayo down at the farm. "The hostages got away. Don't let them get past you."

"We won't."

He disconnected, then watched his men pull the front wheel from Pili's SUV to put onto his truck, wondering how it was that so small a girl had done this on her own.

Impossible. No doubt the Fargo woman had directed her every move.

Didn't matter. He was through working with Tarek. Once he got his money, he was going to kill them both.

CHAPTER THIRTY-NINE

A leader who does not take advice is not a leader.
— KENYAN PROVERB —

Remi gripped the steering wheel, driving as fast as she dared around the sharp hairpin turn. She checked the side mirrors, grateful that they were no longer being followed.

"I could've driven," Nasha said. "We'd have gotten away quicker."

"I know," Remi said, looking over at her. Had it been the Land Rover, there was no doubt. The cab of this much larger truck was an entirely different matter altogether. Remi doubted the child could even reach the gas pedal. Still, the fact she'd single-handedly set up the spikes in front of the kidnappers' cars and stolen the keys amazed Remi. Thanks to Nasha, Remi figured they had at least a ten-minute head start. The kid was barely tall enough to see over the dash—and was, at the moment, trying not to be strangled by the shoulder strap of the seat belt. "But these roads aren't smooth like ones in Jalingo. And driving a Land Rover is a lot easier than this big truck."

"Maybe."

The vehicle hit a pothole, the bump jarring her insides, rattling her teeth. "See?" Remi said.

"I would have missed that."

Smiling, Remi checked her mirrors again. Still clear. After another ten minutes, she pulled over.

"Why are we stopping?"

"We need to come up with a plan."

"We can't go to the farm, can we?"

Remi looked at her. Nasha had already experienced her share of separation and death and that made her far more astute than the other girls. "Do not tell Zara what you're thinking, okay?"

"Mr. Fargo will know what to do."

"I hope so."

She and Nasha got out of the truck. Remi looked up the steep mountainside, unable to see any headlights through the trees above. They walked to the tailgate and Remi pulled up the canvas, saw the girls huddled next to Amal in the back.

As soon as they saw Nasha, they surged forward, jumping out of the truck, hugging her.

"Quietly," Remi reminded them and drew Amal to the side. "How are you holding up?"

"I didn't have a seizure," she said. "I was worried about Nasha. I just felt I had to do something to distract them."

"Nicely done, then. It worked." She looked up the hill again, listening. So far, nothing to suggest they were being followed—yet. "We're going to need a lot of luck. With only one road in and out to the main highway, we'd need a way to get past Zara's farm. I'm not sure we can risk it."

"So how do we get out of here?"

"Our best bet may be going out on foot, through the forest."

"I'd rather take my chances with the forest than kidnappers."

"I have to agree with you. Let's talk to the girls." Remi told them what she was hoping to do, that they'd all be setting out on foot.

Zara lit up. "If we go farther down the road, we can warn my father."

Remi and Amal exchanged glances, Remi saying, "I'm not sure that's a good idea."

"Why not?" the girl asked.

"You saw the guns those men had?"

She nodded.

"I don't think they'd hesitate to kill anyone who got in their way."

"But they didn't kill us . . ." She looked over at the other girls, perhaps hoping for some agreement.

Remi reached out, clasping her hand. "Only because we were supposed to be their hostages. I can't say that about anyone who helps us. If we leave the truck behind, we can set out on foot and maybe find a different way. To the village. Or at least help."

Zara's eyes welled up, but she nodded, saying, "My father says the footpath could take someone all the way to Cameroon."

Maryam added, "It crosses the road leading up to the school. There's a sign warning to watch for hikers."

They all turned toward Remi, waiting for her to weigh in. "If they come searching, that sign's going to make it easy to find us. And leaving the truck there is like putting out an even bigger sign saying *Here We Are*."

Nasha looked up at Remi. "What about the dirt trick? Like you did when the Kalu brothers came after us? We could pretend to go one way, then go the other?"

Remi was about to explain that the only reason that had worked was because they'd only needed a short space of time to hide in order to defend themselves—never mind that she and Sam had both been armed. This was . . . different.

Or was it?

"Maybe we can trick them. Gather round, girls. I have an idea."

CHAPTER FORTY

If you have escaped the jaws of the crocodile
while bathing in the river,
you will surely meet a leopard on the way.
— AFRICAN PROVERB —

Pete stood in the dark, his ear to the air vent, listening. The goats had settled, though he heard an occasional bleat. What he didn't hear was the sound of men tromping across the gravel. Or talking. All of that had stopped after the shouting, the roar of their vehicles as they sped off.

Still, he waited, wanting to make sure. He wasn't about to risk anyone's safety.

Wendy moved behind him, putting her hand on his shoulder.

He reached up, grasping her fingers in his. Though the two had been dating exclusively ever since they'd started working for the Fargos, once the girls had moved into the school, they'd both agreed that any displays of affection in front of the young and impressionable students were best kept to a minimum.

"Anything?" she whispered.

"I think they're gone."

"What about Mrs. Fargo and the girls?" she asked.

He put his finger to his lips, trying to listen, and glanced behind Wendy, the dim light revealing twenty pairs of eyes watching their every move. The caretakers, Monifa and Yaro, sat on the blankets with them, trying to distract the girls with a halfhearted game of cards. Fear had invaded the space as they waited to hear about their missing fellow students and Nasha, who had somehow slipped past everyone when Remi left. Pete smiled at the girls, then turned his back to them, facing Wendy. "Stay calm. They're watching you," he said quietly. "I'm going up."

"But Mrs. Fargo said—"

"She's gone. And we have no idea if she was able to call Mr. Fargo before they took her and the girls. Every minute we delay calling means they'll be that much farther away. We need to let Sam know. And the only way to do that is from up there."

Wendy agreed, her smile anxious.

Going against their employers' wishes wasn't easy. He and Wendy, having worked for the Fargos for this long, knew the dangers that seemed to follow the treasure hunters, especially considering how many millions of dollars' worth they'd recovered over the years. That was not the career that Pete or Wendy would have chosen, no matter how much money, both content with their much simpler California lifestyle, surfing and boating, when they weren't helping Selma with her research for the Fargos.

But the school was different. Planning and helping to build it had brought Pete and Wendy even closer, and they found their lives enriched by working with the girls. Perhaps that's why, for the first time since they'd started dating, Pete began to picture a very different life with Wendy. One that entailed something more than having a good job that allowed them time to play at the beach.

He wanted time with her.

If he couldn't have that, the next best thing was knowing that she, and everyone at the school with her, was safe. Which made his decision that much easier. He looked at the girls. "I'm going out to call for help."

They nodded. Monifa looked over at her husband, then Pete. "Maybe you should take Yaro."

The caretaker patted his right hip, where his gun was holstered.

Not knowing what he might find up there, Pete nonetheless said, "Turn out the light, and no talking, until the door's closed again."

When Monifa switched off the battery-powered lantern, plunging the tunnel into darkness, Wendy wrapped her hand around Pete's neck, pulling him toward her. "Be careful," she said, kissing him.

"I will." He climbed to the top, feeling for the latch and sliding it over, listening for any source of noise as he pushed the trapdoor upward about an inch. Hearing nothing but the frantic bleating of the goats, Pete climbed out.

Yaro followed. "Something's spooked them again."

The two men drew their guns. When Wendy closed and latched the door, Pete nodded at Yaro and slipped out of the shed.

Perhaps he'd misread the signs that the bandits had left. But other than the goats, the rest of the courtyard was empty, the sickle moon casting faint illumination across the flagstones and planters. Pete and Yaro crossed over toward the mess hall and edged their way out to the front of the school, alarmed when they saw an orange glow coming from the front of the building.

They raced back into the courtyard, into the mess hall, grabbing a fire extinguisher off the wall and the portable water pump, wheeling it out to the front.

Heat hit them as the flames raced across the wooden porch, licking up the sides of the dorm. Yaro aimed the extinguisher while Pete primed the pump, pointing the hose at the burning building. The water hissed and turned into steam the moment it hit the flames.

CHAPTER FORTY-ONE

To run is not necessarily to arrive.
— SWAHILI PROVERB —

I daresay, you're worried," Lazlo said, one hand on the dash as Sam drove. "But perhaps you might slow down a tad. It's dark out. The road isn't exactly in stellar condition."

They hit a pothole, the force of impact jarring them against their seats. Sam kept his focus out the windshield. "You're wearing a seat belt, I think you're safe."

"Yes, well, that's debatable. You get in an accident on the way there and Remi and everyone else is out of luck."

Sam, knowing Lazlo was right, let his foot off the gas. "I'm worried."

"Understandable." Lazlo took a deep breath, leaning back in his seat. "I'll ring Selma to see if she managed to get ahold of that farmer." He dug his phone out of his pocket and made the call, putting it on speaker. "It's me," he said. "I'm with Mr. Fargo. Any word?"

"Not since the last call five minutes ago." She cleared her throat. "I'm afraid I haven't been able to get ahold of anyone. I hate to say it, Mr. Fargo, but unless you want me to call the police, you're on your own."

"No police," Sam said, going over every option he could think of. Back when he was employed at the Defense Advanced Research Projects Agency, DARPA decided to cross-train some of their engineers in covert operations at the CIA's Camp Peary. He'd met Rubin Haywood, a case agent, when they were partnered up for close combat weapons training. Though Sam tried not to take advantage of their resulting friendship, there were times—like now—that he had no choice. "I need to call Rube."

"Already did. Waiting on his return call," Selma said.

"Thanks. We may need his help before this is over."

"I'll let you know as soon as I hear from anyone," she said as Sam's phone started ringing.

"See who it is," he told Lazlo, too intent on driving to answer.

Lazlo picked it up from the console, checking the number. "It's Pete." He held the phone toward Sam, saying, "Go ahead. Mr. Fargo's here."

Pete's voice came out in a rush, saying, "They have Remi and some of the girls."

"I know," Sam said. "For ransom. The kidnappers called from Amal's phone."

"I'm so sorry. We didn't see them coming until too late. Remi went back for the girls who didn't make it into the tunnel."

"Who, besides Remi?" Sam asked.

"Tambara, Maryam, Zara, Jol, and Amal. Everyone else made it. No cell reception or we would've called sooner."

"Six?" Sam confirmed.

"Wait. Seven missing. Nasha. She wasn't in the tunnel with us."

"You're sure she's not somewhere on the grounds? What about the shed? She called me from Remi's phone. I think it died on her—"

"No," Pete said. "I haven't seen her. If she was here, she'd find me, I'm sure."

Sam, checking the clock on the dash, hoped she was hiding somewhere safe. "We're almost two hours away. About how long ago did the kidnappers leave?"

"Less than fifteen minutes ago. Our supply truck's gone, so I'm guessing they took that to move the hostages. I doubt they've made it down the hill yet. What do you want me to do until you get here?"

"Keep everyone in the tunnel. We'll reevaluate once I get there."

"Will do. Yaro and I are going to hole up on the roof to watch in case they come back."

"Pete . . ."

"Yes, Mr. Fargo?"

"Be careful."

"I will be."

The phone beeped as the call ended. Sam glanced at the other phone that Lazlo held. "You catch all that, Selma?"

"I did."

"Good. When Rube gets back to you, have him call me on Lazlo's phone. I want mine open in case Remi or the kidnappers call."

A little over an hour later, Sam reached the edge of Okoro's farm, seeing lights in the distance. He let his foot off the gas, trying to get a better look.

"Something wrong?" Lazlo asked, following the direction of his gaze.

"I'm not sure. That farm belongs to the man Selma's been trying to reach. So why isn't he answering his phone?"

"Maybe it died."

"He's got power. He'd certainly be able to charge it."

Sam slowed as they passed the long drive. Instead of heading left up toward the school, he continued on the main road until he passed the stand of eucalyptus trees, then parked out of sight. He grabbed his gear bag from the back.

Lazlo strapped on a holster. "You're sure this is a good use of our time? The school—"

"Pete and Yaro are there. They'll call. But something's wrong." He lifted the night vision binoculars, saw several figures moving around the grounds. "Not a good sign," he said, handing the glasses to Lazlo.

The professor focused them. "Exactly what am I looking at?"

"Men. Who don't belong there."

"How do you know?"

"I'm fairly certain Okoro's farmhands aren't in the habit of carrying rifles to guard his tea crop." Sam suspected they were using the farm as an outpost to watch traffic in and out of the school. What he didn't see was the supply truck, which he assumed the kidnappers had taken to hide their hostages in as they fled.

Lazlo lowered the glasses. "By my estimation, the kidnappers left the school well over an hour ago. If these men are working with them, shouldn't they be long gone by now?"

"That, Lazlo, is a very good question. Let's go find out why."

CHAPTER FORTY-TWO

Restless feet may walk into a snake pit.
— AFRICAN PROVERB —

S am and Lazlo moved in on foot through the thick eucalyptus grove that grew up alongside the farm. Thankfully, the dagger-shaped leaves that had fallen from the trees and left to rot on the ground acted like a sound-dampening barrier. When they neared the edge of the grove, Sam held up his hand, motioning for Lazlo to stop.

The two armed guards stood watching the east side of the property, looking in the direction of the road leading up into the hills to the school. Sam watched them for a few minutes.

Lazlo shifted beside him, whispering, "Shouldn't we go now while their attention's diverted?"

"Patience. I want to make sure it stays diverted." About two minutes later, one of the men started walking toward the farmhouse directly across the route he and Lazlo would have taken. Sam waited until he was around the corner, then motioned for Lazlo to follow. They edged along the side of the barn and hid behind the tailgate of an oxidized blue Toyota pickup parked between the two buildings. Sam peered over the tailgate toward the house. Someone inside walked past the backlit window.

Definitely too short to be Okoro.

"Wait here," Sam whispered. "I want a better look."

Lazlo nodded.

Sam checked both directions, then ran to a rain barrel beneath the downspout next to the window, crouching behind it. He started to rise when one of the guards rounded the corner making a beeline toward the pickup where Lazlo was hiding.

Sam, tracking the guard with his gun sight, motioned for Lazlo to remain where he was. The guard stopped by the driver's door, pulled it open, and reached inside, retrieving a bottle of water. But instead of taking it with him back on his rounds, he stood there, drinking. As much as Sam wanted to take the guy out right then— and he might have, had he thought doing so would get the man to finish his drink—he wasn't about to start a gunfight. Not until he knew how many people he was dealing with and whether or not the girls were anywhere on the premises.

The man capped the bottle, tossed it onto the seat of the car, and closed the door. Rather than returning to the front of the farm, he walked toward the open barn door. Just a few more feet and he'd have tripped over Lazlo to get past him. Sam moved his finger from the trigger guard to the trigger, increasing the pressure with each step the man took. Someone called out from the front and the guard stopped, pivoted, walked quickly in that direction.

The moment he turned the corner, Sam glanced at Lazlo, who was leaning his head on the rear bumper of the Toyota, clearly rattled. Finally, he looked over at Sam, giving him a thumbs-up.

Sam nodded, then moved to the window, peering in. Zara's father sat in a wooden chair, his hands bound behind him, his lower lip cut and swollen, staring defiantly at two armed men inside the room. Okoro's three farmhands were seated on the floor next to him, looking scared but unharmed.

Four hostages. Four gunmen. Two inside, two outside.

Returning to the rain barrel, he motioned Lazlo over.

Lazlo hurried across the dirt drive, crouching beside him. "I daresay, you and Mrs. Fargo do this all the time," he whispered, watching Sam unsnap the pouch on his belt that held the speed loaders for his Smith & Wesson. "But . . ."

"But what?" Sam said.

"I was rather hoping we'd get through this without killing anyone."

"That ship sailed the moment they kidnapped the girls, never mind my wife."

"I had a feeling you were going to say that."

"If it helps, they'll probably try to kill us first."

"I feel better already."

Sam clapped his shoulder. "You'll be fine. Now, let's go get those two guards."

CHAPTER FORTY-THREE

Where a woman rules, streams run uphill.
— ETHIOPIAN PROVERB —

L ike Amal, Remi held a thick clump of long grass to cover the footprints of the girls who'd gone on ahead—Amal working her way up the steep, moonlit trail toward the trees, while Remi worked her way back to the truck to speed the process. With as many men as Makao had working for him, it wouldn't be long before they had their tires changed.

Remi swept her gaze over the portion of the trail visible from the road, satisfied that the prints were no longer so obvious. "I think we're good," she said.

Amal glanced behind her, the girls long gone from sight. When she looked down at Remi, her smile faltered. "You are coming back . . . aren't you?"

"That's my goal," Remi said. The last thing she wanted to do was add to Amal's stress and possibly induce a seizure. "But if I don't, keep going, no matter what. And trust Nasha's instincts. I have a feeling she's done this before. Now hurry."

As Amal disappeared into the trees, Remi looked up at the sign marking the hiking trail, then the four-inch-thick wooden post. The last piece of evidence. She climbed into the truck, putting the gear-shift in reverse, backing until she heard a loud *crack* followed by a thwump as the sign fell into the shrubs at the side of the road. She got out, threw some brush over the stub, and dragged the sign from the bushes and hauled it into the back of the truck.

Though she wanted to throw more brush over the trail, the rumble of Makao's approaching vehicle just up the hill told her she was out of time. She jumped in the truck, shifting to drive. About a quarter mile downhill, she reached the second sign that indicated *Lower Trail*. Parking just beyond it, she shut off the motor, pocketing the keys as she hopped out, wishing she had the time to remove the *Upper Trail* sign from the truck and hide it somewhere in the forest. If she was lucky, they'd give the cargo area a cursory glance, see it was empty, and head down the lower trail into the valley, allowing the girls enough time to get to safety.

The revving engine grew louder, and she waited until the beam of headlights swung around the curve, illuminating the back of the truck. Careful not to look into the headlights and ruin her night vision, she did her best to appear shocked at being discovered—remaining a second longer than prudent to make sure they saw her.

The tires skidding across the dirt as they sped up, then braked, gave her hope that her plan had worked.

Racing down the trail far enough to draw them in, she doubled back and hid near the road behind some low bushes. She needed to be able to get back up that hill.

And if she couldn't, so be it. As long as the girls made it, she'd be good with whatever happened next. Dropping completely flat on the ground, she closed her eyes against the settling dust, evened her breathing, and listened to the sound of the men as they tromped down the footpath, searching for her.

"This way," one of the men shouted. "She moved off the trail."

CHAPTER FORTY-FOUR

By the time the fool has learned the game,
the players have dispersed.
— ASHANTI PROVERB —

Makao looked up at the Forest Service sign and down the trail where the Fargo woman had disappeared. "Get a flashlight."

Jimi retrieved one from the truck, handing it to him. He shined it on the ground at the trail's entrance, seeing waffle-style footprints leading from the back of the Fargos' truck and onto the trail. He followed for a short distance, but the prints disappeared about twenty feet in.

Interesting. He stomped his foot on the ground, then checked to see if it left a print in the thin layer of dust on the hard-packed earth. Not much of one, which made him wonder if the girls, weighing much less, could possibly have gone that way without leaving a mark.

Somehow, he doubted that, and he shined the light into the thick growth on either side of the trail to see if they were hiding there.

Realizing it would take them all night to search beyond the immediate area, he returned to the road.

"Where else would they go?" Jimi asked him.

"Good question. Bring the map," Makao said.

The wind rattled the corners of the paper as he spread it out on the open tailgate of his pickup. He held it down with one hand while

Jimi angled the flashlight toward it. The location of the school was marked with a red X. Neither it nor the road they stood on appeared anywhere on the map, probably because both were privately funded. But a dotted red line clearly marked the winding hiking trail that led into the protected national park forest. It appeared that someone could follow it from the main road near the farm all the way up into the reserve and on to the Cameroon border.

He glanced over at the lower trail where he'd seen the Fargo woman disappear. Why no other footprints? He wouldn't put it past her to lift every child from the path, then have them walk for a time off trail to hide their prints. The question was whether they were headed down to the farm or doubling back up to the school. "Pili, you and Den follow the trail to the end and keep an eye on both sides in case they're hiding."

The two men headed down the trail, their flashlight beams swinging across the path and into the trees. The sound of distant gunshots brought them to a halt. "What was that?" Jimi asked.

"The farm," Makao said. "Find out what happened."

Jimi made the call while Pili and Den continued down the serpentine trail carved into the thick forest.

It didn't make sense that seven women and girls could disappear so quickly—which made him wonder how well his men had checked the bed of that truck.

He walked over, lifted the canvas, the beams from his headlights shooting in. At first, he saw nothing but his own shadow cast across the cargo area. As he started to turn away, he realized something was in the back of the truck. He reached in, pulled a thick post up and over the tailgate, cursing when he saw the large Forest Service sign bolted to its top reading *Upper Trail*.

"Pili, Den," he shouted. "Change of plans. Get in the back of the truck with the others."

"They're not answering," Jimi said as the two men jogged back up the trail.

Den glanced at the sign hanging out of the back of the Fargos' truck. "Where are we going?"

"We're getting our hostages back."

CHAPTER FORTY-FIVE

Ears that do not listen to advice
accompany the head when it is chopped off.
— AFRICAN PROVERB —

S am stepped over the slain guard, planting the barrel of his gun
in the back of his new hostage. "Anyone tell you that smoking's hazardous to your health?"

Lazlo eyed the dead guard with distaste. "What happened to
killing him quietly?"

"This seemed more expedient." The guards had been surprisingly uninspired to carry out their duties, lighting up their third
cigarettes instead of patrolling the grounds. Sam decided to hurry
matters along. The disadvantage, unfortunately, was that with the
gunshots they'd announced their presence. Sam forced his hostage toward the bungalow-style farmhouse, saying, "Let's hope
one of your friends comes out to see what happened." He leaned
in close, adding, "I need one of you alive. I don't much care which
of you it is."

The man said nothing.

Lazlo glanced into the window. "What if they don't come out?"

"I go in after them."

"I was afraid you were going to say that."

"Good news is, you get to stay here."

"What if something happens to you?"

"Find Remi and the girls, make sure they're all safe." Sam

watched the front door of the house, wondering what was taking so long. Those gunshots should have brought them out by now. He gripped the guard's collar. "What's your name?"

"Deric."

"Deric, tell them you need help."

"They won't come."

"You better hope they do or it'll be the last time you walk. Now call them out." Sam jammed the barrel against his spine. "And make it convincing."

"Urhie," he shouted. "Joe. I need you both. Hurry."

Sam glanced over at Lazlo, who stood by the window, watching the room with the hostages. Lazlo gave the OK sign and pointed toward the door.

Good. They were coming.

Sam sidestepped, making sure Deric was between him and the door.

"Fargo," Lazlo said. "Only one's leaving. He took a hostage."

"You know what to do."

Lazlo took a deep breath, steeling himself.

Sam dragged his prisoner back, whispering into his ear. "Save a hostage, save your life."

"It'll never work. He'll kill you first."

"You better hope otherwise because I'm not the one who's going to die tonight."

The knob turned, the door opened inward, silhouetting the man holding a gun on Okoro.

"Easy," Sam said. "I don't want to hurt anyone. Just want to exchange hostages, then find my wife and the missing kids."

"Good luck. You have one, I have one. My friend Urhie has three more." Which told Sam that the missing girls weren't there. "Gun. Down. Now," Joe ordered, pressing the barrel of his semiauto into Okoro's temple.

Sam slipped his finger into the trigger guard, letting the weapon swing down, dangling it from his index finger. Slowly he held it out, proving he was no longer a threat. "Here you go," he said. "Where do you want it?"

"Give it to Deric."

"How about I give you Deric." Sam drove his foot into the back of Deric's knee, shoving him forward. As expected, Joe forgot about his hostage, aiming for Sam, who by this time had swung his Smith & Wesson upright. The butt landed against Sam's palm, he gripped it, and fired. Joe stumbled back, letting go of Okoro, falling to the ground. Deric scrambled for Joe's gun. He grabbed it and aimed.

Sam fired. Deric fell back, lifeless.

Three more shots rent the air.

Sam turned to see Lazlo at the window, staring in shock, his gun pointed into the room.

"You okay?" Sam asked.

"He was going to kill them."

Okoro leaned against the wall, looking faint. Sam aimed at the two fallen men, making sure they were dead, recovering Joe's weapon before moving to the window next to Lazlo. Inside, the three remaining hostages looked as shell-shocked as Lazlo, unable to take their eyes from the dead man on the floor.

Sam looked over at Okoro. "How many gunmen?"

"Four."

"We're good. For now."

"What do you mean 'for now'?"

"Maybe we should go inside, where we can sit down." He surveyed the road that ran across the north end of the farm, leading up into the hills toward the school. Typically, it was at least a forty-minute drive down that winding road to there. Assuming the kidnappers left when Pete first called them, they should've been long gone. What didn't make sense is why these men were still here. And now they were dead. He looked at Lazlo, handing him the key fob for the Land Rover. "Take one of Okoro's men with you to get the car. Hide it behind the barn. Warn me if you see any vehicles coming from that direction."

Lazlo nodded, appearing grateful that he was remaining outside.

Sam envied him in that moment. Informing a father that his only daughter was a kidnap victim was not something to look forward to.

CHAPTER FORTY-SIX

*Those who move are the ones who see
the lion's footprints.*
— AFRICAN PROVERB —

Remi heard the second volley of distant gunshots coming from the direction of the farmhouse. The timing would put Sam in the vicinity. Though she wished she had some way to contact him, she had every confidence that he was the one doing the shooting. The thought buoyed her spirits, something she desperately needed since Makao had failed to take her bait and returned to look for the upper trail.

Remi waited several minutes. When she no longer heard the sound of his pickup, she worked her way through the shrubs to the road, coming out beside the supply truck. Moonlight caught on one of the bullet holes in the side panel from their first encounter with Makao's gang. If Nasha hadn't escaped the Kalu brothers by hiding in the truck, they might have fallen prey to Makao back then.

A twist of fate had brought them all together.

As much as she worried about Sam and Lazlo, the girls were her first priority.

She needed to get back to Makao before he and his men found that upper trail. Though the truck would get her there faster, she didn't dare risk it. Instead, she jogged the quarter mile up the hill, dismayed to discover he'd parked almost on top of the trail's entrance.

Makao stood near his open driver's door, the engine running, while all of his men seemed to be searching the road above them, the surface lit by the pickup's headlights. She ducked behind a tree, watching through the branches as they tromped around, knowing that the only tracks they'd see up there were hers from when she dragged the sign to the back of the truck.

"Well?" Makao called out.

"This looks like where the truck stopped," Jimi said, pointing toward the side of the road, perilously close to where the sign had once stood. "You can see the tire tracks where it pulled off."

Makao joined them in front of the truck, the headlights casting a gigantic shadow of the four men up the hillside.

"Why would it pull off here?" one of the others asked.

"Why do you think?" Makao said. "The Fargo woman set us up. She let the girls out here somewhere, broke the sign off, and led us on a goose chase. The trail has to be there somewhere."

Had he parked just a few feet back, he would have easily seen the brush covering its entrance.

Even better, they were blinded to anything behind the truck. She edged toward it, doing her best to stay in the grass on the side of the road, hoping to avoid leaving footprints.

When she reached the tailgate, she eyed the path just a few feet to her right. A single tree trunk was all that stood between her and the upper trail. She ducked behind it when Makao returned to the truck, reaching inside for a flashlight. He turned it on, shining it across the ground, then up onto the hillside, searching for evidence of their escape.

Remi pressed herself against the tree, edging around it to keep it between her and him. Two more steps and she'd be on the path— and in the open for a good distance, the brush too low to hide her even if she belly-crawled up to where the forest thickened. Watching the men, she blindly felt around with her foot, hitting a fist-sized rock. Scraping it toward her, she repeated her search until she had several gathered at her feet. Squatting, she picked them up and tossed one of the larger ones over the top of the truck to the other side of the road.

The stone landed in a bush, rattling the branches.

"Hear that?" one of the men said.

"What?" another asked.

"Quiet," Makao ordered as Remi lobbed a second stone high over them. It landed on the other side, thudding, then rolling down the hill. "There," he said.

"I hear it." The men rushed to that side of the road, pointing their guns and flashlights into the brush. She threw one last stone and ran up the trail and across the open space as the beam of a flashlight swung across the road, hitting the trees in front of her.

She dove to the ground, then peered through the leaves, seeing Makao almost standing at the trail entrance.

"Something moved up there," one of the men said, drawing his gun. Another aimed his flashlight into the shrubs, blinding her.

Crack!

CHAPTER FORTY-SEVEN

The fool speaks, the wise man listens.
— ETHIOPIAN PROVERB —

A bush pig scrambled down the hill past Makao.

"Idiots," he said, then looked at the scuffs in the dirt near the back of his truck, trying to decide if one of his men made them when they were jumping out or if they could've been caused by girls searching for a trail. He swept the beam of light across the trees and shrubs growing on the right side of the road, his attention catching on what looked like a waffled footprint in the dirt near a tuft of broken dried grass. None of his men had walked down that far, so the print wasn't theirs. He moved closer and crouched down. Same waffle print he'd seen on the lower trail. Too small to be a man's, too large to be a girl's.

Remi Fargo, no doubt, returning to the scene of the crime.

He aimed his flashlight uphill, knowing if she went to the trouble to double back, the trail had to be here somewhere. Sure enough, he saw more signs of disturbed vegetation and partial footprints in the dirt.

Each had the same waffle pattern.

Jimi joined him. "Find something?"

Makao pointed with his flashlight. "Wasn't the Fargo woman wearing hiking boots?"

"Definitely." He squatted, taking a better look. "You think she let the girls out here, then drew us farther down the hill, pretending to take that lower trail?" Jimi laughed as he stood. "Smart woman."

Makao hated to admit it but Jimi was right. Remi Fargo had outwitted them. In fact, the more he thought about it, the more he realized how much she'd actually manipulated their movements from the time they were kidnapped until the moment he had found the sign in the back of the Fargo truck. He was not going to underestimate her again. "That trail those girls took has to be around here somewhere."

Eventually, they found the entrance by tripping over the stump once belonging with the sign. Had his truck not been parked practically on top of it, they might have noticed it sooner. The Fargo woman was tenacious, following him back up the hill—he'd give her that. What he wouldn't do is point out that they'd been bested by a woman. That was bound to stoke their anger and turn them trigger-happy.

Not a good combination when his hostages were worth more alive than dead.

He shined his light on one of the waffle boot prints. "That belongs to Remi Fargo. I have a feeling she's experienced. Be careful. If she moves those girls off the trail, you could pass them right by and not even know it."

Pili glanced at the three men beside him. "Maybe we should wait at the school until morning. There's beds and food."

"And if they called the police, that's the first place they'll come looking," Makao said. "For the missing girls and for you. If you have to rest, find a place nearby out of sight. But know that the longer you wait, the farther they'll get."

"You're not going with us?"

"Jimi and I are going down to the farm to find out what happened there." He looked at each of them in turn. "Do not let anything happen to those hostages. They're worth nothing if they're dead."

The four men climbed up the hillside. Jimi followed Makao to his pickup, taking the passenger's seat as Makao got behind the wheel, while the other two jumped in the back. Makao's phone buzzed in his pocket and he pulled it out, looked at the screen, recognized the Tunisian number. He dropped the phone in the cupholder, ignoring the call. The phone buzzed again and Jimi reached for it.

"Don't answer. It's Tarek," he said. "I don't want him to know what's going on."

"He's not going to like it if he finds out."

"Who says he's going to find out?" he said as he maneuvered the truck back and forth on the narrow road until he was facing downhill.

Once they reached the lower trail where the Fargos' truck was abandoned, he turned off the headlights and continued on at a much slower pace.

"Why'd you turn off the headlights?"

"Making sure we get down this hill alive and past that farm. It'll be hard to collect a ransom if we're dead."

"You're driving a white pickup. They're bound to see it once you're on the main road. It'll be safer with the lights on."

Makao ignored him, driving as fast as he dared on the straightaway, then slowing to a snail's pace at the next curve, his eyes straining to make out any details in the road.

"Pothole," Jimi said.

Makao cursed when the front end dipped down, slamming into the dirt road. At this rate, they were never making it down the hill. He finally turned on the headlights, hoping whoever was at that farm wasn't watching.

CHAPTER FORTY-EIGHT

However long the night, the dawn will break.
— AFRICAN PROVERB —

Myriad emotions flashed across Okoro's face as he listened to what Sam was telling him. "You say my daughter is one of the hostages at the school?"

"With my wife," Sam said. "Had we known anything like this would happen, we never would've—"

"No." He stood, fists clenched, directing his rage at Sam. "I was told she'd be safe up there."

"You have every right to be angry," Sam said.

"One thing I know about Zara. She would never blame the people who helped her live her dream. She would blame the people who stole it." His jaw muscles ticked as he held Sam's gaze. "Who are they? Boko Haram? Fulani terrorists?"

"We're not sure."

"I'm going to find these men. And I'll kill them if any harm comes to my daughter."

Lazlo burst into the front door, out of breath. "Lights . . . Headlights."

"Where?" Sam asked.

It took him a moment before he could answer. "Coming down from the hills."

Sam and Okoro ran outside, then down the drive, until they had a view of the road that ran across the north edge of the property. Sam caught a glimpse of headlights about three-quarters of the way down the hillside before it was lost in the trees again. "We may have about ten minutes before they get here." He turned around, looking at the dead guards lying outside the mud-sided building, wondering if he should hide them.

There wasn't time. The vehicle was coming fast.

Sam passed out the long guns taken from the dead men. "Don't shoot unless I give the order."

Okoro and his three farmhands followed Sam. "I say we just kill them."

"As much as I agree with you," Sam said, stepping over one of the dead men, "alive will be better."

"Why?"

"Because they might provide valuable information about where the girls are."

Lazlo rejoined them. All five men set up behind the dead gunmen's pickup, aiming at Makao's white Toyota as it pulled into the long drive and stopped about two hundred yards out.

"Do you think they saw us?" Lazlo asked.

As if in answer, the vehicle suddenly reversed, tires spinning in the dirt as it backed to the road and sped off.

Sam stood, watching as the red taillights disappeared around the bend, not relaxing until he saw the Toyota cresting the hill past the bend in the road. "Something alerted them."

Lazlo held up one of the phones from the dead guard. "Missed phone call, would be my guess."

"I'm going after them," Sam said, walking behind the barn.

"Not without me," Okoro replied, following him and Lazlo.

Sam had no sooner slid behind the wheel than his phone rang. Amal's number showed on the screen. "It's Makao," Sam said, then answered.

"Show me my money or you'll never see your wife again."

The words echoed through Sam's brain and he clamped his mouth shut when what he wanted to do was reach through the phone and strangle the man who dared to threaten him with Remi's life. He took a slow, calming breath. "That much money takes time," Sam said. "It could take a couple of days."

"Even for someone like you?"

"Yes."

A few seconds of silence, then, "How much can you get me by tomorrow morning?"

"I'll need to call my banker. Give me about ten minutes."

"Five." The line went dead.

Sam looked out toward the hills, going over the conversation in his head, a glimmer of hope blooming.

"What did he want?" Okoro asked.

"Money. He wanted to know how much I could get by to-morrow."

"Tomorrow?" Lazlo said. "That bloody well smacks of desperation. You think Mrs. Fargo and the girls got away?"

"It's starting to look that way." Sam glanced up to the sky, the stars still bright, dawn hours away. "We better not get ahead of ourselves. If they're desperate, that makes them unpredictable and dangerous. Call Pete. Tell him to keep those girls hidden until we can get help up there."

"Will do."

Sam called Selma to give her an update.

"Guarded good news," she said.

"If Makao doesn't have the girls, we need to find them before he does. Have you heard back from Rube?"

"Yes. He's pulling in a few favors with his Nigerian military contacts. A helicopter with a search and rescue team is headed your way first thing in the morning, along with some extra men to stand guard at the school until the matter's resolved. I'll send an email with any-thing else. In the meantime, get some rest."

"Thanks, Selma. I'll get back to you tomorrow."

Sam called Makao next. He picked up on the first ring. "I can get you one hundred thousand dollars by tomorrow night. Now let me talk to my wife or one of the girls."

"You'll talk to them when we have the money. You know how to reach me."

Sam's phone beeped as the call ended. "Things are looking up. We'll have a helicopter in the morning and we can start our search then."

"Why wait?" Okoro said. "We should be heading up there to look for them now."

Sam, understanding the man's panic and knowing the real dan-ger came from making a mistake from being too tired, said, "What I do know is there could be more of his men up there. The last thing we want to do is walk into a trap. We need to wait for morning. I'll take the first watch."

"I'll watch with you," Okoro said. "We let the others sleep. I doubt I'll be able to."

The two men walked out to the front of the house. After several minutes of strained silence, Okoro looked over at him. "I should never have agreed to rent my property to you."

"If I'd ever have thought any danger would come to the girls, I'd never have agreed to build the school. We took every precaution—"

"Not enough, it seems," Okoro said quietly. The two faced the long drive, looking out at the hillside that led up to the school.

Sam studied the dark forest, worried, wondering where Remi and the girls might have taken refuge. The park was a collage of habitats, everything from grasslands and swamps to woodlands and rain forests, and all manner of wildlife that might be found therein. "What sort of dangers are they facing?"

"Much depends on where they go. The biggest threat would be

the Fulani herdsmen. Some of them are no better than Boko Haram. Killing anyone who threatens the land they've claimed for livestock."

"Remi would know to watch out for them."

Okoro looked at him. "You seem to have a lot of confidence in this wife of yours."

"For good reason. The only other person I'd trust to keep those girls safe is me."

"One thing I don't understand," Okoro said. "If this Makao doesn't have my daughter or your wife, why are you promising him money?"

"To keep him connected to us," Sam said. "If I had to guess, he's hoping to cut his losses and run. I'm going to kill him, and every one of them, before that happens."

Okoro's smile was grim. "At least we agree on something."

CHAPTER FORTY-NINE

Earth is the queen of beds.
— NAMIBIAN PROVERB —

Once Remi caught up with Amal and the girls, she pressed them at a fast clip for a couple of hours until their exhaustion became too hard to ignore. Without rest, they were prone to make mistakes and that was a danger. Jogging ahead, she found a clearing that was far enough from the trail, the entrance well camouflaged to keep them from readily being seen.

"I'm cold," Jol whispered. "And hungry."

"Me, too," Maryam replied.

"Scoot together," Remi said quietly as they sat at the base of a large tree. "You'll keep warmer. We'll try to find some food when it's light."

"I have food," Nasha said. She slipped her pack off her shoulders, unzipped it, and pulled out a stale roll, two very bruised bananas, and an apple. The girls split the bananas among them. Remi sat down next to Nasha. "What other kinds of treasures do you keep in that pack of yours?"

"My school board," she said. "And your phone."

She pulled out the phone and gave it to Remi. As expected, the battery was dead. Remi handed it back to her, saying, "You think you can hold on to this for me?"

Nasha said yes and returned it to her pack, carefully zipping the pocket.

The four older girls made a bed of dried leaves, curling up tightly next to one another. Amal leaned up against a tree trunk, Nasha in her lap, the child clutching her backpack close to her chest. Remi took the first watch, standing at the edge of the clearing. The forest was anything but quiet. The rustle of leaves in the canopy above mixed with the chirps and buzzing of nocturnal creatures and insects. A snap of a twig just outside the clearing broke the otherwise peaceful sounds. Just as Remi was regretting that Nasha hadn't been able to get her backpack—and the gun within—a leopard wandered in. It looked over at them with only mild interest in its glowing eyes before slinking off into the night—hopefully, in search of far easier prey.

Come morning, she was going to need to find a very big stick. Breathing a sigh of relief, she moved closer to the girls. But in the three hours she stood watch, the leopard didn't return. She switched places with Amal, warning her about it just in case.

Nasha stirred, opening her eyes, as Remi shifted the girl into her lap. "How will Mr. Fargo find us?" Nasha whispered.

"Because he's very, very smart," Remi said. "Like you."

Nasha snuggled in closer, asleep within seconds.

Not so Remi. She looked up, a break in the canopy revealing the bright stars set in the black sky. *Where are you, Sam . . . ?*

Years ago, they'd met by chance at the Lighthouse Cafe in Hermosa Beach. And while she wouldn't call it love at first sight, by the end of the night she knew he was the one. He'd walked her to her car, telling her that he'd see her again—soon.

"You sound pretty sure of yourself," she'd told him. "Exactly how will you find me?"

"Do you know anything about constellations?" he'd asked.

Considering that her college major had an emphasis on ancient trade routes, she knew a lot about them. "A bit," she'd replied.

"That star there," he said, pointing up into the sky. "The one at the end of the Little Dipper."

"The North Star?"

"You find that, you'll find anything." He stared up at it a moment, then looked over at her. "It'll always lead me to you."

"What if we're in the Southern Hemisphere where we can't see Polaris?"

He laughed, leaned down, and kissed her for the first time. "Just in case, a phone number works."

She'd never given her phone number to anyone—and definitely not to someone she'd just met at a bar. But she had that night. And she ended up marrying the man.

Ever since, the North Star had brought her comfort. It did now, even though she couldn't see it. Somewhere out there, he was looking for her. He'd find her. He'd find all of them. And everything would be right in the world.

All she had to do was keep the girls safe . . .

"Mrs. Fargo."

Her head filled with fog, she turned away, trying to capture the dream she'd left behind. She and Sam were running down the beach with their German shepherd, Zoltán.

"Mrs. Fargo," Amal whispered. "There's someone out there. You need to wake up. Now."

CHAPTER FIFTY

The heart of the wise man lies quiet like limpid water.
— CAMEROONIAN PROVERB —

Sam, Lazlo, and Okoro left for the school at dawn, while Okoro's farmhands, armed with the dead men's AK-47s, remained behind to guard the property. Sam, at the wheel of the Land Rover, took his time, worried about missing any signs of the girls as he drove.

Okoro sat in the back, leaning forward between the two front seats to see out the windshield. "How positive are you that this Makao did not have them in his truck when he drove down the hill last night?"

"Yesterday, I'd agreed to pay him a million dollars. Last night, he's suddenly asking for any amount I can get."

"But he could also demand that if something had happened to them. If . . ."

They were dead, Sam finished silently. That was always a possibility, but not one he was willing to entertain. "All we can do is go on what we know. We know Makao's truck came down that hill. If Remi and the girls weren't in it, then they're still on that mountain."

Lazlo looked up from his phone. "Weather report's forecasting rain for the next three days."

"Starting when?" Sam asked.

"Later today, with a severe weather advisory the next two days."

"Let's hope it holds off long enough to track them."

Sam kept his eyes on the dirt road, the steep switchbacks slow-going, even if he wasn't concerned about driving over some vital clue. Twenty minutes later, they rounded yet another sharp turn, this time coming face-to-face with their supply truck, seemingly abandoned.

"Stay behind me," Sam said, drawing his gun, wanting to make sure they weren't walking into a trap.

He surveyed the trees to the left of the truck, listening to the sounds, hearing nothing but the multitude of birds. When he approached the vehicle, he noted two sets of footprints near the driver's door, one being Remi's, the other set belonging to a man. He followed Remi's footprints to the cargo bed, where he saw the broken post sticking out the back. Remi had continued past there down the trail, as did several men after her.

What Sam didn't see were footprints belonging to the children.

Okoro stared down the empty trail. "Where would the girls be if not here with your wife?"

"I have a pretty good idea." Sam pulled the signpost from the back of the truck, matching it up to the scuff mark on the bumper. "If you're running for your life, you don't stop to pick up a broken sign. If you're hoping to buy some time, you'd definitely want to hide it."

"Buy time for what?" Okoro asked.

"For Amal and the girls to get away on the upper trail while Remi led the kidnappers here." They followed her waffle boot prints into the woods. About twenty yards in, her tracks veered to the right, then disappeared altogether. Sam checked farther along the trail to make sure she hadn't simply been walking close to the edge but only saw the heavier marks left by the men who were undoubtedly searching for her. Remi probably hid while the men pursuing her walked right past. The undergrowth was too thick to see where. "Let's check back up on the road. See if she came out."

It wasn't hard for Sam to find where she emerged from the forest and continued uphill. "Time to see where this leads," he said, hearing a helicopter somewhere above them. He looked up, saw a military-green aircraft in the distance. No doubt the reinforcements Rube had promised.

Okoro followed close beside Sam. "You're sure there were no girls with her?"

"Positive," Sam said. "If I had to guess, she was in a hurry or she'd have found somewhere else to hide that sign besides the back of the truck."

"But there are tread marks here," Okoro said, pointing to where another vehicle had clearly stopped behind the supply truck, then turned around, heading back. "They discovered her plan. What if they followed her?"

Sam took a closer look at the tracks where the vehicle had backed up and made a three-point turn before heading uphill. "Other way around. She followed them."

"How can you be sure?"

Sam nodded to the pattern in the dirt. "Remi's print is on top, not the other way around." They tracked her path up the road, while Lazlo followed behind in the car. About a quarter mile up, they found the stump of the broken sign that marked the trail's entrance. Remi had definitely taken the trail up, as had several men after.

"No kids," Okoro said, sounding worried.

"Brush marks," Sam said. "To hide their footprints." He looked over at Lazlo, who was sitting in the car, the engine idling. Sam looked up at the sky as the beating of rotors grew louder. "Let's follow this while it's still fresh."

Lazlo locked the car and joined them. Sam took one last look around, wanting to make sure that he hadn't missed anything. The same heavy boot prints were in every direction on the road below them, leading Sam to believe the kidnappers had spent some time in the dark searching for the trail's entrance. The sight gave him hope that it was enough to allow Remi and the girls to escape.

"Considering all that's gone on," Okoro said as they started up the hillside, "you seem confident."

"Confidently hopeful," Sam replied. "If anyone has the skill to get the girls to safety, Remi does."

Lazlo agreed.

The trail was easy to follow in the daylight, and from what Sam could tell, Remi either didn't have time or wasn't too worried about trying to cover her tracks, most of which were trampled on by the men pursuing her—four, apparently. "How far would this trail take them?" Sam asked Okoro as a flock of green birds burst from the trees, then settled back into the canopy.

"To Cameroon, should they continue through the park to the border. Several days' walk in good weather. If it floods . . ." His voice faded, no doubt thinking about his daughter.

"We'll find them," Sam said, and the three men quickened their pace.

After about a mile, the trail was covered by a long stretch of trampled leaves, obscuring any footprints. Remi's distinct waffle pattern picked up on the other side, along with the men following it.

"I don't see the children's tracks," Okoro said.

"Or Amal's." Sam looked back, recalling that their prints were visible just before the dead leaves covered the path. "Wait here."

Sam jogged ahead, following Remi's trail. Eventually, it stopped. The kidnappers, however, continued on in that direction. Sam returned to find Lazlo examining the leaves scattered along the trail.

The professor picked up a few of them. "These are damp, the ground beneath bone-dry."

Okoro crouched beside Lazlo and looked up at Sam. "Would your wife have covered the path to disguise it?"

"In a heartbeat," Sam said. There was enough brush and fallen leaves on both sides of the trail to obscure the direction they might have taken. "Remi hid the girls off the trail and doubled back, trying to throw the kidnappers off."

"You're positive?"

"I'd stake my life on it."

Unfortunately, Remi's trail turned cold. They could have gone any different direction. Okoro stood in the middle of the forest, his face looking broken. "Zara," he shouted.

His voice echoed across the rocky terrain, then died.

The only answer was the snarl of a large jungle cat somewhere deep in the forest.

CHAPTER FIFTY-ONE

Despite the beauty of the moon, sun and the stars,
the sky also has a threatening thunder
and striking lightning.

— AFRICAN PROVERB —

Deep in the bracken, Remi and Amal put their arms around their young charges. The steady babble of a nearby mountain brook covered the sound of the girls' panicked breathing as the four kidnappers walked within just a few feet of where they hid. The distant echo of Zara's father's voice calling out to her a second time caught Zara by surprise. She shifted, rustling the fronds. One of the kidnappers stopped, looking around. After several tense seconds, he moved on.

A tear slid down Zara's cheek and Nasha reached up and placed her small hand on the girl's face. Zara looked down at her, tried to smile, then pulled her in close.

Remi waited until the men were no longer in sight before leading the girls in the opposite direction. Though she was hoping they could double back to the trail, and the school, after that morning's close call, she worried it might be too dangerous. She surveyed the horizon, noting the dark clouds stirring above the wind-whipped treetops. The helicopter they'd heard earlier was no longer audible, but there was no doubt in Remi's mind that it would eventually return. And when it did, they needed to be somewhere in the open, not an easy feat considering how they were trying not to be seen by the kidnappers. Her eyes swept over the trees to a ridge high on the mountainside. "If we can get up there, we'll have a better chance of being found."

"How long do you think it'll take?" Amal asked.

"As the crow flies, not long. But we have to take the scenic route." Remi and Amal led the girls along the creek, following it through the woods, the terrain turning rougher and steeper the longer they traveled. When it became apparent that the girls were too exhausted to continue on, she slowed the pace. Soon, they emerged from the thick forest onto a rough path along rugged cliffs overlooking a vast meadow. When Maryam slipped, scraping her arm on the rocks, Amal rushed over and helped her to her feet. Blood streamed down the girl's arm and Amal held her hand over the wound. "Not too deep. I'll patch this up and you'll be fine."

With so little cover from the sparse trees on the rocky incline, Remi worried about stopping. But pushing them any farther without a break upped the risk of serious injury. Spying some low-lying shrubs about fifty yards up the trail, she pointed toward them. "We'll rest there," she said. Not the ideal location, but better than sitting out in the open.

While the girls huddled together, Amal took one of Nasha's stolen nails from her backpack and used it to tear strips from the bottom of her shirt for a bandage. Remi searched for a fallen tree limb, finding one about six feet long and the thickness of her wrist.

"Is that for the, uh, walk?" Amal asked when she brought it back. Neither of them had told the girls about the leopard. They had enough to worry about without being stressed about wildlife.

"Multi-use," Remi said. "A good stick always comes in handy." She hit one end on the ground, feeling a solid vibration travel up the shaft to her fingers. After removing the smaller branches, she hefted the weight of it in her hand. Smiling to herself, she walked out toward the cliff's edge to survey the area and plot out their course. If they could find a way down to the meadow, then cross over where the river narrowed, they might be able to cut out the craggy ascent from this side of the mountain. A few feet beyond them, she found a wide fissure in the cliff face leading to a ledge below. From this angle, it looked promising. If they climbed down the fissure, it might open up to a navigable route along that lower ledge. The thought died when she glanced up at the dark clouds and saw how quickly the weather was changing. Rain and rock made for treacherous climbing, especially with novices. Better to go the long way, she thought, returning to the girls.

The poor things, nearly asleep, were covered head to toe with dirt. As much as she wanted to give them more time, she didn't dare. "Up and at 'em."

They hauled themselves to their feet. Remi, about to offer words of encouragement, stopped when she heard voices carrying toward them from lower down the slope. Their meager cover would leave them vulnerable. She put her finger to her lips, warning the girls.

Up or down? The choice of which direction turned dire.

She judged the distance to the trees above. They'd never make it in time. The only place was down to the ledge below. "This way," she whispered, urging them toward the cliff. They balked when she told them they'd have to climb down the narrow channel between the granite slabs. "It looks scary. But it's easier than you think. You put your hands and feet on one side and push your back against the other, using the pressure to hold yourself up. Like Santa in a chimney."

Amal stepped to the edge. "I've done this before. I'll show them."

The younger woman lowered herself between the rocks and worked her way down, clearly experienced at climbing. Even so, she hesitated at the end of the fissure, perhaps gearing up for the several-foot drop to the ledge below. The moment she was safely on the ground, Remi turned to the girls. She was not surprised when Nasha volunteered first, intuitively finding toe- and footholds until she reached the end. Amal was there to help her make the jump onto the ledge. After seeing how easily Nasha managed the climb down, the others quickly followed.

Remi took one of the branches she'd torn from her stick to brush away the footprints near the cliff's edge and scattered leaves over the top to help disguise them even further. She was about to climb into the fissure when she caught sight of a number of fist-sized rocks that had tumbled down the mountainside near the base of the boulder the girls had rested against.

She quickly arranged them into an arrow aimed at the mountainside route she had considered taking earlier, then handed her walking stick to one of the girls before lowering herself into the crevice. And none too soon. The voices on the trail grew louder.

She dropped to the rocky ledge, grateful to find that the overhang, though not quite a cave—and definitely not tall enough to stand beneath—actually offered some protection from the rain. She guided the girls beneath it, as far back as they could fit. Above them, the men started a heated argument as to which way they should go.

"That way," one said. "Before the rain starts."

"Pili," another called out. "Does that look like an arrow?"

Remi glanced up, shocked to see that one of the men was practically straddling the fissure. He leaned forward. She pressed back against the girls as he spit almost straight down at them.

"Look at that," he said. "It looks like—"

"Listen," Pili said. "I think I hear that helicopter again. Get to the trees. Before they see us."

She breathed a sigh of relief as they moved off, their voices fading. A sharp gust of wind swept across the cliff face and moaned through the rock fissure. As if in answer, a cow mooed plaintively down in the valley. Remi signaled for the girls to remain where they were, then edged out, looking between the large boulders. A herd of white longhorn cattle grazed in the meadow below.

Remi glanced upward, grateful to see no sign of the kidnappers on the trail above. Nasha crept out next to her, pointing to the approaching helicopter. "Look. It's coming this way."

Remi returned her attention to the aircraft, knowing that even if someone was looking exactly this direction, they were hidden by the line of boulders at the edge of the cliff. Somehow, they'd have to get up top.

A sharp crack echoed across the valley.

Nasha ducked back, throwing herself at Remi.

The other girls looked up, thinking it was thunder.

Crack! Crack!

"Stay down," Remi said as the helicopter suddenly veered off.

"What happened?" Amal asked.

"Someone down there's shooting at them." Remi wrapped her arms around Nasha, feeling her heart beating hard against her chest. "Are you okay?"

She looked at Remi through a sheen of tears, her hand shaking as she brushed them away. "They're the ones who killed my parents. And my aunt."

"Who did?" Remi asked.

"Boko Haram."

CHAPTER FIFTY-TWO

If you don't know where you're going,
any road will take you there.
— UGANDAN PROVERB —

Pete watched the Land Rover bouncing up the dirt road toward the school, surprised that Lazlo was by himself and anxious to hear word on what they'd found on their way up the hill. Behind him, the military guards patrolled the gate. When one of the soldiers aimed an automatic rifle at the approaching vehicle, Pete called out to him. "It's okay. He's a friend."

Even so, the point guard didn't lower his weapon until the car cleared the gate and Lazlo got out, at first shaking hands with Pete, then pulling him into a hug. "I can't tell you how glad I am to see you."

"Where's Mr. Fargo? I thought he and Okoro were coming back with you."

"We heard gunshots and he changed his mind."

"How far away?"

"Mountains, rock—echoes. Almost impossible to tell. He thought it might have been northeast of where we were."

"Well, glad you're back," Pete replied, leading him to the office.

"The children? How are they?"

"Holding up fine. Worried about their friends, of course, but— kids."

"Resilient?"

"More so than the rest of us. It helps that they saw nothing, being in the tunnel during the worst of it. They're in class. We figured it was best to try to keep everything as close to normal as possible. To the children, it's almost an adventure. Especially after the helicopter touched down, dropping off half their squad," he said, indicating the soldiers manning the front gate.

"I must say, good show on getting them to safety."

"It wasn't me," Pete said. "Mrs. Fargo's the one who sounded the alarm. I'm not sure I'll ever get over the guilt of letting her convince me that she should go out after the missing girls alone."

Lazlo gave him a friendly clap on the back as the two men walked up the steps onto the porch. "Mere mortals like us simply get in the way. Why do you think I'm here instead of with Mr. Fargo?"

"I know you're right . . ."

"In the time it would take us to assess the danger, the Fargos have already come up with ten different plans on the off chance the other nine fail."

Pete laughed for the first time since the attack as he opened the door to the office.

When Wendy saw them, she jumped from the chair to wrap Lazlo in a hug. "I'm so glad you're here."

"There, there," Lazlo said, seeing that she was close to tears. "We're all fine. That's what counts."

"You have good news, I hope?"

"As Selma says, guarded good news." He spied the tall thermos on the desk. "Is that coffee, by chance? I could use a cup." Wendy found a mug and filled it for him as he told them about the supply truck abandoned near the lower trail. "Sam believes it was a decoy and that Mrs. Fargo fled with the girls on the upper trail into the Gashaka Gumti preserve. They're following. How far behind, I don't know. But I expect he'll call as soon as he's ready to start the air search."

"Thank goodness," Wendy said. "It was horrible not knowing.

Pete came out, found the supply truck gone, the building on fire, and that SUV left outside the gate on its rims. Trying to figure out what happened—"

"My understanding is," Lazlo said, "Nasha saved the day."

"I can't tell you how relieved I was when Pete told me that she'd somehow called Mr. Fargo," Wendy replied. "All I knew was that she was with us one minute, gone the next."

"I wish we knew more," Lazlo told her. "But the call cut off abruptly. We assume since she's not here with you, she's with Mrs. Fargo and the other girls. Mr. Fargo's almost positive they managed to escape. But we think they're still being pursued."

Pete saw the toll that statement took on Wendy. And not just because of Remi. Wendy considered each child in her care as part of her family. He clasped his hand around hers. "If anyone can keep those girls safe, Mrs. Fargo can."

"I know," she said as Lazlo's cell phone lit up with a video call from Sam.

"Do you have a map?" Sam asked. Zara's father stood behind him, both beneath a thick canopy of trees filled with a chorus of birds. "Remi and the girls left the trail. I'm hoping to find the most logical route."

Pete glanced up at the area map tacked to the wall behind the desk, dismissed it as not being detailed enough. "Wendy, do we still have the topographical map from when we were searching for the school site?"

"In the file cabinet," she said, retrieving it from the top drawer.

They unrolled the long tube of paper, tacking it to the wall next to the other map. "Any idea where you are?" Lazlo asked.

"I'd say about two miles in . . ." Sam aimed his phone so they could see the area. On the left, the mountainous forest rose into a blanket of clouds. On the right, the granite-studded valley stretched out to the horizon.

Pete looked at the map. The school was marked with an X and the trail was marked with a dotted line.

Wendy traced it with her finger, approximating where Mr. Fargo might be. "If we're reading this map correctly," she said, "it looks like the trail follows a riverbed, then veers off."

"Remi might follow it for a source of water," Sam said.

"Let's hope she didn't head that way," Pete replied. "If the rain is as bad as predicted, there's a good chance of flash floods."

As if in warning, the first few raindrops started to fall.

CHAPTER FIFTY-THREE

The rain does not recognize anyone as a friend;
it drenches all equally.
— NIGERIAN PROVERB —

Sam and Okoro moved out into the clearing once the military Mi-17 helicopter landed, the two men ducking as the rotors whipped the rain and mud around them to a frenzy. There were four soldiers on board, along with the pilot and copilot.

"Welcome aboard," one of the crew shouted, handing them both helmets with headsets. The pilot glanced back at Sam as he settled into the seat and buckled the restraints. "Understand you're experienced at this."

"Search and rescue in California," Sam said.

He acknowledged and guided the craft upward, giving Sam an unparalleled view out the port side door of Gashaka Gumti park and the surrounding area. At first all he saw was the endless treetops of the surrounding forest. But when he caught sight of Okoro's farm, as well as the road leading up to the school, he was able to orient himself to the clearing they'd just left. "That's where we lost the trail," he said, pointing out the rain-splattered windshield.

The pilot turned the craft. "Any idea where they might be headed?"

"My wife would know we're searching for them. She'd definitely head for open ground. We also heard gunshots this morning coming from the northeast. I'm assuming that was the kidnappers."

The pilot and copilot exchanged looks. "They were shooting at us," the pilot said. "But I'm not sure they were the kidnappers."

"If it's the same group who attacked us on the road," Sam said, "they're armed with AK-47s."

"I think the group we ran into were cattle rustlers. They were guarding a large herd. We'll do a flyby and you can see for yourself." He looked over at his copilot. "We better get moving before this weather takes a turn for the worse."

Sam nodded, then turned toward Okoro, noticing his gaze was fixed out the window. "Remi will keep them safe."

Okoro said nothing.

Sam looked out his own window, praying they'd find them soon.

The helicopter banked to the right, heading northeast, following in the general direction of the meandering creek that Sam and Okoro had seen on their first search. Eventually, it was lost in the thick growth. The pilot ascended, hovering high over the southern portion of the park. Lightning arced across the gray sky. "Up ahead, at the end of the valley," the copilot said. "See the cattle?"

One of the soldiers riding in the back handed Sam a pair of binoculars. Thunder rumbled as he looked out the window, seeing a thick forest and glimpses of the rocky banks of the tributary through the trees. A long grassy meadow stretched along the bottom of the valley. At the far end, he could just make out the steep cliffs jutting up from the valley floor into the forest. When he focused on the base of the cliffs, he saw the white cows. "Definitely a large herd down there."

"The herdsmen were the ones who shot at us."

"What are the chances our kidnappers are doing double duty as cattle rustlers?" Sam asked.

"If they're dressed like Fulani herdsmen, we've found our guys."

"You're sure they were shooting at you?"

"No doubt."

Disheartened, Sam handed the binoculars to Okoro as the helicopter continued in that direction. He took a look and returned the glasses to Sam, saying, "A week ago, a herd was stolen by armed Fulani. It would probably take them that long to get all the way out here."

The aircraft, caught in a sudden gust, shifted violently. The co-pilot looked back at Sam. "Hate to say it. Turbulence is picking up. We're going to have to turn around. Wait for the squall to pass. Soon as we can get back out, we'll do so."

The helicopter passed high over the Fulani cattle. Sam, not willing to lose one second of possible search time, focused his binoculars, seeing the armed gunmen who were tracking them with their rifles as they flew overhead. The helicopter banked away and Sam swept the binoculars across the cliffs, catching movement about midway down. "I see something."

The pilot hovered as best he could, allowing Sam to focus.

The soldier sitting next to him looked through his own pair of binoculars. "Cat."

It took Sam a moment to make out the reddish brown fur of the African gold cat. Smaller than a cheetah, it blended into the cliff face—so much so that he was sure that wasn't what caught his attention. But when he looked higher up, searching, a blinding flash of lightning, followed by a torrential downpour, impeded his view.

CHAPTER FIFTY-FOUR

Evil knows where evil sleeps.
— AFRICAN PROVERB —

The rain beat against the windows of Makao's apartment while he waited for word on the hostages. He and his crew had driven five and a half hours straight back to Jalingo after the debacle at the school but had heard nothing since. Every minute that passed, Makao saw his profit slipping away. Anxious, he called Pili's phone, but it went straight to voice mail. Again.

He looked over at Jimi, who'd fallen asleep on the sofa, while his other two men had crashed on the floor next to him. They didn't seem bothered. Must be nice. He was too keyed up to sleep, though he'd been the one who drove all night to get there.

"Call, already," he said, pacing. He looked over at the phone, stolen from that Amal woman, wondering if Fargo suspected anything when he'd called last night about the ransom.

Of course he did. Which made it all the more important to find those missing hostages.

When Tarek first hired Makao, he'd mentioned very little about the Fargos other than to say they'd be an easy mark. After a bit of quick research, Makao had thought the same. He knew better now. He also knew they were too rich and well known for law enforcement to look the other way. If Makao's men didn't find the hostages, not only was he going to lose his share of the ransom, he was going to have to relocate yet again.

A gust of wind rattled his front window, drawing his attention. Parting the blinds, he saw Kambili Kalu getting out of a car parked out front.

"Jimi . . ." He kicked Jimi's foot. And those of the two men sleeping on the floor. "Get up," he said as Kambili stormed toward the apartment. "All of you."

Makao drew his gun, intending to shoot the man in his tracks. But as he reached for the front door knob, the door burst open, splinters flying from its shattered frame. Startled, Makao jumped back, tripped over one of the still-sleeping men. Before he could right himself, Kambili rushed in, aiming his semiauto at Makao's head.

"Kamb—"

"Drop your gun," Kambili ordered, "or I'll kill you right here."

Makao slowly lowered his weapon to the ground, surprised to see Kambili's left eye swollen nearly shut. "What's this about?"

Kambili towered over Makao, glaring. "You killed my brothers."

"No," he said. "It wasn't me, I swear. Where'd you hear that?"

"You see my face? Yesterday, the man who did this told me."

Makao shot a look over to Jimi, who seemed as shocked as he was by the revelation that Kambili knew what had happened. The rest of his crew who hit the Fargo caravan were dead, which meant there was only one way Kambili had learned of this.

It had to be from Fargo himself.

What Makao couldn't figure out was how Fargo could possibly have known who the Kalu brothers were. "I assure you that whoever told you this was lying. There has to be some reason this man would want to blame me. What'd he tell you?"

"He came to my home, looking for one of my boys."

"For what reason?"

"He wanted to know what village he'd come from."

Makao, seeing Jimi slowly move his hand to his holstered gun, was torn between letting him kill Kambili and wanting to know what Fargo was up to. From everything he could tell, Fargo was a straight shooter, his business dealings above board. Why, then, would a man like that purposefully seek out a man like Kambili just to find out about one of his thieves?

It didn't make sense—until he caught sight of Jimi's injured arm. He looked down at his own bandaged hand, recalling how that girl had jabbed them both with the road spike as she raced out the door. Suddenly he wondered if Jimi had been mistaken about losing those keys. "One of your pickpockets?"

"My best one."

"Where is this kid?"

Kambili seemed taken aback by the simple question. "Ran away. Two days ago, after he got caught trying to steal a Land Rover."

"The man who killed your brothers was driving a Land Rover," Makao said. "Isn't that right, Jimi?"

He nodded in agreement.

"Why would this man kill my brothers?"

"To pin it on me and start a war between us."

"You expect me to believe that?"

"Why would I lie to you? We have an agreement, you and I. But I know how we can get back at him."

"How?"

Makao smiled when Kambili lowered the gun. "Jimi, take the boys to lunch. And find someone to fix that door," he said as rain splashed its threshold. "Mr. Kalu and I have some business to discuss."

"WHAT BUSINESS?" KAMBILI ASKED AFTER THE OTHER MEN LEFT. HE had, thankfully, put his gun away.

"About your pickpocket." The cut on Makao's hand started to throb with the memory of how she'd clawed him with that tire spike. "Tiny thing, darts around like a gazelle fleeing a cheetah?"

"Nash? He's my best pickpocket."

Which explained how she got the keys from Jimi. "That pickpocket was definitely a girl."

Kambili stared a moment. "You sure we're talking about the same boy?"

"Why else would the Fargos have taken her to a school for girls?"

"A girl . . . Always thought he was small. What about him—her?"

"Tell me everything you know about the kid."

"Comes from a village up north. His—her uncle paid for her and some other boys to come here because of Boko Haram."

"How do I find her uncle?"

"One of my boys, Chuk, came from the same village. They were friends."

"Good. We'll need him to get to the Fargos. Here's my plan . . ."

CHAPTER FIFTY-FIVE

You may be disappointed if you fail,
but you are doomed if you don't try.
— AFRICAN PROVERB —

Remi left Amal and the girls to search for better shelter. Eventually, she found a deeper overhang where they could ride out the storm without worrying about being seen by the kidnappers from the trail above. The climb to the top of the cliffs from there would be easier for the girls. But the crevice they'd shimmied down seemed to be a channel for runoff and she worried that if the steady rain continued, what was now a thin stream would soon turn into a full-fledged waterfall.

Judging by the sky, they had a very narrow window before the storm started up again. The rain, however, concerned her less than the severe wind gusts that could easily knock them off balance. After a quick perusal of the area, making sure she wasn't invading the home of some jungle cat, she returned to the girls. "We don't have much time. Let's get moving."

Amal gave her an odd look as she and the older girls stepped aside. Nasha, the child that Remi had come to think of as her warrior princess, sat with her arms wrapped around her knees, rocking back and forth.

"Nasha." Remi held out her hand.

"It's never coming back," Nasha said, to no one in particular.

"The helicopter?" Remi smiled. "Of course it's coming back."

Unfortunately, the other girls keyed in on Nasha's fear, their concern moving to the patch of angry gray sky above them. "Why'd it leave?" Jol asked. "It was almost all the way here."

Nasha's eyes welled with tears. "Because Boko Haram were shooting at them. They'll never come back. They can't."

Remi kneeled down next to Nasha, drawing her close. She'd never seen the girl this frightened. "I don't think they're Boko Haram at all. I think they're Fulani cattle rustlers." Though she'd heard tales of some Fulani herdsmen being equated with Boko Haram, killing anyone they deemed a threat to their pastureland, she wasn't about to mention that fact now. The girls had enough to worry about. "They probably thought that helicopter was trying to bring them in for stealing the cows."

Jol turned in panic toward Remi. "They won't kill us, too, will they?"

"No," Remi said, looking at each girl in turn. "I won't let anything happen to any of you."

"You can't promise that," Nasha said, pulling away from her. "You don't even know."

Zara's eyes widened. "You're scaring me."

"You should be scared. They killed everyone in my house. The only reason I didn't get killed was because I got scared and ran away."

Thunder rumbled in the distance. Remi stood. "We have to leave."

Nasha shook her head, turning away, tears running down her face. "I don't want to go."

Jol crouched down in front of her. "We can't go without you." She tried to pull Nasha to her feet.

"We're just girls," Nasha whispered. "They have guns."

Maryam crouched down beside Jol. "But you tricked the Kalu brothers."

"Because I was pretending to be a boy," Nasha said. "If I was being a girl, they would've . . ." She wiped the back of her hand across her eyes, then looked away. "It doesn't matter."

Zara, perplexed, said, "But you saved us. You're the brave one."

"I'm not. I'm afraid all the time," she said. "I'm afraid right now."

The girls stared at her, their eyes wide with surprise. Zara's sought Remi's. "Are you ever afraid?"

"Of course," Remi said, anxious. "What matters is what you do with that fear."

"I'd run away," Zara said. The other girls agreed.

Nasha said, "I wanted to when Mr. Hank said I stole those nails. I didn't steal them. I found them." She gave a firm nod to prove her point. "It's his fault we're here. If he hadn't gotten sick, Mr. Fargo wouldn't have had to leave. He would've saved us."

Amal offered her a timid smile. "We got in trouble because of me. Something happens and I shut down. You saved us because you didn't run away."

"But I wanted to," she said, her voice small as she wiped away tears.

"Sometimes," Remi said as a gust of wind swept in, "that's the right thing to do. The secret is to know when." She held out her hand, breathing a sigh of relief when Nasha grasped it. What she couldn't ignore was the sound of rushing water deep within that crevice and the growing stream filling their path. "Watch your step," she told the girls.

Remi led, Amal brought up the rear. Though the trek to their new shelter hadn't taken long, it was slow-going with all the girls in tow. The runoff from the mountain above channeled down the numerous crags. Rivulets of water splashed across the ledge, creating treacherous silt-covered fissures that gave way, ready to catch the unwary traveler.

About thirty minutes into their journey, one of those rivulets widened considerably, washing a two-foot gap in the trail. Remi stopped, poked the other side with her walking stick, felt solid rock, and jumped across. She turned, holding her stick out toward Nasha. "If you slip, don't let go of the stick. I'll pull you up."

Nasha grabbed the staff but hesitated as thunder echoed across the mountains.

"It's okay," Remi said.

Nasha jumped. Each of the girls followed. The sky let loose, rain pelting them, as they continued up the cliff. As they neared the shelter, Remi stepped over a narrow rivulet, then turned to make sure the others saw it. She called out, her voice lost in the rush of wind, but Nasha nodded, easily stepping over. Jol followed. As Nasha's foot hit the other side, the ledge disintegrated, plunging her downward in a torrent of water and mud.

CHAPTER FIFTY-SIX

He who learns, teaches.

— ETHIOPIAN PROVERB —

The girls screamed as the ground disappeared beneath Nasha's feet. Remi grabbed her arm and dragged her back as the crevice widened at an alarming speed. When she looked down, she saw Jol about twenty feet below, precariously balanced on a narrow outcropping of rock.

"Don't move," Remi shouted to her, then turned her attention to the other girls. She held the stick out across the open space. "Grab it, Maryam."

"What about Jol?"

"I'll get her."

Maryam wrapped her fingers around the thick staff but didn't move, her eyes locked on her fallen friend.

"Don't look down. Look at me. You can do it."

She gave a hesitant nod and jumped.

When everyone was across, Remi shouted to Amal, "The cave's not much farther. I'll be right behind you as soon as I get Jol."

Amal nodded. "Let's go, girls. They'll be fine."

Remi moved to the edge of the gap and slid down the cliff, the progress slow as she braced herself with her walking stick in some spots and blindly felt for solid finger- and toeholds in others.

Finally, she reached Jol, the poor girl's eyes wide with fright. "Are you okay?"

She nodded.

"Take my hand," she said, reaching down. She wrapped her fingers around Jol's slim wrist. When she was safely in front of her, Remi instructed her where to place her hands and feet as they slowly worked their way up to solid ground. Several times Remi searched the horizon, praying the helicopter would return while they were there on the open cliff where someone might actually see them. But as they ducked to the ground with each wind shear that threatened to rip them from the ledge, she knew help would not be arriving by day's end.

At least they'd have a safe and fairly dry spot to spend the night, she thought as she hustled Jol beneath the overhang. Amal tore off more strips from her shirt, wrapping one around a cut on Nasha's leg, and another on Jol's right forearm, scraped raw from her fall.

Remi, grateful the injuries weren't worse, took the first watch.

As night fell, Amal suggested the girls try to get some sleep, but they were too keyed up to rest. After a while, Jol said, "Mrs. Fargo, you promised to tell us about your treasure hunting."

Remi looked back, just able to make her out in the dim light. "Tomorrow maybe."

Jol turned to Amal. "Have you ever found any treasure?"

"Once. When I was a little girl."

The girls clasped their hands together, chorusing, "Tell us. Tell us."

"It happened back when I spent the hot summers at my grandmother's home."

"Where did she live?" Maryam asked.

"Near Bulla Regia. In the heart of Tunisia."

"Where's that?" Nasha asked.

"Tunisia? Way up north at the very top of Africa. It's much hotter there than here in the mountains. Hot like the desert, but my grandmother's house was shaded by a large olive grove that's been there for hundreds of years."

"Hundreds?" Tambara said.

"Many hundreds," Amal said. "And in that house was the lid of an old charcoal burner that had a Sator Square palindrome engraved into the metal."

"What's a *palindrome*?" Nasha asked.

"Words or phrases that can be read forward or backward. *Madam* is a one-word palindrome. The Sator Square is a five-word palindrome—*sator, arepo, tenet, opera, rotas*. It's supposed to be magical."

"Why?"

Tambara put her finger to her lips. "Shhh."

"It's a good question," Amal said. "In this case, I think whoever was using it wanted the people to think it was magic. When the charcoal burner was lit, it would shine the words onto the wall or ceiling of a very dark room, probably to make people think something very mystical was going on. Anyway, when my grandmother was a girl, her grandmother used to tell her bedtime stories of the lost treasure of the last Vandal King. His treasure was hidden somewhere in our olive grove." The girls leaned forward as she lowered her voice. "The day my grandmother found that Sator Square, ten people had passed it by, not one of them seeing it right there in front of them."

"Why didn't they see it?" Maryam asked.

"Because the treasure," she said, looking at each of them in turn, "is protected by a curse. If the wrong person takes it, they or someone they love will die a horrible death."

"Why didn't your grandmother die?"

"Because the ancient oracles were charged with watching over the missing treasure," she said, lowering her voice, "until one who is of royal blood could return it to its rightful place."

The girls' eyes widened as she imparted this bit of news, Nasha asking, "Are you an oracle, too?"

Amal smiled. "I'm not sure they were ever real to begin with. My mother told me that our overly creative storytelling comes from our oracle blood."

Nasha crossed her arms. "So you do believe in oracles?"

Amal laughed softly. "Intuition, yes. The rest of that stuff? Not so much."

"Did you ever find anything?" she asked.

"No. And though I was hoping I'd discover the lost treasure from the last Vandal King, the only thing I ever found were bits of potsherds. Nothing so wonderful as the piece my grandmother unearthed, but it was enough to feed my love of archeology."

"I want to be an archeologist," Maryam said. "Maybe I can find treasure."

"Me, too," Tambara said, Jol in agreement.

Zara shook her head. "I want to teach."

The four girls turned toward Nasha, who gave a slight shrug, saying, "I don't know what I want to do yet."

Tambara's smile held a hint of awe. "You're good at sneaking around. You could be a spy."

"She can't be anything," Zara said, "unless she goes to school."

"I am going to school," Nasha said, turning a determined gaze toward Remi. "Aren't I?"

"Everyone is going to school," Remi said, wondering if they'd have a school to return to. "Time to get some rest. We have a long walk ahead of us in the morning."

The girls settled down, then slept. Remi sat down next to Amal, whispering, "You did a nice job distracting them."

"They're so brave. And that one," she said, looking at Nasha.

"Amazing. I hope you're able to find out where she's from and get her into the school."

"I hope so, too," Remi said with a calmness she didn't feel. Watching the growing water running across the front of their shelter, what she really hoped was that the ledge they'd used to get here would still be there come morning.

CHAPTER FIFTY-SEVEN

Hope is a good thing and good things never die.
— AFRICAN PROVERB —

Rain pounded on the roof of the school's office, then poured across the overfilled gutters like a waterfall, flooding the ground in front of the door. Sam looked out the window at the soldiers standing beneath the porch, refusing to come into the building even though Sam offered it.

He turned back inside where Okoro, Pete, and Lazlo sat, studying the topographical map of Gashaka Gumti and the surrounding area. Pete gave a tired sigh. "I don't see any other direction they would've taken."

"I agree," Okoro said. "Northeasterly along that creek. Which worries me."

"Why?" Wendy asked.

"The river." He traced his finger from the path he and Sam had taken, up toward the mountains. "If they followed as we believe, along this stream, they'll come out here. Their only choice is through this valley where we saw the Fulani herdsmen. That or up into the mountains."

Pete studied the map a moment. "Couldn't they go around?"

"They could," Okoro said. "But they'd have to cross the river. In this weather, that wouldn't be advisable. Flooding."

"Remi," Sam said, "would know that."

Wendy leaned into Pete. "But if they were being chased, she'd take the risk."

"She would," Sam said. Which made the search for them even harder. Remi would do whatever it took to keep those girls safe, even if it defied logic. "Either way, she'd know we'd be sending out a search party. She's going to head to where they can be seen." He walked back to the window, looking out at the front of the school in the growing dark, where, beyond the gate, he could just make out the abandoned SUV that sat in the middle of the muddy road. "Has Rube gotten back to us with who that vehicle belongs to?"

"Not yet," Pete said. "He was still waiting on information from his contacts."

Sam called Rube's number. "Hope I'm not disturbing you?"

"Nothing that can't wait," Rube said. "I figured you'd be out searching or I would've called earlier."

"Weather break," he said. "About that truck left behind?"

"Hold on." A few seconds later, he was back on the line. "Sorry. Had to clear the office." Sam heard him shuffling through papers. "The truck belongs to a Pili somebody-or-other. I've got the file here somewhere. He's got an extensive criminal history in Taraba State."

"What sort of history?"

"Mostly robbery. No connection to these Kalu brothers."

"What about this Makao?"

"If it's Makao Oni, he's wanted out of Lagos State after the police tied his gang to a string of murders about a year ago. That, at least, gives Taraba State a place to start searching now that they believe there's a connection to Pili. They're gathering intel on his known associates in hopes of finding out where they might be hiding out. Hold on . . ." A few minutes of silence followed before he was back on. "I've got a couple of fires here to put out. Just know that the guards and search team are yours until they round up everyone involved. They're committed to bringing everyone home and making sure the school is safe. I'll get back to you if I hear anything else."

"Thanks, Rube."

Sam disconnected and immediately called Selma, this time on video, deciding she looked as tired as he felt. In her fifties, her short hair worn in spikes, she looked at him over her dark-rimmed glasses, which she wore on a chain around her neck.

"Anything new on your end?" he asked.

"Nothing related to the kidnappers," she said. "I do have a bit of information on that village where you think Nasha's uncle lives. There was an article that came out a little over a year ago, about an attack by Boko Haram, which fits the time line of when you think she was brought to Jalingo. Whether or not her uncle survived is unknown. The article isn't too detailed, other than mentioning that after the terrorists burned down half the village, the military was brought in to roust them from the area."

"That's a start. Soon as we find them, we'll follow up."

Wendy walked in a couple of minutes later. "Dinner's ready."

Though Sam wasn't the least bit hungry, he knew he needed to eat. If the weather prevented them from doing an air search, he was going out again on foot.

CHAPTER FIFTY-EIGHT

Do not follow a person who is running away.
— KENYAN PROVERB —

As soon as it was light, though it was still raining, Remi led the girls out onto the ledge. The path continued between two massive boulders twice as high as the others, flanking either side of the trail. The flat-topped rocks created a natural overhang that gave some protection from the rain. Remi had the girls wait there while she continued on a short distance to see if the Fulani were still waiting below. Heading down through the meadow and then up the other side would save significant time. When she climbed out far enough to see into the valley, she realized that avenue of egress was no longer an option. The river was rapidly encroaching across the meadow, the current too strong to cross. Their only choice was to continue onward and upward.

Back when Wendy and Pete had first proposed the school, Remi recalled them telling her about the location they'd found, an isolated plateau that would protect the compound from any flooding during the rainy season. Out here in the wilderness, what might flood was anyone's guess, especially considering the nonstop rain.

She returned to the girls, looking at the overhang and the rivulets of water coming down from the mountain above. They couldn't depend on the search team finding them in time. If they didn't get off that cliff, they'd soon be standing in a waterfall.

The higher they climbed, the more she regretted her decision. The realization she'd made a terrible mistake came too late. What had been tiny rivulets earlier were turning into wide swaths ripping down the cliff. The path they were following was now inches deep in water. "We need to go back," Remi said.

"Where?" Amal asked.

"What was that?" one of the girls asked.

Remi heard shouting from the path below. They'd run right into the kidnappers.

Amal stared in horror. In the few seconds they'd stood there, the growing runoff turned brown, then thickened, as water and dirt rushed down from the mountainside, turning the tiny stream into a swirling current of mud and debris.

They were trapped.

Remi searched for a location to hide the children so that she could draw the men away. "There," she said, pointing to the top of one of the massive boulders.

"How?" Maryam asked, craning her neck. "It's too high."

"Amal," Remi said. "You first. You can help the girls."

Remi kneeled and Amal climbed on her shoulders, using the boulder to balance herself as Remi stood, lifting her. Amal then pulled herself onto the boulder. Remi repeated the process with each girl, Amal gripping their arms as they scrambled up.

It wasn't until they were all safely on top that they realized Remi had no way up herself. A couple of the girls started crying. Remi put her finger to her lips. "Be brave and stay flat, out of sight. I'll be fine."

The kidnappers' voices grew louder, one of them complaining about the muddy trail.

The water was now several inches deep, swirling around Remi's ankles. She was taking a calculated risk, hoping that centuries of runoff would continue in the same direction as it always had, between the mountainside and the boulders. With the rain beating down, she poised herself near the craggy rocks. As the four kidnappers rounded the corner, she started running through the shallow stream. One of them ordered her to stop. Halting, she slowly turned, saw their automatic rifles pointed toward her. Remi planted her walking stick to balance herself in the quickening torrent. "Help," she called out.

Pili and his men trudged up the hill toward her. A sound like the far-off surf of the ocean grew in intensity. Before they realized what it was, a muddy river roared toward them. They turned, trying to outrun it. Remi scrambled up the rocks, using her stick to brace herself against the boulder as the current rose to her knees. It wasn't the water she worried about, it was anything carried along with it. Within moments, tree branches and rotting logs swept down from the mountain, some getting stuck in the rocks, until the force of the surge knocked it loose. A tree trunk as thick as a telephone pole hurtled straight toward her, missing by mere inches as one end struck the massive boulder. The other end angled toward Remi, creating a barrier that protected her for a few short minutes, until the far end swung out. The onrush sent it slamming against the mountain on the other side, bridging the flood. Seconds later, fast-moving debris caught against it, the water rising and threatening to rip her into its swift current.

CHAPTER FIFTY-NINE

With a little seed of imagination,
you can grow a field of hope.
— NIGERIAN PROVERB —

High above the forest, Sam lowered his binoculars, leaning forward to look out through the rain-splattered windshield. A downdraft caught the helicopter, sending him back against his seat as the pilot wrested control of the craft.

"Sorry, Mr. Fargo," he said.

"Circle around again." Sam scrutinized the valley. They'd made two trips over the area, seeing nothing but cows slowly moving through the floodplain to higher ground. What he couldn't see was anyone attending them. The Fulani herdsmen had either abandoned their stolen cattle or they were taking shelter from the storm.

One of the soldiers pointed. "I see someone. In the tree near the waterfall."

The waterfall that hadn't been there yesterday, Sam realized.

The pilot maneuvered the helicopter around. Sam caught sight of a man draped high in the branches of a tree growing at the base of the cliff as though he'd been swept down the precipice.

Sam focused his binoculars on the flooded field directly below the tree jutting out of the cliff, saw several men lying lifeless at the bottom. Definitely not the Fulani. "Can you get us in closer? I'd like to see the source of that waterfall."

The pilot continued his ascent, giving them a view of the entire valley and the multitude of swift-moving swollen tributaries and streams feeding the river below.

"Mr. Fargo," Okoro said. "You look worried. If those dead men are the kidnappers, surely that's good news?"

"I hope so," Sam said, wondering how close those men were to Remi and the girls when they were swept away. "Can you follow that waterfall to its source?"

"I can try." The helicopter swung around. Rain beat down on the windshield, while a gust of wind sent drops of water across the glass, making it difficult to see. An army of chimpanzees raced down the mountainside, drawing their attention. "Something's spooked them," the copilot called out.

Sam, following their movement, wondered if the sound of the helicopter had disturbed them. He peered through the trees, seeing movement behind them.

The pilot ascended over the treetops, allowing a better view of a massive boulder between the mountain and the swollen creek.

"There," Sam shouted.

The pilot banked toward them.

Sam counted, came up one short, despair so overwhelming he had difficulty breathing. Remi was missing.

As the aircraft neared, Sam realized the debris from the flash flood had formed a dam near the boulder. Water seeped through on the side closest to them, but there were too many trees hiding their view. "Check upstream."

They flew over the boulders, the girls waving wildly, trying to get their attention. The other side looked like a muddy lake about to overflow. And there, braced against a boulder as though holding back the flood, was his wife. She squinted up at them, then gave the cliff above her a pointed look.

A couple of the chimpanzees from the fleeing troop hovered in the trees, looking the same direction as his wife—as though they sensed impending doom. Sam watched them a moment, then eyed the water swirling almost to Remi's knees. The swift runoff continued rushing down from the cliff above, the deep brown water filled with silt washing between that boulder and the base of the mountain. "We need to get them off that rock."

"Copy," the pilot said. "I think I can come in from the other side. Anyone injured? We can rappel down and bring them up one by one."

Sam focused his binoculars on the flat-topped boulder and up just beyond them and saw a flurry of small rocks and plants slipping down the mountainside. Sam glanced at the two soldiers and Okoro. "If you can touch down on the edge of the boulder, between the four of us back here we can extract them twice as fast."

"What about your wife?"

"I can rappel down, bring her up at the same time."

The copilot looked back at him—whether to object or agree, he didn't know. He was already snapping into the harness and attaching it to the hoist while the two soldiers readied themselves for the rescue.

The moment the helicopter was within a few feet of the boulder, the first soldier jumped out, grabbed Nasha, and lifted her to Okoro. The second soldier operated the hoist as Sam jumped out. Sam moved to the edge of the boulder, looking down at Remi. Her red hair whipped about her face as she looked up at him, signaled him to get the children to safety first.

Sam turned, helping to lift each girl alongside the other soldier. Amal and Zara were last. Once they were safe, Sam moved to the edge of the rock, the rain beating against him, and lowered himself over the side.

Remi reached for him and he clasped his hand around her wrist, pulling her toward him. The moment she let go of the stick she'd been using to help brace herself, the debris sucked past the boulder with an astounding force. Within seconds, the entire side of the mountain slid down, trees and mud crashing against the boulder.

Sam wrapped his arms around Remi as the helicopter rose, the rope jerking them from the rock.

It swept them up and away, Remi holding tight to Sam. "About time," she shouted over the rush of air.

"You didn't exactly leave a trail of crumbs."

"Only because I knew you'd find us." She kissed him—and she didn't stop until they were pulled into the helicopter and safely on their way back to the school.

CHAPTER SIXTY

*If you keep your head and heart going
in the right direction,
you don't have to worry about your feet.*
— AFRICAN PROVERB —

The storm continued east, the rain nothing but a light drizzle by the time the helicopter touched down just outside the gates. Once they were on the ground, Sam and Remi hung back while Wendy hugged each girl, then directed them toward the office, where an army medic stood waiting to triage their injuries.

Nasha took one look at the man as he started to unwind the dirty bandage around Maryam's arm and darted back toward Remi. "I don't want to go in there."

Remi crouched down in front of her. "You need that cut on your leg looked at and a clean bandage."

Amal held out her hand. "I'll go with you."

Nasha turned a suspicious glance toward the office, then looked up at Amal. "You promise you'll stay with me?"

"Promise."

She took Amal's hand and the two walked off, while Wendy hustled the uninjured girls toward the dorm to get cleaned up. When she saw Remi, she gave her mud-stained clothes a thorough once-over. "I'll wait for that hug until after you've showered."

Sam put his arm around his wife's shoulders. "You do look like something the cat just dragged in from the jungle."

Remi arched a brow at him.

"Assuming," he added quickly, "the cat had extremely discerning taste."

"Nice recovery, Fargo," Remi said as he leaned in for a kiss.

Wendy, Pete, and Lazlo laughed.

AN HOUR LATER, SAM AND REMI CARRIED THEIR LUNCH TRAYS TO THE adults' table, taking a seat across from Okoro and Amal. Amal slid the coffee carafe toward Remi. "I swear, it's the best you've ever tasted."

Remi poured herself a cup and passed the carafe to Sam. "Nothing like a couple nights in the jungle to remind you of the finer things in life." She took a sip, savored it a moment, looking at Amal over the rim. "Did you get in touch with Renee?"

"Just before lunch. Wendy lent me her phone."

"I'm sure she was relieved to hear from you."

"We didn't really get to talk. She was in the middle of an interview with a police detective when I called. Something about a break-in at the dig site. She said she'd call back after she picks up Hank from the airport."

Remi lowered her cup to the table, looking at Sam. "What break-in?"

"Forgot to mention it," he said as some of the students at the tables started clapping. "I was a bit preoccupied, if you recall."

They turned to see Maryam, Zara, Jol, Tambara, and Nasha walking in the door. Zara smiled, then lifted Nasha's hand, holding it up like the winner of a prize fight. "The fifth Musketeer," she shouted.

The clapping and cheering intensified, even more so when Nasha, clearly overwhelmed by the attention, brushed tears from her eyes.

Sam put his arm around Remi's shoulders. "Look at that. Our street urchin, all grown up and being recognized as a hero."

It was a moment before Remi could speak. She cleared her throat and blinked as though something had gotten in her eye. "Please tell me you were able to find out where she came from?"

"That's the one thing that went right with my trip to Jalingo. Selma's been working on it. I was hoping that Pete and I could head out there once things settle down. But that's going to be a while. Before anything else happens, we have to notify every parent of every student . . ."

Remi took a ragged breath. "I wonder how many will pull the girls from the school?"

"You can't blame them if they do," he said, feeling Okoro's gaze on him. He was actually grateful when the lieutenant and half his squad walked in for lunch, disrupting the conversation. Sam invited them to their table. The three soldiers declined, having to return to their posts, but the lieutenant joined them.

Amal rose. "You can have my seat."

He raised his brows at her. "I don't usually have that effect on people."

She laughed. "It's not you, don't worry. I volunteered to help Wendy frost a few dozen cupcakes to celebrate the girls' return."

"Considering you were one of the returnees, I'm surprised they're making you work."

"Trust me," she said, picking up her tray, "I have an ulterior motive. Dark chocolate frosting. I plan on piling it extra thick on my own cupcake."

He watched her a moment, smiling, before turning back toward Sam, his expression turning somber. "I'm glad we have a few moments. I've been in touch with Taraba State investigators. They're asking that we extract the bodies . . ." He stopped, looking at Remi, mistaking her emotion over seeing Nasha's recognition for an aversion to hearing about the dead kidnappers. "My apologies, Mrs. Fargo. I'll save the more gruesome aspects until after lunch . . . There's one thing bothering me," he said to Sam. "You're isolated up here. How did they know of the school's existence?"

Sam had wondered the same thing. No doubt their ambush after leaving Jalingo was connected. Beyond that, he wasn't sure. "It's possible they found out about the school from one of the locals in Gembu. Pete and Yaro get their supplies there."

"You should mention that to the investigators. They may find it useful."

"We appreciate it," Sam said, glancing at Okoro. "As much as I hate to say it, we may have to rethink keeping the school open. The last thing we want is to endanger the children in our misguided belief that we're doing the right thing."

"If I may suggest, Mr. Fargo, wait until all the facts are in," the lieutenant said. "This school, and more like it, are very much needed in our country."

"It's heartbreaking." Remi's gaze followed a group of girls as they grabbed a jump rope from a basket by the door, then ran outside. "We were so close to finishing the second dorm to bring in new students. Wendy and Pete have worked so hard. To see it all end like this . . ."

Sam hated the defeat in her voice. He knew she was blaming herself for what happened. And the grim look on Okoro's face wasn't helping. Sam could well understand the mix of emotions running through the man after the kidnapping. Clearly, he and Okoro needed to sit down and have a long talk about the school.

The lieutenant, thankfully, changed the subject to the weather, commenting that rain wasn't expected for at least another week. "A few days of sunshine and hard work," he said, "you'll be back on schedule."

As much as Sam wanted to share his enthusiasm, he couldn't. Pete and Yaro needed to personally contact each family to inform them about the kidnapping. Most lived in far-flung villages, hours apart. Who knew how many students would be left once the parents were notified. Even if there were any remaining, rain was expected within a week and they'd never get the dorm done in time. "Let's hope so," he said as a low rumble emanated from somewhere outside, the sound growing louder by the moment.

Two soldiers raced past the cafeteria door toward the front of the school. Remi looked over at Sam in alarm. "What on earth?"

CHAPTER SIXTY-ONE

If you educate a man, you educate an individual,
but if you educate a woman, you educate a nation.
— AFRICAN PROVERB —

S am and Remi hurried out of the cafeteria, past the girls jumping rope in the courtyard. At the front of the school, they were
surprised to find the soldiers directing several military vehicles
into the now crowded graveled yard, where the poor chickens
clucked and scurried as they sought refuge far from the trucks.

"What's going on?" Sam asked Pete as he strode across the drive
from the office.

"I have no idea."

When Okoro and the lieutenant joined them, the lieutenant nodded at the closest truck as a dozen soldiers jumped out the back.
"These men are here to reinforce your gate."

"That's a lot of men," Sam said.

"So it is . . ." The lieutenant smiled as Wendy joined them. "But
you also have a lot of dorm to finish before the rain starts up
again."

Wendy stared in disbelief as the soldiers began unloading flats of
roofing shingles. "You know what this means?" she asked Pete, her
eyes brimming with emotion.

He put his arm around her. "We might make our deadline after all?"

"No," she said. "We have to make more cupcakes. Look at all

the extra dinner guests." She stood on tiptoes, kissed Pete on the cheek, and ran back toward the cafeteria.

"Why?" Sam asked the lieutenant. "Not that I'm against it."

"As I mentioned earlier, we need more schools like this. Especially for girls." He looked over at Sam, then Remi, his smile fading. "About those aerial photographs, Mrs. Fargo. It shouldn't take more than a few minutes, but we'd like to be certain the men who died after being washed off the cliff are the same who followed you."

"I'd be glad to help," Remi said.

The two walked off toward the office, the silence growing awkward despite the activity in the yard. Finally, Sam looked at Okoro. Asking about the continued use of his property so soon after the kidnapping seemed opportunistic, but Sam hated to see all this work go to waste if Okoro planned to rescind his permission. "There's no good time to talk to you about this. After everything that's happened, we understand if you—"

"I made a promise. That hasn't changed."

"Thank you. We appreciate that."

"Zara?" Pete asked. "Will she still be attending?"

"I think you need to ask Zara that question," Okoro said, watching the men unload the truck. He looked at Pete, his dark eyes unreadable. "Her mother gave up everything to marry me and live out here in the middle of nowhere. But it was a choice she willingly made. She would want her daughter to have that same choice."

"And what about you?" Pete asked. "What do you want?"

"I want my daughter to be safe." He was quiet a moment, smiling to himself. "My wife used to tell me there'd be no sons of Nigeria if there are no daughters of Nigeria."

"Wise woman," Pete said.

"Very." Okoro nodded at the truck. "She'd also say that we should help those who are helping us."

Pete looked relieved. "Definitely."

The three men walked over to the truck, helping to unload the shingles. On their way back, Sam saw Lazlo watching Nasha jumping rope, chanting "*Sator, arepo*—daughters of the sun. *Tenet, opera, rotas*—convey me to the light . . ."

One of the girls quit turning her side of the rope. "That's not a jump rope song."

"It's the only one I know," Nasha said, crossing her arms. "I learned it from Amal."

"Start over. We'll sing one for you." Soon, Nasha was happily jumping to a song about a teddy bear turning around.

Curious about Lazlo's interest, Sam asked, "Since when have you found jump rope so intriguing?"

"Not even in my youth, Mr. Fargo. But the song strikes a chord . . ."

"Teddy bears?"

"The Latin ditty she was singing before that."

"Will it make the work go faster?" He nodded toward the trucks being unloaded.

"On my way," he said, his gaze still on the girls.

As Sam left the courtyard, he glanced toward the office, where Remi and the lieutenant stood, Remi holding a tablet, nodding as she pointed to something on the screen. A few minutes later, she was on her phone. She looked up, and waved him over.

"Renee," Remi whispered, then listened intently to whatever her friend was saying. "Of course. We won't say anything to Amal until I hear back from you. We can head out first thing."

"For what?" Sam asked as she disconnected.

"That break-in at their dig site. It was definitely Warren."

"Why are we going there? The police should be handling that."

"He's dead, Sam. They found him at the bottom of the villa."

"Did he fall?"

"That's what Renee thought. But the police don't seem to be

treating it like an accident. The only thing that leaves is suicide. She doesn't want Amal to know until she's sure about what happened. We have to go back."

She gave him her *this is nonnegotiable* look just as someone started laughing from the roof of the dorm. He glanced that direction, seeing a couple of soldiers laying flats of shingles across the decking. Between Pete, Wendy, and their new guardian angels, there was really very little he, Remi, or Lazlo could do here. He pulled his phone from his pocket. "I'll call the flight crew and let them know. Next stop, Tunisia."

CHAPTER SIXTY-TWO

What you help a child to love
can be more important than what you help him to learn.
— AFRICAN PROVERB —

Early the next morning, Remi stood next to Amal and Lazlo as Wendy and Monifa brought the children out to the front of the school to say good-bye. Before Remi or Amal could even think what to say, the girls ran forward, each working her way in for a hug. Jol, Zara, Tambara, and Maryam waited until the other girls cleared, then wrapped their arms around both women.

Remi stood back, smiling at them. "We had quite an adventure. You were all marvelous."

"Yes, you were," Amal said. "But let's not do it again anytime soon."

The four laughed and backed away as Wendy stepped in, saying, "Okay. Let's give them some space. They have a long trip ahead."

A moment later, Pete and Yaro stepped out of the office, both with small duffels slung over their shoulders. With Makao and his gang still on the loose, the Fargos weren't taking any chances. They decided to caravan to Jalingo, Pete and Yaro in the truck, Sam, Remi, Amal, and Lazlo in the Land Rover. With the school well guarded, Pete and Yaro planned on spending the night in Jalingo and picking up the beds they'd ordered for the new dorm the following morning.

Sam loaded their bags in the back, closing the tailgate. "Are you ready, Remi?"

"Wait," she said. "Where's our youngest Musketeer?"

Wendy nodded toward the office. Nasha sat on the porch steps, a stick in her hand, tapping it on the ground. When she looked up and saw Remi watching her, she snapped the stick in two.

"Give me a minute." Remi walked over to the office, sitting down next to Nasha. "Why didn't you want to come say good-bye?"

Nasha shrugged but wouldn't meet her eyes, instead watching Pete and Yaro, who were tying down the back of the canvas on the truck.

Remi looked over at them, then back at Nasha. "I'm not sure when I'm going to see you again."

"Doesn't matter." She tossed half of the broken stick to the ground. "No one ever comes back."

As much as Remi wished she could promise to find Nasha's uncle—or, at the very least, find who might be responsible for her in his absence—she wasn't about to raise her hopes only to have them dashed again. Still, she had to say something. "You know, sometimes people want to come back, but things happen. It doesn't mean they ever stopped loving you."

"What kinds of things happen?"

"Maybe they got in an accident and they didn't have a way to call you. Or they didn't have enough money." Remi laid her hand over Nasha's. "But that's not going to happen to me. I'm coming back. I just don't know when."

"Never. Like everyone else."

"Someday," Remi said. "I promise."

Nasha's response was to whack the remaining half of her broken stick against the wooden step.

"I have a friend who needs my help," Remi continued. "Just like

I needed yours when we were in trouble. I promised her. You wouldn't want me to break that promise, would you?"

"No . . ." She hit the step one more time and looked up at Remi, her eyes troubled. "But what if you were mad because your friend did something wrong? Could you break your promise then?"

"I'd try to find a way to make it right. Because that's what friends do."

She tossed the stick, her dark eyes shimmering. "Why can't I go with you?" she said, her voice breaking. "I'll try to be good."

Remi's heart twisted as she put her arm around Nasha's thin shoulders. It was a minute before she could even get past the lump in her throat. "I'm going to miss you most of all,"

Nasha threw herself at Remi, pulling tight. "I'll never forget you. Never."

"I know." Remi held her for several seconds, then gently pried her loose. "Now, go say good-bye to Amal. She's going to miss you, too."

Nasha wiped the tears from her cheeks and ran across the gravel, jumping into Amal's outstretched arms. Where she disappeared to after that, Remi didn't know. When they were in the car, pulling out of the gate, Sam looked over at Remi. "Something in your eye?"

She glanced in the side mirror, watching all the girls racing past the army trucks toward the gate, waving good-bye. "A lot of somethings."

THEY WERE HALFWAY TO JALINGO WHEN REMI'S PHONE RANG. Expecting it to be Renee with news about what had happened to Warren, she was surprised to see Wendy's number on the screen when she answered it. "Did we forget something?"

"It's Nasha. I haven't been able to find her since you left. Did she say anything to you?"

"She was upset we were leaving."

Sam looked at her. "What is it?"

"Nasha. They can't find her." Remi turned on the speaker and shifted in her seat, looking back at Amal. "Did she say anything to you?"

"Just that she'd miss me. What about up in her tree?"

"We've searched everywhere," Wendy said.

Remi glanced out the rear window, seeing the supply truck behind them. "Oh no . . . Sam, stop the car."

Sam braked and again looked at Remi as Pete pulled to a stop behind them. "You don't think . . . ?"

"Think what?" Wendy asked.

"Hold on," Remi said. They got out of the Land Rover and walked back toward the truck.

Pete hopped out, following them around to the cargo bed. "Something wrong?"

Sam unhooked the canvas covering, pulling it up. "Stowaway," Sam said.

Nasha braced herself in the corner, a look of determination on her face as she stared back at them. "Are you mad at me?"

"She's here, Wendy. We'll call you back." Remi dropped her phone into her pocket. "Nasha . . . I thought you liked it at the school."

She bit at her bottom lip, then in a rush said, "I have to go back to Jalingo."

"Why?"

"I promised. My friend's there all by himself."

"Chuk?" Sam asked, surprising Remi he even knew who Nasha was talking about.

Nasha nodded.

"We can't leave him there," Remi said.

"No," Sam replied. "I'm just trying to figure out the logistics. I don't think Kambili's going to willingly give him up. If we're lucky, we'll find him out on the street."

But once they reached Jalingo, the street where they'd first been accosted by the boys was surprisingly empty of pickpockets. Sam took a quick look around. "Pete, we'll need you to stand guard while Remi and I go in. The rest of you wait here."

As they walked off, Remi heard Lazlo saying to Amal, "I've been meaning to ask you about this jump rope rhyme you taught to Nasha. A bit of Latin, I believe."

"Latin? I don't recall teaching her any."

"Pity, that. It reminded me of something. Nasha, what was that rhyme . . . ?"

Remi, figuring Lazlo was reflecting on his lost youth, hurried after Sam and Pete. A few minutes later, they descended on the Kalu shop, only to discover that Kambili wasn't there.

But neither was Chuk.

"He's with Kambili," one of the boys said.

"And Scarface," another added. "They're taking him home."

"Home?" Sam looked over at Remi.

"Lucky for us, we've brought the cavalry."

CHAPTER SIXTY-THREE

———

A snake can shed its skin but it still remains a snake.
— AFRICAN PROVERB —

The village was much smaller than Makao had anticipated, but he hoped they'd be able to use that to their advantage and quickly find the girl's uncle. The sooner they found him, the sooner they'd be able to lure the Fargos into his scheme.

"How do you know the man?" Makao asked, looking in the rearview mirror at the young boy sleeping in the backseat.

"Never met him," Kambili said. "Word got out that I took in homeless boys."

"Out of the goodness of your heart. They forget to mention the way you help them is by turning them into street thieves?"

"They'd starve to death if not for me."

More like Kambili would starve to death if not for the kids, Makao thought, ignoring the stares of the people as he drove past. One problem with a village this small was that everyone knew everyone. He and Kambili would definitely stand out. "We need to think of a good reason why we're searching for this guy."

"Trying to bring Jonathon Atiku's nephew home."

"Niece."

Kambili shifted in his seat, looking back at the sleeping boy. "What about him?"

"What do I care? Take him back with you when we're done. We

need to find Atiku's farm. Once we have Atiku, we can contact the Fargos and give them our ultimatum. When they bite, we move in."

It didn't take long to drive the length of the village. There was one dirt road through the center, and there were a number of burned huts in the south part of the village. Most of those that still stood were made of mud, some with corrugated tin roofs, others with thatched. "Wake him," Makao said.

Kambili reached back, slapping Chuk's knee. "We're here."

The boy stirred, sitting up. He looked around, confused. "Where are we?"

"This is your village, isn't it?" Makao asked. "Where does Nash's uncle live?"

Chuk shrugged. "I don't know. This doesn't look right."

Makao, seeing a woman carrying a jug on her way toward the well, rolled down his window. "We're looking for Jonathon Atiku."

She shook her head and quickened her pace. After several more attempts to ask other locals, Makao and Kambili got out, Kambili pulling Chuk from the cab, holding his hand tight as they walked along the street. Chuk seemed baffled, unable to determine where the Atiku farm was located. "Everything looks different," he said, staring at the burned-down huts.

Makao tried offering money to some of the locals for information. Even then people backed away.

"I don't understand," Kambili said. "Why won't they tell us what we want to know?"

Makao stepped in front of a young man, holding several bills out to him. "Where do we find Jonathon Atiku's house?"

The young man gave Makao an odd look. "It's your money," he said, grabbing the bills. "This way." He led them past a few huts and pointed to the east. "That's his farm. A year ago, Boko Haram burned it because he hid the boys working his fields."

There was nothing left but a blackened shell of crumbling walls.

"Where is he?" Makao asked.

"Dead, I guess." He backed away, then ran off.

"Hey." Kambili started to follow.

"Let him go." Makao looked down at the boy, noting the fear in his eyes. "Where would Nash's uncle go?"

"I don't know. I'm hungry."

"Me, too," Kambili said.

They walked to the market, ate, and asked a few more people, finding them all unhelpful. The terrorists had instilled in them a distrust of strangers.

"Wasted trip," Kambili said as they returned to Makao's truck.

He was about to agree when he glanced down the street and noticed a familiar-looking vehicle at the far end of the road. Not wasted at all.

The Fargos were there.

CHAPTER SIXTY-FOUR

Only a wise person can solve a difficult problem.
— AKAN PROVERB —

After Sam pulled into the village, he parked alongside a bungalow, where a too-thin dog lying beside it in the shade watched them with wary interest. The dog wasn't the only one watching. Even if Pete had not rolled in behind them with the supply truck, they might as well have installed a neon sign on the top of their vehicle announcing *Virtual Strangers*. The rented Land Rover was decades newer than any of the vehicles owned or driven by the local residents. The same held true for Makao's white Toyota pickup, which Sam had noticed the second he'd driven onto the lone, dusty road.

Remi fished the binoculars from Sam's pack, peering through them. "Makao, Kambili, and—"

"Chuk," Nasha said from the back, leaning forward. "You were right, Mr. Fargo. Kambili brought him home."

Not quite how Sam would've phrased it, but he wasn't about to mention that to Nasha, who had yet to realize the significance of Kambili's and Makao's presence in her uncle's village.

No doubt in Sam's and Remi's minds, though. Those men were after her uncle to get to the Fargos.

Remi passed the binoculars to Sam.

He focused on the two men who were standing in front of the

Toyota. The boy, Chuk, started backing away. Kambili grabbed him by the shoulder, then dragged the kid to the truck, opened the back door and shoved him in.

"Lazlo," he said, keeping his focus on Kambili and Makao. "Do you remember that story I told you about the time Remi and I were in Juárez with a couple of our friends?"

"Yes . . . Wait. Surely you don't mean . . . ?"

Remi, her Sig Sauer already drawn, looked back at him. "You're welcome to take my spot?"

"Dear heavens, no." Lazlo gave a tepid smile and opened the Rover's door. "Come along," he said to Amal and Nasha. "I have yet to see a Fargo car make it through unscathed."

"What're you talking about?" Sam slapped the dash. "Not a mark on this thing."

Lazlo turned a dubious expression Sam's way as he held the door for Nasha and Amal. "I'll call Mrs. Fargo's phone when I'm there."

As the professor hurried the two away, Nasha asked him, "What does *unscathed* mean?"

"It means you don't want to be anywhere near their car when the fighting starts."

Sam kept his attention on Makao as he and Kambili stood in front of their truck. "Ready?"

"Ready," Remi said.

He called Pete, giving him a quick rundown, then let the car idle forward until they were about fifty yards away from Makao's pickup. Not unexpectedly, Sam's phone rang. He answered. "Can't say I was expecting to hear from you again, Makao."

"You have something I want. Money. I have something you want."

"Which would be . . . ?" Sam asked.

"We were hoping for the girl's uncle but feel certain you'll settle for the boy."

"What makes you think we want him?"

"You came this far, didn't you?"

Sam sensed Remi bristling. He checked her phone, sitting in the cupholder, waiting for Lazlo's call. "How much?" he asked Makao.

"The same as before. One hundred thousand dollars. When you wire it to my account, I'll give you the boy."

Finally, Remi's phone lit up. Lazlo was in place. "No need," Sam said. "I've got the money here."

"You expect me to believe you have that much cash with you?"

"I had it delivered by special courier when I thought you had my wife." Sam didn't give him time to think. "Keep the boy in the open where I can see him. Meet me halfway. I'll bring the money to you. If you're satisfied it's all there, you send the boy to me."

A stretch of silence followed, then Makao said, "Agreed. But keep your hands where I can see them or you won't make it back to your car."

The phone beeped as Makao disconnected. Sam saw him talking to Kambili, who nodded in response to whatever he was saying.

"Let's hope this works," Sam said.

CHAPTER SIXTY-FIVE

Love never gets lost;
it's only kept.
— AFRICAN PROVERB —

Remi handed Sam a Bluetooth earpiece. He placed it in his ear
and tucked his Smith & Wesson into the back of his waistband.
Remi called his phone, telling him, "Be careful. I'm calling
Lazlo now."

He nodded when her voice sounded in his earpiece, then opened
his door, holding up his empty left hand. Remi handed him his backpack. He lifted it by its strap with his other hand, making sure
Makao knew he wasn't holding a gun.

"I'm almost there," Lazlo said.

Remi opened her door a few inches, bracing one foot on the
frame, aiming her Sig in the direction of Makao's truck. "Sam, stay
to the left."

Sam walked slowly toward the two men, glad to see the few wary
pedestrians quickly running from the street out of sight. And no
wonder. As many burned-out shells of houses Sam had seen on his
way in, he knew the people here were no strangers to violence.

Makao and Kambili waited at the front of their truck, Chuk
just behind them. When Sam reached the halfway mark, he tossed
the backpack on the ground and held up both of his hands. "It's
yours." Sam backed away to the left, making sure Remi had a line
of sight.

Makao pushed Kambili. "Go get it."

Kambili reluctantly moved forward.

C'mon, Lazlo . . .

"Here," Lazlo said.

Sam saw him standing just behind the mud-sided building, waving at Chuk. The boy looked over at the professor, but then, surprising Sam, moved closer to Makao.

Sam heard Remi sigh. "I don't think Chuk realizes that we're trying to save him. Lazlo, you're going to have to grab him."

"I've got a better idea," Lazlo said, ducking back behind the building. "Buy me a few more seconds."

That's all they had left. Once Kambili reached the backpack, and realized the only cash it contained was probably a bit of change in the front zippered pocket, they were done for.

"Think of something, Fargo," Remi said.

Sam held up both hands. "You sure you trust him?" he called out.

"Why wouldn't I?" Makao said.

"Wasn't asking you," Sam replied. "I was asking Kambili."

Kambili stopped, looking back at Makao. "What's he talking about?"

"Don't listen to him," Makao said. "He's doing this on purpose."

Lazlo was back, this time with Nasha. Unfortunately, when Chuk saw her, Makao unknowingly stepped between them. Sam kept his gaze on Kambili. "Makao killed your brothers. What makes you think he's not going to kill you the moment you grab that backpack?"

"He's lying," Makao said.

"Am I?" Sam took a second step that direction, still holding his hands up.

Chuk backed up and darted toward Lazlo and Nasha.

Makao tried to grab the boy. "They tricked us," he shouted, aiming at Remi.

Her shot was nearly simultaneous to his. Makao staggered back toward the truck.

Sam drew his Smith & Wesson as Kambili spun around, gun in hand.

Sam fired.

Kambili dropped to his knees. Red bloomed on his chest as he fell facedown on the ground, still gripping his weapon. Sam kept his gun trained on the man, approached, kicked Kambili's weapon away and leaned down, checking his pulse.

Dead.

"Fargo," Remi shouted. "Makao's getting away."

Sam looked up in time to see the white truck backing up. He ran to the Land Rover to give chase, then stopped, seeing the odd tilt of the car as Lazlo, Nasha, Amal, and Chuk emerged from between the buildings. "Bad news," Sam said, examining the damage.

"We could go after him," Pete said, indicating the supply truck.

Sam spied the dust cloud in the distance. Had it been a smaller truck maybe? "You'd never catch him."

Nasha crouched beside Sam and looked up at Lazlo, asking, "Is a flat tire *unscathed*?"

"When it comes to the Fargos? Quite."

Eventually, the villagers started wandering out, a crowd gathering around the group, while they waited for the police to arrive from Mubi.

"Nasha?" A man pushed through the crowd, stopped, and stared in disbelief. "Nasha . . . Is that really you?"

Myriad emotions swept across her small face, but she didn't move. "You . . . You said you were coming back for us . . ."

"I did. I looked for you. The man I paid to drive you, he told me . . . It doesn't matter now. You're here . . ." He held his hand out toward her, his smile broken. "Come. Give your old uncle a hug."

Chuk nudged her forward.

That was all the encouragement she needed. The man scooped her up in his arms, hugging her tight. "My Nasha . . ."

Remi smiled at them. "All's well."

Sam, holding the tire iron, went back to removing the lug nuts when his cell alerted him to a text. He pulled it from his pocket, reading the message from Makao. *I'm going to get her.*

"Remi . . ." Sam handed her the phone.

She read the text, met his eyes, then looked at Nasha, saying, "I don't know which her he's talking about, but we're not leaving ours behind, until he's caught."

"Exactly what I was thinking."

CHAPTER SIXTY-SIX

A child who is carried on the back will
not know how far the journey is.
— NIGERIAN PROVERB —

How to protect Nasha presented a problem. Although Pete had suggested she could return to the school with him, her uncle was against the idea of allowing her to live so far away—or accepting any sort of charity, after they offered to pay him to move. "Farming is the only thing I know. I've always told Nasha that life is what you make of it, but what lesson does that send my niece if I simply accept a handout because she had the good fortune to cross your path?"

That was something neither Sam nor Remi could argue with. Remi looked over at Nasha and Chuk, both out of hearing range as they tried to coax the dog from his coveted spot in the shade. Surprisingly, it was Amal who came up with a great suggestion. "She could come stay with me and my mother. A temporary visit to Tunisia."

Remi smiled at Nasha's uncle, hoping he'd agree.

"I'd say yes," he replied, "except what little identification she had was lost in the fire."

Sam and Remi exchanged glances. "Rube," they said at the same time.

"He works for the government," Remi explained as Sam called him at the CIA to arrange for an emergency visa.

When everything was settled, they told Nasha about the trip—but not about her uncle's refusal to let her attend their school. "We'll change his mind later," Remi said to Sam once they were on their way.

FORTY THOUSAND FEET IN THE AIR, THEY FINALLY HAD A CHANCE TO relax—up to a point. Remi was left with the task of telling Amal what had happened to Warren. Amal sat at the table across from Remi, Nasha in her lap, while Sam and Lazlo occupied the two aisle seats. When the child fell asleep, Amal didn't seem to notice how quickly the men excused themselves from the table, Lazlo proclaiming that he was in desperate need of a nap, Sam saying something about talking to the pilots about flight plans. Amal looked down as the girl stirred but didn't waken. "I'm surprised she could sleep, as excited as she was about her first plane trip. Then again, after everything that's happened, I may sleep for a week once I get home."

Remi smiled at her. "Are you sure your mother doesn't mind? We could always take her with us to the hotel. She might enjoy time by the pool."

"I think my mother's more excited about Nasha's visit than Nasha is."

"That may change when she's faced with such a bundle of energy and curiosity." Remi's smile faded as she thought about how best to broach the subject. "There's something I need to talk to you about."

Amal looked up in concern. "What's wrong? Is it Dr. LaBelle?"

"She's fine. It's Warren."

"The embezzlement. Has he been arrested? It's all a terrible mistake, I'm sure of it."

"He's dead."

"Dead . . . ?"

"I'm so sorry. I know you were friends."

She stared at Remi, her brow furrowing. "I don't understand . . . How?"

"Renee found him yesterday morning. She asked me not to say anything until she knew the details. She was worried about the stress. That you might—"

"My seizures."

"Yes . . ."

Amal's eyes started to glimmer with unshed tears. "What happened?"

"I'm not sure. Renee found him at the bottom of the excavation. She thought he might have fallen."

"The broken deck . . . ?"

"No. I think that had been ripped out. The police are looking into it. It's possible it was a terrible accident. Maybe he didn't realize the decking was damaged."

"My mother didn't even tell me."

"I'm sure she was worried."

"She's very protective. Too protective." Amal looked out the window for several long moments toward what promised to be a spectacular sunset, not seeing any of it. When Nasha stirred in her arms, she looked down at her, then back at Remi. "I think I'll ask Nasha not to tell my mother about the kidnapping. She'll only worry more."

"I'm sure Nasha will keep your secret until you're ready to talk about it."

Sam returned from the cockpit, taking a seat next to Remi. "I want you to know how sorry we are."

Amal nodded, brushing the tears from her eyes. "Do you think it was suicide? The guilt he must have carried to take his own life."

"I don't know," Sam said. "Whatever it is, we'll get to the bottom of it."

CHAPTER SIXTY-SEVEN

Life is as you yourself make it.
— GHANAIAN PROVERB —

Bulla Regia, Tunisia

I feel like we're intruding," Remi said in the car as Sam parked in the graveled drive of the university house Renee shared with the other archeologists.

She must have been watching out the window because a moment later Sam saw the front door open. Renee, leaning on one of her crutches, stood at the threshold, looking at them. "Don't forget, Remi. She called you. You're here for moral support."

"I know. Remember, nothing about the books. I don't want to add to her stress." She leaned over, kissed him, then slid out of the car.

Sam didn't follow. Instead, he pulled out his phone, pretending to be studiously reading an email, in order to give them a few moments of privacy. He hadn't known Warren all that well, but from what Remi told him, Renee had been close to the man.

After a few minutes, Remi waved him over and he walked up to the door, offering his condolences.

"Thank you," Renee said. "It helps to have old friends around. And thanks for bringing Remi out. Especially after everything the two of you have been through."

"That's what friends are for," Sam said, earning a smile from his wife. "Have the police said anything else?"

"No," she said, using her crutch to cross the room, taking a seat on the couch. "I'm sure I'll hear more today. Amal's crushed. Hank, thank goodness, is keeping his head about him, even though I left him stranded at the airport. After finding Warren, I totally forgot I was supposed to pick him up."

"What happened?" Remi asked.

"Where do I even start?"

"The beginning," Sam said.

"That would be the phone call from José about the break-in." She pulled her phone from her pocket, showing Remi a photo. "The theft of Echo."

"They took the whole floor?" Remi asked.

"Worse," she said as Remi handed the phone to Sam. "They hacked out her face. You can see it in the next photo. We were lucky they didn't completely destroy the floor taking it out. There was a significant crack running along the tree she's leaning against, which sort of helped them."

Sam enlarged the photo on the screen, seeing a young woman in white, her hair pulled back with bands in a classical Grecian style, peering at something just beyond the tree she hid behind. He scrolled to the next photo, where Echo's face had been hacked out. Though the mosaic was many hundreds of years old, the colors were still vibrant. "Let's hope the police find it."

"Items sold on the antiquities black market don't often resurface."

"You think Warren stole it?" Remi asked.

She nodded. "The police believe he was trying to steal another section of the mosaic the next day when he died. They found the chisel beneath his body."

"An accident?"

"So it would seem. After the other suspicious happenings around here, I did some searching on my own. I found a listing for Echo on a website that I know Warren's used in the past. In hindsight, I should've called the police the moment I saw the listing. But Hank didn't want to wait. He was hoping to get there before the mosaic disappeared. Who knows what else they stole after digging around in the rubble." She gave a sigh. "Needless to say, Hank's still upset about it."

Hank walked in from the hallway, overhearing her. "I'm just grateful you weren't hurt. Who knows what might have happened had you caught him in the act." He gestured to Sam and Remi. "It seems we've all had our share of problems. LaBelle told me every-thing the two of you have been through. I can't imagine how har-rowing that must have been for everyone involved."

"For now, everyone's safe," Sam said. "We're hoping they catch whoever was behind it."

"Let's hope they do," he said.

Renee used her crutch to pull herself up. "Who wants a cup of coffee?" she said, her smile overly bright.

"Sit," Hank said. "I'll get coffee for everyone."

"How's your ankle?" Remi asked as he left.

"Much better." She lifted her pant leg, showing off a bruise that was turning yellow. "The doctor wants me to rest it a few more days."

"So listen to him," Hank called out from the kitchen.

"Easier said than done. I'm almost on a first name basis with the police, with everything that's gone on."

"Hank's right," Remi said. "You need rest. Come stay with us. You can keep me company by the pool. It'll give us a chance to catch up."

"As divine as that sounds, I have a video conference with the uni-versity tomorrow and a ton of paperwork."

Remi leaned forward, lowering her voice conspiratorially. "Just angle your phone camera so they don't know you're actually pool-side drinking Bloody Marys. Besides, Sam has a meeting himself to-morrow, so you can keep me company."

"I can't," Renee said as Hank returned.

"Seriously?" Hank handed her a mug of steaming coffee. "How often do old friends drop by?" He looked over at Remi, saying, "I'll personally drop LaBelle off at your hotel tomorrow morning. Sometimes she's overdedicated to her job."

"It's settled," Remi said, taking her friend's hand in hers. "You're coming to stay with me."

Sam leaned back in his chair, watching Renee LaBelle's face. Curiously, she seemed less than enthused at Remi's announcement. Which was odd, considering the two women were fast friends.

Back at their hotel later that night, he pointed this out to Remi.

She dismissed his assessment entirely. "After finding Warren dead, I doubt anyone would act normal. Honestly, Fargo, I think you're being a bit paranoid."

"Pragmatic, not paranoid," he replied. "There's a discrepancy in the books, Warren's dead, and, like it or not, you've got to talk to her about it. Tomorrow."

CHAPTER SIXTY-EIGHT

While the sun is shining, bask in it.
— AFRICAN PROVERB —

Late the following morning, beneath the shade of a large umbrella, Remi and Renee settled into their lounge chairs, two Bloody Marys on the table between them.

Remi picked up her glass, looking over at her friend. "Tell the truth. Aren't you glad you came?"

She took a deep breath. "I needed this. Every time the phone rings, I jump. I haven't been able to sleep since I saw Warren at the bottom of the villa, his blood all over the mosaic, and all I kept thinking about was that this is all my fault."

"How can it be your fault?"

She again picked up her drink, stirring the stalk of celery in the glass. "As I said, the police think he came to steal another piece of the mosaic when he fell. The deck repair wasn't quite finished. It is now, but I should have had made sure it was done before I left."

"That's hardly your fault."

"How could he have been so desperate that he couldn't come to me if he needed money? I know it wasn't drugs, so what was it that drove him to steal?"

"Maybe he had a gambling problem."

"Maybe . . ." The two women sipped their drinks in silence, staring out at the pool, where a middle-aged man was swimming a slow lap down the length. "What I really need is to get back to work. I'm worried the university's going to find out about Warren's death, the embezzlement, my accident, then cut their funding and send us all home before we finish."

Hearing the worry in her voice, Remi decided to hold off asking any more questions about the books or about Warren. "Forget everything else. Tell me about the villa." For the next hour, they let their imaginations run wild about what they might find beneath all the rubble once it was cleared. Hearing her friend so animated over the project reaffirmed Remi's belief that she'd taken the right course of action. Plenty of time to address the embezzled funds later.

When the waiter appeared, they ordered refills of their drinks. Remi watched him walk across the grounds toward the gate, stopping to talk to two men, one wearing a white shirt and black slacks, the other in khaki pants and a green shirt. She wouldn't have given them more than a look in passing except that the hotel employee suddenly looked in their direction, giving Remi the distinct feeling that she and Renee were the topic of conversation. "Do you know either of those men?" Remi asked.

Renee shaded her eyes and shook her head. "No clue."

Curious, Remi watched as the two strangers walked through the gate. They seemed familiar, but she couldn't place them.

The two men smiled as they neared, yet their implied friendliness failed to reach their eyes. Remi looked around for something she could use as a weapon. The only thing remotely adequate were Renee's crutches—unfortunately, on the other side of the lounge chair out of reach.

It wouldn't have mattered. The men quickly closed in, one grabbing an abandoned towel from the back of a poolside chair as he walked past. He used it to cover the gun he pulled from beneath his shirt.

"Come with us," the man said, the barrel of his gun level with Remi's head. "And don't make a sound."

CHAPTER SIXTY-NINE

Noise and hunting don't go together.
— AFRICAN PROVERB —

Nothing on Makao?" Sam asked, looking down at his phone, which was propped against the lamp on the desk for his video call. Pete shook his head. "Not yet. But they're following up a few leads on some of his known friends. I did get some good news, though. Yaro was telling Okoro about Nasha's uncle. When Okoro heard how Boko Haram invaded the village and burned down his farm, he suggested leasing a part of his tea fields to him. That way, Nasha can still attend the school, and he'll be a lot closer. He's agreed to come look at Okoro's land to discuss a possible lease, then take a tour of the school."

Lazlo, seated on the couch behind Sam, absorbed in something on the screen of the computer tablet he was holding, looked up at the news. "Good show," he called out.

"Remi will be glad to hear that," Sam said, glancing out the fourth-floor window. The hotel room overlooked the pool where Remi and Renee had taken up residence beneath an umbrella under one of the tall palms. What he didn't expect to see was two men standing over the women, one with a towel draped over his hand. Had the man been a waiter, Sam might not have been so concerned. But the hotel staff wore uniforms, and neither man looked as though he was dressed for lounging around the pool.

"Once things settle down," Pete said, "Yaro and I plan to head out and—"

Sam drew his gun and rushed to the balcony.

"Mr. Fargo?" Pete called out. "What's going on?"

"Remi's in trouble. Lazlo, call the police." Through the palm fronds, he saw both women rise from their chairs, the two men taking up a position on either side. He heard Lazlo on the phone, but he knew the police would never get there in time. Nor would he, for that matter.

Those men would have his wife and Renee out the gate to the parking lot before he ever made it downstairs.

He aimed at the man closest to Remi, the one holding the towel, but the breeze gusted. The row of palm trees swayed, obscuring his vision. If he waited until they cleared the trees, his trusty .38 wasn't going to cut it. There were too many guests scattered about on lounge chairs. And he didn't dare leave the balcony to retrieve his wife's Sig.

"Remi," he shouted.

The man next to Remi looked up. She rammed her elbow into his side and swept upward, knocking his gun from his hand. He pushed Remi and dove for the weapon. Sam fired at the ground.

The gunman jerked to a stop. A few guests looked around, unsure what the sharp noise was. Sam fired about a foot behind the second kidnapper. The shot ricocheted, hitting the planter behind him. Guests screamed. Remi pivoted, grabbing one of Renee's crutches, swinging it against the other man's knees. As he stumbled forward, the first gunman lunged at the two women. Remi swung the crutch again, knocking him into the stone planter. He scrambled to his feet and dashed after his partner.

Several hotel employees ran out, surrounding the women, helping Renee to a chair. Lazlo was still on the phone as Sam raced to the stairs, taking them down two at a time. He burst through the door to the pool. "Remi."

"I'm fine," she said, looking at him. "We're both fine."

She looked at Renee, then walked over to Sam, speaking quietly. "Just a run-of-the-mill kidnapping attempt."

"That part seemed obvious. I'm just trying to figure out—" He stopped when one of the hotel managers came running toward them.

The man looked as though he might faint. "Is anyone hurt?"

"No," Remi said.

"They came in asking if there was a Western woman at the hotel pool. They said they'd hit her car and wanted to talk to her."

Sam exchanged a look with Remi, before asking, "At the pool?"

"Yes, sir."

"Their exact words?" Sam asked. "It's important."

He indicated the gate where the conversation had taken place. "They said they'd hit a car parked out front and asked if the two women at the poolside belonged to it. I told them I couldn't give out that information. I assure you, had I suspected anything was amiss, I would never have returned inside." He looked at Remi and her friend. "I am very, very sorry."

Remi smiled at the man. "We're both fine, I promise. Perhaps, though, you could call the police?"

"Of course." He bowed several times, backing away, and stopped in surprise at the sight of the police walking through the gate.

"Lazlo," Sam explained.

"A shame they didn't get here about two minutes sooner. The kidnappers might've run right into them."

After the report was taken, with assurances from both the police and the hotel staff that the area was normally very safe, the three retreated to the Fargos' suite, where Renee called Hank to let him know what had happened.

"Hold on," Hank said. "I think we have a bad connection. Can't hear a word you're saying. Let me move to higher ground and call you back."

Renee's phone rang just a few minutes later, this time a video call. Hank's face filled her screen, the ruins of Bulla Regia behind him. "Tell me I heard wrong, LaBelle. I thought you said someone tried to kidnap you."

"They did," she said.

"But you're okay? Where were you? I thought you were at the hotel."

"We were. At the pool. But we got away."

"Thank heavens. How'd you manage that?"

"Remi grabbed one of my crutches and whacked the guy. And then Sam shot at them from the balcony. They both took off."

His mouth dropped open. "From the balcony? Thank goodness he was even there." He cleared his throat. "How are you otherwise?"

"I'm fine . . ."

Sam drew Remi to the side, out of their hearing. "There's no way this is some random kidnapping. I think Makao's got tentacles all the way to Tunisia."

"That may be the case," Remi replied, "but I'm not sure this has anything to do with Makao."

"What makes you say that?"

"I remembered where I saw those two men before. In the restaurant the afternoon of Renee's accident. I think this is the second time they've tried to kidnap us."

CHAPTER SEVENTY

*One who has been bitten by a snake
lives in fear of worms.*
— AFRICAN PROVERB —

You're sure those are the same two men?" Sam asked.

Remi, not wanting to alarm Renee, who was sitting just a few feet away, kept her smile intact. "Almost positive."

"That changes about everything. It definitely makes you wonder what Warren was really involved in."

The officers took statements from the Fargos and Renee, talked to a couple of poolside witnesses, and asked for any surveillance videos management might have. After they left, Sam, Remi, and Renee retreated to the restaurant for lunch.

Renee, Remi noticed, kept shifting around in her seat anytime anyone walked in or out of the restaurant. "You're safe now," Remi said.

"How do you know anyone here isn't one of them?" she asked, then nodded out the window toward the pool. "Or anyone out there?"

Remi again smiled. "Sam has his back to the wall. No one's getting in or out without him seeing."

When their food was served, Renee picked at the meal, unable to eat. Finally, she pushed her plate away. "I'll call Hank to pick me up. I can't stay here after this."

"I'm so sorry," Remi said, wishing she could reassure her friend that this was an isolated incident, not likely to repeat itself. "But we can take you back, can't we, Sam?"

He drew his attention from the door, looking over at them, along with their unfinished plates. His plate was empty. "Might be for the best. Why don't you two go up to the room, get her things, and meet me out front."

They were on the road within fifteen minutes.

RENEE, QUIET DURING THE DRIVE, PERKED UP AS THEY NEARED THE archeological park. "Since my ankle keeps me out of the field, I can definitely get some paperwork done. I don't suppose you want to sit down with those books now, do you?"

Sam looked back at her in the rearview mirror. "If you think you're up for it. It's not like Remi and I have anything better to do."

"Good. That'll be a weight off my shoulders once we get everything reconciled."

Sam pulled up in front of the small house at the bottom of the olive grove. The three walked up the graveled drive to the door, where Renee inserted a key in the lock. "You'll have to forgive the mess," she said, standing aside to let them in. "They sort of tossed the place during the burglary."

"Anything stolen from the house?" Remi asked.

"Not that we can tell, thank goodness."

Once inside, she leaned her crutches against the wall, switched on the portable air conditioner, and sat at the desk. "Pull up a chair," she said.

Sam and Remi took the seats opposite her, while she swiveled around to look at the bookshelf on the wall behind her. "Okay, where is it?" She leaned forward, scrutinizing the shelves, pulling out several green ledgers, turning around and placing them on the desk in front of her. She opened each one, scanned the first page, then shoved it aside. "That's odd. I don't see it. The ledger with the discrepancies in it."

Sam and Remi exchanged glances.

Renee looked up, her expression worn, tense. "I'm just so sorry to have roped you into this."

"It's not your fault," Remi said, kicking the side of Sam's shoe, "is it, Sam?"

"Of course not." He turned to the window. "You know, while you two look for the missing book, I think I'll head down to the site, see what Hank's up to. I haven't really had a chance to talk to him since we've been back."

Remi watched him walk out the door, wondering what he was really looking for.

CHAPTER SEVENTY-ONE

*If you observe attentively,
you will even find wisdom in shadows.*
— AFRICAN PROVERB —

S am strolled down the rocky path and through the open gate,
where Amal, Osmond, and José were kneeling at a shallow excavation. Nasha sat next to Amal, watching as the team gently
brushed the dust of centuries away from small protrusions in the
dirt. At one point, Amal handed her brush to the girl, showing her
how to work it without displacing the shards.

Nasha looked up, saw Sam, and held up the brush. "Look. I'm
being an archeologist."

He crouched down beside them to see what they were working
on. "Find anything yet?"

"Miss Amal says they're broken pieces of pottery. They look like
rocks to me."

"Keep working," Sam said. "You never know what you'll find . . .
Is Hank around?"

Nasha rolled her eyes, her tone one of frustration as she said,
"Yes. And he won't let me go down there to see the mosaic."

Amal angled her head back toward the gated-off excavation.
"Finishing up the repairs to the scaffolding. Unless he somehow
tiptoed past us, he's still down there. I can run over and get him, if
you like."

"I can use the walk. Happy hunting."

THE DAMAGED DECKING HAD BEEN REMOVED FROM THE ENTRANCE and was piled in a stack near the gate. Sam passed it by, then backtracked, picking up one of the broken deck boards, which still had a nail sticking out of it.

He tossed it aside and picked up another. And another. After finding two broken boards that appeared to have been partially sawed through, he walked to the entrance, where a ladder poked up. "Hank?"

"Down here."

Sam peered in. "I take it the police finished their investigation?"

"So it seems." Hank stood in the light of a lamp clamped to a sawhorse. He lifted the light's extension cord, stepping beneath it, to look up at Sam. "Come on down. The deck's been repaired. It's safe."

"Did you happen to see the cut boards?"

"Cut?"

"As in partly sawed through."

"No . . . You're sure it's not something that happened when the crew came and tore it out?"

"Doubt it." Sam climbed down the ladder onto the now solid scaffolding. "This is where they found Warren?"

Hank nodded. "I was at the airport, waiting for LaBelle to pick me up, when she found him." He pointed to the pile of rubble. "That's where he fell. I've dumped water over the bloodstains, but the masonry is rather porous, so I figured I'd remove the, uh, more obvious pieces. I'd hate for LaBelle to have to see it when she's able to come down. Slowly clearing this out."

"By yourself?"

"Thought it was the right thing to do. Couldn't really ask José or Osmond. Warren was like a father to them." He leaned down, picking up a large chunk, placing it in a wooden box.

"I'd be glad to help."

"I'd be glad to accept. If you're sure you're up to it. I can't imagine wanting to do much of anything but drink after the morning you and your wife had."

"All's well," Sam said. "We can't ask for more than that."

The two worked side by side, clearing out some of the rubble to get to the bloodstain on the mosaic beneath.

Eventually, the conversation died as they concentrated on the labor. Sam placed a heavy remnant into the now nearly full box and brushed the dust from his hands. "That must have been some earthquake, to wipe out an entire city like this."

"I expect it was." Hank picked up several small pieces, placing them gently on top of the other remnants they'd collected, then scrutinized the area. "I think it looks safe enough, should any of them wander down. This is about as far as we can go with this load. That bucket and pulley were what we were using to clear it out. But they haven't been repaired yet."

"Who built it? The decking?"

"Local contractors."

"Good thing Dr. LaBelle is so petite," Sam said. "Can you imagine if you'd been hauling up all this rock when that accident occurred?"

Hank eyeballed the wooden box. "That could've been deadly for anyone standing beneath it . . ." He looked over at Sam. "I could see Warren stealing something, but revenge? I would never have thought that of him."

A shadow darkened the entry above them.

They looked up to see Amal and Nasha looking down.

"Everything okay?" Hank called out.

"Fine," Amal said. "My mother wants to know if you, the Fargos, and Lazlo would like to come over for dinner tomorrow night. If so, I need to leave a bit early today to catch a bus to the market."

Hank grinned. "I can't speak for the Fargos, but I'd be delighted."

"So would we," Sam said. "Remi's at the house with Renee. I'm sure she'd be glad to drive you in. It'll give her something to do."

"Thank you. I'll go ask."

"Her mother's an amazing cook," Hank said to Sam after she left. "Poor thing, usually has to take the bus. Can't drive due to her seizures." He pulled off his gloves, tossing them onto the rock pile. "Well, not much more we can do down here today. Eventually, I'll get the pulley system fixed and I can actually start moving this out. At least it no longer looks like a crime scene." He started for the ladder, adding, "I expect now is as good a time as any to go over the books."

"Dr. LaBelle couldn't find them."

"I know right where they are. I'll show you."

They climbed out and walked to the house. When they entered the front door, Hank made for the bookshelf where Renee had been searching less than an hour before. "It was here, I'm sure of it."

"When's the last time you saw it?"

"LaBelle and I were sitting in here talking about it the morning of her accident. I suppose it's highly possible Warren came in and took it while we were at the hospital." They found the women sitting at the kitchen table. Hank pulled out the chair next to Renee and sat. "How are you? You're not hurt from—"

"No," Renee said. "Just stressed. Remi made me chamomile tea. It's helping." She gave him a tired smile. "What'd you need?"

"I was trying to remember the last time we saw the ledger. The morning of your accident, wasn't it?"

"Definitely." She grabbed her crutches. "Let's go take another look."

They followed her into the front room and she took a seat at the desk, swiveling the chair around, searching the shelves again, pulling several identical-looking ledgers from the shelves and placing them on the desk, going through them one by one.

Remi looked at Sam. "Why the grim expression, Fargo?"

"Hate to say it, I think someone sabotaged the deck."

"Warren . . ." Renee said. "Had I known that, I might've pushed him myself—" She stopped midsentence when Amal walked in the door.

"Where's Nasha?" Sam asked her.

"With my mother." She looked at the bookshelf, her face turning ashen. "Excuse me. I forgot something in the field."

Before anyone could comment, she hurried out the door.

CHAPTER SEVENTY-TWO

If you listen to the noise of the market,
you won't buy anything.
— AFRICAN PROVERB —

Remi watched through the window as Amal hurried off. "Wonder what that was about?"

"Perhaps," Hank said from behind her, "a little post-traumatic stress leftover from Nigeria? It'd certainly explain her odd behavior since she's been back."

Sam put his arm around Remi's shoulder. "You can find out what's going on when you pick her up later."

"Me?"

"I volunteered you to drive her to the market this afternoon."

"HOW'S NASHA?" REMI ASKED AS SHE DROVE AMAL INTO TOWN A couple of hours later. "She hasn't complained that you're keeping such a close watch on her?"

"I'm not sure she's noticed. Everything here's so new and strange to her."

"Glad to hear that. And how are you doing? You seemed a bit upset when I saw you walk into the office earlier."

"Oh. Sorry. I . . . I left my new phone in the field."

Certain Amal wasn't being truthful, Remi let it slide. "Send us the bill. Sam and I intend to pay for it."

"You don't have to do that."

"This is an argument you won't win. The only reason Makao got your phone was because you were at the school, as a favor to us."

When they reached the market, Remi parked. Amal checked her watch, then led Remi through a few narrow streets, stopping in front of the bright fruits and vegetables displayed in front of a store. "First thing, dates. Then *malsouka*."

"*Malsouka*? For *brik à l'oeuf*?" Remi asked. Though it had been years and years, Remi had never forgotten the triangle-shaped deep-fried pastries filled with tuna, capers, and egg that she and Renee had enjoyed during their study-abroad trip. "One of my favorite memories of Tunisia."

"I hope you'll like these. My mother adds a touch of crumbled goat cheese. Nasha's beyond excited about helping her make them."

"Can't wait to try it."

She and Remi wandered toward the next stall, where Amal picked up a fig, replaced it, and checked her watch once again.

"Are we okay on time?" Remi asked.

"Sorry. I think it's a nervous habit when I'm out shopping. I'm always worried about missing the bus." She quickly gathered a dozen dates, paid for them, and smiled at Remi. "Since we actually have extra time, there's a wonderful little shop not too far from here that I've always loved but never had much time to visit. Dr. LaBelle says it reminds her of an old-fashioned general store. It has a little bit of everything."

"Sounds fun. Maybe I can find something for the girls back at the school."

The two women worked their way through the pedestrians, then around the corner. "Here," Amal said, stopping in front of a two-story shop painted a deep turquoise. Racks of postcards and trinkets were displayed out front. Inside there was, as Amal said, a variety of goods, and she immediately gravitated toward the corner where bright bolts of cloth were stacked on shelves. She pulled out one, feeling the smooth texture of the material. "I'm tempted to get a few yards." She smiled again. "I bet they have better gift items upstairs. I'll meet you up there after I look over the material."

"Take your time." Remi passed by the tables filled with textiles and sewing notions, taking the winding tile stairs to the upper floor. A breeze swept in through the open arched doors of the balcony, causing the wind chimes hanging outside to tinkle merrily. A rack of wooden puppets on strings stared back at Remi. She thought of the girls at the school, wondering if they were too old for such a thing.

The chimes stirred again, drawing her to the balcony. Some were made from colored glass, others from brass bells. Those, she decided, would make for a nice gift, hanging in the trees outside the school. She started to reach for the bells but noticed Amal in the street below her, quickly walking away. As the young woman reached the corner, she looked back toward the shop.

Curious, Remi hurried down the stairs and followed. When she arrived at the corner, she looked around it. Amal, who had been striding at the same fast pace as Remi, had stopped about midway down the street and was knocking on a door. She started to turn away but stopped, pulling something small from her pocket—a slip of paper, possibly—and holding it toward whoever answered the door and she was talking to. After a bit of back-and-forth, she nodded, then started in Remi's direction.

Remi hurried back to the shop and up the stairs, picking up a horse puppet. Amal appeared just a couple of minutes later and Remi asked, "Find what you were looking for?"

"Sadly, no. I think I'll wait. Did you find anything?"

Remi held up the puppet. "As cute as this is, I think the girls might be a bit too old."

"Even Nasha?"

"Old beyond her years." She replaced the puppet and picked out a couple of wind chimes. "These, however, will be perfect for the courtyard trees."

"I agree."

They walked downstairs and Remi paid the merchant. As they left the shop, she looked over at Amal. "Your bags. Where are they?"

"I asked the shopkeeper to hold them while I looked around. I'll run back in and get them." A moment later, she returned with both shopping bags and the two women walked through the market. Amal seemed quieter than usual.

"Everything okay?" Remi asked.

"Fine. Just a bit tired. I was up early."

They passed a shop filled with incense, several sticks burning outside to lure in visitors, no doubt. Remi breathed in the pungent, sweet scent. "I'd forgotten how wonderful the market can be. So much to see . . . In fact, I thought I saw you taking off."

Amal stopped. "I . . ." She took a deep breath and looked at Remi, her smile fading as the scent of incense grew overwhelming. "I . . ." Her knees buckled and she sank to the ground, landing in a heap between her bags.

"Amal." Remi kneeled down beside her, checking for a pulse. Relieved when she found one, she scooped Amal into her arms as the passersby gave them wide berth. "Amal," she said, nearly choking on the strong incense herself as the smoke drifted up and over their heads.

A tall man with white hair and a goatee stepped out of the shop, saw them. "Do you need help?" he asked in French.

"I think she needs fresh air."

He nodded and picked up Amal, carrying her to a bench a few doors down. Remi grabbed the shopping bags and followed. "*Merci, Monsieur . . . ?*"

"Cussler," he said. "Would you like me to call the medics?"

"I think we'll be fine. Thank you."

He waited until he was sure Amal was okay, then returned to the shop. Remi patted Amal's cheek as the younger woman came to. "Are you okay?"

It took a moment before Amal answered. "I . . . I think so. One of my attacks, no doubt. One minute we were walking, the next I felt as though I'd stepped into another world. At first, I was looking down at water, seeing my reflection. But I realized I was really beneath the water, looking up." She sat up on her own, looking toward the shop. "I should know better than walking too close to that incense. I never could abide the stuff. It always made me feel . . . But this was different. Like a sense of panic."

Panic? Or more of a distraction because she knew that Remi had followed her?

CHAPTER SEVENTY-THREE

A patient person never misses a thing.
— SWAHILI PROVERB —

A mal seemed anxious," Remi said, calling out from the bathroom.

Sam, seated on the sofa in their hotel suite, heard Lazlo knock at the door. "About what?" he asked, getting up to answer it.

"I have no idea. From the moment we arrived to the moment she snuck off, she wasn't her usual self. Definitely hiding something."

"She never said where she went?"

"Not a word. And I couldn't really press the point when she fainted. I was more worried about getting her home after that."

"If we get a chance, we can ask her tomorrow at the dinner."

Remi walked out, clipping a barrette in her hair, as Sam and Lazlo took a seat at the table. "I'm not sure she'll even admit to it. I tried bringing it up again right before I dropped her off at her mother's house and she totally evaded the subject. It's all very strange," she said, then smiled at Lazlo. "Did Selma get back to you?"

"I just rang off with her. Unfortunately, the investigator you've hired has failed to find anything on Warren. If the man was in dire straits before he died, he hid it well. But Selma mentioned he has a few leads left."

"Let's hope they pan out," Remi said.

"What about Makao?" Sam asked.

"If Remi's shot actually hit him—"

"It did," she said with a firm nod.

"He hasn't shown up at any hospitals in Nigeria. Nor at any airport."

"Does she have any good news?"

"Possibly. She was able to dig up an address on that black market website that may give you enough to work with. Apparently, she matched up the listing from the stolen mosaic piece to a shop that specializes in hard-to-find antiques. Open by appointment only."

"Imagine that," Sam said as Remi took a seat next to him at the table.

"I'll text the address to your phone."

"You're not going with us?"

"As unexciting as that sounds," Lazlo replied, "I'm going to spend the rest of my afternoon doing some research. I'm intrigued by this jump rope song that Nasha was singing. I never could resist the lure of a hidden treasure, even if there is a curse attached to it."

"Your loss," Sam said. He brought up the address Lazlo sent on his phone's map and showed it to Remi.

"That's not too far from where Amal and I were today," she said.

In fact, it was very close, they realized after heading out. Remi pointed to the wind chimes tinkling from the balcony above them as they walked past. "She made a point to tell me I needed to look at what they were selling on the upper floor. No doubt to keep me from seeing her leave."

"Let's find the address," Sam said, following the directions on his phone.

When they turned the corner, she said, "That's definitely where Amal was. I'm sure of it."

"There?"

"About midway down on the right. I stood here, watching her."

They continued onto the narrow street. Sam stopped in front of the address listed on his phone's map. "Is this it?"

"Definitely the same place."

Sam rapped on the door. When there was no answer, he approached someone who was sweeping the area in front of the adjoining shop. "Excuse me. Do you know what sort of business this is?"

The man stared blankly.

Remi repeated the question in French.

"*Antiquités,*" he replied.

Remi thanked him and he went back to his sweeping.

"I have to say," Sam said, "I didn't expect that from Amal."

"There's got to be a good explanation."

Sam studied the shop for a few moments. "Ask him if anyone will be there if we return this evening. We'd like to talk to the owners."

Remi repeated the question. "Unfortunately, no. The shop is closed at night. He believes the man who owns the place lives out in the country, but he has no way to contact him."

Sam looked at the man, nodding. "*Merci,*" he said. "We'll stop by tomorrow."

He and Remi left. At the corner, he stopped to look back at the shop.

"Tomorrow?" Remi asked, almost in disbelief.

"Give or take a few hours."

Just after midnight, in fact. As in the past, they used a Bluetooth earpiece with their cell phones to communicate. They strolled down the narrow street where the antiquities shop was located, glad to see the area was completely deserted, every window dark. That bode well. Last thing they needed was a witness who might call the police.

When they reached the shop, Remi stood as lookout while Sam picked the lock and opened the door. Once they were inside, he checked for a control panel on the wall but found none.

"You'd think they'd have an alarm," Remi said as he locked the door behind them. "Especially if they're dealing in stolen antiques."

"Maybe they're not worried about anyone stealing from them." He took a quick look around. The front room was filled with artwork, Roman vases, and knickknacks artfully placed upon the antique furniture.

Remi lifted an Etruscan vase. "No wonder they don't have this place alarmed. These are fake."

"So why is a place dealing in fraudulent antiques selling the real deal?"

She returned the vase to the shelf. "Who's to say they aren't trying to sell these as the real deal?"

"I'll check down here, you check upstairs."

Sam began his search in the front room. Finding nothing of interest, he moved down the hall to a small office, seeing a scarred mahogany desk covered with papers. Invoices, he realized as he shined his flashlight across them. Apparently, the Roman antiques they were selling out front were made in China.

As he looked them over, he heard a scrape coming from the floor above him. "Remi? Everything okay?"

"Fine. Looks like this is mostly inventory, still boxed up. Guess where all their antiquities come from?"

"China?"

"How'd you know?

"Psychic," he said, finding a piece of paper tucked in the corner of the desk blotter. He slipped it out, saw what looked like a hand-drawn map of the archeological park with an arrow pointing at the far end.

LaBelle's site.

He put the map into his pocket and opened the top desk drawer, finding several more invoices clipped together along with a note that said *Envoi*.

"Sam." Remi's soft voice in his earpiece held a note of tension. "There's someone coming."

He grabbed the stack, rolled it into a tube, and shoved it into his back pocket, then drew his gun. "On my way." He moved into the hall, gun at the ready. "I don't hear anything, Remi. You're sure?"

"I'm at the balcony. They're walking this way from the corner," she said. "Hold on . . . Definitely coming this way."

"How many?"

"Two. They're at the door."

CHAPTER SEVENTY-FOUR

Don't seek to hurt any man;
but if any man seeks to hurt, you may break his neck.
— AFRICAN PROVERB —

S am heard the sound of keys dropping, then someone fumbling
with the lock.

Finally, the door opened.

Sam slipped behind an antique bureau and edged his way around
it, keeping it between him and the two men as they entered. One of
the men stumbled down the hallway, his words slurring as he said
something about using the bathroom. The other stood a few feet
away, pulling a pack of cigarettes from his pocket. He dropped the
pack, swore, and leaned down to pick it up. Sam couldn't be positive, but he looked like the same man who tried to steal Renee's
purse at the ruins.

"Hamida? . . . That you?" the man said as his unfocused eyes
landed on Sam's shoes. Slowly, he straightened, reaching for his gun.
"You're not Ham—"

Sam, gripping his revolver like a set of iron knuckles, drove his
weighted fist into the guy's jaw. His head snapped back, slamming
into the wall, his gun firing into the ceiling as he slumped to the
ground.

"Tarek?" Hamida called out as Remi appeared in the stairwell.
"What's going on out there?"

Sam took her hand as Hamida stumbled from the hall.

"Sorry." Sam guided Remi through the doorway. "Looks like your friend had a bit too much to drink."

"You . . ." He tried to draw his gun from his holster.

Sam rushed out, pulling the door closed.

Crack!

Wood splintered behind him as he raced after Remi. A second shot rang out as they turned the corner, the sharp retort echoing between the buildings.

"That was close," Sam said once they reached their car.

"You realize who they were? The two from the hotel."

"Had I known earlier, I would've clocked the other guy, too."

"Considering they tried to kidnap me," she said, buckling her seat belt, "your restraint is exemplary."

"Only because we were the ones breaking in. Not exactly the time or place to kill anyone."

"I suppose you're right. It would take a lot of explaining." She sighed. "I just can't see Amal being involved in this."

"Well, she's involved somehow. Which means we're going to have to confront her about it. Especially after finding this." He handed Remi the slip of paper. "A map to the house—and the dig site where Warren's body was found."

Remi turned on the cab light for a better look. "Oh no . . . There has to be a logical explanation."

"I can't wait to hear it. I also found a bunch of invoices for assorted antiquities that were possibly shipped out. It'll give us a good place to start our search for the stolen fragment."

He handed Remi the roll of papers. She looked at a few and put them in the glove box. "I hope you're wrong about Amal. She was so good with the girls. I couldn't have asked for a better companion when Makao and his thugs broke into the school."

"You can question her tomorrow."

But Amal wasn't at the dig the following afternoon when Remi and Sam arrived, nor was she at Renee's house when they checked there.

Renee, no longer using her crutches, invited them to the kitchen table for coffee. Hank was at the stove, stir-frying rice and vegetables, the scent of hot olive oil filling the room. José was at the sink washing his lunch dishes. He nodded in greeting as he set them wet in the rack. "Heading out," he said when he'd finished.

"Sit," Renee told Sam and Remi, bringing over a pot of coffee and two mugs. "It's sort of a free-for-all at mealtime."

"So I see," Remi said. "Where's Amal? Isn't she usually out in the field in the afternoon?"

"Usually," Renee said as she poured their coffee. "Did she say anything to you, Hank?"

He turned off the burner and looked back at them. "She took the day off to help her mother with the big dinner tonight. Anything wrong?"

"Probably not," Remi said. "She had one of her episodes yesterday at the market."

"But she usually recovers pretty fast," Renee said.

Hank scraped the vegetables and fried rice into a large serving bowl and carried it to the table. "Have you eaten yet? We have plenty."

Sam and Remi declined.

"LaBelle. Aren't you forgetting something?"

"Yes. Be right back." She left the room, then returned a moment later, handing Sam the missing ledger. "I found it last night. Somehow, we looked right past it."

Sam opened it, turning the pages, studying the entries while they ate.

"What is it?" Remi asked when she noticed him pausing and turning back to the previous page.

"A few pages are missing."

Renee set her fork down. "That's impossible. There was nothing missing when Hank and I went over them together."

"When was that?" Sam asked.

"When we first discovered there was a problem."

"They're not there now." Sam opened the book wide. "You can see where they were torn out."

"The burglary," Hank said. "We couldn't figure out what was taken. That had to be it."

"Warren?" Renee leaned back in her chair, looking sick to her stomach. "I know I shouldn't speak ill of the dead, but why can't he just leave us alone?"

Sam looked up from the book. "Where'd you end up finding it?"

"With the other ledgers," Hank said. "It was out of order."

Sam checked his watch and stood, tucking the ledger beneath his arm. "I'd really like to take a closer look at this, but not right now."

"You're leaving?" Renee asked.

"We have a few errands to run before dinner tonight. We'll check in with you later."

Remi, picking up on Sam's hint, turned to Renee. "If we get done in time, maybe I'll swing by and we can visit some more." She followed Sam out the door. Once they were in the car, she asked, "Why are we rushing out?"

"This," he said, handing Remi the ledger. "The dates of the missing pages are right around the same time Amal came to work at the site. I want to get a copy of it to Selma. I think we need a fresh eye."

Remi looked through it while Sam drove. "Please tell me you don't think Amal's behind the embezzlement and artifact theft?"

"I have no idea. I'm just pointing out the obvious. After her odd reaction yesterday when she saw us looking for the journal, then the secret meeting at the market, we have to admit Amal is far more involved in this than we thought."

"I refuse to believe that."

He glanced over at her as she studied the ledger. "Refuse all you want, Remi. Something is going on with her. Remember when we saw her out at the ruins on our first day? You asked her about it. She denied being there."

"Maybe it was a misunderstanding."

"Maybe. But the guy I saw tonight looked an awful lot like the guy who stole Dr. LaBelle's purse that same day. My suggestion? Watch her closely at dinner tonight. And keep an open mind."

CHAPTER SEVENTY-FIVE

A small house will hold a hundred friends.
— AFRICAN PROVERB —

"My mother, Yesmine," Amal said, smiling at a woman who looked very much like she could have been Amal's older sister. "This is Mr. and Mrs. Fargo and their friend Professor Lazlo Kemp. The Fargos are the couple who've financed the excavation."

"So glad you could join us," Yesmine said, smiling at them. "Amal's told me so much, I feel as if I know you all quite well. Please, come in. My home is your home."

"A very nice home," Lazlo said.

Nasha raced in from the kitchen. "You're here. Wait until you see what I helped make."

"I can't wait," Remi said, wrapping her in a tight hug. As she let go, her gaze caught on the aged-bronze Sator Square sitting on the mantel. "The famed charcoal burner lid," she said, walking over for a closer look. Slightly bigger than her hand, she marveled at the workmanship. "I hear this is why Dr. LaBelle expanded the search for more Bulla Regia ruins."

Yesmine beamed. "My daughter's a very good storyteller."

"Amal regaled us with stories about this when we were"—Remi checked Amal, saw her worried expression, recalling that she hadn't told her mother what had happened at the school—"discussing archeology to the kids," she finished, noting the look of relief in the young woman's eyes. "It's a lovely piece."

Nasha's eyes sparkled. "It's a palindrome square. *Sator, arepo . . .*" She hopped as though skipping rope and suddenly stopped. "I don't remember the rest."

Yesmine glanced at the artifact. "My mother found it when she was a girl."

"Amal tells me there's supposed to be a curse tied into all of this," Remi said.

Yesmine laughed. "I'm not so sure about that. Like Amal, my mother was a bit of a storyteller herself. But yes, supposedly a curse that kept others from finding the ancient scroll buried by one of the Vandal kings." Her eyes sparkled as she looked at the artifact, then at Remi and Sam. "The curse will bring death to any who try to take the scroll for their own. If I remember, it's only one of royal blood who can return it without invoking the curse."

"Which," Amal said, "I've never understood. It can't just be a Good Samaritan, it has to be a royal Good Samaritan."

"Were your grandmother still here, she'd tell you that there was always a reason for those oddities in the old tales, even though it might not be obvious to the storyteller."

"I miss her," Amal replied as someone knocked at the front door. She walked over to answer it.

"As do I," Yesmine said as Renee, Hank, José, and Osmond walked in. "My mother had much to do with nurturing Amal's love of archeology."

Renee laughed. "Thank goodness or we'd all be out of a job."

Osmond, his face beaming, handed a bouquet of flowers to Amal.

She thanked him and turned to her mother, saying, "How sweet. Osmond brought you flowers again."

"Again?" Remi whispered to Sam.

Poor Osmond appeared crestfallen. Nasha tapped Amal on the

arm, looking as if she was about to correct her as to who the bouquet was for. But Renee held up two bottles of chilled sparkling water, since neither Amal nor her mother drank alcohol. "We need something to toast with."

"Perfect," Yesmine said. "This way. It's such a nice evening, I thought we'd eat outside."

Twinkling lights strung across the branches of the nearest olive trees cast a festive glow across the picnic table draped with a white cloth. Amal and her mother brought out plates stacked high with the deep-fried *brik* triangles, followed by bowls of couscous, spicy chicken, and other Tunisian dishes.

When everyone took a seat, Nasha slipping in between Remi and Amal, Amal's mother raised her water glass. "To good friends, old and new."

Sam and Remi raised their glasses. "To good friends," they said.

Renee raised hers, saying, "To the best graduate students a professor could ever hope for."

Amal smiled and cocked her head, down the hill and through the dark grove, toward the house Renee rented for their crew. "Here's to hoping this dig lasts for a long time. No long bus rides for me."

José laughed, saying, "Hear! Hear!"

"'Hear! Hear!' What does that mean?" Nasha asked Amal.

"A short way of saying that's exactly what we want to hear."

Hank gave the final toast. "To good food. I vote we eat before it all gets cold."

"Hear! Hear!" Nasha said. Everyone laughed. And, with that, they passed the dishes.

Remi was surprised when Yesmine handed her the plate of *brik*, saying, "Amal tells me this is a favorite of yours?"

"My memory of it, it's been years." Remi took two and passed the dish to Sam, then Lazlo. "Not since I was here with Renee back in college." She took a bite and closed her eyes, savoring the explosion of flavors and tang of goat cheese. "Even better than I remembered."

At one point during the dinner, Nasha elbowed Remi, grinning. She apparently had noticed the same thing that Remi had. Osmond spent almost the entire time stealing glances at Amal. It was clear he was smitten with her.

Amal seemed totally unaware of his attention.

Well into their meal, the conversation turned toward the new fragments the graduate students were uncovering. "Unfortunately," Amal said, "it's nothing as wonderful as the Sator Square my grandmother found. I'm not that lucky."

"Nonsense," Renee said. "If not for you walking into my class that day, then writing your thesis, we'd never have found that subterranean chamber to begin with."

"You got that right," Hank said. "LaBelle would still be digging in exactly the wrong spot on the exact opposite side of the archeological park if not for you. It's a shame that Warren almost ruined it for the rest of us."

"Speaking of," José said. "I heard the police don't think he fell at all."

Hank lowered his water glass to the table. "Where'd you hear that?"

"One of my friends at the British works," José said.

Renee glanced at Remi. "I suspected something like this. The police have asked me to come down to the station tomorrow morning. No doubt to tell me it was"—she gave Nasha a quick look, noting she seemed more interested in the *brik* triangles on her plate than the conversation at the table, Renee lowering her voice anyway—"self-inflicted, would be my guess."

Remi turned toward Sam. "We're not letting her go down there by herself."

"Remi's right. We'll go to the police with you."

"Let me," Hank said.

"You're needed here," Renee told him. "The Fargos have more experience with this sort of thing. Offer accepted." She gave a tired sigh. "I vote we change the subject. I actually have some good news. The university received an endowment and they intend to funnel some of that money into the archeology department—once everything's sorted out, that is," she said with an apologetic smile toward Remi.

They tossed around ideas about where that money would best be put to use. Eventually, the conversation drifted into the happenings at other sites in the archeological park.

Osmond pulled out his phone, accessing a video. "Did any of you see the prank that the Brits pulled off? They hung a plastic skeleton on fishing line in the entrance to the amphitheater . . . Watch."

Nasha gasped. "Were they scared?"

"Very," he said, passing the phone to Renee, who held it so she and Lazlo could see it together.

"Brilliant," Lazlo said.

Renee laughed. "This is great. Where's Amal? She needs to see this."

Her mother looked up at them. "I think she was clearing dishes."

Remi's gaze wandered toward the olive trees and she was surprised to see a light at the bottom of the hill where none had been just a few minutes before. She nudged Sam with her knee. "I think someone might be in the office."

Sam looked that direction. "You're sure it isn't a reflection?"

"I don't think so."

He studied it a moment longer, then stood, holding his hand out to his wife. "After all this great food, I need to stretch my legs. It's a lovely night for a walk."

"Exactly what I was thinking," she said.

Lazlo bowed his head to them and launched into a tale of the treasure he hunted for but never found in Laos, drawing everyone's attention.

But Nasha saw them and followed. "I want to go for a walk."

"Nasha?" Yesmine called. "Ready to help me with the dessert?"

That did the trick. As she raced back to the table, Sam and Remi strolled through the yard, ducking below the low-growing branches of the olive trees that surrounded it. The laughter and conversation faded as they continued down the slope through the grove, toward the small house rented to the archeologists.

About twenty-five yards away, Sam saw a flash in the window. "Definitely something going on inside there."

"If everyone's up at the party . . ."

"My thoughts exactly," he said, searching the front of the house. The door and windows were shut. Nothing looked disturbed. "Let's check around back."

As he and Remi stopped at the corner, he peered around it, then pointed.

The door was open.

CHAPTER SEVENTY-SIX

*Tell your friend a lie. If he keeps it secret,
then tell him the truth.*
— AFRICAN PROVERB —

S am drew his gun, moved to the threshold, and motioned for
Remi to wait at the door. Whoever was in there wasn't too
worried about being overheard. He entered the kitchen, walked
down the hall to the dining room, stopping at the arched entrance to
the front of the house that the archeologists used for an office. When
he looked around the corner, he saw Amal picking through the
books on the shelves. He called her name.

She jumped, turning toward him, her hand flying to her heart.
"You scared me."

"What are you doing?"

"I . . . I wanted to find the missing ledger."

"Is there anyone here with you?"

"No, of course not."

Remi joined them, shocked to see Amal. "What on earth?"

The young woman gave them a sad shrug. "I know this looks
bad, but it's not what you think. I came down to search for the missing ledger. I wanted to prove it wasn't Warren who was stealing."

"Renee found it and gave it to us. There were pages missing."

Amal's mouth dropped open. "I didn't know. But you have to
believe me, I only wanted to help."

Sam moved to the window, peeking between the slats of the

blinds, seeing Renee and Hank heading down the hill toward the house. "Yes, well, I'm not the one you'll have to convince."

Amal jumped up from her chair to look out the window. "Oh no. What do I tell them?"

"The truth," Remi said.

She looked at them in desperation. "I can't."

"What about the market?" Sam asked.

"The market?"

Remi said, "When you took off on your own and knocked on that door."

Amal seemed surprised she'd been caught. "I . . . When I found out that's where he tried to sell the stolen artifact, I had to see for myself."

The front door opened and she clamped her mouth shut. Hank stood at the threshold, Renee right behind him. "What's going on?" Hank asked.

Remi smiled at them. "Amal was asking about the girls back at the school and if they'd found Makao. She didn't want her mother to overhear. For obvious reasons."

Sam had no idea why his wife decided to defend Amal, but he wasn't about to sideline her efforts. "We thought we'd have more privacy down here."

"Without the lights?" Hank said, turning them on.

Renee moved past him, her focus on Amal. "You haven't told your mother what happened?"

"How could I?" Amal said. "If she knew, she'd never let me out of her sight again."

"True. I doubt she would," Renee said. "And she's going to figure out something if she discovers you're not at the dinner."

"She's right," Remi said. "We probably should have left this conversation until tomorrow." She moved to Sam's side. "Why don't we head back up to the house before we're missed."

Thankfully, Nasha had kept Amal's mother occupied, helping to serve dessert, and hadn't noticed their absence, and Lazlo was still entertaining the two young men with treasure hunting stories. When the dinner ended and they bade their good-byes, Amal walked Sam, Remi, and Lazlo to their car. "Thank you for not saying anything."

Remi clasped the younger woman's hand. "We'll finish this conversation tomorrow. It's important."

"Of course. I know." When her mother and Nasha appeared in the doorway, Amal stepped back, waving at them as they drove off.

"Nice dinner," Lazlo said from the backseat. "How was your little adventure?"

Remi buckled her seat belt. "Interesting. Just not sure what to make of it. It was Amal."

Sam glanced over at her. "Exactly why did you stop her from explaining what she was up to?"

"A time and place for everything, Fargo."

"And what was wrong with that time and place?" he asked, driving down the hill.

"It was clear she was uncomfortable talking about it in front of Renee and Hank."

"You think?"

"I want to know why first."

Sam had learned long ago not to question his wife's instinct even when it defied logic. "Tomorrow," he said. "Because like it or not, Amal is involved in whatever's going on." He slowed at the sight of an SUV parked at the side of the road at the bottom of the hill—one he might not have seen had it not been for the moonlight reflecting off the vehicle's roof.

"What's wrong?" she asked.

"Up ahead."

"That's an unusual parking spot." Remi opened the glove box, pulling out her gun. "Shall we investigate?"

Walking up to a car in the dark was a good way to get killed. "Let's drive by, see what happens."

"Brilliant plan," Lazlo said.

"Spoilsports," Remi said.

Sam continued past, his headlights sweeping across the car as they approached the curve—too quick to make out much more than two men sitting inside. "I wonder if those are our friends from the market."

"The kidnappers from the hotel?" Remi fingered her gun. "Wish I'd got a better look."

The vehicle pulled out the moment they drove past. "You might get a second opportunity. They're following us . . . Better duck, Lazlo. Never know what might happen."

Lazlo slunk down in his seat. "Remind me again why I decided to tag along?"

CHAPTER SEVENTY-SEVEN

Wisdom does not come overnight.
— SOMALI PROVERB —

Sam checked the rearview mirror as he drove down the hill, leaving the olive groves behind. So far, the dark-colored SUV was keeping its distance. "Why follow us? If it's the same two who tried to kidnap you and Renee, it's not like they don't know which hotel we're staying at."

Remi looked over at him and cocked her head toward the back-seat and Lazlo. "If that's supposed to make us feel better, it doesn't."

"Just stating a fact."

Lazlo cleared his throat. "There's a lot of empty highway between here and the hotel. Maybe you could drive a bit faster?"

"Remi," Sam said, ignoring him. "There's something incredibly wrong about all this."

"Besides the fact we're being chased by kidnappers?"

"Nigerian kidnappers, Tunisian kidnappers. What does any of it have to do with Warren and the embezzled money?"

She pulled her attention from the side-view mirror to look at him. "I'm not sure this is the time to worry about any inconsistencies. They're gaining on us."

"Make sure your seat belts are buckled tight." Sam hit the gas pedal. The Audi RS shot forward, leaving the other car far behind. There was no way the SUV could match their speed on the curves without rolling over. Even so, he didn't relax until they reached the city, then the hotel, where security had been beefed up to quell the fears of the other guests after the earlier kidnapping attempt.

As they strolled past the armed guards at the front entrance, Sam took Remi's arm and looked at Lazlo, saying, "You have to admit, no one's getting past the guards in the lobby."

Remi smiled at the uniformed men as Sam held the door for her and Lazlo. "Back to the 'something incredibly wrong' thing," she said as they crossed the lobby toward the elevator. "Exactly what do we have wrong?"

"The order of everything." He pressed the elevator button. The door opened and they stepped on. "Like I said before, I think it all started here. Someone here contacted Makao and his gang."

Remi looked at him as they rode up to the top floor. "Warren? But he's dead."

"Yes," Lazlo said. "But that doesn't mean he didn't start this nightmare. Only that he's not the one finishing it. And if anyone wants my opinion, I quite suspect that he didn't fall. Nor did he kill himself. It'd be nice to know what evidence they have."

"Exactly," Sam said. "I'm worried that doesn't bode well for Dr. LaBelle."

Remi glared at him. "This is all your fault, Fargo."

"How's it my fault?"

"None of this would've happened if you hadn't discovered that someone was skimming money."

"I distinctly recall you helping me."

"Well, I wouldn't have had I'd known Renee might get arrested. I'm not letting my friend go to jail for something she didn't do. You need to do something."

Lazlo pulled his key card from his wallet. "As knackered as I am, I'll let you two work out the details. I'm going to bed."

"Good night, Lazlo," Remi said as he continued down the hall.

She turned back to Sam, her green eyes troubled. "So how are you going to fix this?"

Sam put the safety lock on the door behind them and took out his phone, saying, "Renee doesn't need me to fix this. She'll need an attorney."

"And where are you going to find one of those at this hour?"

"I'm not. But I'll bet Rube has a connection at the U.S. embassy who can help until we do find one."

AS PROMISED, RUBE SET UP A MEETING WITH AN OFFICIAL FROM THE embassy, Brian Torres, at a coffeehouse not too far from the police department. The solemn-faced official was there when the Fargos, Lazlo, and Renee arrived.

"Thanks for coming at such short notice, Mr. Torres," Sam said.

"As requested, I was able to make a few inquiries into the nature of why the police are interested in seeing Dr. LaBelle. Why don't we sit?"

As they walked toward an empty table, Renee leaned toward Remi and, lowering her voice, said, "Are all embassy officials this serious?"

"I think it's in the contract."

Once they were seated, Renee said, "I'm assuming, Mr. Torres, that this is all routine and my friends are being overcautious."

He showed no emotion. "In this case, their instincts are correct. The police believe that Warren Smith was murdered."

"Murdered?" She stared at him a moment. "Who would do that?"

"Possibly someone who had a grievance with him. I'm sorry to say, Dr. LaBelle, they believe that person is you."

"Me? But . . ."

"They plan to arrest you when you arrive at the police station. I will, of course, accompany you."

Renee gripped the tabletop. "Why would anyone think I killed him? We were friends."

Sam said, "They must have some sort of evidence beyond a suspicion?"

"Her prints," Torres replied. "On the murder weapon."

"What murder weapon?" Remi asked. "I thought he fell."

"He did. After he was stabbed with a chisel." Torres focused on Renee. "The chisel was found beneath his body. Any chance you know how your fingerprints ended up on it?"

"I picked it up."

"When?" he asked.

"After I discovered someone removed Echo's face from the floor."

"The police didn't take the chisel for evidence?" Remi asked.

"I didn't find it until after they left. I was more worried about the damage to the mosaic. I just picked it up. I wasn't thinking it would be used for murder the very next day." She turned toward Torres. "So, how do I get out of this?"

"You don't. At least, not the arrest. But our presence will go a long way in making sure you're taken care of and treated fairly. It helps that you're known and respected in the community."

Remi moved her chair closer, placing her hand on top of Renee's. "I'm sure it'll all get cleared up soon. We'll get the best attorney we can."

She nodded, her lips tremulous. "Thank goodness you're both here."

"We're not leaving Tunisia until we get to the bottom of it. Right, Sam?"

"No. Definitely not. What's our next step?" he asked Torres.

"Think like a prosecutor. Figuring out the motive is a good start."

"What about the embezzlement?" Renee said. "The money we think Warren stole from the archeological dig."

"Which," Torres said, "must have made you angry when you found out."

"Of course it did."

"Angry enough to kill him?"

"No."

"That's what the police think. My point, Dr. LaBelle, is that once you find out why someone wanted Warren dead, you'll be that much closer to figuring out who murdered him." He looked at Sam. "After talking with Rubin Haywood last night, I have a feeling that this is where I need to excuse myself and give you some privacy."

"I'll wait with you," Lazlo said. "I could use a bit of fresh air."

"Privacy for what?" Renee asked Sam.

He waited until the two men walked out the door. "When it comes to finding answers, sometimes the most expedient route isn't necessarily the most legal route. Especially if the police are involved."

Renee slumped back in her chair. "I can't let you two risk everything you've built . . ."

"Too late." Remi gave her hand a squeeze, then looked at Sam. "Let's call Selma and see what she's put together for us."

CHAPTER SEVENTY-EIGHT

Ears are usually uninvited guests.
— AFRICAN PROVERB —

While Sam called Selma, Remi consoled her friend, wishing she had a way to reassure her that all would be well. "I think Sam's right. There's no way Warren's murder is about the embezzled money."

Before Renee could comment, Sam placed the phone on the table so the three of them could hear and see Selma on the video call. "No doubt," Sam said, "our untimely arrival in Tunisia might've put a damper on whatever they were after."

Selma agreed, saying, "Even Lazlo thinks there's something more to this dig."

Remi concurred. "He has a nose for these things."

"If we're lucky," Selma continued, "one of those invoices you found belongs to the missing piece of mosaic. Find that mosaic, you might find out who's behind this."

"What invoices?" Renee asked.

"In this case," Sam said, "the less you know—"

"I'm going to be arrested for murder, so if given the choice between the expedient route and the legal route . . ."

"Point taken." He told her about the midnight visit to the antiquities shop.

Renee listened intently. "That sounds like the same place that

Hank went to look for the mosaic. It was already sold by the time he got there. What I don't understand is what led you there?"

"It was actually Remi and—"

Remi, not wanting to add to Renee's burden by implicating Amal, kicked Sam's foot and said, "It was supposed to be a surprise. We wanted to find Echo so you could get the mosaic repaired. Right, Sam?"

"Right," he said, recovering quickly. "The invoices are all antiques and art houses."

"And what?" Renee asked. "You're just going to walk in and ask them?"

Remi smiled. "In a roundabout way."

Renee's brows rose as she looked from Remi to Sam. "How long have you been planning this?"

"Since last night," Remi replied. "Selma put together a legend for us, like the spies use. I can't wait to see what she's come up with. Auction house? Buyer for a museum?"

"Or," Selma said, "Mr. and Mrs. Longstreet, a well-to-do husband and wife in search of the perfect antique."

"Longstreet," Remi said on hearing her maiden name. "Has a certain ring to it, don't you think, Renee?"

Sam moaned, then asked Selma, "You couldn't come up with a better name?"

"Smith was taken."

Sam gave a mock sigh. "There'll be no living with her over this. So, Selma, who are the Longstreets this time around?"

"Since we had some good success with your import/export business when you were searching for the Gray Ghost, I tapped into that website and changed it up a bit, moving you from Texas to Boston. This time, you're searching for antiquities for your winter home in the South of France."

"Old money," Remi said. "Always a good sign."

"In this case, the Longstreet fortune was made during Prohibition, smuggling alcohol, which is why you're not averse to the bending of the rules—should they decide to search your names on the Web. By the way, I looked up each of the five businesses from the invoices. They all deal in questionable goods."

"Perfect," Remi said. "We're all about the gray area." Her smile faded at the tension she saw in Renee's face. Remi gave her a thorough hug. "You'll be out in no time."

"Maybe not that soon," Renee said. "But knowing you and Sam are here, and Mr. Torres will be with me when I turn myself in, I feel a whole lot better."

WITH RENEE SAFELY IN THE HANDS OF THE EMBASSY, THEY GOT TO work immediately. Lazlo played chauffeur, parking just out of sight—ready backup in case anything went wrong. They struck out on the first two locations. As Sam and Remi entered the third establishment, which billed itself as an art gallery, a young woman sitting at a mahogany desk looked up at them, her expression vacant. "*Vous désirez, s'il vous plaît?*"

Remi's demeanor was equally vacant as she perused the interior. Though French was one of the many languages she spoke fluently, she often found it useful to pretend she knew only English. "You were recommended by my interior designer," she said and looked at the woman. "I was told that if I wanted authenticity, this was the place to visit."

The woman sized them up, no doubt trying to decide if they could afford to shop there. "One moment, please. I'll get the manager, Monsieur Karim." She disappeared down a hallway at the back of the store and returned about two minutes later with a white-haired man in a dark suit.

He smiled at them both, then directed his attention to Sam. "May I help you find anything in particular?"

"You'll have to ask my wife. I'm just here to write the check."

"Of course. And so I may know whom I have the pleasure of assisting . . . ?"

"Sean Longstreet," Sam said, "and my wife, Rebecca."

"A pleasure to make your acquaintance. Please, come in, feel free to look around." He followed them about the room as they stopped to admire figurine after figurine. "And where are you visiting from?"

"Boston," Remi said. "We were in Italy for business. My husband's, of course. I came along for the shopping."

"What sort of business, if you don't mind my asking?"

Sam said, "SRF Import/Export."

"Import/export." Karim glanced at the young woman, who was waiting just outside the hallway near the back of the store, giving her the slightest of nods. After she left, he clasped his hands together, smiling. "And what brings you to Tunisia?"

"A side trip," Remi said, picking up a small statue of a satyr. "A friend of mine found some stunning antiques in your country. I'm hoping to find something equally stunning for my own home." She returned the statue to the shelf and gave a disinterested look around the room. "I was hoping for something to hang on the wall."

"Perhaps something like this . . ." He led her toward the back of the shop, pointing to a large embossed copper plate mounted on a stand. "This one is a sublime example of a Roman charioteer, circa early seventeenth century."

Remi reached out, touching the small card set in front of it that listed the price at seventy-five hundred dinars, which put it over twenty-five hundred dollars. "It's beautiful," Remi said, "but not quite what I'm looking for."

"And what is it you're looking for, madame?"

"Something that will give the room more of an ancient Roman villa look. Rustic, but with a much needed pop of color." She sighed. "Sadly, while in Italy we didn't have time for a proper shopping trip and all we found were cheap reproductions."

"And your budget would be . . . ?"

"Budget?" Remi looked at him. "If I find the right piece, I'm willing to pay whatever it takes to acquire it. I don't suppose you can recommend a shop that carries the rare, authentic pieces?"

Sam, doing a splendid job of looking bored, frowned at his watch, then looked at Karim. "I hate to cut this short, but we're under a time constraint. Is this all you have?"

Karim hesitated the barest of instances. "Let me check to see if any of our new stock is ready for sale. Sometimes we set pieces aside for the more discriminating buyer. I'll return shortly." He walked to the hall. "Leila?"

The young woman stepped out of the office. Remi moved closer, pretending interest in a nineteenth-century vase while listening to Leila telling him in rapid-fire French that her internet search brought up their import/export business and the profiles of its very wealthy owners.

"*C'est une bonne nouvelle,*" he replied and turned their direction, his grin wide. "My assistant tells me we do have some items new to our inventory and not yet out on the floor. This way, please. I think you'll find what you're looking for back here."

CHAPTER SEVENTY-NINE

A man does not run among thorns for no reason;
either he is chasing a snake or a snake is chasing him.
— AFRICAN PROVERB —

Monsieur Karim led Sam and Remi down the narrow hall to a room with a digital lock. He stood so that he blocked the keypad from their view as he entered the code. It clicked and he pushed the door open. "Perhaps you'll find something in here more to your liking."

The Echo mosaic was set on a small easel to their left next to an Etruscan vase and numerous pieces of jewelry displayed on black velvet. Remi, however, turned to the right, leading Sam past several Roman busts on pedestals. She stopped to look at them and shook her head. "No," she said, moving past. "I'm not sure I want them watching me."

She paused to look at a mariner's brass astrolabe, then wandered over to the table, admiring the jewelry, finally stopping before the fragment of Echo's face. "I love the vibrant colors in this mosaic. Is she anybody important?"

"I believe, madame, that she is thought to be a wood nymph."

"It's very charming." She leaned in for a closer look. "You're sure it's genuine?"

"This artifact is from one of the subterranean villas in ancient Bulla Regia. It's a fine specimen, thought to be from the Hadrianic era."

Remi studied it for a few more seconds before continuing around the room, admiring other objects, eventually returning to the mosaic. "I do like this the best. I think it would look perfect in my solarium. How much?"

"One hundred thousand."

"Dinar?" Remi asked.

"Dollars."

"U.S.?" Sam asked in mock disbelief. "For a handful of stones set in a chunk of plaster?"

"But I want it," Remi said.

"Will you take fifty?" Sam asked Karim.

"I'm authorized to go as low as seventy-five."

"Is it stolen?" Remi asked.

"Madame, I assure you the provenance is without question."

Remi furrowed her brow. "That's not what I asked. I need to know how to declare this for Customs."

"What my wife means is that getting things out of one country and into another, as I'm sure you're aware, can sometimes be problematic."

"Of course. With the purchase, we'd be willing to provide a receipt with a separate cash value—and, if need be, a letter of authenticity from one of our local artists, declaring it to be an original reproduction."

"Hmm . . ." Remi pretended to study it, then looked at Sam. "What do you think?"

First and foremost, that they'd been there far too long. He looked at his watch. "I'm not the one who wants the thing. Whatever you decide, make it quick. We have a plane to catch."

Remi smiled at the man. "I'll take it. How soon can you have it boxed up?"

"As soon as we receive payment. Cash or wire transfer only."

"Wire," Sam said.

"If you'll follow me, I can give you the details for the transfer." He led them to the front of the store, where the young woman pulled a card from the mahogany desk, holding it out.

Sam took it. "I'll call my banker and have the money wired over."

The man beamed at them. "We'll prepare it for shipment. If you'll wait here, I won't be but a few minutes."

As he returned to the back room, he addressed the young woman. "Please see to our guests while I package their purchase."

While Remi pretended to be absorbed in the various antiques around the store, Sam texted Selma to make the transfer. Not quite fifteen minutes later, Lazlo texted that two men were approaching, one with a black eye. Sam positioned himself at the front of the shop, staring with presumed disinterest out the window, seeing Remi's would-be kidnappers about to descend on them.

Sam looked over at the young woman seated at her desk. "We're on a tight schedule. Do you know how much longer?"

"I'll check," she said.

The moment she left, Sam walked over to Remi and drew her behind an antique armoire. "Company," he said quietly, indicating the front window.

She looked that direction. "What do you suppose they're doing here?"

"I expect we're about to find out."

Sam and Remi edged their way around the armoire as the two men walked into the gallery, then made their way toward the back. The young woman blocked them as they tried to get down the hallway. "Monsieur Karim," she called out. "Tarek and Hamida are here." She looked up at Tarek's bruised face. "What happened to you?"

"None of your business. Karim," he shouted.

The older man stepped out. "I wasn't expecting you today."

"We've decided to remove the mosaic and list it elsewhere," Tarek said.

"Unfortunately, it's already sold. Today, in fact."

That brought the pair up short. "Who bought it?" Hamida asked.

"The couple waiting up front."

"What couple?"

"They were here a minute ago. Maybe they stepped out. But should you be worried, I sold it for twice the asking price."

"The nerve," Remi whispered and elbowed Sam. "We need to do something before we lose that mosaic."

"Are you kidding? I just paid seventy-five K for that thing." He pointed to the hallway. "I'll distract them. You text Lazlo to call the police, then get Echo."

Remi nodded, walked over, and positioned herself next to the wall, pressing back so she wouldn't be seen. The moment she was in place, Sam walked toward the shop entrance, calling out, "I'm sorry, were you looking for me?"

CHAPTER EIGHTY

Do not provoke the anger of a strong man.
— AFRICAN PROVERB —

Several thoughts flashed through Tarek's mind as he looked down the hall and saw Sam Fargo standing in the doorway. First and foremost was that he should have paid more attention to Makao's warning. The Fargos were far more dangerous than the typical people they were used to bilking and robbing. Second was that he was going to relish wiping that smug, taunting look off Fargo's face. "After him."

Fargo slipped out the door, but Hamida hesitated. "Shouldn't we wait for Ben?"

"Now. Before he gets away." He pushed Hamida that direction and turned toward Karim. "I'll be back."

Still sore from his earlier encounter with Fargo, Tarek followed at a much slower pace, waving to Ben, who was parked in their SUV down the block. Fargo crossed the narrow street, then darted into an alley, Hamida on his heels. By the time Tarek rounded the corner, the two men were faced off. Hamida was built like a bulldozer. He'd have no difficulty taking down Fargo.

A good thing, because it took a moment for Tarek to catch his breath once he caught up with them. "You're not"—he gulped in air—"taking . . ."

"Spit it out," Fargo said. "I'm in a hurry."

How Fargo wasn't winded, he had no idea. "Taking that mosaic . . ."

Fargo edged to his left.

Hamida followed him. "You broke into our office."

"Feel free to tell the police," Fargo said. "They should be here any minute."

Tarek wrapped his fingers around the grip of his holstered pistol.

Fargo closed the distance, driving his fist into Tarek's stomach. Pain shot through him. He doubled over. Hamida charged, but Fargo sidestepped, pulling Tarek in front of him. Hamida's fist struck Tarek in the ribs and he dropped to the ground, unable to breathe. When Hamida went for his gun, Fargo grabbed his wrist and spun it around. A sickening crunch sounded as Fargo rammed his shoulder into Hamida's hyperextended elbow. He fell to the ground, his bloodcurdling scream drowning out the faint sirens heard in the distance.

Ben sped down the alley in the SUV as Fargo grabbed Tarek by the collar, ready to drive his fist home. He heard the screech of tires, looked up, saw the SUV bearing down on them, and let loose of Tarek, jumping out of the way.

Ben skidded to a stop, pointing a gun out the window, as the sirens grew louder.

"Forget him," Tarek called out. He opened the back door and dragged Hamida to his feet. He shoved the injured man into the car and scrambled in after him. "Go."

Ben hit the gas, speeding out of the alley past the police cars converging on the street in front of the gallery.

When they were safely past, Tarek sat up, ignoring Hamida as he groaned in pain.

Ben looked back at him. "What now?"

"Find someone who can fix Hamida's arm. Then kill Fargo."

CHAPTER EIGHTY-ONE

A close friend can become a close enemy.
— AFRICAN PROVERB —

A pity you couldn't have held them until the police got there," Remi said to Sam once they were back at their hotel.

"All it would prove is that they were middlemen in selling a stolen artifact. Proving they're behind the murder's going to take more effort. One thing's clear. Amal's got some serious explaining to do. She's already lied to us before. When you saw her out at the ruins our first day here."

"I'd forgotten about that," Remi said.

"Tarek and his men are playing for keeps. We're past trying to spare anyone's feelings."

Lazlo, who was examining the mosaic of Echo's face, looked up at them. "I daresay, he has a point."

Remi started pacing the floor. "I know. And we've also got Nasha to think of. Her uncle's flying in tomorrow to take her home. I'll feel more comfortable once she's back in her uncle's care."

Sam nodded at the open parcel on the table. "Let's put it in the safe at the front desk."

"Maybe," Remi said as she helped Lazlo repack the mosaic, "we could invite Amal to dinner. It won't seem so intimidating."

Sam thought Remi was being far too polite, but he learned long ago that her lighter touch often yielded good results.

She put the phone on speaker and placed the call. "Oh, Mrs. Fargo . . ." Amal was clearly crying. "Dr. LaBelle was arrested. She . . . For murder." She started sobbing.

"We know," Remi said. "Which is why we need to talk."

They agreed on a location, and Amal was waiting for them when they arrived later that evening. Her eyes were red, her lids heavy, but she smiled at them as they entered. The four sat in awkward silence until the maître d' seated them at a table. A waiter brought them drinks and took their orders.

Amal waited until he left. "The police can't possibly believe that Dr. LaBelle killed anyone?"

"Apparently, they do," Sam said. "The best way to help her is by telling us anything you know about what's been going on around here."

"About what?"

"You can start with the day we saw you out at the ruins, and why you lied about being there when we ran into you at the hospital. Was Warren with you?"

She shook her head. "No, I swear. It was a tour to earn money. I only lied about it because Hank had asked me to stop giving them. He didn't want strangers around our dig site. I . . . I thought he might get upset and I didn't want to add to Dr. LaBelle's problems."

"What about the shop at the market?" Remi asked. "I saw you knocking on the same door where the stolen mosaic ended up. You were talking to someone."

"Oh . . ." She sank back in her chair. "That was Warren. About him, I mean. When Hank told me that he'd gone there to sell stolen artifacts, I had to see for myself. No one answered. But a man in the shop next door came out. I showed him Warren's photo."

"And what'd he say?" Sam asked.

"He recognized him." Her eyes filled with tears. "You have to understand, Warren was like a father to me. I didn't want to believe Hank, but when that man at the shop said he'd seen Warren there, that's when I realized . . . I was such a fool. He was using me to learn what I knew about the secrets of . . ." Amal covered her mouth and looked up at the ceiling, trying to compose herself.

Remi slid a glass of water closer to her and she grasped it, taking a sip.

"What secrets?" Remi asked.

"About the Vandal King." She lowered her glass to the table, her hands wet from the condensation. She stared at them a moment and picked up a napkin, wiping her fingers, then used the white square of cloth to dab at her eyes. "He was using me to find the map."

Lazlo, who seemed to be only half interested, perked up. "Map? What sort of map?"

CHAPTER EIGHTY-TWO

There can be no peace without understanding.
— SENEGALESE PROVERB —

According to family legend," Amal said, "there's a map leading to the cursed treasure stolen by the last Vandal King."

Sam wasn't near the history expert Remi and Lazlo were, but he tended to pay attention when treasure was involved—and the Vandals had accumulated a lot of it during their various raids throughout Europe, including the Sack of Rome. "Wasn't all that treasure confiscated after the Byzantine Army defeated the Vandals?" Sam asked.

Lazlo, his eyes alight with interest, nodded. "I seem to remember something about the conquered Vandal King and all his amassed wealth and spoils being paraded before the Emperor while he quoted—or misquoted—something from Ecclesiastes, wasn't it?"

"Vanity of vanities," Remi said, *"all is vanity."* Her knowledge of ancient history far surpassed anything Sam knew, which was why he wasn't surprised when she added, "If memory serves, the Emperor Justinian returned the Vandal Treasure to Jerusalem."

Lazlo said, "Why would anyone give up that sort of fortune?"

"He believed the treasure stolen from the temple was cursed and any city that housed it would eventually be destroyed."

"Guess there was some truth in that," Sam said as their waiter set a plate of *banatages* on the table, the scent of the fried meat-filled potato croquettes tempting. "Look at Bulla Regia, flattened by an earthquake." Once the young man left, Sam turned his attention back to Amal. "So, we're talking about a completely different treasure?"

"Correct," Amal said. "Different treasure, different curse."

Lazlo, suddenly interested again, asked, "A different treasure?"

"Well, not a treasure so much as something that was treasured. A rare scroll, taken about a hundred years before the fall of the Vandal Kingdom. This particular scroll was not to be held by any one man. It was for the people."

"And the curse?"

"Cast upon the Vandals after the scroll was stolen."

"Stolen by whom?" Sam asked.

"The Vandal King, Genseric. His army invaded North Africa in 430 A.D., laying siege to Hippo Regius. Of course," Amal continued, "it varies as to why the scroll was stolen and from whom. One tale is that he stole it from Bishop Augustine's library, though there were probably far more valuable books to be had. Another is that Genseric sought a way to influence the Moors and gain the upper hand during his invasion of North Africa and so stole the treasured scroll from the Moors, then threatened its destruction if the city didn't surrender."

"The scroll?" Sam asked, intrigued. "Was it biblical?"

"No, philosophical. Meant to bring peace and harmony to the world. Beyond that, I have no idea."

"Parmenides," Lazlo said. "I knew it rang a bell. The child, Nasha, was chanting bits of it back at the school."

"Philosophy?" Remi's brows rose. "I never expected that of you."

"You're correct in that respect. It, and the professor who taught it, have haunted me since university. To think I might be rewarded for sitting in that torturous class day after day . . ."

"Back up a bit," Sam said. "Who or what is Parmenides?"

"Parmenides," Remi replied, "was an early sixth century B.C. pre-Socratic philosopher. He's considered to be the founder of metaphysics, ontology. You know, existence, being—that sort of thing."

"Eleatic philosopher." Lazlo rubbed his forehead. "I have a vague recollection of my professor telling me there'd be no Plato if not for Parmenides. Some even suggest the chap contributed to our knowledge of atomic theory."

Sam was about to comment when Remi said, "But what Parmenides is known for in particular is a poem, 'On Nature.' Only fragments of the work have survived."

"A poem?" Sam said. "You're trying to tell me that Warren was killed for a poem?"

"Not a poem in the true sense," Remi said. "Early teachings were done in verse to help with memorization."

Lazlo looked at Sam in disbelief. "If this missing scroll is this poem 'On Nature,' it might well be the complete poem. And if the complete poem has somehow survived the millennia, it's quite likely to be the only existing copy. I daresay, it explains the inordinate interest in what would normally be a bog-standard archeological dig in the midst of other bog-standard archeological digs."

"True," Remi said. "What little is known about Parmenides' works are from surviving fragments."

"Quite right. No scholar has ever seen the poem in its entirety," Lazlo continued. "Fragments alone—should they consist of the missing verses—would be worth a lot of dosh. The entire poem? On the black market? I'd say ten, fifteen million at least. And that's a modest estimate. Anyone who might get his hands on the complete poem would be *playing a blinder*, in cricket terms."

"A home run," Sam said. Which meant those thefts and break-ins had less to do with any curse or random bits of antiquities to sell on the black market and more to do with the value of the Parmenides Scroll. It certainly explained the tenacity of whoever was behind all of this. And possibly why Warren was killed. Sam took his fork and cut one of the *banatages* in half, watching the steam rise up from the meaty filling. "One question," he said to Amal. "Is there any chance that Dr. LaBelle knew of any of this?"

"The curse, a scroll, and the map—yes. But Parmenides? It's the first I've even heard of it. And I'm supposed to be the Keeper of the Map."

"You?" Lazlo said.

"If you believe old wives' tales, that is."

"Indeed, I do. Exactly what do you know about this map and curse attached to it?"

"The curse was cast by the High Priestess after King Genseric hid the scroll. Sadly, that's all I know about it, the part my grandmother taught me, where only one who is of royal blood can return the scroll to its rightful home."

"What happens," he asked, "if it's a non-royal who finds the scroll?"

"Anyone not worthy dies a violent death."

Remi grinned. "Guess it's up to you, Fargo." She gave a conspiratorial wink to Amal. "He's distantly related to the British Crown."

Sam laughed. "Far enough down the line we'd need a computer to calculate. Especially with this new bunch of royal grandkids being born."

"Royal is royal," Remi replied. She helped herself to one of the appetizers, then passed the plate to Amal. "Where were we?"

"She's the Keeper of the Map," Sam reminded her.

"It's not just the map," Amal said. "Again, and only if you believe those old legends, I'm the direct descendant of the Priestess/witch who cast that curse."

Lazlo's eyes practically gleamed at her announcement. "I'm ready to hear every one of those old legends."

Before she could launch into one, Sam asked, "Did Warren know about this connection?"

"It wasn't really a secret. He was one of the first people I told. I have to admit, he was very keen on the idea of looking for it."

Remi and Sam exchanged glances. Sam knew Remi was thinking exactly the same thing that had crossed his mind. Ancient maps are valuable. Even more so when they lead to ancient treasures. And that usually drew all sorts of unsavory characters into the mix.

"Amal," Sam said. "What about Dr. LaBelle? And Hank? What'd they have to say about it?"

"I don't think Dr. LaBelle ever took it seriously. Not the curse or the map. She was all about preserving the mosaic floor and the architecture."

"And Hank?"

"He was more concerned about Dr. LaBelle. Doing whatever she wanted." Amal's dark eyes looked troubled. "How do we make this right? If I'd ever thought that talking about family history would start any of this . . ."

"Understandable," Sam said. "But learning the background will only help."

"How?" she asked.

"Because now we know what we're dealing with. Which means we can force Tarek and Hamida to play their hand and we can expose them to the police."

CHAPTER EIGHTY-THREE

A big fish is caught with big bait.
— SIERRA LEONEAN PROVERB —

As the waiter once again left the table, Remi said, "One problem, Fargo. How do we know they're the only ones involved?"

"We don't," Sam said. "Which is why we don't discuss this with anyone until the time is right."

"Oh no." Amal looked from Sam to Remi. "I hate to even suggest it, but what if it's Osmond or José? They both live in the house with Dr. LaBelle and Hank. Those two would know every move they made, including the trip to Nigeria. And José's always borrowing money."

"Money," Lazlo said, "is always a strong motivator. Did anyone else find it odd that out of all the people at the dinner table, José alone knew that the police had determined Warren's death wasn't an accident?"

"We need a plan," Remi said.

"Something that will bring the players into the open," Sam said. "The best way to set it up is at the house when everyone's there."

"That's hardly a plan, Fargo."

Amal looked disappointed. "Neither of you have any idea how to draw them out, do you?"

"No," Sam said, reaching for the last of the *banatages*. "But that's not unusual."

Lazlo gave her a grim smile. "They do better under pressure."

"I don't," Amal said. "But I do have an idea. What if I had one of my attacks and revealed a certain location and drew them to it?"

"That could work," Remi said, imagining the possibilities.

Sam turned a bemused look Remi's way. "Sorry. How does that help?"

"Visions, Fargo. Amal sees things that aren't there."

"Not sure that clears it up."

"You heard her. She's a direct descendant of the ancient oracles." Remi eyed Amal. "That's where you're going with this, isn't it?"

"Yes. I pretend to have one of my visions about where the map's supposed to be."

"Brilliant," Lazlo said. "One question. Any chance your family legends have ever hinted at the actual location of this map?"

"Sadly, no," Amal replied.

"I've got an idea," Remi said. "What about something hidden in all that rubble? There must be a ton of it down there."

Lazlo nodded. "Entirely plausible that something might be hidden beneath it."

"If we really want to make it realistic," Remi said to Amal, "you should reveal it in a riddle, since that's how the ancient oracles used to talk. Assuming you think you can sell it, that is."

"I think I can."

"Perfect. What about tomorrow morning? They're expecting us to show up for coffee."

"One big flaw in that plan," Sam said.

"What flaw?" Remi said. "Amal said she could pull it off."

"We have to pick up Nasha's uncle from the airport tomorrow morning."

"Not a problem." Remi smiled at Amal. "We'll do it the moment we get back."

Amal's smile in return did not reach her eyes.

———

THE FOLLOWING MORNING, WHEN SAM PULLED INTO THE DRIVE IN front of the archeologists' house, Remi looked out the car window and sighed as he parked. "I feel guilty coming over here to drink coffee while Renee's sitting in jail."

"She knows we're doing everything we can," Sam said. "When we get back from the airport, Amal can pretend to have her vision."

"And while you're gone," Lazlo said as they got out of the car, "I'll have Hank give me a proper tour of the underground villa. Familiarize myself with the area before we implement our plan."

"Or look for a map?" Sam said.

"If, by chance, I stumbled across it, I wouldn't be disappointed."

"No doubt."

Hank, looking worn, let them in. "Have you heard anything about LaBelle, yet?"

"Unfortunately, no," Sam said.

"Neither have I. I only wish there was something I could've done," he said, leading them into the kitchen, where José and Osmond sat at the table. "Had I not gotten sick at the school, I could've come back here with her. She wouldn't have been alone when she found Warren. They would've believed her and gone after the real killer."

"It'll work out," Sam said.

Hank brought a coffeepot and three mugs to the table, then went back to the stove and dumped a plate of chopped potatoes into the frying pan. They sizzled as soon as they hit the surface, the scent of onion and bacon filling the air. "We're having a bit of a late start, but you're welcome to join us for breakfast."

"No, thank you," Remi said. "We've eaten."

"I haven't," Lazlo said. "I'd love a plate."

Hank used a spatula to stir the potatoes. "Off to the airport this morning?" he asked, looking back at them.

"Sam and I are picking up Nasha's uncle," Remi said.

"Ah. Not you, professor?"

"No," Lazlo said as someone knocked at the back door. "Thought I'd stick around here. Mr. Fargo mentioned that you might need some help clearing some of the rubble."

"I'll take any help I can get." Hank tipped his head at Amal and Nasha as they walked in. "Breakfast?"

"Yes," Nasha said.

Amal laughed. "You just ate."

"I'm still hungry."

Hank looked at the coffeepot, then at Amal. "Stir the potatoes. I'll put another pot of coffee on."

Amal took the spatula from him. "Any word yet on Dr. LaBelle?" she asked, adjusting the flame.

"No," he said. "I don't know how long these sorts of things take. Do you, Mr. Fargo?"

"I wish I did. I'll try to call the embassy and see if we can get an update after we get back from the airport."

The pan flared. Amal stepped back as smoke filled the stovetop.

Hank rushed over, turned off the burner, and covered the frying pan with the lid, smothering the fire. "Are you okay?" he asked. When she didn't answer, he waved his hand in front of her face. "Amal . . . ?"

Nasha stepped closer to Remi. "It's happening again."

Amal stared, unseeing, out the window toward the olive grove, then in a soft, monotone voice said, "Beyond the pagan tombs . . . Before Saturn's temple, he points to the water. Beware . . . Death to he who is not worthy."

"Amal?" Hank said again. He took her by her hand, leading her to the empty chair next to Lazlo.

Remi glanced at Sam and then Amal, unsure what to think.

A few seconds later, Amal blinked and looked down at the spatula in her hand. "What's going on? Why do I have this?"

Hank took the spatula from her, setting it on the table. "I think you had one of your seizures."

Lazlo, watching the entire episode with interest, said, "Actually, I think you were giving us a location of some sort."

"I don't remember . . ."

"You were saying something about the temple ruins."

Hank went back to making the coffee. "We've been out there a million times."

"Exactly where are these ruins?" Lazlo asked.

José pointed out the window in the direction Amal had been looking. "Down the hill, past the olive grove. But unless someone thinks they can move a few tons of marble, there's nothing to be found out there."

"Exactly what were you looking for?" Sam asked.

José shrugged. "I'm not sure anyone really knows. Os, weren't you talking about it?"

Osmond, busy texting on his phone, glanced up in surprise. "What? No. I just remember everyone talking about a map, not what it led to."

Once the coffeepot started up, Hank joined them at the table. "I'm not sure anyone really knows. It's . . ." He looked at Sam. "You don't think it has anything to do with what's going on with LaBelle, do you?"

"It's worth mentioning to the police," Sam said. He checked the time on his watch. "We better hit the road if we want to get to the airport in time." He and Remi rose. "You're sure you want to stay, Lazlo?"

"Quite."

CHAPTER EIGHTY-FOUR

Do not look where you fell but where you slipped.
— AFRICAN PROVERB —

"I'll pick you up in five minutes," Tarek said, then pocketed his phone.

Hamida, groggy from the pain pills, stirred on the sofa. "Who called?"

"No one," he replied, doubting Hamida would remember they'd had a conversation at all. "I'll be back in a couple of hours."

As he walked out the door, the sight of Hamida's thick cast reminded him how dangerous Fargo was. The only thing that was going to stop that man was a barrage of bullets—and Tarek looked forward to making it happen.

A time and place for everything. First, he had a debt to collect.

When he arrived at Ben Ayed's apartment, Ben was waiting out front, holding a hard-shell briefcase. Ex-military, an expert in hand-to-hand combat, Ben was also a former sniper, which made him invaluable should things not work out as planned.

The pair drove out to the archeological park, then continued past it until they reached the back road, parking in the same location Tarek had chosen that night he'd followed—and lost—the Fargos. The temple ruins were located beyond the olive grove on the same property belonging to the graduate student's family. It was a hike from this direction. The hilly terrain beyond the vast grove meant there was no easy route to the ruins and excavation site. But the road would allow them to approach without being seen from the archeologist's house.

Tarek parked and looked over at the briefcase on Ben's lap. "I hope you brought extra ammo."

"More than enough." Ben opened the case, loaded up three magazines, and inserted one into his Vektor SP1 9mm, the South African version of the Beretta 92F. He pulled back the slide, chambered a round, then slid the gun into his holster, the magazines into his belt pouch, pulled his shirt over that, and shoved the gun case beneath the front seat. "Doubt I'll need that much."

"Don't be so sure," Tarek said, checking his own weapon. "If the Fargos get back before we're done, you'll change your mind."

"If you're so worried, why not wait?"

"Because I have a reputation to protect. What good is my word if I allow one person to get away with dictating the terms of repayment?"

"A shame that whole ransom thing didn't work," Ben said as they started the long walk toward the ruins.

The very thought of it angered Tarek. What should have turned a profit ended up wasting both time and money. The plan had been doomed from the beginning—his fault for not doing a better search of the Fargos' background. And as much as he'd like to recoup his losses, he was willing to write it off in exchange for putting a bullet in Sam Fargo's head. The original debt, though?

Not a chance he was willing to let that go. The only way to ensure that no one ever tried to take advantage of him was to send a very clear and unmistakable message.

He didn't care how old or how young, male or female—if the money wasn't there, he was going to put a bullet in every one of their heads.

CHAPTER EIGHTY-FIVE

Life is lived forward, but understood backward.
— AFRICAN PROVERB —

The timing of Amal's seizure bothered Sam, but Nasha's presence prevented him from discussing it with Remi, who managed a simple "That was odd" as the three got into the car, then drove to the airport.

"I'm glad Lazlo's there to keep an eye on things." No doubt, they'd sort it out after they got back.

"How was the flight, Mr. Atiku?" Sam asked once they were in the car on their way to Bulla Regia.

"Much smoother than my last trip."

Nasha's eyes widened. "I didn't know you've been on a plane before. It was my first time."

"Many years ago when I was in the army . . . Will we see Professor Lazlo? Chuk's parents wanted me to personally thank him for helping to get Chuk away from Kambili. He was—what's the American term?—fly man."

"Wingman," Sam said as he slid in behind the wheel.

"What's a wingman?" Nasha asked.

"A helper," Sam said.

"Was I a good wing girl?"

Sam glanced at her in his rearview mirror. "The best. Maybe even better than Lazlo."

She beamed as she sat back in her seat.

"Buckle up," Sam said as he pulled away from the curb.

A few minutes into the trip, his phone rang.

Remi looked at it where it sat in the console. "Wendy," she said. "Probably wants to make sure we picked up Nasha's uncle. She's turned into a regular mother hen, taking care of those girls."

Sam laughed. "That she has."

He navigated through the airport traffic while Remi spoke to Wendy. After a minute of back-and-forth, she said, "I'll put it on speaker and you can tell him yourself . . . Go ahead."

"Something wrong?" Sam asked.

"More like perplexed," Wendy replied. "Remember the missing nails?"

Sam surveilled Nasha in the rearview mirror, then her uncle. "I thought we'd decided that was all water under the bridge."

"We did," she said quickly. "But Yaro found about forty or more boxes of nails buried in the dirt pile behind the shed. He thinks that—"

Nasha sat up, gripping the seat back. "I didn't take them, Mr. Fargo."

Sam cleared his throat loudly. "Did I mention you're on speaker and Nasha and her uncle are sitting in the backseat?"

"That's why I'm calling," Wendy said. "I believe her."

"Why do I detect there's more to this than Nasha's hurt feelings?"

"Because everything she took when she first got here had to do with food or little things that she found and claimed. And all of it went straight into her backpack. Hiding forty boxes of nails—I'm not sure she could've carried them by herself. As many as Yaro found, they probably weighed as much as she did."

"Weren't they in boxes?"

"Yes. But they were all hidden inside a large burlap sack, which would make the load a bit heavy for a girl her size. And then there's the bottle of pills."

"I didn't steal those," Nasha said. "I found them."

"What kind of pills?" Sam asked Wendy.

"Some morphine derivative. Amo . . . Avo . . . I don't recall."

A feeling of dread worked its way into Sam's gut. Praying that he was wrong, he checked his mirror and pulled to the side of the road. "Wendy, I need to see that bottle. It's important."

"I'll get it and call right back."

The moment she disconnected, Sam looked over at Remi. "Call Lazlo."

Nasha's uncle leaned forward. "What's this about Nasha taking things?"

"I only took things no one wanted."

"Voice mail," Remi said. She left a message for him to call immediately, then texted the same.

A minute later, Sam's phone lit up with the video call. Wendy's face filled the screen. "Here it is, Mr. Fargo." She held the bottle in front of the camera, the black letters on the label clear and crisp.

Sam's gut twisted at the sight and Remi caught her breath. "Apomorphine," Sam said. "That's not a pain pill. It's an emetic to induce vomiting." He shifted around in his seat. "Nasha, where'd you find them?"

She crossed her arms, tucking her chin to her chest, refusing to meet his gaze.

Her uncle placed his hand on her shoulder. "My sweet Nasha. If you know something, you need to tell them."

She looked at Sam, then Remi, her eyes shimmering with tears. "I didn't steal anything."

"I know you didn't," Sam said.

Remi, her voice soft, asked, "Where did you find the pills?"

Tears streaked her cheeks as she looked at her uncle. "Do I have to tell?"

"If you know the answer," he said.

Nasha brushed her eyes with the back of her hand and looked at Sam. "I found them on the floor in the office bathroom."

That was the last thing Sam wanted to hear. "You're sure this is the same bottle that you found?"

She glanced at the phone screen, where Wendy held the small container. "Yes."

"Thank you, Nasha. You've been a big help."

"A wing girl?"

"More than you know."

Her uncle put his arm around her. "There, there. No need for tears."

Sam put the car in gear and slid into traffic, calculating the driving time from the airport to Bulla Regia. "Try Lazlo again."

As before, it went straight to voice mail.

CHAPTER EIGHTY-SIX

The persons we eat with are the ones to kill us.
— AFRICAN PROVERB —

The villa floor was flooded when Lazlo, Hank, and José arrived later that morning. "What . . . ?" Hank said, standing on the deck, looking down.

"Osmond," José said.

Hank gave an exasperated sigh, kicking at the hose that Osmond had hooked up to the water tank and draped over the deck into the opening. "I told him to wet the floor, not drown it." He pulled out the hose, seeing nothing but a dribble of water coming from the nozzle. "Glad LaBelle's not here to see this," he said, climbing down the ladder. "Looks like the entire tank ended up down there."

Lazlo and José followed him to the first level. They leaned over the railing, seeing a couple of inches covering the floor below. "You have to admit," Lazlo said, "it definitely brings out the colors of the tiles."

"It does at that." Hank turned on the lamp that was clipped to the rail, its long orange extension cord swinging below them.

Lazlo moved around the tool bucket and stepped over a coil of rope to get to the rail. José, however, didn't see it, losing his footing momentarily. He stepped back, caught himself on the railing, bumping the lamp clamped to it. "Glad that didn't go over," he said, righting the lamp, then peering over the edge. "Hate to see what would happen if it hit the water."

Lazlo returned his attention to the mosaic. "Simply stunning. Imagine what it would've looked like back in the day."

Hank nodded. "I expect they'd have a couple of chairs on the far wall so one could sit and admire the beautiful floor."

"Or sit and admire where this map is hidden."

Hank glanced at Lazlo. "You think there really is a map down there?"

"I have no idea. But I always say, no time like the present to look." As Lazlo shifted his feet, bits of dirt and gravel from the platform dropped into the water, the surface rippling as it hit. He watched, fascinated by the subtle changes the moving water had on the pattern of the mosaic, especially the blue and white tiles, which he assumed were originally meant for the reflecting pool in front of the temple.

"You know what I find odd," Hank said. "The artist didn't include Narcissus' reflection in the mosaic. That's a big part of the legend."

Narcissus, on the bottom step of the temple, seemed to be looking at his hand draped into the water. "Perhaps," Lazlo suggested, "beyond the artist's skills? The reflecting pool is rather digital-looking in comparison to the detail of the temple, the trees, and . . ."

"And what?" Hank asked.

"Quite extraordinary . . . The blue and white squares in the reflecting pool. It's a pixelated version of the temple."

José agreed. "Like a digital photo that's been enlarged."

"The six columns, the portico, the pediment . . . And Narcissus' reflection."

"Where?" Hank asked.

Lazlo said, "Close your eyes and look through your lashes—it'll smooth out the pixels. See where Narcissus is pointing? The reflection of the stairs? Those tiles on that side are actually darker. Could it be . . . ?"

"Be what?" Hank asked.

"I daresay, it's a hidden staircase."

Hank squinted. "Son of a gun . . . It was here the whole time. In the temple ruins."

"We need photos." Lazlo patted his pocket. "Left my bloody phone in the kitchen," he said as a shadow darkened the opening above them.

They looked up to see Amal looking down at them.

"Just in time," Hank said. "I think we've found the map."

José nodded. "A hidden staircase."

Hank's attention was on Amal. "Something wrong?"

"No. Just that Professor Kemp left his phone in the kitchen."

"Oh, good show," Lazlo said. "I wanted to take pictures."

José moved to the edge of the platform, grabbed the ladder, and started down to the bottom level. "I've got my phone. I'll take some photos."

Lazlo looked at him, then back up to Amal. She had yet to move. "I say, are you well?"

"Fine," she said and climbed down the ladder.

Below them, José sloshed through the water.

Hank's attention was on Amal. "Where's the professor's phone?"

"In the kitchen. I didn't want to pry. I . . . I just thought he should know."

Something in her voice caught Lazlo's ear. He looked in her eyes and saw fear.

"Don't move, professor," Hank said, his gun drawn and aiming at Amal. "You might be willing to sacrifice your own safety, but not someone else's. Hand me your gun, then down you go."

"I don't have a gun," Lazlo said, holding his hands away from his body. "Whatever you're thinking, we can get past this. It's just money."

"Yes. And your employers have plenty of it. Had Fargo simply allowed his wife to be kidnapped, as I'd first planned, I'd have my ransom and no one would be the wiser. I could've safely returned the embezzled funds, paid my debt to Tarek, and we'd all be happy."

"You set up the kidnapping? Not Warren?"

"I owed Tarek a fortune." He glanced at Amal. "I doubt anyone would've noticed the occasional missing artifact I used to help fund my own search for the scroll until the Fargos arrived."

"Why?" Amal said, her voice filled with disbelief. "We were all in this together."

"Together? You don't get rich working for the university. Just ask LaBelle. Had the Fargos not discovered the missing money, I could've continued my search uninterrupted. I was almost home free, until Warren started looking into everything."

Amal stumbled back against the ladder, her face paling. She started mumbling unintelligibly.

Hank ignored her, instead pointing his gun at Lazlo. "Get the rope."

Lazlo picked it up, eyeing the tool bucket.

"Just the rope," Hank said and jerked his jaw at Amal. "Tie her hands behind her back. Make sure it's tight."

"You'll be okay," Lazlo said softly, wrapping the thick cord around her wrists, then knotting it. "Just stay calm."

If she heard him, she gave no indication. Her stare seemed vacant. She didn't try to move, just continued muttering *"sator, arepo, tenet, opera, rotas"* over and over.

Hank ordered Lazlo to move away and grabbed the rope, drawing Amal to his side. "Down you go, professor. Don't make any sudden moves."

CHAPTER EIGHTY-SEVEN

*When one man's curse falls on a person,
another one breaks it.*
— AFRICAN PROVERB —

A cloud of dust kicked up as Sam skidded to a stop outside the archeological site. Osmond came running out of the house as he and Remi threw open their doors. "Amal's down there. She saw the text on Professor Lazlo's phone."

"Get in the car," Sam told him. He looked over at Remi. "Drive everyone up to Amal's. Get her mother, call the police, and get them out of here."

"Be careful," she said.

He was halfway across the field before Remi had even backed out of the drive. When he reached the dig site, he crept onto the deck, thankful when he heard voices. With the sun overhead, there was no way to approach unnoticed. Hank would see his shadow—unless he was too preoccupied.

"Fargo," Hank called out. "Just in time."

So much for luck. "Lazlo?" Sam shouted, wishing he had a better view inside.

"Hank has a gun."

"Pointed at your friend, Fargo. Keep that in mind as you come down."

Sam, relieved to hear Lazlo's voice, moved to the edge. It wasn't until he started climbing down that he could actually see Hank in the shadows at the end of the platform, holding Amal in front of him. She seemed to be staring at nothing, her lips moving as she mumbled softly to herself. Hank, on the other hand, aimed his gun into the depths of the villa at Lazlo, who sat next to José atop the pile of rubble, both men blinded by the light clamped to the railing.

Hank glanced at Sam. "Warning. I'm a good shot. First wrong move, I'll kill your friend. Empty your gun. Nice and slow."

Sam calculated and dismissed the possibility of taking Hank out first. He drew his weapon. Holding it barrel up, he opened the cylinder, dumping the rounds into his hand. "Harmless," he said as he lowered the Smith & Wesson to the wooden planks.

"Behold," Amal shouted, looking upward. "The Sign of Saturn."

In the second of distraction, Sam pocketed the bullets, then held up his empty hands. "Just don't hurt anyone."

"Where's your wife?"

"With Osmond. Taking Nasha and her uncle to Amal's to get her mother out of here. I'm sure you must have heard the car drive off."

"For your sake, I hope you're right." Keeping Amal close, Hank aimed his gun at Sam's chest. "Down you go, Fargo. Next to the professor."

As Sam walked to the ladder, Hank sidestepped, keeping a wide berth between them. Sam grabbed the first rung and lowered himself over. "Whatever trouble you're in, it's not too late."

"If only that were true. No one was supposed to get hurt. But they killed Warren anyway."

"Then let me help."

"There's nothing you can do," he said, his voice taking on a panicky edge. "Tarek wants the map. I have to give it to him. You understand that, don't you? He'll kill me if I don't."

Sam reached the bottom, landing in at least an inch of water. "He'll kill all of us."

"Not if I give him what he wants." He led Amal to the side,

looped the rope over the railing, pulled it into a knot with his free hand. He looked down at Sam, motioning with his gun. "Over there. Hurry. I don't have much time."

Sam sloshed through the water and climbed up onto the rock pile next to Lazlo, hoping that Hank would simply leave. Sam tried to look past the glare of the lamp shining down on them, catching sight of the man's silhouette as he started pacing above them.

Amal's chanting grew louder. "Saturn holds the wheels . . . The balance between Rhea—wealth and abundance—and Lua—destruction and dissolution . . . Hear, O Usurper of the Vandal Treasure, Lua rains death upon you."

"Quiet," Hank shouted. "I can't think."

"*Sator, arepo, tenet, opera, rotas . . .*"

Hank pulled the lamp from the railing, smashing it against the side of the scaffolding. A flash of sparks reflected on the water as the bulb shattered. Then, surprising Sam, Hank started lowering it over the edge. "What're you doing, Hank?"

"Making sure you don't move. This shouldn't take long. I'll give them what they want." The long orange extension cord slapped against the scaffolding as he inched the lamp toward the flooded floor. The reflector shade hit the tile and he carefully brought it to rest, the exposed socket just above—and precariously close to—the water's surface. "I expect the slightest ripple might cause a shock."

"Hank," Sam called out as the man climbed up the ladder. "Let me help you."

But all he heard in response was Amal's chanting. "*Sator, arepo, tenet, opera, rotas . . .*"

CHAPTER EIGHTY-EIGHT

A bird with fire on its tail burns its own nest.
— AFRICAN PROVERB —

S am focused on the lamp sitting in the water just inches from the scaffolding.

Lazlo followed the direction of Sam's eyes. "Can't we just throw something at it, short it out?"

"That pipe Amal's tied to leads straight down into the water. We can't chance it."

José, his feet tucked up high, his arms about his knees, was rocking in place. "Are we going to die?"

"No," Sam said.

"What about a human chain?" Lazlo said.

"That might work."

He looked up at Amal, who was struggling against her bonds. Definitely not in the throes of a seizure. "Let's do this."

They stood. Lazlo grasped his hand. He was about to lean forward when Amal said, "Hank's coming. *Sator, arepo, tenet* . . . "

A shadow fell across the water in front of Sam.

"*Opera, rotas* . . ."

"Amal?" Remi climbed down the ladder.

"Mrs. Fargo," Amal said, her voice loud and sure. "Thank goodness. I thought you were Hank."

"Remi," Sam said. "The lamp. Cut the power."

She unplugged the extension cord from the socket mounted by the entrance. Its length snaked down and splashed in the water.

Sam jumped from the rocks, ran to the ladder. When he reached the upper platform, Remi was already working at the rope binding Amal. "Where's Hank?" he asked, grabbing his gun from the platform, then reloading it.

"I have no idea. He was gone when I got here."

"My mother?" Amal said.

"She's safe. Osmond drove everyone to the British works. They're supposed to wait there until the police get here." She stood as Lazlo and José came up the ladder. "What on earth . . . ?"

"My fault," Lazlo said. "I left my mobile at the house. Hank and I were here and . . . I believe I found the bloody map."

"Where would he go?" Remi asked. "His car's still out there."

"I have a fair idea," Sam said, starting up the ladder. "Everyone wait here until it's safe."

"Not likely," Remi said, climbing up after him.

Lazlo looked over at Amal and José. "If I can make a bold suggestion, find Hank's car keys and get out of here. I'm going with the Fargos."

"But why?" Amal asked.

"That's a very good question," he said and climbed up after them.

SAM DUCKED BEHIND THE WATER TANK JUST IN TIME TO SEE HANK running into the olive grove. A moment later, Remi, then Lazlo, emerged from the excavation site. The two joined him.

Remi followed the direction of his focus. "Where's he going?"

"If I had to guess, the temple ruins. Any chance you two will take my advice and stay here?"

Remi scoffed. "Like the advice you gave me telling me to stay at

Amal's house? Had I listened, you'd still be trying to get across that flooded floor without electrocuting yourself."

"A few more seconds, we would've gotten out on our own. Right, Lazlo?"

"Or gotten fried," Lazlo said.

Remi grinned. "You're stuck with us now. What's Hank after?"

"The map," Lazlo said. "He seemed agitated about getting it to Tarek. Or some such."

"That he did." Sam thought about the night they left the dinner party and saw Tarek's SUV parked on the side of the road out behind the ruins. "I'll bet Tarek's on his way—if he's not already here. And Hank's meeting up with him."

Remi patted her holstered Sig Sauer. "I vote we follow."

"Lazlo?"

"I vote no."

"Two-to-one." Sam nodded toward the trees. "We go after him."

"It's always two-to-one," Lazlo said as he followed them. "Why bother to vote?"

They kept low as they moved toward the olive grove, hiding behind a thick trunk on the edge of the orchard. "There," Sam said, pointing down the hill. Hank emerged from the orchard into the narrow valley where a line of ancient olive trees with massive twisted trunks stretched between the orchard and the ivy-covered ruins at the base of the hill.

"He's definitely headed toward the temple," Remi said.

"The hidden stairs," Lazlo said. "I saw it in the mosaic."

"You'd think he'd at least take a shovel."

"Whatever he's doing," Sam said, "he's in a hurry." Though Hank was walking in the direction of the temple, he kept looking out to his left.

Sam studied the hillside, at first not seeing anything, until a movement near the crest caught his eye. "Tarek."

Remi stood behind him, looking over his shoulder. "A shame you didn't take out his elbow, too."

"Hindsight. Looks like he brought a new friend." He returned his attention to Hank, who was now running down the hill, waving his hand at the two men. "What is he doing?"

"Sam, I think they're aiming at him."

"Whatever happens, Hank's brought this on himself."

"I know, but Renee . . ."

The pain in his wife's voice made it particularly difficult to let Hank just walk into danger. As much as Sam felt Hank deserved everything he got, Remi would hurt because her friend would hurt. "Hank," he shouted.

If anything, Hank quickened his pace. He waved his hands again. "I've found it. I found the map." He was halfway down the hill, his stride fast and steady, when Tarek stepped out in the open. "I know where it is."

Hank," Sam shouted. "Get—"

A gunshot cracked.

Hank fell to the ground.

CHAPTER EIGHTY-NINE

He who pelts another with pebbles
asks for stones in return.
— AFRICAN PROVERB —

Getting to Hank without breaking cover was going to be an issue, Sam realized as he, Remi, and Lazlo worked their way down the hill toward an avenue of poplars that led from the olive grove to the ruins. The nearest tree to Hank was about thirty feet behind him. Still, if Sam could drag him back there, he might have a chance.

"No signal," Lazlo said, looking at his phone.

Sam calculated the distance to the first tree in the line. "Cover me."

Remi fired. With each successive shot, he ran to the next tree, and the next—all about ten feet apart—until reaching the one closest to Hank. A small hillock of dirt was the man's only protection from the two gunmen, who'd taken cover behind a couple of boulders up on the hill.

Sam waited for Remi's signal. The moment she fired, he raced out, then dove next to Hank. He braced his Smith & Wesson on the ground and fired twice.

Several shots followed, dirt flying up in his face.

Far too close for his comfort. "Let's go."

"Save yourself." Hank gripped his thigh, blood seeping from his fingers. "They won't kill me."

"If you don't get that bleeding stopped, they won't have to." He looked across the barren dirt toward the orchard where Remi and Lazlo hid, Remi firing the occasional shot to keep the gunmen in check. "Put your arm around me," he said.

Crack! Crack! Crack!

Remi's shots echoed across the hillside. She paused, then fired again as Sam dragged Hank to his feet, bracing him while they ran toward the nearest tree.

Once behind it, Sam lowered Hank to the ground. "Give me your belt," he said as a barrage of shots hit the massive trunk.

Hank fumbled at the buckle. Sam pushed his hand aside, tugged the belt from the loops and wrapped the leather strap around Hank's thigh above the wound. "Don't move," he said and edged out.

Crack!

The shot hit the tree, bark flying, as Sam ducked back.

"Maybe if I give myself up," Hank said, "they'll stop shooting. They only want the map."

"Any chance they realize the map is in the mosaic at the bottom of that villa?"

"No."

"Too bad. They're likely thinking they'll pluck it from your dead hands."

"I . . . I . . . hadn't considered . . . that . . ."

His face looked a lot grayer, his wound still bleeding. Sadly, Hank might have been better off had Sam left him in the field rather than racing for cover, causing his heart to pump faster.

The only way to save him was to take out the gunmen. Even if the police arrived in time, they'd never know to come around the back and hike in from the road the same way Tarek had. They'd sweep in from the front. Assuming they didn't mistake Remi for a shooter, they'd probably be picked off by the gunmen the moment they emerged from the trees.

He studied the hillside where they were holed up. Remi was the better shot, but it'd be impossible for her to get closer. If he could get up high enough and come at them from the right side, he might have a chance.

But how?

To his left, the row of trees led back up to the olive grove. To his right, they led to the ivy-covered ruins. Two more trees flanked either side of the temple. If he could get to that farthest tree, he could work his way past the ruins, then up the hill.

It'd have to be a perfect setup and execution or it was likely to be his last move.

Neither he nor Remi had an unlimited supply of ammo, which meant she was going to have to figure out a way to draw their fire without taking unnecessary shots. He looked at her, hoping that she'd figure everything out when she saw him moving.

If not, it was going to get interesting.

CHAPTER NINETY

Cleverness is better than strength.
— AFRICAN PROVERB —

About twenty-five yards of open space between the orchard and the ruins was all that separated Remi from her husband, who was crouched down behind an olive tree next to Hank. "What's the outlook?" Lazlo asked.

"Looking good," Remi said. Panic bred unpredictability, and she needed Lazlo as calm as possible. As many shots as the gunmen had taken, she had to assume they had no shortage of ammunition. Hidden behind their boulders and bushes high on the hill, they definitely had the advantage.

Which meant either she or Sam had to move to a different position if they wanted to take them out.

Just as she was wondering if she could somehow get to the top of the orchard and come at them from a different angle, she saw Sam signaling her. He pointed to his eyes, then to the hill. If he could climb up the hill to the trees behind the ruins, he'd have a better angle and be closer.

At least she hoped that's what he was planning. If she was wrong, she was going to waste the last of her ammunition.

She counted the number of trees he'd have to get past compared to the number of shots she had left.

If they didn't waste any, they had a good chance to pull it off.

"He's going the wrong way," Lazlo said.

"Let's hope not." She fired and ducked back. While the bushes and boulders in front of the gunmen kept her from seeing their exact position, that didn't prevent them from seeing her. Unless they suddenly decided to pop their heads above cover, the most she'd be able to do was keep them cornered for a short while.

That was going to present a slight problem.

Sam still needed to get past that temple and up the hill. "What we need," she said more to herself, "is a highly efficient way to distract them."

"What about Hank?" Lazlo asked. "Shouldn't we try to get him out of there?"

Remi's attention strayed toward the injured man, noticing that he was no longer moving. "I don't think that's going to make much difference at this point."

"Victim to the curse, I daresay."

Remi looked across the field toward Sam, who waited at the last tree. She needed to think of something. And fast. "Lazlo, any chance you can find a stick about two feet long without breaking cover?"

"There are some broken branches behind me." Lazlo ducked down and grabbed one. "What are you going to do with it?"

"You're going to hang your shirt on it and hold it out."

"Me?"

"Or you could do the shooting."

He slipped out of his shirt. "You realize that if this doesn't work and I somehow survive, Selma will kill me if something happens to you."

She had a feeling Selma would kill her if she let anything happen to Lazlo. The two seemed to be growing a strong attachment to each other. "Let me know when you're ready."

"My stick is dressed."

"On my signal, wave it beside the tree. Preferably, shoulder height, and far enough out for them to think it's a person."

Sam was nearly to the end of the ruins.

"Now."

CHAPTER NINETY-ONE

You must act as if it is impossible to fail.
— ASHANTI PROVERB —

A barrage of gunfire from the crest filled the small valley as Sam raced up the hillside toward the last tree—which had seemed a lot closer when he was on the other side of the ruins. It wasn't until he was safely behind its thick trunk that he looked toward the olive grove to confirm that Remi had indeed managed to draw their fire away from him and toward her.

With little time to admire his wife's handiwork, he focused on the gunmen.

"Give up, Fargo," Tarek shouted. "You've got nowhere to go."

"How's Hamida?" Sam called out. "He didn't look so good last time I saw him."

"Your mistake, letting us go."

"Priorities. I was in a hurry."

Crack!

Dirt blasted up about two feet to the right of his tree. Provoking Tarek seemed to be working. "You know what I think? You had better aim that night you were drunk."

Crack! Crack!

Tree bark splintered across his face.

Tarek laughed. "That'd be the sharpshooter who took Hamida's place."

Sam fired and ducked back. Tarek stopped laughing.

Sam checked the cylinder of his gun, saw the expended rounds, then looked out across the field toward Remi. If there was ever a time he needed her to read his mind, this was it. But just in case, he shouted in her direction to make sure she heard. "Hey, Tarek. You ever play poker?"

"Shouldn't you be praying? Step out. I promise to make it quick."

"Number one rule," Sam shouted. "Never let them know when you've got an ace in the hole." He glanced across the field at his wife. *C'mon, Remi . . .*

And there it was. Movement from the orchard drawing their attention.

Tarek and his partner fired at Lazlo's shirt, the rat-a-tat-tat sounding like a war zone.

Sam sidestepped the tree, squeezed the trigger, killing the sharpshooter.

"Drop the gun, Tarek."

Tarek froze. He started to lower his weapon, then suddenly stopped. "Poker . . ." A sly smile spread across his face as he took a step forward, raising his gun. "You're out of ammo."

Crack!

The man faltered, crumpling to his knees. "I . . . thought . . ."

He fell to the ground.

"Thought wrong," Sam said as he walked up. He had put a bullet in the man's head. He leaned down and took the gun from his lifeless hand.

Sam picked up the other shooter's gun, making sure he was dead, and walked down the hill. Remi raced out of the orchard toward Hank, Lazlo close behind as he tugged on his bullet-riddled shirt.

"Hank," she said, kneeling beside him. "Are you okay?"

He looked up at her, his face ashen. "I'm sorry," he said, trying to raise his hand but lacking the strength. "Tell LaBelle . . . I'm sorry . . ."

Within moments, he was dead.

"We better wait at the house," Sam said.

Amal saw them as they emerged from the orchard and ran out. It was clear she'd been crying. "How could he do this?" she asked. "Pretending to like Dr. LaBelle. It'll break her heart."

"We may never know," Remi said.

"What if you hadn't come along, Mrs. Fargo? What if . . . Maybe some of this is my fault for not realizing—"

"He conned all of us," Remi said, putting her arm around Amal's shoulders. "Who knows how long he was setting this up?"

"Remi's right," Sam said. "It's only a matter of time connecting the irregularities in the books to his actions."

Amal gave a slight nod as a faint siren sounded in the air. "I think I'll wait inside until the police come."

She walked off, leaving Sam, Remi, and Lazlo standing alone in the field.

"I feel bad for her," Remi said. "First the kidnapping at the school, then this. Still, she reminds me of Nasha in a way."

"How?" Sam asked.

"Extremely resilient in the face of insurmountable odds. I'm not sure the average graduate student could've handled everything the way she has."

"I hope you're right," Lazlo said as the shrill sirens nearly drowned out his voice. In a moment, they were surrounded by the police.

CHAPTER NINETY-TWO

---

*One who causes others misfortune
also teaches them wisdom.*
— AFRICAN PROVERB —

THREE DAYS LATER . . .

Y ou must be glad that they found Makao," Renee said as she sat
with the Fargos and Lazlo at the kitchen table. The police investigation into the shooting had consumed much of their time
with endless rounds of questioning, phone calls, and visits to the Fargos' hotel, and they were told to expect still more interviews in the
coming days as the detectives pieced together everything Hank had
done. Renee, at least, was finally home. "He's dead?"

"Very," Remi added.

Lazlo gave a small smile as he rose and moved toward the window.
"Apparently, Mrs. Fargo's shot caused a serious infection. Had he
sought proper medical care, he'd be rotting in prison instead of a grave."

"I'm sure that was foremost in his mind," Sam said.

"Regardless," Remi continued. "It's making life for Pete and
Wendy a lot easier. Wendy's hoping that with the military clearing
out, the school can get back to a normal routine. More importantly,
Nasha and her uncle can go home."

José walked into the kitchen, a tilt of the head to them as he
made for the coffeepot. "Did Dr. LaBelle tell you that we found a
wire yesterday?"

"Where?" Sam asked.

Renee brought up a photo of the battery-operated listening device on her phone, showing it to Sam. "Taped right here underneath this table. We turned it over to the police."

"What I don't get," José said as he poured coffee into a mug, "is why Hank would plant a wire when he was here the whole time?"

Sam examined the photo, then passed the phone to Remi. "It gave him a way to let Tarek know what was going on without it being obvious he was the one passing on the info."

"I feel terrible," Renee replied. "How did I ever believe Warren was guilty? How did I never realize how deep in debt Hank was?"

"Because Hank went to extreme pains to cover it all up."

Lazlo drew himself from the window, looking back at them. "Now that it's all proverbial water under the bridge, is it too soon to see if there's any truth to this vision of Amal's?"

"You're serious?" Sam asked. "You realize she only came up with that vision to help us find the mole."

"Whether the vision's real or not," Lazlo said, "there's a valuable scroll out there. And Narcissus is definitely pointing to an oddity in the reflecting pool in the mosaic. That deserves looking into."

"I'm with Lazlo," Renee said. "It's just the thing our crew needs to get past all of this." She picked up her phone. "I'll text Osmond and Amal to see if they want to head down with us to the ruins. If it's not there, we cross it off as a possible location for the scroll and move on to the next."

"What do you say, Fargo?" Remi smiled at her husband. "Shall we make a last stab effort? Who knows what we might find."

"Why not?"

AN HOUR LATER, AFTER THEY VISITED THE VILLA TO TAKE A CLOSER look at the mosaic—just in case it really was a map—the entire group, including Nasha and her uncle, traipsed through the olive grove toward the ruins. As they emerged from the trees, the blue sky above them, Remi was glad that there was little evidence of the shoot-out that had gone on just a couple days before, since it would only add to Renee's stress.

"Doesn't look like anything much, Dr. LaBelle," Nasha said, stopping.

"A mudslide covered part of the ruins," Renee told her. "The rest is covered by ivy. But once you know what to look for, it changes everything. That row of trees, for example," she said, pointing to the ancient olives that Sam had hidden behind with Hank, "actually follows the road that leads to the ruins. You'll see some of the pavers as we get closer. And those two olive trees growing at the base of the hill flanked the front of the temple. If you look carefully behind the tree on the left, you can see part of the steps leading up to it. And the area in front of both trees," she added, "where nothing's growing, would've been the reflecting pool. On a moonlit night, the entire temple would've been mirrored upon the surface."

Nasha looked over at her. "How can you tell all that from what looks like nothing but dirt, rock, and bunch of old ivy?"

Renee laughed. "Part imagination and part because that happens to be what's depicted in the mosaic down in the villa we're restoring."

A light breeze rippled through the grove. Remi brushed back her hair as she moved beside Renee. "Now that you mention it, I can picture the resemblance to the mosaic. The right tree is the one Echo was hiding behind. And to the left of it, Narcissus was lying on the bottom step, pointing into the water . . ." She turned to Lazlo. "But a hidden staircase in the reflecting pool? Beneath the water? I doubt any scroll would survive. Unless, of course, we're looking for something chiseled on a tablet."

"Not necessarily," Lazlo said. "I doubt that reflecting pool has seen water in centuries. Dr. LaBelle would know better, but I suspect the temple was in ruins before either Hilderic or Gelimer reigned."

Renee studied the hillside as they walked that direction. "Sadly, I have to agree with Remi. There's not much hope if it was indeed buried."

"The Dead Sea Scrolls survived in clay pots," Lazlo said.

"Which were in open caves," Renee replied. "But buried beneath the reflecting pool? I'll be happy if we find a few fragments in a pot."

Mr. Atiku looked down at Nasha as they walked. "You actually have roots here in Tunisia."

"Me?"

"You're Nigerian on your father's side, but your ancestors on your mother's side were Numidian."

"What's Numidian?" she asked.

"Parts of ancient Tunisia and Algeria."

Nasha stole a glance at Amal. "Maybe we're long-lost cousins."

"Maybe."

When they reached the temple, Renee stopped everyone in front of the stairs, then looked out over the vast space they'd just crossed. "If this is the spot Narcissus is pointing to, I'm not sure how anything would've survived. Amal, are you sure this is what you saw in your vision?"

She took a slow look around the area and gave a sigh. "I don't even remember speaking. But I'll take a walk around and see if something comes up."

"I'll go with you," Osmond said.

Amal waited for him, and the two walked down the steps, Osmond saying, "Maybe we need to start another stove fire. You seem to be triggered by the smoke."

She burst out laughing.

Renee joined Remi, who was standing beneath the shade of an

ancient olive. "I so hope we find something before you and Sam have to leave."

"Well, even with Rube's help, I think we'll be here for several days. The police still haven't signed off on the shootings." Remi nodded at Amal as she and Osmond wandered off. "One good thing came out of all this. Looks like she finally noticed him."

"Let's hope so. It'll be nice to see her like her old self."

Two hours later, they hadn't found anything near the stairs that appeared to house a hidden staircase. Renee looked out over the ruins. "José, bring up the photo of the mosaic. There's got to be something we're missing."

CHAPTER NINETY-THREE

Looking for something can get in the way of finding it.
— AFRICAN PROVERB —

José had loaded the photos of the mosaic onto a tablet and he pulled it from his backpack. As everyone sat on the steps in the shade of one of the olive trees, taking turns looking at the tablet, Nasha wedged herself between Remi and Lazlo for a better view. "That doesn't look like a map."

"It's a secret map," Remi said.

"How?"

Lazlo enlarged the photo, bringing up the area of the blue and white tiles. "This is supposed to be a pool of water in front of the temple." He pointed to the flat field in front of them. "It used to be there."

"How do you know it's water?"

"Because the temple's reflected in it. See the columns?" He looked over at her, then back at the screen. "And here, where Narcissus is pointing at the reflection, which is darker than the reflection on the other side. It looks like steps."

Remi studied the reflection in the mosaic while Lazlo spoke. The six temple columns depicted at first looked identical in height and width. But now that Lazlo pointed it out, she realized the base of the second column on the left contained far more blue tiles. "You're absolutely right. It does look like stairs. If the map's accurate and we're sitting where Narcissus is sitting, the stairs would be located somewhere out there in the pool."

Renee looked over Remi's shoulder, then turned to Amal. "What was it your grandmother told you? I mean, besides the show you put on to distract Hank?"

"Something about the Usurper finding the scrolls from the Underworld through the eyes of the penultimate king."

"What's *penultimate* mean?" Nasha asked.

"Second to the last," Amal said.

"Like the column that's different from the others?" she asked Lazlo. "Second to the last?"

"Exactly like that column."

Nasha's eyes sparkled at the praise in his voice.

"Where was I . . . ?" Amal furrowed her brow. "Something about the Festival of Saturnalia and he'll lose that which he holds dear *until all that is left is shadow, and naught remains but vanity.*" She stood. "My grandmother and I used to explore down here together. Maybe if I follow the same route, that'll stir up memories of what she told me." Nasha saw her walking down the stairs and quickly followed.

As they wandered toward the other end of the ruins, Lazlo returned his attention to the photo. "Oracles and riddles. The festival around Saturnalia was all about role reversals . . ."

"Saturnalia." Remi smiled. "You're brilliant, Lazlo. If the penultimate king sees it from the Underworld, he's looking up. Vanity, water, Narcissus . . . And, Amal had a vision where she was looking up through the water." She nodded at the photo on the tablet. "Alice through the looking glass."

"Remi," Sam said. "We've already gone down that rabbit hole."

Renee looked at Lazlo. "Is it always like this between those two?"

"Always."

"If," Sam said, "it has to do with obscure history and leaps of logic, then yes."

Renee laughed. "I'm with Sam about the leaps of logic. How's a children's book going to help?"

"Not a book," Remi said. "The concept. We know the ancient Tunisians put water on the floor to act like a swamp cooler in the summer. If we're correct about a map being hidden on the floor, the artist would've known this and used it to his advantage. He would've also known that Saturnalia was a festival that had to do with role reversals. It fits with everything we're seeing here."

Sam nodded at the photo. "The only thing I see is Narcissus pointing to the water."

"Forget about where he's pointing, Fargo. Think about where he's looking—at his reflection. Remember, everything's opposite."

"Quite right," Lazlo said. "If Hilderic's the penultimate king looking up from the Underworld and the Usurper is Gelimer . . ."

"Who," Remi said, "would be looking in the same direction as Narcissus—and us . . ."

"We were searching in the wrong part of the ruins."

"No doubt about it," Remi replied. "Anyone looking at that mosaic would assume that Narcissus was pointing to the reflecting pool. He was pointing to the reflection. The reflection of the hidden steps, which should be behind him in the temple."

Lazlo's eyes gleamed. "Quite right, Mrs. Fargo. But don't forget about Saturnalia, which seems to have been brought up frequently in these old legends passed down by Amal's family. According to the rules of the festival, we can safely assume that the hidden steps are on the opposite side of that depicted in the mosaic. It's not here behind us at all. It's over there."

Everyone looked in that direction, seeing nothing but the ancient twisted ivy vines that seemed to be holding up the ruins. The wind gusted, rustling the leaves, causing a soft, plaintive wail deep within the temple. Then, just as suddenly, it died and all was quiet.

"That was spooky," Renee whispered.

"Nasha . . . ?" her uncle said, his voice laced with concern. "She was with Amal. Where are they?"

Remi shaded her eyes from the glare of the sun. The two had been standing on the edge of the ruins just a few minutes ago. "Maybe that wasn't the wind at all."

"Nasha . . . Amal . . ."

Sam and Remi ran to the other end of the ruins, seeing nothing but the thick vines and the marble beneath. They called out again, but no one answered. "Let's split up," Sam said. "Half take the right side of the ruins, half the left."

After several minutes of searching without finding the pair, they reconvened in front of the ancient temple. Nasha's uncle shaded his eyes, searching the hillside leading up to the olive grove. "Could they have gone back to the house?"

"We would've seen them," Sam said.

He was just about to suggest they make another pass around the temple when he heard Nasha's voice coming from beneath the tangle of ivy as though she were singing a jump rope rhyme. "*Sator . . . arepo . . . tenet . . . opera . . . rotas.* Behold . . ." She parted the thick vines, peering out, surprised at the sight of everyone watching her. "Is something wrong?"

"Where's Amal?" Remi asked.

"Down there." She pulled the ivy curtain wider, revealing a passageway that led into the hillside behind the crumbling temple. "Amal was showing it to me. It's where she used to go when she was little."

Relieved, Sam took his phone, turned on the flashlight, and checked the passage. One of the fluted columns had collapsed onto the hillside, providing a trellis over which the ivy had climbed, hiding the entrance from prying eyes. In fact, had Nasha not pointed it out, Sam doubted they would've been able to find it behind the vines at all. "Amal?"

"Here," she called out.

Sam led the way, discovering Amal sitting on the floor of a small cave.

She narrowed her gaze against the intrusion of light. "Sorry. I just wanted to show Nasha where I used to play when I was her age. I'd mostly forgotten about it." She looked around the small cavern, then stood. "This is where I used to come to escape. It always relaxed me, sitting in the dark."

Nasha scurried in and sat next to her, looking equally at home.

Lazlo was drawn to the inscriptions carved on the cavern walls. "If nothing else, I'd say we're on the right track."

"Ancient graffiti," Amal said.

"Indeed . . ."

Remi followed the direction of Lazlo's gaze. "Sam, bring that light closer."

He aimed the beam at the spot Remi and Lazlo were focusing on. Scratched into the wall was a graffito that looked very much like the temple in the mosaic. And below it, what looked like a staircase set directly below the penultimate column on the right-hand side.

The very column they'd passed under on their way into the cavern.

CHAPTER NINETY-FOUR

A man who is patient is rewarded.
— AFRICAN PROVERB —

Nasha had been excited about the find, until she realized how long it would take to do the excavation just to find the hidden steps—assuming they really existed. Suddenly the prospect of returning to Nigeria with her uncle seemed far more tantalizing than the countless days of carefully removing centuries of dirt and crumbling ruins just to find them. When it came time for her and her uncle to leave for the airport an hour later, she didn't protest.

Standing just inside the terminal, Remi was faced with saying good-bye to her. But unlike their previous parting at the school, this time when Nasha hugged Remi her face was filled with joy. "You won't forget me, will you, Mrs. Fargo?"

"How could I?" Remi said. "You stole a piece of my heart."

"No I didn't. You gave it to me."

Remi's throat closed up, and it was a moment before she could speak. "Keep it safe for me?"

Nasha pulled her backpack from her shoulder, patting it. "Right here."

"Nasha," her uncle said. "It's time."

She nodded, then followed her uncle toward security, turning back to wave at Remi and Sam just before they disappeared into the crowd.

Remi leaned her head into Sam's shoulder as they left the terminal.

"We'll see them again," he said.

"I know. Soon, I hope." Her phone buzzed in her pocket and she pulled it out. "This should help distract me from that ache in my heart. Renee thinks they may have found the secret entrance. Looks like home will have to wait."

GROUND-PENETRATING RADAR HELPED RENEE'S TEAM MAP THE actual remains of the chamber hidden beneath the ancient mudslide. Once they'd removed several feet of dirt from that side of the temple, they were able to get to the pedestal belonging to the fallen penultimate column. The entire process of working the site was slow and tedious, but when they had uncovered the base, they found that the marble flooring was darker and cracked, whereas the rest of the temple floor appeared to be yellow marble, all still intact.

José documented their progress with photos and a measuring rod. Once he'd finished, he helped Sam, Lazlo, and Osmond carefully lift the top half of the broken slab and then the bottom. Crumbling stairs led down beneath the temple into a tunnel carved from the rock.

Remi moved next to Sam, staring into the narrow passage below the temple floor, while José took more photos. He stepped back and Sam turned on the flashlight, holding his hand out to Remi. "Shall we?"

"Thought you'd never ask."

They led the group downward, Sam's flashlight reflecting off inscriptions carved in the rock walls much like the ones they'd found in the cavern hidden behind the ivy. They followed the passageway beneath the temple and eventually emerged into a cavern much larger than Amal's. At first, it appeared empty, until Sam lowered the beam of his flashlight. Two chests sat at the far wall, the wood rotted, the contents partially spilling out to the cavern floor. The near-black patina of the tarnished silver plates, goblets, and bowls made it difficult to see the exquisite workmanship hammered around the edges. The other chest held spoons and a few pieces of jewelry, also tarnished with age.

"Okay, so not a king's ransom," Renee said.

"But a worthy find nonetheless," Lazlo replied.

Remi moved closer. "So why would the Vandal King hide it?"

"Perhaps," Lazlo said, "it was hidden from the Vandals when they invaded North Africa."

"We may never know," Sam said.

"Amal, look at that." Remi pointed to the other side of the cavern. Sam aimed his light at a square oxidized-bronze charcoal burner. "That looks like it matches the lid on your mantel."

As they moved closer, they noticed a tall, lidded cylindrical vessel made of bronze, standing behind it. Simple in structure, there were no markings anywhere on its surface except a Greek inscription in chased silver on the lid that read

Alítheia kai armonía.

"Truth and harmony," Remi translated.

Lazlo moved closer. "Truth—from Parmenides' poem 'On Nature,' perhaps?"

Amal took a breath. "If my grandmother's stories are correct, this is what we were meant to protect."

Renee, her attention on the vessel, circled around it and the charcoal burner, leaning in close. "Exquisite. We need photos, José."

He opened his camera bag and set up his tripod and took photos from several angles around both artifacts. When he finished, Renee examined the taller vessel. "The moment of reckoning. Who wants to open it?"

Sam said, "You should do the honors."

"Me? If not for you and Remi, I wouldn't be here."

"Remi?" Sam said.

"Sorry, Fargo. Or are you forgetting there's a curse?"

José laughed nervously behind them. "I don't want to die a violent death."

"Me neither," Osmond said. "Look what happened to Hank."

"Lazlo?" Sam said. "You're the one who translated the map."

"I'll be glad to look. After you break the curse."

Remi laughed. "Open it, Fargo. His loss."

"Or gain," Lazlo called out. "Depending."

Renee nudged Sam forward. "Aren't you the one with royal blood? Just be careful. It's over fifteen hundred years old."

Sam looked at Amal. "Any warnings from the oracle?"

"Sorry. Fresh out of prophecies."

"Have at it, Fargo," Remi said. "Before the curse changes its mind about your royal lineage."

Sam approached the cylinder, lifted the lid, and peered in.

"Well?" Remi asked.

"It's here. The scroll."

CHAPTER NINETY-FIVE

A happy man marries the girl he loves,
but a happier man loves the girl he marries.

— AFRICAN PROVERB —

La Jolla, California
Goldfish Point

S am opened up that morning's newspaper as the light ocean
breeze swept across the balcony where he and Remi sat drinking their coffee. Neither was surprised by the article that came
out in the Lifestyle section of the paper, describing the historic find of
the silver hoard and the Parmenides Scroll in Tunisia by Dr. Renee
LaBelle, all of which was turned over to the Bardo National Museum
in Tunis by Amal's family. Of the treasure, it was Parmenides' entire
poem "On Nature" that was the greatest find since it had previously
existed only in fragments. The mudslide sealing the tunnel had
helped to preserve the scroll intact and it was the world's only surviving copy.

Sam reached for his coffee cup, pausing when he saw Remi over
the top of the newspaper. A soft smile played on her face as she
tucked an errant strand of auburn hair behind her ear. At the moment, she was absorbed in something she was reading on her tablet.
Sam lowered his paper, content to simply watch her. After everything they'd been through over the years of their marriage, it was the
quiet moments like this that he appreciated most.

Eventually, she noticed him staring at her. "What," she asked, "do you find so intriguing?"

"Besides you?"

She leaned over, kissed him. "Look what Wendy just sent. A class photo."

Remi turned the tablet toward him and he saw everyone grouped in front of the new dorm. Pete and Wendy stood on one side of the girls, Monifa and Yaro on the other. While there were several new faces, he recognized most of the girls, including Okoro's daughter, Zara. Beside her stood Maryam, Tambara, and Jol. But he had to smile at the sight of Nasha—front and center—wearing her little blue backpack.